Slave
to the Rhythm

To Jodie,

love from,

Jane Harvey-Berrick

Jane Harvey-Berrick
♡
9·7·16

HARVEY
BERRICK
PUBLISHING

Slave to the Rhythm

Copyright © 2016 Jane Harvey-Berrick

Editing by Kirsten Olsen and Alana Albertson

This ebook is licensed for your personal enjoyment only. It may not be re-sold or given away to other people. If you do, you are STEALING.
I only distribute my work through iBooks, Amazon, Nook, Kobo and Create Space. If you have received this book from anywhere else, it is a pirate copy, it is illegal, and you've really spoiled my day.
Thank you for respecting the hard work of this author.
All rights reserved.

Jane Harvey-Berrick has asserted her right under the Copyright, Designs and Patents Act 1988 to be identified as the author of this work.
This book is a work of fiction. Names and characters are the product of the author's imagination and any resemblance to actual persons, living or dead, is entirely coincidental.
All rights reserved; no part of this publication may be reproduced or transmitted by any means, electronic, mechanical, photocopying or otherwise, without the prior permission of the publisher. Jane Harvey-Berrick has asserted her moral right to be identified as the author of this work.

Cover design by Hang Le / www.byhangle.com
Cover photograph by Allan Spiers / www.allanspiers.com
Cover model: Kevin H

ISBN 9780992924676
Harvey Berrick Publishing

DEDICATION

To every artist who has smiled through the blood, sweat and tears
hoc feci

ACKNOWLEDGMENTS

To Kirsten Olsen, editor, friend, confidant, chocolate aficionado.
To Trina Miciotta for her editing and unfailing support.
To Hang Le for her beautiful cover and never-ending creativity.
To Sheena Lumsden for her friendship and all her work behind the scenes.
To Neda Amini for her marketing expertise and enthusiasm for all things books.
To Alana Albertson, friend and author, who shares my love of dancing, glitter and sequins, and made sure that Ash knew his mambo from his salsa.
To Lea Jerancic who checked all things Slovenian while she was checking out Ash.
To Rhonda Koppenhaver who made sure my Chicago references were on the money.
To Dina Farndon Eidinger and Audrey Thunder—you know why ;)
To Selma Ibrahimpasic, Savanna Phillips, Lelyana Taufik, Melissa Parnell and Sarah Lintott for letting me shamelessly exploit their names.
And to Fuñny Souisa, for loving the idea of this story from the start.

Thank you Stalking Angels. You know how much you mean to me and you never let me down.

Tonya Bass Allen, Neda Amini, Jenny Angell, Lisa Clements Baker, Nicola Barton, Jen Berg, Mary Rose Bermundo, Reyna Borderbook, Sarah Bookhooked, Megan Burgad, Kelsey Burns, Gabri Canova, L.E. Chamberlain, Tera Chastain, Elle Christopher, Beverley Cindy, Paola Cortes, Nikki Costello, Emma Darch-Harris, Megan Davis, Jade Donaldson, Drizinha Dri, Mary Dunne, Dina Farndon Eidinger, Jennifer Escobar, Fátima Figueira, Kelly Findlay, Andrea Flaks, Andrea Florkowski, MJ Fryer, Raquel Gamez, Evelyn Garcia, Carly Grey, Helen Remy Grey, Nycole Griffin, Rose Hogg, Kim Howlett, Selma Ibrahimpasic, Carolin Jache, Andrea Jackson, Jayne John, Ashley Jones, Heidi Keil, Rhonda Koppenhaver, Hang Le, Wendy Lika, Sarah Lintott, Sheena Lumsden, Kathrin Magyar, Trina Marie, Susan Marshall, Sharon Kallenberger Marzola, Marie Mason, Bruninha Mazzali, Aime Metzner, Nancy Saunders Meyhoefer, Sharon Mills, Kandace Milostan, Ana Moraes, Barbara Murray, Bethany Neeper, Clare Norton, Luiza Oioli, Crystal Ordex-Hernandez, Celia Ottway, Kirsten Papi, Melissa Parnell, Ana Carina Pereira, Savanna Phillips, Cori Pitts, Vrsha Prose, Ana Kristina Rabacca, Rosarita Reader, Heather Sulzer Regina, Lisa Smith Reid, Carol Sales, Gina Sanders, Rosa Sharon, Jacqueline Showdog, Johanna Nelson Seibert, Sarah Simone, Adele Sloan, Fuñny Souisa, Erin Spencer, Dana Fiore Stusse, Lisa Sylva, Lelyana Taufik, Candy Rhyne Threatt, Audrey Thunder, Ellen Totten, Natalie Townson, Amélie White Vahlé, Tami Walker, Lily Maverick Wallis, Jo Webb, Krista Webber, Shirley Wilkinson, Emma Wynne Williams, Caroline Yamashita, Lisa G. Murray Ziegler.

And the Fanfic readers who were there from the start.

♥

Other Titles by Jane Harvey-Berrick

Series
Slave to the Rhythm (Rhythm series #1)
Luka (Rhythm series #2)

The Traveling Man (Traveling series #1)
The Traveling Woman (Traveling series #2)
Roustabout (Traveling series #3)

The Education of Sebastian (Education series #1)
The Education of Caroline (Education series #2)
The Education of Sebastian & Caroline (combined edition)
Semper Fi: The Education of Caroline (Education series #3)

Standalone Titles
The New Samurai
Exposure
Dangerous to Know & Love
Playing in the Rain (*novella*)
The Dark Detective
At Your Beck & Call
Summer of Seventeen
Lifers
Dazzled
One Careful Owner

PROLOGUE

Heat and noise.

The deep bass reverberated through the floor, through the table and chairs, the empty bottles on the table trembling as the music pulsed.

The dry, desert air was humid inside the sealed room, a room that never saw daylight.

The casino was alive 24 hours a day, seven days a week. Men and women with the bloodshot eyes of those who had been at the slot machines for too many hours were replaced with the young and young at heart who wanted to dance the night away, the sweat stains and smudged makeup hidden in the pockets of darkness among the strobing lights.

My friends were on the dance floor, lost in the music, rolling their hips, stroking the air above their heads with languid arms, grinding against each other to the determined, demanding music. I could see the eyes following their movements, the loose jaws, the wet lips.

A part of me envied them—the part that always envied people who could be so free, and if I'd loved them less, envy might have turned to resentment.

The reunion had been planned for eight months, and even though the timing had turned out to be a cosmic joke, I refused to miss out. Despite everything, it was good to see them. Old friends who had seen me at my best and worst.

I stared longingly at the bar, wishing that a Mimosa would materialize in front of me. But none of the scantily dressed waitresses even noticed me sitting by myself.

I was used to being alone. I worked from home and rarely saw the people I called colleagues, and that suited me just fine. But it's one thing to choose to be by yourself; it's completely different to be alone in a crowd.

I glanced back to the heaving dance floor, smiling as a cowboy with a large Stetson and no rhythm limbered up behind Vanessa, trying to attract her attention with his awkward but well-meaning gyrations.

My eyes skated away with embarrassment at his lumbering gait, and that's when my gaze was drawn to another man. And this one caught and held my attention as surely as I caught and held my breath.

He was dressed in black, a snug shirt tucked into dress pants, an easy elegance that made him seem like a thoroughbred among carthorses.

His movements were sinuous with suggestive grace, one fluid action flowing into the next. His hips thrust and rolled, his long legs flexed and straightened, his arms moving rhythmically, fingers extended. He held himself erect, his chin dipping only slightly so his eyes could fix on his much shorter dance partner. Even from this distance I could see that he was focused, like a wild animal stalking his prey. His eyes were feline, too, slanting up slightly at the corners, emphasizing his sharp cheekbones.

His spiky dark hair was gelled at the front, but almost military at the back, showing off his long elegant neck and the broad muscles that writhed beneath his short-sleeved shirt, the shadow of a tattoo peeping out.

He was tall, and the black clothes he wore emphasized his slim silhouette. It was hard to tell his age, his unsmiling face clean shaven and intense, he could have been anything from twenty to thirty.

For a moment, he disappeared into the swirling mass, and I leaned forward to catch another glimpse.

The crowd parted and the illusive dancer reappeared. I saw his partner for the first time: a short, doughy woman with perspiration dripping down her face and too-tight dress.

They didn't fit, the man and the woman. I sat back in my chair, watching, intrigued.

I suppose I'd spent a lot of time, on the sidelines. Life had made me an observer. So I'd made a study of male beauty in all its forms: the jock, the joker, the emo, the player, the hot and dangerous. I was a connoisseur, you might say, but only from a distance. Perhaps that made me a voyeur.

But this man—he was in a class of his own. I was mesmerized watching the strong, graceful lines he created, the perfect symmetry of his perfect body, his subtle strength and obvious talents. He was beautiful. And that made me sad.

His intense, serious gaze was utterly focused on his partner, and envy bubbled up inside me. I tried to push it away, but I couldn't drag my eyes from the dancer. He rotated his hips, his body fluent and effortless, always in motion. The thought crossed my mind that if he fucked the way he danced, his partner was in for a night she'd never forget.

But then the woman's steps faltered, and she edged her way from the dance floor, sucking in lungfuls of air, her fingers sinking into broad hips as she rested her hands.

The man followed, asking a question, and the woman shook her head, half laughing as she nervously backed away from him. When she retreated, he pressed closer, wrapping his long fingers around her wrist, his eyes narrowed.

I leaned forward again, then glanced around, wondering if anyone else had noticed the drama unfolding in front of me.

They seemed to be arguing, and the woman's sweaty face was red and worried. But then the man held up his hands in surrender, releasing his prey.

I relaxed back into my chair, feeling almost as much relief as the short woman who was retreating in the direction of the bathroom.

The man stood, watching the woman leave, and I was surprised to see frustration on his face. Not disappointment, not annoyance. He wasn't offended, his ego wasn't dented. If anything, he seemed angry with himself.

It was odd. Nothing in their behavior hinted that they were close. It looked like a hookup, but why had he chosen someone who was so far below his own league?

It occurred to me that perhaps he was one of those men you read about in Vegas, a gigolo in all but name. It hurt my heart a little to think that such a beautiful man might use his perfect body in such a way. I didn't want to be disappointed when everything else about him was just so … perfect.

The man ran his hands over his hair as he searched around the room, his eyes ticking off the women he saw, some internal checklist that remained hidden to all but him.

But then his eyes flickered to me, probably because I was still watching him, and a wide smile stretched his full lips. The smile, so totally unblemished from a distance, didn't reach his eyes, and when he approached me, I was immediately on guard.

"Hi, I'm Ash. Are you by yourself?"

It was hard to be sure over the pounding music, but it sounded as if he had an accent. Something Eastern European, perhaps Russian? Polish?

I gave him a polite but closed smile, a cool smile that hid all warmth, a smile for slow servers and rude cab drivers. A smile for men I didn't trust.

"No. I'm here with my friends."

The man looked around him, then shrugged theatrically.

"I don't see them. Would you like to dance?"

And he held out his hand, obviously assuming that I would say yes.

I laughed. "No, I'm not dancing."

He frowned, his hand still suspended between us.

"But you like to dance?"

I stopped laughing and stared, my gaze sinking into his, puzzled, annoyed.

"What makes you think I like to dance?"

He shrugged again and his hand fell to his side.

"You're in a nightclub, and you're not drinking. So you must be here to dance. Please, dance with me."

He held out his hand again, but I shook my head impatiently. "Then go find someone who will dance with you."

His eyes widened with surprise, and then he grinned as he leaned on the table, his perfect face inches from mine. "Maybe I want to dance with you."

"Then you'll be waiting a long time."

He cocked his head to one side and I noticed a small beauty spot, shaped like a teardrop beneath his left eye—a perfect imperfection. Up close I could see that he was younger than I'd thought, younger than me perhaps, maybe early twenties. My eyes dropped to his lips and then to his throat. I could see a thin silver chain around his neck.

"I'm a good dancer," he said, looking almost wounded at my continued refusal.

He wasn't lying, but my anger, smoldering beneath the surface, ignited.

"I'm not dancing!"

"But everyone comes here to dance," he insisted, his intense dark eyes so focused, it was unnerving.

"Not me," I insisted.

He was making me anxious now and I glanced around for my friends.

"You'll have a good time."

"I don't doubt it," I snapped, losing patience. "Your last friend seemed to enjoy herself immensely."

A dull red flooded his cheeks and he looked away.

His reaction surprised me. I'd hurt his feelings, but I wasn't sure why.

"Maybe I'd like to dance with a pretty girl for a change," he said softly, glancing up at me from beneath long dark lashes.

His intense stare and pleading eyes were hard to resist. Oh, he was good. Calling me 'pretty', pretending to be upset that I wouldn't dance with him. But then I felt a little guilty, too. You can't fake flushed cheeks. I would have guessed that it was simply the exertion from dancing, but when I met his gaze, his expression was almost desperate.

"You are missing out."

My mouth tightened and the gates to my sympathy slammed shut.

"Laney, is this guy bothering you?"

I breathed a sigh of relief as Vanessa and Jo strode toward me, their lips pursed, eyes flashing dangerously.

Ash looked nervous, his glance flicking between my friends and the bouncers by the exit. He started backing away, his hands held out from his sides.

"I just asked her to dance, that's all. I wasn't doing anything wrong."

Jo threw him a disbelieving look and stood with her hands on her hips.

"Do you want to go back to your room now?" Vanessa asked.

Suddenly feeling emotional and overwhelmed, I nodded silently as Jo continued to glare.

Vanessa walked behind my chair and handed me the pashmina that had been hanging on the back. Then she unlocked the brakes on my wheelchair and pushed me away from the table.

Ash's mouth dropped open.

"Still think I'm pretty?" I asked, as my eyes filled with tears.

CHAPTER 1

Forty days earlier...

Ash

"Name?"

I'd been waiting in line, passport in hand, for 50 minutes. Fifty long, boring minutes, waiting for my life to start over.

I followed the shuffling line, a few nerves, but mostly waves of excitement spiking through me. I felt as if something didn't happen soon, I'd crack wide open and all the chaotic, pent-up energy would come pouring out.

But then the line moved along a few steps and I could look out of the window. Seeing the orange haze of a million electric lights that lit Las Vegas made me smile and my heart jumped up a notch. Soon. I'd be a part of it, living the dream, achieving everything.

"Name?"

"Aljaž Novak."

The Immigration Officer frowned at my passport.

"It says here that your name is 'Al-jazz'."

Outside my own country, that happened a lot.

"It's pronounced 'Ali-ash'."

He squinted at the passport again.

"Purpose of your visit?"

I couldn't help standing taller when I answered, pride in my voice.

"I'm here on business. I have a job. As a dancer in a theater."

He didn't seem particularly impressed as I showed him my H-1B Specialty Occupations work visa.

He studied the papers skeptically, then finally handed them back.

"These give you permission to work for one month," he said, looking at me sternly.

I nodded, trying to look as serious as he did, withholding a need to touch the St. Christopher I wore.

Then he handed back the passport and waved me through.

I let out the breath I'd been holding.

The visa I had was used for dancers and fashion models in transit, that kind of thing. My new boss had explained that it was easier to apply for a long-term visa when you were already working in the country.

At the end of the stark, white corridor, the space opened up into a vast baggage collection area with hundreds of people milling around, searching for their possessions. I'd been in line for so long, that my suitcase was already waiting for me, slowly circling the carousel along with dozens more.

The bag was heavy, up to the maximum 20 kilos, and contained just about everything I owned. I'd sold most of my possessions once I knew I was leaving Slovenia. When it came down to it, there wasn't much I wanted to keep—some of my trophies, a few photographs—and those I left with Luka before he went on tour.

Most of the things I'd packed were for dancing: six pairs of dance shoes, rehearsal clothes, Latin pants, shirts … things like that. I heaved my suitcase to the floor, then trundled it toward the exit and the sprawling arrivals hall.

I blinked, gazing around me at the sea of movement. The place was full of energy, bursting with people, slot machines going off, and a small crowd was laughing at an Elvis impersonator, a few singing along.

I felt like I'd come home.

Moving slowly through the airport, I scanned the unfamiliar faces until I saw him.

The man was enormous, swollen with heavy muscle that had partially gone to fat, and wearing a badly-fitting suit where rolls of flesh bulged out. His cold, lizard eyes skated over me then back again as he slowly lowered a sign that simply said 'Novak'.

He was one intense guy and not what I'd been expecting. But I walked toward him confidently and held out my hand. He ignored me, moving away with a rubbery bounce that contradicted his massive frame. I could tell that he'd trained, probably as a boxer, if the flattened nose and scar on his cheek were anything to go by. Still an asshole though. He reminded me of Conan the Barbarian, but without the warm personality.

I followed him through the airport to a minivan waiting outside. He jerked his head as an instruction to get in, then muttered something in Russian.

My mood lifted when I saw four girls sitting inside. Each had a large suitcase like mine, and I guessed that they were dancers, too. The one nearest me was really hot. Things were definitely looking up, and my excitement returned.

"Hi, I'm Ash!"

I spoke to the stunning blonde, giving her my best smile. She seemed happy to see me too, and replied in heavily accented English.

"Hey, I'm Yveta. This is my friend Galina," and she pointed to the brunette sitting next to her. "The redhead, I think is Marta. I don't know the other."

Two of them gave quick, nervous smiles, but when the other one turned to look at me, I was surprised to see how young she was. She reminded me of Luka's little sister and I wanted to ask her if she was okay, but she turned to stare out of the window again.

"I don't think she speaks English." Yveta shrugged. "Or Russian."

I shoved my suitcase into the only free space and settled into a seat.

"Is that where you're from?"

Yveta smiled. She really was stunning.

"Yes, and Galina. But Marta is from Ukraine. Where are you from?"

"Slovenia."

"You are dancer?" Her eyes drifted over my body appreciatively, but her next remark stopped my thoughts as they slid toward the gutter. "Exotic?"

Was that her idea of a joke? I shook my head.

"No. Latin, ballroom, contemporary."

Yveta seemed amused. "I think we dance what they tell us."

I wondered if something had gotten lost in translation.

"No, I have a contract."

Then Conan climbed into the minivan and everyone fell silent. He leaned across the narrow aisle, glaring at us.

"Passports," he growled.

I hesitated as the guy loomed over Yveta. I really didn't want to give him my passport, but I didn't want to make enemies on my first day either. Especially when he looked as if he could crush my skull with one hand.

I'm not a small guy at 6' 2", and dancing professionally isn't for weaklings—not when you're supporting or lifting your partner all day long. Plus, I worked construction when I wasn't competing. But Conan must have weighed close to 300 pounds, and looked mean with it, the long scar on his cheek adding to the air of menace.

I told myself that he wanted my passport so my new bosses could get the longer-term visa they'd talked about, but still … I wasn't happy.

No one wanted to argue with him, although the girls looked at each other, huddling closer together.

Their gazes shifted to me, and I knew that they were waiting to see if I was going to do or say something. I shrugged and handed over my passport.

Conan snatched it, tucking it into his jacket pocket as he collected the others.

Then he squeezed into the driver's seat and the minivan rumbled to life. Yveta frowned with disappointment, then stared out the window, completely ignoring me for the rest of the ride. It left me feeling irritated and uneasy. Not a great start to my new life.

But as we drove from the airport toward the glowing mecca of Las Vegas, I couldn't help smiling. Russian women were moody—everyone knew that. Not like my people, who were hard-working, honest and passionate, in a country so small it was a common joke that everybody knew everyone.

Both my parents were from the old Yugoslavia, although my mama grew up in London. She returned when Slovenia won independence in '91. I was born nine months later.

I think she would have liked to go back to Britain to live but never got the chance. So instead, she made a point of speaking English to me. It had been a while.

She'd loved dancing, so I guess that's where I got it from because I was nothing like my father. Thank God.

Las Vegas was a river of colored lights as we swept past. From my window, I saw the exotically named hotels: the Monte Carlo, Aria, Bellagio with its famous fountains; Caesar's Palace, the Mirage, Palazzo—old European names in a new world of loud, bold colors and 24/7 energy. I was home. That's how it felt.

But when Conan finally slowed the minivan, it was at an ugly concrete tower—definitely one of the cheaper hotels—which was a real letdown. I hoped their theater was as good as they'd promised. That was all I cared about.

Conan pulled into a service entrance lined with dumpsters and empty crates, and I could see the disappointment on the girls' faces, as well. Watching our arrival were two men in chefs' uniforms who stamped out their cigarettes as soon as they saw the minivan and slunk inside, the heavy kitchen door slamming behind them. It looked like they didn't want to be seen by Conan. A bad feeling began to brew inside me.

Conan heaved his bulk from the front seat and left without a word.

When he didn't return immediately, Yveta and Galina whispered to each other anxiously.

"What do we do?" Yveta asked.

"Looks like we've arrived," I shrugged, smiling with a reassurance that I didn't feel.

The girls seemed relieved and smiled back, including the one who hadn't spoken yet. Even in the unlit minivan, I could see that she was much younger than the others—maybe only 15 or 16. That was young to be away from home in a foreign country. It happened, especially with dancers, because you started early and your career was short.

I was about to speak to her when a door in the hotel opened, sending a path of light toward us. Our cue.

I slid open the minivan door and jumped out, happy to stretch after 24 hours of traveling.

The air was warm and dry, and if I craned my head back, I could see stars beginning to appear in the sky.

Conan arrived back, following another guy in a suit.

The new guy walked toward me, his hand outstretched, and spoke with a Russian accent as we shook hands.

"Welcome to Hotel Royale."

"Thank you."

Then he turned to the girls still sitting in the minivan, their faces drained of color in the gloomy parking lot.

"Come, ladies," he laughed. "Don't be shy."

The four girls climbed out and stood behind me, peering anxiously at our new boss.

"Do you all have cell phones?" he asked. "Please let your families know that you have safely arrived. For security reasons, I'll have to collect your cells, but they will be returned to you later."

I paused, halfway through an email to Luka, even though I knew he didn't check his messages that much when he was on tour.

"You want our phones?"

The man scanned me quickly, then gave a cold smile. "It will be returned once it's been processed."

First my passport, now my phone? I really didn't like that idea. But I didn't have any choice, so I finished the email and handed it over.

He tossed it to Conan who dropped it into a plastic bag with the others. I really hoped that the screen hadn't been damaged. It was a new iPhone.

Silently, we followed them inside. It was creepy, and I felt Yveta close behind me. I reached out to hold her hand.

She clung on, her skin cold and clammy even though the night air was warm.

We trudged through the hotel along a series of service corridors until we arrived at a battered elevator and crowded inside. I was surprised when the car started moving downwards, stopping three floors underground. It really felt like we were trapped. Yveta was holding on tightly and I wanted to say it was going to be okay…

When the doors opened, there were two more heavies in suits waiting for us. That was a lot of muscle to escort five dancers.

"Women that way."

Yveta hesitated, then gave me a small unhappy wave as she trailed after the others.

Conan jerked his head at me to follow him.

I hoped that I wouldn't have to be around him too much, he was a scary dude. I'd been expecting to meet the artistic director, Elaine something. But having that asshole's cold stare on me felt like insects crawling across my skin.

I followed him through more corridors until we ended up at a large kitchen. Two Asian guys were sitting at a table playing Poker, but when they saw Conan, they scooped up their cards and slunk out. That was definitely weird. They acted like they had a reason to be scared of him, and it made the hairs on the back of my neck stand up.

Conan pointed at a chair and left.

Welcome to America.

When no one came to get me, I wandered around the kitchen, searching for something to eat, but other than an apple and some cheese, there were only things that needed cooking.

I must have fallen asleep at the table because I was woken by the sound of high heels tapping across the floor.

"Are you Mr. Novak?"

I sat up straight and looked over my shoulder.

The woman was tiny, perhaps fifty years old, with bleach-blonde hair and false eyelashes edged with miniature rhinestones that caught the light. Even from ten feet, I could smell the acrid scent of fake tan that she'd tried to hide under a heavy dose of perfume.

She huffed impatiently. "Are you Mr. Novak?"

I nodded slowly, replying with a croak. "Yes."

"Finally! We've been waiting for you. You were expected at the theater."

"I'm sorry, I didn't know. A big guy with a scar on his cheek brought me here."

The blonde woman shuddered.

"Oleg! Ugh, don't mention that creep's name."

She jerked her chin at my suitcase.

"Well, come on then."

I followed her out of the kitchen, still hungry and feeling jetlagged.

"I was a dancer," she said cheerfully, strutting along the corridor. "Exotic—I'm too short to be a real Las Vegas showgirl. Now, I work backstage and look after the boys and girls."

"How long have you been here?"

She shrugged. "A while. I'm Trixie Morell." She grinned at me. "I was born Doris Wazacki, but that's showbiz for ya!"

She marched ahead, leading me through an unmarked door with air conditioning ducts humming overhead.

Finally she stopped at a numbered keypad and punched in a code.

"This is the staff wing," she threw over her shoulder. "The long-timers have their own apartments, but we get a lot of people on short-term contracts. As well as us show folk, it's where the kitchen and wait staff live. It's safe."

Safe? Why would it be unsafe?

After another corridor, she pushed open the door to a small bedroom with a tiny attached bathroom.

Half of the room was plastered with posters of Hollywood icons from Greta Garbo to Judy Garland, and one of the twin beds was covered in men's dance clothes.

So my new roommate was a dancer.

"You'll meet Gary later," Trixie said, ignoring my silence. "He's very possessive about his things, so don't borrow anything without asking. In fact, don't touch anything at all. He can be a bit of a bitch, but you'll get used to him."

I almost smiled. After my last fight with my father, it was the least of my worries.

"Leave your things here. Oh, bring your dance shoes—something you can audition in."

"Audition? I thought I had the job?"

She shrugged. "Elaine told me you were auditioning."

I was worried. I'd spent a lot of money on my flight here—no one had said anything about an audition.

I dropped my suitcase on the spare bed and dug out a pair of Latin shoes and dance pants. Trixie watched the whole time while I dropped my jeans and changed. She didn't even bother to look away. I'm not shy about my body, it was just off-putting.

I took one last look at the room, then followed Trixie as the door closed behind me with a soft click.

She led me to the wings of a large stage and I could smell sweat and greasepaint, hear the sounds of rehearsals as we drew closer.

"Not too shabby, eh?" said Trixie proudly.

I had to agree. It would be the largest stage that I'd ever danced on. I could tell that it was professionally designed and had a sprung floor that looked new.

This was what I'd come for.

"Ash!"

A woman in towering heels and a clinging leotard strode toward me, her breasts bouncing, and an enormous set of ostrich feathers fixed to her hair.

"Yveta?"

I smiled as she kissed me on both cheeks.

Trixie interrupted, frowning, and shooed Yveta back to the stage.

"Friend of yours?"

I shrugged. "We've met."

"And?"

"We arrived at the same time."

Trixie pressed her lips together but I wasn't sure what was bothering her.

"Hmm. Come and meet Elaine—she's the Artistic Director. She'll be pleased to see you. She's one man down since Erik left..."

I glanced at her, but Trixie didn't finish her sentence.

"Elaine! I've got your new boy at last!"

The Artistic Director was a tall, thin woman with the hard body of a dancer and a face that could chisel granite.

Her eyes were raking up and down the rest of my body, professionally assessing me.

"What's your experience?"

"Two time finalist in Slovenian All-Stars International Ten Dance," I spoke clearly, proud of my achievements.

"Anything else?"

I blinked, nonplussed by her lack of interest—I'd already given her my best result in a prestigious national competition.

"I can dance anything—whatever you need. I've been dancing since I was five."

"How old are you now?"

"Twenty-three."

Elaine sighed. "Right, let's see what you can do."

I wanted to laugh. I was jetlagged, I'd hardly eaten for 12 hours, hadn't slept for 24, and I was stiff from sitting for the best part of a day. I had nothing prepared and had no idea what sort of routine she wanted to see. And from the look on her face, I was already pissing her off. I'd never been less ready for an audition.

Elaine shouted to a technician standing by the mixing board.

"Joe, set him up with something." Then she looked at me impatiently. "What are you waiting for? Go do your warm up."

I knew she wasn't going to give me a second chance. I had to nail this audition or I was out of chances, and I didn't know what that would mean. Would they just put me on the first flight back?

I talked to the technician quickly, Elaine's impatience filling the room while I jogged on the spot, then did some arm swings, sways, trunk rotation, rumba walks and spot turns, stretching my muscles then finishing with some balance exercises. A full warm-up took 15 minutes minimum: Elaine gave me less than ten.

I should be far more prepared than this to dance—Elaine knew it. Which probably meant she didn't want me in her troupe.

I rubbed my throbbing temples—I had to nail this audition.

I nodded at the technician, then pulled off my t-shirt, holding it out like a matador's cape, and strode onto the stage with the sultry, dragging steps of the Paso Doble.

Florence and the Machine poured from the speakers, filling the empty cavern of the theater.

And I became the dance. I was a matador, facing a pitiless enemy.

But I'm not giving up…

I stepped forward with my heels, strong and proud, arms sweeping up from my sides, the t-shirt whirling around my head and tossed away.

I can't count on anyone but myself…

Apel: the Flamenco stamp.

The movements were quick and sharp, staccato, chest and head held high, feet directly underneath my body.

I felt it. I felt it all. Anger and frustration, the drama of the music: *sur place*, separation, attack, the open promenade, the Spanish line—the formal steps flowed through me, but it was emotion, owning the music, feeling the music, living it. I danced and the world stopped. All the pain, all the bitterness, lost in the music.

I leapt through the air, my body shouting the aggression that was sealed inside. Movements proud and strong.

Then the music changed abruptly and Public Enemy's 'Rebel Without a Pause' blasted out. My whole body shifted. From tall and proud, I got low down and earthy, limbs loose and flowing, masculine and raw, unpolished. Smooth transitions were edged with hard finishes, taut arms and angry eyes. Then I threw myself into a handless cartwheel, landing with soft knees and a ton of attitude, finishing with a helicopter spin on my back, ignoring the bite of the wooden floor on my bare skin, then leaping to my feet, almost glaring at Elaine.

The music died away and I stood panting on the stage, sweat pouring down my chest.

Yveta cheered from the wings and I turned my head to grin at her.

Against her will, Elaine was impressed. She jerked her head in a quick nod.

"You can dance."

Elaine led me to the rest of the cast, and I could see right away that there was a clear separation between the girls who were Las Vegas regulars and the people like me who'd been brought in recently. Elaine would have her work cut out turning us into a team.

We were opening in the refurbished theater in four weeks—not an overly long rehearsal period for a two-hour show. There were also singers, a magician and a cool guy who juggled stuff, but still, the core of it was the Vegas showgirls.

Elaine introduced me to the other male dancer, an older guy whose eyes narrowed when he saw me.

"Gary, this is Ash. He's also your new roommate."

So this was the guy with all the posters. He definitely didn't look happy to meet me, resting his hands on his hips and staring without speaking.

Elaine ignored his unfriendliness and told him to walk me through elements of the men's role. There were only two of us, and it seemed we were just there to 'present' the girls, showing them off. Elaine mentioned that she was considering giving one of us a dance duet, which would be far more noticeable than boring chorus-line work. I guess it was too much to hope for a prestigious solo dance. Gary kept throwing me dirty looks, which I ignored. I was going to get that duet.

Rehearsals lasted late into the evening, and it was nearly 1AM local time when Elaine dismissed us, tired and sweaty. I followed Gary back to our room.

"So, you're the new flavor of the month."

I ignored Gary's tone. Jealous dancers … I was used to that. It came with the territory. I'd even known one guy who'd sabotaged a competitor's dance shoes. Shit happens.

"I'm just new."

"Hmm, well, I have seniority, so don't forget that, showboat."

His comment pissed me off. "I don't showboat."

Gary sneered out a laugh.

"And I'm not a friend of Dorothy."

It had been a few years since I'd spoken English, and I didn't get the reference right away. But then I noticed the Judy Garland poster on Gary's side of the room.

I could care less that Gary was gay, but I wasn't going to put up with being accused of showing off.

"It was an audition," I said flatly. "If I didn't get in, I'd be sent … home."

Gary's frigid stance softened slightly.

"Where are you from? You speak really good English."

"Koper in Slovenia. It's about 100 km from Ljubljana."

"I have no idea what you just said, sugar lips."

Twenty-four hours ago, I would have been irritated by the nickname—now I didn't give a shit. Perspective is everything.

"Slovenia. It was part of Yugoslavia until 1991." I saw the blank look on Gary's face. "In Europe."

"Right. Do you have a King and Queen?"

I shook my head. "No, we're a Republic."

Gary looked disappointed. "No queens? Pity. So, where did you learn English? Or is that what you speak in … wherever it is you come from?"

I raised an eyebrow at him.

"Nope, no queens. And we speak Slovene in Slovenia."

"Whatever. I'm going to take a shower and get some sleep," he said, without much interest.

I nodded. Sounded good to me.

I stared out of my bedroom window, trying to see the stars. But the only view was of concrete.

CHAPTER 2

Ash

As dawn filtered through the window, I woke, having slept only a few hours, still tired and sluggish.

I stumbled to the bathroom, turning the shower to scalding hot. Some of the tension in my body eased as I enjoyed my first hot shower in two days.

I'd just finished and was staring into the steamed-up mirror, trying to decide whether or not to shave, when Gary breezed into the bathroom.

"Damn! You're wearing a towel. Don't give me that look, Mr. Hotpants. There have got to be some perks to rooming with a prima donna."

"Whatever you say, Toto."

"Are you saying I'm a little bitch?"

I stared at him coldly, but was surprised when he grinned at me and winked.

Then Gary flapped his hands, shooing me out of the bathroom. "By the way, nice tat."

I automatically glanced down at the tattoo covering the top of my left arm. The dark, swirling lines were decorative but meaningless, unless you knew how to read them.

The tattoo was just something else that my dad hated about me. To older people like him, tattoos were seen in terms of permanence and regret, but to me it was a map of my life and experiences; memories inked into skin.

I'd be adding to it soon. I didn't know what yet, but when I did, yeah...

Changing into a clean t-shirt and cheap sweatpants, I sat on the bed, wondering what the day would bring.

I looked up to find Gary staring at me, an odd expression on his face.

"How's the jetlag?"

I shrugged. "Won't stop me dancing."

Gary grinned. "I hear ya! I danced the whole of the Harlequin in the *Nutcracker* with a metatarsal fracture."

"You dance ballet?"

Gary's chest inflated. "Since I was four years old. I'm just waiting for my genius to be recognized," and he sighed.

I dropped my gaze. Gary was the wrong side of 30—there was no big break around the corner for him now. A dancer's life was short—ballet dancers especially. Like top athletes, optimum potential was reached early. After that, you could coach, teach, or go do something else and dream about your glory days. Gary knew this.

"And you're a ballroom boy," Gary continued.

I nodded.

"How did a guy like you get into that?"

"A guy like me?"

"You know? All brooding alpha; all dark looks and oozing testosterone—which is a total turn on, by the way, especially with your bubble butt."

I blinked, still a little slow at catching Gary's rapid fire words, then a grin spread across my face.

"You're crazy, man."

"Crazy for you!" Gary screeched, clutching his chest. "You have no idea what a relief it is to have a hunk to look at," his voice dropping back an octave. "Erik had a face that said 'spank me' … you know, total butt face."

"I thought I was a showboating prima donna?" I reminded him.

"Psh! I'm over it. Come on, let's eat—I'm starving."

I hadn't eaten for nearly two days, but I didn't mention that.

The hotel's staff dining room was the place I'd been taken to the night before. It was small and basic, with narrow benches under metal tables. But the food looked and smelled fantastic, with piles of bacon, scrambled eggs and the weird stuff Americans called 'biscuits', bowls of fresh fruit and yogurt.

I was tempted to eat everything in sight, but I knew that was a sure way to end up puking during rehearsals.

Reluctantly, I made up a small plate with two pieces of bacon and a spoonful of eggs, as well as some fresh fruit and a glass of water.

I also took a couple of bananas for fuel later.

Gary introduced me to two other showgirls who were living at the hotel: Grace and Honey, friends from California. Both were attractive, with the same build—very tall and thin with medium-size tits that looked natural.

I was enjoying some low-level flirting until Yveta and Galina arrived, staking a claim by sliding into the empty places either side and kissing both cheeks in the European way.

"*Dobroe utro!* Sleep good?"

I nodded and smiled. "Hey, Yveta, Galina! This is my roommate, Gary."

"We've met," Gary said waspishly.

Yveta nodded curtly and Galina ignored him altogether. I wondered what the story was between them. They hardly knew each other.

The girls left the table briefly to grab some fruit to eat later, but their breakfast was a glass of hot water with a slice of lemon in it.

They were already thin and I wondered if they were anorexic—it was common in the dance world for men and women.

Instead, Yveta watched everyone else eat, her eyes hungry, while she sipped her hot water.

There were other hotel staff eating at the same time, but they kept to themselves.

After many coffees, we all headed to the theater for rehearsals.

The other showgirls arrived, the ones who didn't live in the hotel, complaining about the early hour. Gary told me that most of them had more than one job, and worked until two or three in the morning. A 10AM start was almost unheard of in Vegas.

Elaine's assistant ran us through some basic warm-up exercises until our muscles were loose. I was surprised to learn that I was one of only two people in the troupe who didn't have a background in ballet. It didn't bother me, but it made me think that someone other than Elaine had initiated my travel here.

The warm-ups weren't that different from ones I was used to, and I was confident that I could do the job I'd been hired for. I'd nailed my audition, I knew that much.

Neal, the assistant, had me and Gary do some upper body strengthening, push-ups and planks to help with core training to protect our backs when we lifted the girls.

Classical ballroom doesn't have lifts, but I'd always enjoyed the showdances where 'illegal lifts' were allowed. Even before my balls dropped, I'd wanted to be strong enough to do lifts. I was a big guy for a dancer, but even a girl who weighed a hundred pounds soaking wet could take a toll on your body if you didn't stay strong and have great balance.

The showgirls here were all more than averagely tall—over 5'10" as a minimum. And although their costumes were almost non-existent, their headdresses could weigh up to 30 pounds.

Either way, that was a lot to lift and I wasn't used to it. The theater arts girls I'd worked with before were all under 5'2". This was going to kill me.

I pushed hard, trying to make sense of the crazy world I'd been dropped into. *This* I understood—dancing, working to appear effortless on stage.

"Ash, take five," said Neal, throwing me a towel.

Surprised, I glanced past Neal and saw Trixie heading in my direction, her hard face unreadable.

"Boss wants to see you, Yveta and Galina this evening after rehearsals," she said, pointing a sharp fingernail at the three of us.

I grit my teeth. "Oleg?"

Trixie gave a delicate shudder. "No, the big boss. Mr. Volkov wants you in his suite at ten. I'll meet you in the lobby to take you up."

As she strode away she called out, "Dress nice!"

Yveta threw me a look. "What do you think he wants?"

"To meet his new staff, I guess."

"Maybe we'll get our phones back," she said hopefully.

The thought cheered me up, and I concentrated on finishing my workout, then followed Elaine's instructions as we began preparations for the show.

As one of only two guys among 14 women in the troupe, my role was simple: present seven girls, which meant leading them onto the stage so they could do their showgirls routine, while Gary presented the other seven. Easy. Boring.

All that Elaine wanted was a samba promenade. I'd been doing that since I was six. But when Yveta reached for me and smiled, I couldn't help throwing in a couple of sexy *botafogos* that made her giggle.

"Stop! Stop! Stop!" Elaine yelled. "What are you doing?"

My grin dropped. *Fuck!* This was no time to mess around.

"Sorry, Madam Director," I said formally.

"Hmm, no, I liked it," she said thoughtfully. "It's cheeky. Keep it in. Gary, show me your *contra botafogo* with … new girl … Galina!"

Gary looked taken aback, but then gripped Galina's hand and led her into the dance, cocking an eyebrow at me. I knew what he was saying: *Anything you can do…*

"Yes, I think we've got something here," Elaine said to herself. "Ash, solo spot *volta* with a reverse turn, whisk, and side samba walk. Yveta—keep up."

And she did.

By the end of the rehearsal, the four of us had developed a kind of dance-off, with each of us competing against the other couple to pull off increasingly intricate and difficult steps. Elaine was delighted and things were looking up. Not as boring as I thought it was going to be.

"The audience will eat this up. Good work people."

My gray t-shirt was dark with sweat and Yveta's make-up was smudged, but we grinned at each other. Even Gary didn't seem unhappy, although he found something to bitch about.

"Four years," he griped. "Four years, and I've never even had a sniff of a duet or solo spot until you come along, showboating your tight ass."

I winked at him, and Gary had to look away to stop the smile that was threatening to break out.

Honey strolled over, patting at her damp chest with a towel.

"Grace and I are going for drinks at the Venetian. It's happy hour—draft beer for three bucks, margaritas for five. Wanna come?"

"Are you asking all of us or just Mr. Hot-pants?" sniped Gary.

Honey sighed then gave a wide smile. "All of you, of course."

I was surprised, but pleased. "I'm in."

After showering and taking my workout clothes to the staff laundry, I went with Gary to meet the girls for drinks. It looked as though they were several margaritas in already.

Yveta poured herself onto my lap as soon as I sat down, while Honey and Grace exchanged amused glances. Gary sighed loudly and rolled his eyes.

I had to hold Yveta's hips firmly to stop her grinding on me. The attention was fun and she was hot, so I can't say I didn't enjoy it. Affairs between dance partners were common, but I also knew how they could negatively affect the dynamics of a performance if the relationship went bad, and Elaine had hinted at a larger role for us in the future. I couldn't fuck this up just because I had a chance of getting laid.

Yveta sighed into my neck, her warm breath bathing my skin. I shook my head, reminding myself that life was complicated enough right now.

Unfortunately, my dick wasn't paying attention to anything except the sexy woman snuggling against my chest and sitting with her hot pussy over my crotch. It had been a while.

Carefully, I shifted Yveta from my lap and gratefully took a sip of the cold beer that a waitress brought.

"Fine," huffed Gary. "I'll pay for one beer, Mr. Hot-pants, then the bitches can buy your drinks."

"You're the biggest bitch," laughed Honey.

"I'll drink to that," Gary said, raising his glass.

It was so damn easy to sit in a bar and have a few drinks and talk about dance. It made the easy hours pass too quickly and it was time to go and meet Volkov. My mellow mood slipped when Yveta told me that the new boss's surname translated as 'Wolf'.

Gary raised his eyebrows.

"I've worked here four years and I've only met the boss once. I wonder why he wants to meet you?"

His glance was speculative, but I saw concern there, too.

I shrugged, trying to hide the fact that my heartrate had kicked up a couple of beats.

"I don't know. But as long it's not that creepy bastard Oleg, I don't care."

Gary pressed his lips together but didn't say anything else.

Yveta was a happy drunk, but at nearly six foot, she wasn't the lightest weight to prop up. She sobered slightly when Galina reminded her that we had an appointment, but giggled all the way back to our hotel, wobbling dangerously in her high heels, until I clamped my arm around her waist and steered her through the early evening crowds with Galina's help.

Galina's English wasn't as good as Yveta's, but she told me that they'd met at a dance academy in St. Petersburg and had been friends ever since. It was Yveta's dream to be a Las Vegas showgirl.

She was silent for a moment, glancing at me nervously.

"I don't like it here."

Then she lowered her voice, even though we were on a noisy, crowded street.

"Where are those other girls, the ones who arrived with us?"

"I don't know."

"But it's strange, yes?"

I didn't know what to say to that.

Her lips trembled and she looked as if she might cry.

When we arrived back at the hotel, I waited outside the ladies' bathroom while Galina tried to sober up her friend some more.

Trixie saw me leaning against the wall and hurried across, her high heels click-clacking on the marble floor.

She stared critically at my chinos and plain white shirt, then gave a sharp nod. Her eyes narrowed as Yveta and Galina exited the bathroom.

Yveta seemed a lot more sober when she saw Trixie's grim expression, throwing a nervous glance at Galina, who looked as if she was about to pass out.

Without a word spoken, we followed Trixie to the elevator, watching in silence as she keyed in a private code for the Penthouse.

"Don't speak unless Mr. Volkov asks you a question, give yes and no answers, and smile."

She'd missed her calling as a cheerleader.

When the elevator doors swept open with a soft thwump, we were facing two heavy-set men with dark suits and emotionless faces, guarding a pair of thick oak doors with ornate handles.

They ignored the wide smile that Trixie sent their way.

"Mr. Volkov is expecting them," she said, sweeping her arm toward us.

The bodyguard with pale icy eyes held the door open so we could pass inside. He could have been Oleg's twin: not a reassuring thought.

I'd been expecting an office for a business meeting, but instead we were standing in an expensive suite with thick carpet and muted lighting.

The air was heavy with cigar smoke and I could smell weed, too.

Squinting through the clouds, I counted three men and a woman, all lounging on the wide Italian sectionals, drinking champagne.

One of the men was out of place in the classy room. He was heavily tatted and bearded, with a leather vest over a black t-shirt, and heavy biker boots on his feet. He also had a massive hunting knife in a sheath at his waist.

The other two men wore suits. I was no judge, but they looked expensive.

Then beside me, Yveta gave a soft gasp and I turned to look at her.

"Marta," she whispered.

The woman sitting on the couch was dressed in a plunging tank top and short skirt, heavily made up, and wearing stripper heels. I wouldn't have recognized her if Yveta hadn't said anything.

But then the biker guy laughed and clapped his hand on Marta's thigh, making her jump and spill her drink. That made him laugh harder as he gripped her leg.

Yveta's smile froze and she bit her lip as she glanced at me worriedly.

"Ah, my young dancers," said the man in the center of the room.

I didn't need to have ESP to know that this was Volkov—the Wolf.

He was well named, with thick gray hair like a mane around his large head and yellow-hazel eyes. He was lean and rangy like a wolf, but it was the way he exuded power that told me he was the man in charge.

"Sit, please," he said, but it was an order.

I sat on the section furthest away from him, trying to ignore Volkov's amused expression.

He waited until the girls were seated before he showed his teeth in a wide smile.

"Sit a little closer. You're so far away over there."

So we all had to stand and shuffle forward awkwardly until we were seated next to our host.

"That's better," he laughed. "Shy showgirls—and boy—who would have thought it?" And he laughed again.

"Now, you must be Yveta," he said to Galina, although I suspected he knew exactly who was who.

It was obvious that he was enjoying playing games with us. The thought put me even more on edge, although I tried to hide it. But at least Oleg wasn't in the room. The relief was short lived.

"And you are Aljaž, of course. I believe you like to be called Ash."

I nodded, and thanked Marta as she handed me a drink without looking at me.

Yveta and Galina were worried, exchanging nervous glances.

"I've heard good things about you," Volkov said, directing his eerie gaze to me. "Elaine is very pleased with rehearsals. She says you'll be an asset."

I forced out a smile, remembering Trixie's orders. "Thank you."

"Aren't you going to introduce me to your new friends, Andrei?" asked the other man in a suit, who'd remained silent until now.

Volkov hesitated for a fraction of a second then smiled coldly.

"Where are my manners? Yveta, Galina, Ash—this is my dear colleague Sergei. He's in charge of security."

Sergei stood to shake hands with us. He was maybe fifty, with steel-gray hair and eyes to match.

He smiled at me, his unblinking gaze crawling across my body.

"It seems to be my lucky night. It must be fate."

I was about to let go when he gave my hand an extra squeeze, his fingers stroking my wrist.

I pulled free, inhaling sharply, but he just smiled wider, his dead eyes shark-like as they trailed over my body in a way that was deliberate and obvious. He could also tell that it made me uncomfortable.

I'm a dancer. I'm used to people looking at my body. After all, it's my instrument, a powerful tool—I want people to look and admire. But it's all about the dancing. Not about people fucking me with their eyes like this asshole.

A lot of people assume that all male dancers are gay. I'm not. Definitely straight. It doesn't bother me what other men do. Getting hit on by gay guys is an occupational hazard when you're a dancer. Most of them back off when they realize that you're straight.

I wouldn't say I was close friends with them or any other dancers because it was too competitive. Except for Luka, my friends were outside the life.

I'd guess that probably six out of ten male dancers are gay, and I don't care whether it's ballroom, ballet or contemporary, but that means that four are straight. So I'm a minority. That gives some guys I've known license to sleep with as many women as they can—real wolves in sheep's clothing. I'm not like that. I'm not a monk either and I've had girlfriends, but it's usually too much drama, so I steer clear. One night stands where everyone knows the score is more my thing, but even then, not all that often. I'm always training, always taking classes. And if I'm not doing that, I'm working. Girls don't stay around if you don't pay enough attention to them.

My dance coach, Lelyana, always said that the drama should be on the dance floor and not in your personal life. I wanted to win more than I wanted to screw around.

But Sergei … I got the feeling that he didn't care if I was gay or straight. And that could be a problem, especially if he was close to Volkov.

I moved back to my seat, trying to relax the tension in my body.

Volkov had already lost interest and turned his attention to Yveta and Galina, chatting easily in Russian.

I wondered what was going on with Marta—and where was the other girl? If she hadn't reminded me so much of Luka's little sister, I probably would have kept my mouth shut.

"There was a girl at the airport..."

A sudden silence made me feel as if a spotlight was on me, and although the room was air conditioned, sweat trickled down my back.

"With Oleg..." I rasped out, my throat dry despite the drink in my hand.

Volkov laughed and glanced at Sergei.

"Oleg has a girlfriend? Why did no one tell me? Should we prepare for a wedding?"

His smile was wintry.

"I'll make enquiries," he said without much interest.

I wanted to say more, but I was nervous. The atmosphere turned arctic and those yellow lamp-like eyes burned coldly.

The biker shifted in his seat, his hand tightening on Marta's leg until she let out a small cry.

Sergei stared at me, his face a wax-like mask, blank and expressionless, but utterly chilling.

I felt my courage shrivel and my body screamed for me to run.

Sitting still, meeting his gaze, those were the mostly insanely brave things I'd ever done in my entire life.

CHAPTER 3

Ash

The meeting with Volkov had left us all shaken. It was clear that Marta wasn't in that room willingly, and she looked terrified. The biker guy had been creepy enough, but those Russians ... not people you messed with.

I hoped I wouldn't see any of them again.

Trixie was waiting outside the suite. She didn't seem surprised when she saw our shocked faces.

"Who are these guys?" I asked quietly as we rode the elevator back to the ground floor.

She gave a grim smile. "Haven't you figured it out yet?"

I had. I just didn't want to believe it.

"Bratva."

Russian mafia.

It was Yveta who had spoken. Trixie stared back, but didn't answer directly.

"It's not always so bad. Mostly they just want to do business, you know."

Galina gripped my hand tightly and I gave it an encouraging squeeze although I felt just as worried as her and Yveta.

"Sergei..." Trixie shivered and lowered her voice to a whisper. "He's a sick bastard. Thank God I'm not his type," and when she glanced at me, her expression was pitying. "And Oleg ... he likes them young. Very young."

She swallowed and looked down.

"They don't usually come to the theater—that's a legit business. You should be okay. Just keep your mouths shut and stay out of trouble. That's the best advice I can give you." She forced a fake smile. "That's showbiz!"

I shook my head, and her smile dropped away.

"You do what you gotta do, kid. Which in this case is nothing. You'll learn."

"But that's crazy!"

"Comments like that will get you killed," Trixie snapped, dropping the ditzy blonde act.

Galina and Yveta were having a silent conversation, although both of them looked scared.

When Trixie left us in the lobby, I turned to them.

"Can you believe this shit?!"

Galina paled even further, swaying slightly.

"Shut up!" Yveta hissed at me.

"But…"

"Listen," she said, grabbing my arm and towing me toward the staff area. "Those are *Bratva!* You don't mess with them. You don't make them angry. Not if you want to live."

Galina swallowed and nodded her agreement.

"Then what the hell are we supposed to do?"

"What we came here for—we dance."

And she marched off, dragging Galina with her. I watched them in silence, wondering if she was right.

I decided I'd talk to Gary. But when I opened the door to our room, it was empty. I waited up for him for a while, but then I remembered he had a date with one of the guys in the band.

Frustrated and disgusted with my own cowardice, I finally fell into an uneasy sleep.

My last waking thought was that I hadn't gotten my cell phone back either.

The next morning, Galina and Yveta avoided me at breakfast. Honey raised an eyebrow.

"Lovers quarrel?"

"What?"

She sat down next to me, a bowl of fruit and yogurt in front of her.

"Why are they giving you the cold shoulder?"

I took a sip of coffee.

"How much do you know about this guy Volkov?"

"Oh," she said, understanding in her expression. "You heard the rumors."

She knew. They all knew.

"It's more than that. We saw…"

"Look, Ash, I've lived in Vegas for a few years now. You hear stuff. It's best to ignore it. Asking questions isn't a good idea."

"That's what Trixie said."

"You should listen to her."

I rubbed my forehead. "But…?"

She rested her hand on my arm and looked at me seriously.

"Ash, asking questions isn't a good idea."

Then she stood up and walked away.

Across the room, Yveta glanced at me briefly, then dropped her gaze back to the table.

Elaine worked us relentlessly all day. She'd decided to add another Latin number to the show, and as there were only three of us who were trained in mambo let alone salsa, it was slow going. We were professional dancers, but still, it's a tricky rhythm to pick up. Salsa is a street dance with no frame, and doesn't even break on the right count. A lot of ballroom dancers despise salsa, but I'd always liked it.

When you're learning, teachers say you only dance three of the four steps, but that's not strictly true. It's a fluid, loose dance, and you're constantly in motion.

The hip action is mostly relaxed, subtle, especially for the men, and your weight is placed onto a slightly bent knee. There are no heel leads, unlike in ballroom, so steps are taken first with the ball of the foot in contact with the floor, and then with the heel lowering when the weight is fully transferred.

Armography has to stay natural or it looks contrived and weird. You have to let your arms react naturally to body movement, and held slightly above waist level.

And there are *a lot* of lifts you can use in a showdance salsa. Elaine must have been trying to kill me and Gary, because it felt like she was working us through every lift she knew, and then inventing a few on top.

"Again!" she shouted. "Grace—more hip action."

Un, dos, tres…

The Ricky Martin song pounded out for the hundredth time. Again. And again.

My t-shirt was stuck to my body and Gary's face was bright red. The girls had sweated through their makeup, even though we all used waterproof cosmetics for that reason. But we'd been at this all day, not just the two hours of a show.

Un, dos, tres…

"Smile!" Elaine roared.

We smiled our asses off, and Honey threw me an apologetic look as I braced myself one more time to lift her into a rollerblind drop.

She wrapped herself into my right side and I caught her rising leg with my free arm, spun around twice, clamped my hand around her lower thigh and let her roll down my body, making sure she didn't hit the floor.

My muscles were straining, and Honey's skin was slippery with sweat. It had been a near miss the last couple of times.

Then Gary dropped Yveta on her ass and she yelled at him in Russian.

Elaine told Yveta to go ice her backside. Then she turned to look at us, all panting like racehorses. I guess she took pity on us because she frowned and shook her head, dismissing us for the day.

"Good job people," she said grudgingly.

I couldn't help smiling—we were on fucking fire, and the audience would be wowed. Yes, we sweated. Yes, we strained. But we smiled through every second. And I fucking loved it.

I high-fived Gary and he slapped the palm of my hand, then winced.

"I don't know about icing my ass," Gary whined. "I need to ice my whole body."

"I've done that before," I sighed, rolling my head to ease my neck muscles.

"Yeah, me too. We can't get that here, but we can use the masseuses if they're not booked by guests."

"Really? That would be amazing."

"I'll call down after we've showered and then I'll ask if…"

Gary's words died as he opened the door to our room.

"What the…?"

I stepped into the room behind him, staring at the devastation.

"Oh my God," Gary whispered, clutching my arm.

All our clothes had been tossed onto the floor, and it looked as though someone had taken a knife to them. But as I looked closer, I realized it wasn't Gary's clothes that had been cut to ribbons—just mine. Everything I owned, every single thing had been shredded, even my shoes.

"I'd better call security," he whispered.

I nodded, robbed of any words I might have said. I started to sift through the rags, searching for anything that they might have left undamaged. But there was nothing.

My iPod was gone, my wallet and ID, even my aftershave had been taken. I sat on the bed, numbly wondering why they hadn't touched Gary's clothes.

But when security arrived, I had a horrible feeling that I knew the answer.

Sergei walked into the room, shaking his head at the mess.

"Oh dear, who could have done such a terrible thing, I wonder? But still, it's my lucky day," he smiled. "I get to see your bedroom."

He smirked at me while Oleg stood watching, and I had to clench my fists to keep the anger inside.

"We'll find the person responsible and make them pay, of course," he said. "I do feel responsible as the head of security. But I'm sure I can make it all better."

His eyes dropped to my t-shirt, still stuck to my body with sweat, and he licked his lips.

"If you don't feel safe in this room, better rooms are provided for staff who show their loyalty," he said, catching my elbow and staring at me.

He trailed a finger along my forearm and squeezed my hand.

Annoyed, I stepped back, crashing my hip against the bed frame.

"I'm not gay," I said quickly, hoping that I was wrong and that he'd back off.

He smiled like he didn't believe me. That pissed me off even more. And it reminded me of my father, which was one of the reasons I was here.

"So? Just think about it as making the boss happy," and he smiled again.

I didn't want him to know that he'd got me rattled, so I crossed my arms over my chest, trying to ignore the way he was staring at my crotch.

"Ah, Aljaž, you really should learn who your friends are."

"What are you going to do about this?" I asked, my eyes narrowing. "Everything is ruined."

Sergei shrugged, his eyes glinting.

"Who knows? Choices, choices."

He paused, his eyes lingering on mine and gave a sarcastic laugh, leaning forward, tapping a finger against his thin lips.

"I can offer you somewhere … cozier? A little more luxury? No? Ah well, that's a pity. I'm sure we're going to be great friends. Think about it overnight. Let me know when you've changed your mind."

And he left.

Gary wiped a hand over his face, his skin a sickly green color.

"That guy is…"

"I know."

He swallowed and glanced at the door.

"What are you going to do?"

"Can I borrow something to wear? I've got some money saved so I can buy…" Then I swore. "They took my credit cards. Fuck it—I'll have to cancel them. Can I borrow your cell?"

Gary nodded and handed me his phone. It took a while to make the calls and while I spoke to the credit card companies, Gary picked up my destroyed clothes and shoved the rags into garbage bags.

It was approaching 2AM by the time we went to bed. Gary wedged a chair against the door. It wouldn't do much, but it made him feel better.

I don't think either of us slept.

The next morning he loaned me some workout clothes. At least I had the dance shoes I'd used yesterday. That was something, but I needed to buy a performance pair along with, well, everything.

I planned to go shopping after work with Gary. He said he knew some discount places where I could get what I needed, and he'd loan me the money until I could get my cards replaced.

But when we got to rehearsals, Sergei was waiting for me. With Oleg.

"I just need to borrow him for a few hours," he smiled at Elaine.

She didn't look happy about it, but didn't argue either. I had no choice but to go with him.

He led me through the staff entrance. It creeped me out to have Oleg walking behind me, wondering what he was going to do because he damn well wasn't there for decoration.

At the kitchen, we halted and Sergei pointed his finger at one of the Asian cooks.

"Him," he said. "He's the one who broke into your room."

The man looked terrified and started babbling in his own language as he backed away. When he turned to run, Oleg grabbed him by his arm and flung him against the wall. And then he punched him. Over and over again he punched him, methodically turning the man's face into raw meat.

The other cooks fled and I stood there, watching a man being beaten half to death.

I did nothing.

I said nothing.

I couldn't do anything except stare in horrified silence.

Oleg dropped the man to the floor, like a carcass from a butcher's shop, then calmly washed his hands.

For the first time in my life, I was seeing more than everyday meanness or stupidity. We all say: *I could kill him for that*, but we don't mean it literally. For the first time, I was staring at real evil.

Cold fingers of fear clawed their way into my chest as Sergei smiled and heaved a fake sigh.

"Koreans—always the same. Ah well, problem solved. Now, what can we do about your clothes? Although I'd much rather see you naked."

And he laughed.

Still shocked, my flesh crawled when he laid his hand on my shoulder, slowly stroking down to my stomach.

Appalled, I stepped back abruptly, but Conan was standing behind me and wrapped a thick arm around my neck, cutting off the oxygen with expert speed.

The pressure on my throat increased each second.

I fought with my whole body, striking out with legs and arms, but it was like hitting granite.

"That's not very friendly when I've done you a favor," Sergei commented as I fought for breaths.

He grinned as he grabbed my junk and squeezed hard.

"I'm sure we'll be friends soon," he whispered against my ear. "Good friends."

My vision was turning black.

Then Conan let go, and I dropped to my knees, breath rasping through my crushed windpipe.

Fury and humiliation heated my blood, but fear cooled it again. I wanted to kill the bastard, but I didn't want to die. *This is a nightmare! Please God, let me wake up.*

The mix of extreme emotions was disorienting.

I shook my head, trying to get my vision back and stop my ears from ringing. Slowly, my breathing started to ease, and Conan hauled me to my feet while Sergei smiled and clapped his hands together like a gameshow host.

"Shopping!"

I was still dazed, but seeing his grinning face, I felt a rush of raw anger, raw fucking anger.

I gritted my teeth, trying to remain calm. Dancing was everything to me and I'd lost count of the times I'd danced through the pain. That's what I had to do right now—dance through the pain. *Survive.*

"Oleg will find a shop where we can get what you need. I would pay good money to see you dance—how fortunate I feel that you work for us." Then he smiled. "Oh dear, you will owe me a lot of money for your new clothes. How on earth will you pay me back?"

His eyes glittered with lust and malice, enjoying the disgust he saw on my face.

I bit the inside of my mouth, tasting blood.

I will get out of here, I told myself. *I will survive this. And then this evil bastard is going to pay. I swear it.*

"Where are we going?" I asked, my voice an expressionless monotone.

I'm not sure what I was thinking. Maybe that if I talked normally to the psycho, he'd … I don't know … behave normally? I didn't want to die in this miserable hotel kitchen.

"You'll find out," he replied dismissively.

He led us out, stepping past the unmoving body of the cook, ignoring him like he was trash. I glanced down, but I couldn't tell if he was breathing or not.

Outside, Oleg climbed into the driver's seat of a limousine. And for the next two hours, we shopped. It was a lesson in submission, and I knew it.

I watched, stony-eyed, as Sergei paraded me through a number of upscale boutiques, choosing the most expensive clothes for me to wear. Each time he'd sigh and raise his eyebrows.

"Oh, dear. Such a debt you owe me. But don't worry: I can be a very generous friend."

He licked his lips slowly and suggestively, as if licking an ice cream … or a dick. I wanted to vomit.

And everywhere was the silent, looming presence of Oleg, his flat eyes shifting continuously, the bulge under his armpit showing that he was armed.

During the entire shopping spree, my mind was whirring, thinking, taking in the spread of Las Vegas, trying to hatch an escape plan.

But Oleg was watching, subtly moving his body to block every exit.

I knew that I had to escape. But I had no phone, no money, no ID. And no contacts—nowhere to turn for help outside this damn city.

Luka was on tour, and my father—he'd made it very clear that he didn't want anything to do with me.

My heart rate rocketed when I saw two men in the uniform of city police. But Oleg's hand moved toward his gun, a clear message, and Sergei edged closer, his stinking breath hot on my cheek.

"That wouldn't be sensible," he chuckled. "And it would be very unfortunate for those pretty girls you dance with."

My body was rigid. I already felt guilty for what had happened to the Korean. I couldn't be responsible for anything happening to the girls.

I forced myself to stay still, but inside I was begging the police to turn in my direction.

When they disappeared from view, Sergei laughed derisively.

"Not the hero you think you are."

He was right. I did *nothing*. I was a coward.

My shoulders slumped in defeat.

Then Oleg's phone rang and I heard him say the name 'Volkov' as he handed his cell to Sergei.

He spoke rapidly in Russian, but still I felt his greedy eyes on me. The way he kept glancing in my direction made me think the conversation was about me.

My head dropped into my hands.

What the hell do I do now?

People were beaten to bloody rags, and people were held hostage, and we shopped.

It was sickening.

Sergei ended his call and uttered a string of instructions to Oleg while we drove to another store. But this one sold dance supplies and I felt a small surge of hope. The familiar scene, the smell of leather, of coconut foot lotion—it reminded me that there was a world beyond this nightmare.

Oleg didn't enter but left us at the entrance, nodding at something Sergei said to him.

I didn't understand what was going on. I knew it was all a game, but if they were just going to kill me, why go through this charade?

It was all mind games, to get inside my head, to break me. I knew Sergei wanted to fuck me. No way. Over my cold, dead body. Although he'd probably enjoy that.

Trying to ignore his hungry stare, I chose a pair of Latin shoes with the regulation two-inch heel, and a pair of patent ballroom shoes—the tools of my trade.

Ballroom shoes look like ordinary men's dress shoes, but instead the soles are suede and they're super light in weight, even with the central steel-shank support and extra cushioning.

I chose the best because cheap shoes can cripple a pro dancer.

My last must-have purchases were a pair of Latin pants and a plain black, long-sleeved shirt with a built in dance-belt. Americans called them mantys—man panties.

But my gut twisted again at the fascination on Sergei's face while I bought what I needed. He was staring at the built in dance-belt which looks kind of like a woman's teddy. It's only strange when you first start wearing them. We all use them: they hold your dick and balls in place, and give a clean line—no shirt hanging out of your pants when you dance.

But he was still staring at me.

And I was worried.

As we left the dance supplies store, I sensed a shift in his mood.

The casual mocking, the insinuation, the sexual comments had given way to something darker.

I've seen every kind of petty meanness as a pro dancer. I've seen costumes slashed, shoes suddenly gone missing. I've seen people deliberately blocked-in or boxed during a competition so they're squeezed into a corner by other competitors and can't complete their routine. I've seen spite and jealousy and every kind of backstabbing you can imagine. I thought I'd seen it all. But looking into his eyes was like looking into Hell.

Oleg opened the limousine's door and Sergei slid onto the plush leather with a gratified sigh. Then he patted the empty seat next to him, and my eyes widened.

"Come sit," he ordered. "Daddy wants to play."

He spread his legs and grinned up at me.

Oh shit!

My feet refused to move, disgust and dread locking me to the spot.

From behind, Oleg launched a kidney-punch, and fierce pain knifed through my whole body. I gasped, collapsing into the back of the limo, my face inches from Sergei's crotch.

"Perfect!"

He laughed, gripping the back of my head and forcing my face against his zipper. He was hard and I gagged, trying to turn my face away.

"So ungrateful," he laughed again.

There was a soft metallic click, and something cold pressed against the base of my skull. I knew it was a gun—knew it although I couldn't see it. I froze, my heart pounding painfully.

"No one can see you through these tinted windows," he said conversationally. "No one can hear you. And guess what? No one will care. Just another faceless, numberless, insignificant immigrant."

He pressed the barrel of the gun so it dug into my flesh as it was dragged down my spine.

"All those pretty clothes I bought for you. Well, now I want you to thank me nicely," he said pleasantly. "It's not much to ask. Is it?"

The pressure was removed from my neck and I sat up cautiously, muscles bunched, ready to run.

Sergei smiled slyly.

"The doors are locked, but feel free to try them. Oh, you're shaking. Poor boy. I'll do it for you," and he rattled the limo's door handles. "See, locked."

He leaned back against the seat, the gun still in his hand, his eyes trained on me. He was enjoying every part of this. He was sick in the head, getting off on the power trip. I thought I was going to die.

"Unzip my pants."

My mouth was dry. I wanted to shout, but all that came out was a feeble croak.

"Fuck you!"

"That's the general idea. Let's start with me fucking your mouth."

CHAPTER 4

Ash

All I could do was glare at him, show him my disgust and hatred. My heart raced as the urge for fight or flight screamed inside me. Sergei huffed with impatience, then grabbed my hand and pinned it against the door with the gun.

"If I have to ask you again, I'll break a finger. I'll keep breaking them until you do what you're told. Or maybe I'll break your feet. You're a dancer: tell me, Aljaž, how many bones are there in the human foot? I know it's a lot."

I shook my head, breath hammering in my throat.

"Fuck you!" I said again, louder this time.

He slammed the gun barrel against my hand, snapping the bones of my pinkie finger.

White hot pain slashed through me and I shouted out, trying to pull away, but he slammed the gun again, and a loud crunch was the sound of my index finger breaking.

"I am not a patient man," he growled, unzipping his pants and pulling out his straining cock. "Suck it!"

"I'll bite off your fucking dick and spit it at you!" I shouted, my vision dipping with the agony from my shattered hand.

I was concentrating on trying not to pass out as I slumped into the corner, my eyes blazing with hatred. I was close to breaking, launching myself at the evil bastard. Only the black barrel of the gun pointing at my stomach stopped me.

I was panting, breaths fast and ragged, lips pulled back in a snarl, wishing I had the gun, wishing I could kill him and take this evil out of the world.

He sighed, pressing a button that lowered the panel between the backseat and the driver.

Sitting in the front was the girl from the airport, the young one, the one whose name I never learned. Tears streaked her face and one eye was swollen shut. Purple bruises colored her arms and neck, and her expression as she stared at me was pleading, desperate. Her mouth moved wordlessly.

Instinctively, I leaned toward her, but Sergei slapped my face casually, bringing my attention back to him.

"Suck me off and do it with a smile ... or I'll let Oleg finish her this time."

Oleg put his massive hand around the girl's neck and started to squeeze. Her eyes bulged, small blood vessels popped, turning the whites of her eyes red, but still fixed on me, still staring, begging me to save her. Her tiny hands clawed at Oleg, but the hulking man just laughed.

"Running out of time," Sergei sing-songed.

"You sick bastard!"

I punched the back of the seat, impotent and furious.

"So my mother tells me," he smiled. Then he glanced at the girl, and his smile widened. "Oh dear, she's turning blue. I don't think she'll last much longer."

The girl went limp in Oleg's hands, but he didn't let go. If anything, his massive fingers tightened around her slim throat and her body jerked.

Vomit burned in my throat, and the musky scent of his dick was putrid in the enclosed space.

The girl's body jerked again and I cried out, but Sergei simply smiled and gestured at his bare cock with the hand that held his gun.

I squeezed my eyes shut so I didn't have to look at the girl. Tears of outrage burned behind my lids.

I leaned forward, taking his dick in my mouth. If I didn't look, it wasn't real.

But I could feel him, smell him, taste him. He thrust hard and I gagged, then felt the roots of my hair rip as he gripped hard, tugging painfully.

"Hmm, I think you've done this before," he purred.

Let the girl live. Let her live...

My eyes watered as his small dick pumped into my mouth. He was getting off on this, I knew it. His dick twitched and when he came with a soft sigh, salty cum pulsed onto my tongue.

I reared back, unable to control the retching as I vomited onto his lap.

He screamed with rage and slammed the gun's barrel against my temple, knocking me backwards so my head bounced against the window.

Stars danced in front of my eyes and I was close to passing out.

"You'll pay for that!" he screeched, then shouted something in Russian.

The car shuddered to a halt and a moment later, pain exploded through me as Oleg grabbed my broken hand, dragging me from the car.

I'm going to die.

The thought was clear and exact. I can't explain, but it was a relief.

My knees hit concrete and I knew that I was drawing my final breath. I spat at Oleg's feet, hatred burning through me as I lifted my head and stared into his eyes. It all seemed so pointless now: all my dreams, everything I'd worked for—it all crumbled to ashes in front of me, and I was going to die on a dirty concrete floor.

A pair of shiny shoes stepped in front of me and the click of a gun's safety being released drew my gaze upward again. I stared at the barrel of Sergei's gun, waiting for the shot, waiting for the explosion of light that would end in darkness. His finger tightened on the trigger and our eyes locked. He frowned, his finger trembling as we stared at each other. My stomach clenched, waiting for the bullet.

But it never came.

And then he was backing away and the car was moving. I blinked, shocked, suddenly viscerally aware. The girl! I scrabbled to my feet, trying to see if she was alive, but the tinted windows did their job, and I was forced to watch as the limousine gathered speed.

I collapsed onto the ground, the concrete cool against my face and hands. I was too tired to move. My eyes closed. I was close to unconsciousness, and I think that would have been a blessing.

But then the memories surged back, and my stomach revolted again, heaving up acid as I spat cum onto the floor. My vision swam and I felt blood trickling through my hair from where Sergei had slammed the gun into my head.

I retched again and again, but my stomach was already empty, I was doing nothing more than spitting phlegm onto the concrete. My eyes streamed and every part of my body hurt, my broken fingers twisted like twigs.

Slowly, I sat up.

I'm alive.

I laughed. And I cried. I don't remember, but I sat there having a complete fucking breakdown.

When I was finally able to stop my stomach from climbing up my throat, I kneeled up shakily and gazed around, blinking in the dim light of an underground parking lot. My bags from the shopping trip were scattered around me. I touched my head with my good hand, and the fingers came away dripping bright blood. The other hand throbbed relentlessly and I held it against my chest, wondering if I could use something to make splints and a sling.

My brain was skittering in a hundred different directions, making it impossible to focus on anything, to do anything. I felt dirty and violated, sickened beyond everything I'd known. The taste of vomit was still in my mouth, and I spat onto the floor repeatedly, shock, pain and spent adrenaline making my body shudder.

I closed my eyes as a wave of dizziness hit, leaning forwards, resting my good hand on my knees, trying to catch my breath.

I will live through this.

Then I stood up straight and screamed out loud: "I will live!"

"Hello? Who's there?"

A woman's voice made me spin around and I nearly lost my balance.

"Oh, is that you, Ash?"

Was I? I hardly knew anymore. I wasn't the same person who'd arrived in Las Vegas. I wasn't even the same as when I'd woken up this morning.

Trixie's heels clicked as she strode across the concrete floor. She was wearing a bright pink pant suit.

It was so surreal that I just stood there staring like an idiot.

My body was ice cold and I was shaking, nauseous.

Her eyes drifted to the blood that masked one side of my face and my hand with the bent fingers, still cradled against my chest.

"Oh," she breathed out. "Did Sergei do that?"

My eyes shot up to hers. "You knew?"

She nodded.

"He called me to come get you."

Her tone became brisk and businesslike. She certainly didn't sound shocked.

"I'm sorry this happened."

"There was a girl," I croaked, my throat still raw. "Oleg had her…"

"Take my advice," she said sharply. "Forget everything you've seen and heard."

"But…"

"You're not listening to me," she hissed. "You've only seen a tiny piece of what they're capable of doing! If you want to carry on breathing, forget *everything!*"

She bent down and picked up my bags, walking away, clip-clopping across the concrete.

I didn't follow.

I should go to the police. Christ, I had to do *some*thing.

"Listen!" she snapped, turning around and glaring at me. "Did you get a photo of it happening? Video it on your phone? No, of course you didn't. There's no proof! And even if someone did listen, you wouldn't last the night."

"He killed her! I know it! Don't you even care?"

"I care about not being next," she said, her voice low and furious.

"Then I'll leave!" I shouted. "I'll get the hell away and then tell someone. I'll buy a ticket online and…"

Her voice was brittle. "They'll be watching you—and you can't trust the police. You'd never make it."

She stared at me, holding my gaze until I scrubbed a hand over my face in frustration. Then she glanced down at my damaged fingers.

"I'll take care of that for you."

I shook my head. "There must be a way out of here!"

"Sure, honey. Feet first." Then she gave a small smile. "Maybe you'll get lucky and Sergei will forget about you. Especially as he's already had you."

"He hasn't *had* me!" I spat out, my eyes narrowed in anger, my gut twisting.

"Oh," she said softly.

"What? What the hell are you talking about?"

She deliberately ignored my question.

"I'm going to get out of here," I growled.

She shrugged again, unimpressed.

"That's what they all say."

When she turned and walked away, I didn't know what to do. I had nowhere else to go. This time I followed.

I tried to take in my surroundings and ignore the pain.

It was gloomy, just a few service lights that filled the space with shadows. Expensive cars were parked in numbered bays: Porsches, Ferraris, an Aston Martin and two Jaguar coupés.

I was scared, really fucking scared. I was lucky to be alive. If I kept asking about the girl, I wouldn't live for much longer. Maybe I should do what Trixie said and forget about her if I wanted to survive. Could I do that? I wasn't sure. The girl, if she was alive, what would happen to her? Where would they take her? I had to tell someone. But I didn't know who I could trust.

Anger and frustration burned inside me and it wouldn't take much for the simmering rage to explode.

And then you'll die. I was a fucking coward.

"Looks like you got some cool clothes," said Trixie, peering into one of the bags.

I stared at her in disbelief as blood continued to trickle down the side of my face.

Twenty minutes ago, I thought I was going to die, now Trixie was smiling and joking in front of me. She didn't want to see the blood or my broken fingers; she didn't want to know that I'd witnessed an assault, possibly a murder, maybe two. I couldn't make sense of it and I shook my head in confusion.

Nothing felt safe anymore.

She took me to the theater's first aid station. I could hear rehearsals on the stage, feel the vibrations of the music.

It spun my mind that this existed side by side with the violence of the last few hours, operated by the same people.

Dance, performing, this was my life. But now the whole thing was tainted.

Trixie frowned, staring at my hand which had swollen to twice its normal size. The fingers that Sergei had broken were turning purple and looked like a couple of Kranjska sausages.

"We'll get some ice for that."

Trixie led me to a stool and told me to sit while she opened a large fridge, pulling out two packs of ice.

I rested my hand between the icepacks while she washed the cut on my head.

"You'll have a scar," she said. "But it's above your hairline. It should probably have stitches…"

Her words tailed off.

"But I'm not going to get them," I finished for her.

"You're learning."

We stared at each other for several long seconds before Trixie looked away.

After some of the swelling had begun to reduce, she eased the ice packs away, and without telling me what she was going to do, grabbed my broken fingers and yanked them back into a straight line.

The pain was off the chart and black dots floated in front of my eyes. I didn't know if I was going to puke or pass out.

In the end, I didn't do either, swaying on the stool while Trixie expertly splinted my broken fingers, then wrapped them in a thick bandage.

I guessed it wasn't the first time she'd had to do that.

"Leave the splints on for a week. Then you'll need to do some exercises so they don't get too stiff. Just like new in five, six weeks."

I nodded, but inside the molten lava of anger was beginning to glow red. Somehow, I'd find a way to take these evil bastards down. Somehow.

"You'd better get to rehearsals."

I didn't move. I just sat there staring at her.

She shrugged and walked out.

I sat for a few more minutes, staring at my bandaged hand, then I walked from the wings onto the stage. Elaine opened her mouth, an angry look on her face. But then she took in the blood on my shirt and bandaged hand. I thought I saw a flicker of emotion behind her eyes, but it was gone so quickly, I couldn't be sure.

"Be ready in ten minutes," she said.

Two broken fingers, a bitching headache and a gash in my head that needed stitches, aching ribs from where I'd been punched, and … I didn't want to think about the rest.

Elaine definitely didn't look happy to see me. Maybe she was worried that Sergei would be around more now. My gut twisted at the thought, remembering what Trixie had said.

When the other dancers saw me, a shocked murmur rippled around the room. Elaine snapped at them, and they all went back to work, throwing me quick, questioning glances.

Yveta looked like she was going to say something but bit her lip and thought better of it. Gary's expression tightened as he eyed the blood on my face and swollen hand, but he didn't say anything either. It was a disease of silence. And I was just as infected as everyone else.

I woke up choking, feeling Oleg's hands around my throat. I lashed out with my feet and someone shrieked.

"Ow! You asshole!"

Panting, my hands shaking, I turned on the small bedside light and found Gary crouched at the end of my bed holding a bloody nose.

"What the fuck is wrong with you?" Gary moaned, then shuffled to the bathroom, dripping blood on the cheap carpet.

I yanked back the covers and stalked after him.

"What did you do to me?"

"What did *I* do to *you*? I'm the one bleeding to death!"

Gary's voice was muffled as held a wet washcloth to his face and a nose that was twice its normal size.

"You were screaming and yelling and wouldn't wake up. I tried to shake you awake and you almost broke my fucking nose!"

Oh shit.

I ran my good hand through sweat-soaked hair. I must have been dreaming. I'd thought that Oleg had come back for me, had tried to kill me, just like…

I didn't want to finish the thought, but the memory of the air being cut off, my throat being crushed—it was wriggling like an eel in the back of my brain.

And her eyes … the girl's eyes: I couldn't stop seeing them, begging me to help her, to save her.

"I'm sorry," I said lamely. "It was a nightmare."

"You're the nightmare!"

I couldn't blame him. It must be shitty when your roommate starts shouting, and you try to wake him up and get punched in the face.

Silently, I grabbed a towel and started scrubbing at the blood stains on the thin carpet. Gary was sitting on the end of his bed holding the wet washcloth to his nose.

I glanced up to catch him staring but he just shrugged.

"What can I say? You're a crazy asshole, but you're still hot."

Looked like I was forgiven. I was working out that Gary's bark was worse than his bite.

I gestured at his nose.

"Is it broken?"

"No," he sighed. "Thank God. My plastic surgeon would throw a fit." Then he glanced at me. "What was the nightmare about?"

"Oleg."

Gary shuddered. "Ugh, that monster. Don't say anymore."

"I think he killed…"

"I DON'T WANT TO KNOW!" Gary hissed at me.

His words made me grimace.

"Nobody wants to know. This place is sick. The fear is like … it's a cancer inside everyone. How can you stand it?"

"It's never been this bad before," Gary admitted flatly. "I'm scared. We all are after what happened to you today. So you know what I'm going to do? Nothing. I don't see anything, I don't hear anything, and I don't say anything."

"But…"

Gary dropped his voice to a whisper.

"People around here disappear. My last roommate, Erik, he was like you—thought he could change the world. One day he was just gone. Officially, he went back to his family in Poland. Unofficially, no one knows."

He shuddered.

"The rumor is that Sergei wants to be top dog, and with Oleg helping him, it could well happen. There's a power struggle going on. And you, my friend, have walked right into the middle of it."

Gary dropped the washcloth onto the floor and climbed back into bed.

"This conversation is done. And if you start screaming again, I'll toss a glass of water over you—it's safer."

Gary threw the duvet over his shoulders and turned on his side, huffing noisily.

I'd just been chewed out by an angry dude in *Hello Kitty* pajamas.

My brain was wired after everything that had happened, but my body was suffering.

I lay in the narrow bed and forced myself to relax. I'd wait, find out how this place worked, and then…

"Hey, Gary!"

"What do you want now?" came a very pissed off voice.

"Can I borrow your phone? I need to send an email."

Gary grumbled some more, but eventually tossed me his phone.

"I'm just going to say this one more time—be careful who you involve in this. These people are dangerous."

I sat with the cell phone in my lap, and tapped out an email to Luka, giving him the basics of what I'd seen and heard. I wasn't expecting to hear right back, because I knew he was on tour, but within minutes, he'd replied, his message short and unambiguous:

Go to the police.

I glanced over at Gary who was snoring loudly, his swollen nose amplifying the sound.

I can't.

After a few more moments, the reply arrived.

I have €1,000. It's yours brother.
Just say the word. I'll buy your flight home right now.

I wanted to tell him to get me a ticket, but without ID, I had no chance. I turned off the phone and lay back.

But every time I shut my eyes, I saw the girl's face. I wanted to claw that memory out of my brain, and after another hour of her haunting me, I was ready to tear out my own eyes. But eventually, sleep pulled me under into dreams that were dark and ugly, slicing at the surface of my mind, icy breaths chilling my skin.

My life hadn't been all sunshine before, but I hadn't been afraid of it. Everyone dies. Everyone. But today, I'd thought it was my turn. That was messing with my head. I barely knew who I was anymore. All I wanted was to feel something other than numbing fear.

Two months ago, my biggest worry was Jana breaking up our partnership. Now, a crazed mafia killer had his sights set on either fucking me or killing me.

The next morning, we carried on as if nothing had happened. Gary's nose was a little swollen, but he didn't mention it.

At breakfast, no one spoke to me and no one wanted to sit near me. Even Gary was unusually quiet.

Then Trixie appeared, and the muted conversation died away.

"Mr. Volkov wants to see you," she said, snapping her fingers.

No one would look at me, although I saw Gary darting a worried glance before his eyes lowered quickly.

I didn't even know how I felt. I didn't know if I expected to live.

This time, Trixie led me to Volkov's office where he sat like at king on his throne.

"Such a shame about that little misunderstanding with Sergei," he said, inclining his head to my damaged hand. "He just can't help himself when he sees a handsome face, although I can't say you do much for me … no offense."

"None taken," I ground out after slightly too long a pause that made Volkov's forehead wrinkle in a frown.

"Hmm, so there's an end to it, no?"

If I was going to say anything, now was the time, but my tongue felt paralyzed.

"Sergei says you owe him money?"

Volkov's voice was even, pleasant, the odor of violence hidden behind expensive cologne.

"I … my clothes were damaged."

"Maybe you'd like to repay him personally?" Volkov asked.

I knew what he was suggesting, and for a moment I thought that I was going to puke, so I said nothing.

"Or perhaps I'll pay him what you owe, and you can pay me. It's possible to get good tips working in my nightclub."

I frowned, confused.

"Tips … for dancing?"

Volkov smiled. "Go have a few drinks in the bar after the show. Let the ladies from the audience buy them for you. Entertain them, make them happy, you know?"

He paused, his yellow eyes cutting into me.

"You don't want to be in Sergei's debt any longer than you have to be. Or mine. But it's your choice."

Now I understood.

I was in Hell.

CHAPTER 5

Thirty-six days later...

Laney

"It's ridiculous! You're not in a fit state to go anywhere!"

Collin was furious, the tendons standing out on his thick neck, a vein throbbing in his forehead as he stood puffing like an angry bull.

"For God's sake, Laney! Just phone them and cancel. It's only Vegas—it's not like it's anything important."

I stared at him, fury making my lips tremble. I hated looking weak when I was so damn angry.

"No, it's not important! I know that! It's just my life. Ordinary life."

Collin jeered. "Don't be so dramatic."

"I'm not. I'm really not, but what difference would it make if I stay here? I'll be the same wherever I go. I may as well enjoy myself. And I've been planning this with Vanessa and Jo for eight months. I *want* to go."

"It's ridiculous," Collin said again, aggravated that I wouldn't agree with him. "I can't just take off and go to Vegas with you. I have work. I have responsibilities. It's selfish of you to take risks with your health."

My mouth dropped open. "Selfish? You think I'm being selfish?"

I was hurt he could think that. Didn't he know me at all?

"Yes, I think you're being selfish. I can't look after you if you go there and..."

"I'm not *asking* you to look after me and I don't *need* you to look after me."

"Of course you do!" he snapped.

We glared at each other across the kitchen table.

That damn wheelchair. It too often defined me.

I took a deep breath. Keeping calm would reassure him, or at least strengthen my argument.

I hated talking about my health. It was all so *boring*.

"I'm not a child. I can manage perfectly well."

Collin dismissed my words with a wave of his hand.

"How? How will you manage getting your wheelchair to the airport? How will you manage your luggage? Have you thought about *any* of this?"

I stared at him, insulted that he thought so little of me, assuming I couldn't organize anything without him. Collin shook his head.

"I'm just thinking of you," he said in a milder tone.

"Stop trying to control me and let me get on with my life," I said quietly.

Collin's knuckles turned white, gripping the coffee cup as if it was a life-preserver.

"Is that what you think? That I'm trying to control you?"

I sighed. "Sometimes, yes. I know you don't mean to be like that … but I'm going to Vegas."

"Fine," he snapped, slamming the cup onto the table so that coffee slopped over his hand. "You don't want me 'controlling' you?"

He made air quotes with his fingers.

"You know what? No problem. I'm done, Laney. I'm so done. All I've ever tried to do is help you and I get shot down every time."

He stood up, his bulky frame towering over me.

"I'm done trying to look after you."

Then he scooped up his jacket and stormed out of the room.

I heard the door to my apartment slam and the silence washed over me.

"I don't want you to look after me," I said to the empty room.

Lame Laney—that's what they called me at school. I wanted a boyfriend, not a babysitter.

Collin was right in one way. There's nothing simple about traveling with a wheelchair. I had to be organized, planning ahead for every eventuality. How many other people pack a puncture repair kit when they travel? Other than cyclists, obviously.

I had to pay for my general practitioner to issue a 'fit to travel' letter because I was having to change my travel plans. I had to hire a cab that could accommodate my chair, one with a ramp or a pneumatic lift. I needed to organize assistance at the airport—and then hope that it was in the right place at the right time. I could have asked my friends or family to help me, but that wasn't the point. I was 29 years old, an independent woman. I didn't want to be reliant on others if I could avoid.

But it helped to choose an airline that would be sympathetic—laws and legislation were often inadequate, no matter what anyone tells you. Goodwill means as much, if not more.

I had to notify the airline service team about the nature of my disability and the kind of wheelchair I used. Hand-propelled ones were simpler than electric chairs, where batteries caused the carrier a headache. Each part of the wheelchair had to be marked with my name in case anything went missing, although I hoped to take the cushion onto the plane with me. And at least I could request a gate check whereby my wheelchair could be directly loaded to the plane's fuselage.

I spent two hours changing my travel arrangements, wincing at the cost even though I had insurance. And I'd learned by experience not to rely on emails; talking to a human being usually produced better results, although not always.

"Ma'am, are you able to walk a short distance?"

The airline's employee was polite, going through her checklist of questions.

"Not today," I sighed.

"That's fine, ma'am. We'll pre-board you. If you could be at the airport three hours before your flight."

I hoped that the airline would upgrade me. Sometimes they did. But if they didn't, I'd requested a window seat. It might seem easier to have an aisle seat … right up to the moment the person by the window needs to get up to visit the bathroom and has to climb over you.

I'd also learned that a window seat gives you something extra to brace against during the landing.

Next, I contacted the hotel to check if a disabled room was available.

"On the lowest floor possible, please."

Elevators are shut down in the event of a fire.

And because I was careful, prepared, I asked the hotel about the width of the doors on their disabled rooms, including the bathroom. There was no point checking in and finding your chair didn't fit through the door.

So far, so good. But although they had a roll-in shower, they weren't sure if a shower wheelchair was available. I politely requested that they enquire, then packed several garbage bags in my suitcase. If necessary, I could wrap my seat cushion and chair back in plastic and make do. It wasn't ideal: garbage bags are slippery to sit on. You might even call it an accident waiting to happen.

And finally, I packed a spare pair of pushing gloves; it's surprising how quickly they wear out from all the extra work.

With my suitcase half full already, I thought about the clothes that a Vegas trip required.

I'd planned to wear my favorite skinny jeans, but loose clothing is far more comfortable when you're sitting all day.

It got boring being sensible.

I didn't always have to use a wheelchair, only on the days (or weeks, or sometimes months) when I had a flare-up. On those days I couldn't walk. On those days, it could hurt to breathe.

Today, I was somewhere in the middle: walking was painful. Even rising to my feet took several minutes while tears streamed down my cheeks, and I gasped in oxygen, willing the burning in my joints to recede, praying for the meds to work and the piercing pain to ebb.

Some days I only needed a walking cane, moving slowly like an old lady, grimacing as I tried—and failed—to pull my shoulders back from the safety of a hunched position.

But other days—most days, in fact—I was just like every other 29 year old, albeit one who wore comfortable shoes and took her meds with an almost religious fervor.

Sitting at my desk, at a table in a restaurant, I could feel normal.

I'd planned to dance with Vanessa and Jo wearing my sneakers, the ones with the special gel insoles. High-heeled pumps had no place in my world most of the time, but this weekend, I'd be able to wear them again.

I glanced at my Louboutins, discarded under the bedroom chair, and smiled, their irreverent red soles flirting with me. I couldn't walk, but I could show off my fabulous shoes.

The irony was not lost on me.

There are certain indignities associated with disability, I thought bitterly. Apart from the doors you can't reach, or the ones that are too heavy to open from a sitting position, apart from the shops you can't enter or move around if you do enter, apart from the ramps that are too steep or badly positioned, apart from the pitying glances, or the irritated looks from people who stumble over and around you, apart from the well-meaning but ill-informed people who talk to whoever is with you but not to you, apart from all of that, there is the horror of the disabled toilet.

Distant, dirty and dire.

There are the bathrooms that defy belief: with steps, with too-steep ramps, with doors that can't be opened from a chair, with no handrails, or handrails that are too high, or ... I could go on, but do you care?

I was red in the face and sweating hard by the time I reached my gate at O'Hare. My arm muscles burned from the exercise, and my neck and back ached. My thighs trembled from the tension of trying to keep my small suitcase balanced on my knees. I was close to admitting that Collin was right—but that meant admitting defeat.

A stubborn streak told me it would all be worth it—Las Vegas would be amazing.

"Are you traveling alone, ma'am?"

The gate stewardess didn't seem unduly concerned, although a little surprised by my lone status.

"Yes," I smiled. "I left my boyfriend at home. It's a girls-only weekend."

The steward returned my smile politely.

"I'll arrange your pre-boarding now, ma'am."

While she picked up her phone to make the arrangements, my good mood took a dive. I very much doubted that I still had a boyfriend to come home to. Collin had been so angry—angrier than I'd seen him in a long time. But what had fueled that anger, I wondered. Why had he been so incensed that I traveled alone? Did he want me to become dependent on him? Couldn't he be happy for me that I wasn't giving up? Use it or lose it: isn't that something to be proud of?

I shook my head. Maybe I was being selfish by making Collin worry. But honestly, what was going to happen in a resort where a credit card could solve every problem?

No. I'd been right to fight him on this. I was already too reliant on other people. I *needed* this weekend. The harder it was to get there, the more important it became.

Hoping it would be a peace offering, I sent a selfie of me by the gate and typed out a short message to Collin.

Nearly there. Love you.

My finger hovered over the 'send' button. I reread the message twice, then deleted the last two words and sent it.

It felt like a marathon to get this far, but despite my anxiety—or maybe because of my incessant planning—the airline hadn't dropped the ball. Three hours later, I was sitting in a window seat watching O'Hare shrink as the plane gathered height, the ugly tangle of concrete buildings and tarmac runways giving way to misty clouds pressing against the Perspex.

Four hours and two movies later, the plane descended through the bank of cloud and the pale baked Nevada landscape rose up to meet me. Dust and sand with small patches of green made way for straight roads and then blocks of high rises. The background of mountains was ghostly and insubstantial in the heat haze.

From my small window to the world, I could see the Pyramid Hotel glittering in the harsh sunlight, a reminder of the desert city's true purpose.

Las Vegas.

The name alone brought a colorful host of expectations, mixed with drama and Hollywood glitz, and maybe a little darkness, memories of movies glamorizing the darker, grittier aspects.

These days, it was marketed as a family-friendly resort, and I was looking forward to spa treatments and lounging by the pool with my friends, taking in a couple of shows and yes, spending a few dollars on the slot machines.

I was excited to see Jo and Vanessa again, but weary too, from worrying, as much as the journey itself, and I still wasn't in my room. An anxious knot started to tie itself in my stomach: would the assistance I'd organized for the transfer be there? Had my hotel really changed the reservation? Was the whole weekend the mistake Collin had described?

"We are now making our final descent to Las Vegas McCarran International Airport."

Mistake or not, I was about to find out.

Once the plane landed with a jarring bump, passengers were leaping out of their seats, rummaging through the overhead compartments and huffing impatiently until the fuselage doors opened.

I watched quietly, waiting until I was the only one left in the cabin. Usually people with wheelchairs de-board first, but since I'd requested a window seat, it was easier to wait until everyone else had gone.

A steward arrived with the airline's lightweight chair to transfer me to the arrivals terminal and reunite me with my stout, black, old faithful wheelchair.

This was the part I was dreading. I moved slowly, grimacing as my joints protested against the movement, flinching when my feet touched the ground.

"Can I help you?" asked the steward, looking askance at my slow and arduous progress from my seat to the wheelchair.

"No, it's better if I do it," I said tightly, lips compressed against the pain. "Thank you."

Flipping up the armrests, I shuffled my backside awkwardly from seat to seat, arms trembling as they took my weight. Then I let out a gasp and a sigh of contentment as I lurched into the chair.

The steward looked as relieved as I did, and we shared a conspiratorial smile.

"Welcome to Las Vegas!"

There are two different expressions people have when they see someone in a wheelchair: pity or distaste.

A small minority, tiny, in fact, treat me just like anyone else: neither more nor less concerned.

And then there are the old friends who have long stopped seeing the wheelchair, and see the person.

"Laney!"

Vanessa's shrieks turned heads across the airport's terminal, and she hobbled toward me, weighed down by an enormous suitcase and five-inch heels.

"Oh my God! Are those Louboutins! I'm so proud of you!" Vanessa cried, hugging the ever-living crap out of me, making me laugh as I winced.

"And how come you're in Old Ironside?" she asked, kicking my wheel.

"No idea," I grimaced. "One of those things."

"Will it stop you drinking?" Vanessa asked, cutting to the chase.

I laughed. "That's a hell no!"

"Thank God! We so need to have some fun!"

Well, I wasn't supposed to mix alcohol and meds, but this weekend was about letting go and relaxing. I'd have one or two drinks, take it easy and be careful. Mostly.

Being drunk in a wheelchair wasn't something I particularly wanted to relive, although the memory made me smile.

Vanessa was obviously thinking the same thing.

"I'll try not to push you into a fountain this time."

I grinned at her.

"Maybe I should get a seatbelt on this thing."

"I could tie you in," Vanessa said with a wink.

"You getting kinky on me, Ness?"

"Nah, you're not my type. Sorry, honey."

"How come you're at the airport—I thought your flight from Seattle landed a couple of hours ago?"

Vanessa rolled her eyes. "It did, but my luggage didn't. I decided to wait for the next flight. Whatever—it's here now. Although I wouldn't have minded the excuse to do some more shopping if it hadn't arrived."

I smiled. Vanessa had an infectious love of life—nothing got her down for long.

"So, what are we going to do first?" she asked. "Slot machines, dinner and dancing?"

Vanessa's smile dropped.

"Oh God, sorry! I forgot about the chair."

I grabbed her hand. "It's one of the things I love about you the most," I said quietly. "You see *me*, not the chair. And you are *so* going dancing! I want to see you strut your stuff and shake your tush. No wimping out!"

Vanessa knelt down on the hard polished floor and carefully wrapped her arms around me.

"We'll have an amazing time," she said, then gave me a sly look. "And what happens in Vegas stays in Vegas. We'll have to find you a hot guy."

I laughed and gestured to the chair. "I don't think there's much chance of that, and besides, did you forget about Collin?"

Vanessa scrambled to her feet awkwardly. "Saint Collin? I wouldn't dare forget about him."

I rolled my eyes at Vanessa's nickname.

"He's not that bad!"

"He's a killjoy. Whenever I meet him I feel like I should go sit on the naughty step."

"You probably should," I laughed.

Then I sighed, remembering the argument before I left.

"I think we're kind of broken up at the moment."

"Kind of? What does that mean?"

I explained the argument and watched Vanessa's eyes flash with anger.

"He really tried to stop you coming, even though he knew we'd be here?"

I shrugged unhappily. "He said I was being selfish."

"What a prick!"

"I don't know, Ness. I wondered … maybe he's right. He worries about me and…"

"No, he's not right," Vanessa said emphatically. "He should be on your side."

"He is, it's just…"

"No, Laney! If you want to skydive out of an airplane, he should be helping you achieve your dreams, not telling you it's too hard, too dangerous all of the time. It's not *his* life—it's yours."

"I know, but…"

"No more buts unless they're tight, sexy ones on a cowboy. Deal?"

She held out her hand, and I shook it—she always made me smile.

"Deal."

Half an hour later we were at the hotel and I felt like I could relax. My room was just as they'd said, with full disabled access. And they'd even found me a shower chair. I tipped the man who took me to my room and decided that if this standard kept up, I'd write to the hotel's management to thank them.

"He was cute," said Vanessa, as she unpacked my clothes and toiletries. "Do you need any help getting ready?"

"You've done enough," I said gratefully.

"Wrong answer," Vanessa said with an arched eyebrow. "Do you need any help?"

I smiled. "I'll be fine. Thanks, sweetie."

Vanessa winked and blew a kiss, before sashaying out of the room. Jo would be arriving shortly, and we were all meeting in my room before going for a few drinks and hitting up the slot machines, then dinner and dancing.

Or dinner and sitting.

Five hours later, I was dragging.

I'd won seven bucks and change on the slots—woohoo!—then enjoyed a wonderful lobster dinner, before heading back to our hotel for dancing and more drinks.

Vanessa and Jo were still going strong and I was determined not to spoil their evening by admitting I was tired.

"Stop being a wimp," I muttered to myself. "You've got the rest of your life to sleep—but right now you're in Vegas!"

I glanced back to the crowded dance floor, my eyes tracking my friends, smiling as a cowboy with a large Stetson and no rhythm staggered up behind Vanessa, trying to attract her attention as he swung his hips randomly, completely out of time to the music. Cute, though.

Then I saw a man who captured my attention utterly.

He was easily the best looking guy in the room, although not the tallest or the most built. But he danced with an easy elegance that made him seem a thoroughbred among carthorses.

My God! That guy can move!

I was surprised when I saw his partner: a short, plump woman who was red in the face and gasping for air. It was hard to imagine them as a couple—even harder to imagine that the sexy guy had picked her up. Although they definitely weren't dancing like brother and sister. Or mother and son. My smile disappeared because only one answer was left.

He must be one of those men I'd read about, a gigolo in all but name. It was a depressing thought.

I watched as the woman stopped dancing, clearly out of breath as well as out of her league, and definitely ready to call it quits. Her eyes darted away from her partner as if trying to find an escape.

When the man grabbed her arm, it was several seconds before he released her, reluctantly backing away. I realized that I'd been holding my breath as I watched the small drama unfold.

I inhaled deeply, still curious about what the man would do next.

He ran his hands over his hair as he searched around the room, his eyes ticking off the women he saw, some internal checklist that remained hidden to all but him.

But then his gaze flickered to me, and a wide smile stretched his full lips. He stalked forward and I automatically pressed myself backward in the chair, defensively crossing my arms.

"Hi, I'm Ash. Are you by yourself?"

I gave him a polite smile.

"No. I'm here with my friends."

"I don't see them." He paused, his full intensity fixed on me. "Would you like to dance?"

He held his hand toward me and my eyes opened wide. Was he expecting to swing me around in my chair? Did he think I was that desperate?

I laughed at his nerve.

"No, I'm not dancing."

He frowned, his hand still suspended between us. "But you like to dance?"

I stared, my gaze sinking into his, puzzled, annoyed.

He hadn't seen the chair?

Isn't this what you wanted? I asked myself. *A man who sees me and not the chair?*

My expression softened as I met his intense dark eyes.

"What makes you think I like to dance?"

His hand fell to his side and he shrugged again.

"You're in a nightclub, and you're not drinking. So you must be here to dance. Please, dance with me."

I sighed with disappointment. Even if he was good looking, the guy couldn't take a hint. I'd made it clear that I wasn't dancing.

He held out his hand again, but I shook my head impatiently. "Then go find someone who will dance with you."

His eyes widened in surprise, and then he grinned as he leaned on the table, his face inches from mine. "Maybe I want to dance with you."

"Then you'll be waiting a long time," I laughed coldly.

But I couldn't help my traitorous eyes tracking over his too handsome face. Golden skin stretched across sharp cheekbones, and his lips looked soft and generous. His black eyebrows were arched over dark eyes. And then I noticed a beauty spot shaped like a teardrop beneath his left eye—a perfect imperfection.

"I'm a good dancer," he said, looking almost wounded at my continued refusal.

My anger snapped. Tiredness, my fight with Collin, and frustration at the damned wheelchair taking away this weekend that meant so much.

"I'm not dancing!"

"But everyone comes here to dance."

"Not me!"

"You'll have a good time."

"I don't doubt it," I sneered. "Your last friend seemed to enjoy herself immensely."

A dull red flooded his cheeks and he looked away.

His reaction surprised me. I'd hurt his feelings.

Then I felt guilty taking out my bitterness on him, but *dammit! Why wouldn't he leave me alone?*

"Maybe I'd like to dance with a pretty girl for a change," he said softly, glancing up at me from beneath long dark lashes.

I didn't believe him. Not even for a second. I gave him a supercilious look and turned my head away.

"You are missing out," he whispered.

My jaw tightened in disgust.

"Laney, is this guy bothering you?"

I breathed a sigh of relief as Vanessa and Jo strode toward us, their lips pursed and their eyes flashing dangerously.

Ash looked nervous, his glance flicking between my friends and the bouncers by the exit. He started backing away, his hands held out from his sides.

"I just asked her to dance, that's all. I wasn't doing anything wrong."

Jo threw him a disbelieving look and stood with her hands on her hips.

"Do you want to go back to your room now?" Vanessa asked.

I nodded silently as Jo continued to glare.

Vanessa walked behind my chair and handed me the pashmina that had been hanging on the back. Then she unlocked the brakes on the wheelchair and pushed me away from the table.

Ash's mouth dropped open.

"Still think I'm pretty?" I asked him, as my eyes filled with tears.

CHAPTER 6

Ash

I pushed away from the table, burning with humiliation and shock.

She was pretty, the girl in the wheelchair. Natural, not fake like so many of the girls I saw in Vegas. Her hair was a warm, honey blonde that had been left straight and shiny. She'd worn a little makeup, but, only mascara and some lip gloss.

I'd been attracted to her even though I knew that she wasn't the type of woman who'd be interested in a guy like me. Not anymore.

I thought about the kind of man I'd become—nothing better than a fucking prostitute. Although I still got to dance.

And then if my evening wasn't bad enough, I saw Sergei pushing through the crowded lobby toward me, Oleg in his wake.

I turned and disappeared into the river of tourists.

Two weeks. That's all it had taken me to be persuaded to turn tricks for money. I disgusted myself.

It had happened after rehearsals one evening. He'd sent another note, demanding money, demanding to meet.

I knew what a meeting would mean: he'd never made any secret of the fact the he wanted to fuck me to clear the so-called debt.

He'd started by leaving messages with Trixie and once with Gary, saying he wanted his money … or 'a dinner date with my favorite dancer'. *No fucking way!* But the money I'd saved from my meager pay was a fraction of what he was asking for—and the amount increased daily. It was extortion—and there wasn't a damn thing I could do about it. It was so fucking frustrating knowing that I had €5,000 sitting in a Slovenian bank, but I had no way of accessing it, despite my best efforts so far.

I'd been avoiding Sergei, but I didn't have the money and time was running out. Gary offered me a loan, but I could tell from the fear on his face that there would be repercussions. I'd thought about it and thought about it, losing sleep over what I had to do.

That first time, I'd gone to a bar far away from the hotel, wanting nothing more than to be left in peace, to drink until I couldn't feel anymore.

But I hadn't been seated at the bar for long when a woman came up to me.

"Drinking alone?"

I looked up, surprised, and realized that she was talking to me.

"Yes," I said, staring at the nearly empty beer that I'd drunk and wishing I could afford more—but not with Sergei's threat dangling over my head, suspended by razor wire.

The woman settled herself onto the stool next to me, her short skirt sliding up her legs.

"Girlfriend stand you up?"

I shook my head.

"Boyfriend?"

That made me look up, my glance sharp and annoyed.

"No!"

She gave a predatory smile and rested her hand on my thigh with a gentle squeeze.

"Just checking. Whiskey? Or another beer?"

This time I really looked at her.

She was attractive, older, perhaps as much as forty, but she took care of herself and smelled good. I remembered what Volkov had said about earning 'tips'.

I closed my eyes against the memory and breathed in deeply. The woman's subtle perfume filled my nostrils and when I opened my eyes again, she was staring at me, a small frown on her face.

"Are you okay?"

Her concern was touching. Yveta and Gary avoided asking me questions like that because they were afraid that I'd answer, saying things they didn't want to hear.

No, I wasn't okay. I hadn't been okay since my plane had landed in this gateway to hell.

"Sorry. Bad day," I answered. Then I forced a smile and watched her eyes light up. "I'm Ash."

"Melissa."

We shook hands and Melissa waved at the bartender for two whiskeys.

"To new friends," she said as we clinked glasses. "Cute accent, by the way."

I savored the quick burn of the whiskey and glanced at my new 'friend', not responding to her comment. I didn't want to talk about it. I didn't want to encourage more questions about me. So I turned it around.

"Are you on vacation?" I asked politely.

"God, no!" she laughed. "Convention—for business. I wouldn't come here by choice." Then she glanced at me. "Sorry, that was rude. But I prefer the beach. What about you?"

"I work here."

"Really? What do you do?"

"I'm a dancer."

Once I'd have been proud to say that, but not now. My voice was empty of emotion.

"Oh, I should have guessed," Melissa smiled, eyeing my body with easy familiarity, a covetous glint darkening her gaze.

After that, it hadn't taken her long to invite me up to her room "for a drink in private." Less than 20 minutes.

She'd been upfront, businesslike, not offering any reason for hitting on me. Maybe there was nothing to explain: she was a single woman picking up a guy in a bar and offering him a good time, no strings.

I swallowed as I tried to get the words out, to ask for money. But then a sliver of doubt made me hesitate. Could she be an undercover cop? Gary had told me that they did this, waiting for the girl or guy to solicit money.

I smiled at the irony: if she was a cop, she was exactly what I needed; if she wasn't, it wouldn't make any difference.

But when we reached her room, there was nothing undercover about Melissa.

The moment she was through the door she shimmied out of her dress, attacking the zipper on my pants before I'd turned the lock behind me.

Melissa was attractive, but a sort of horror that I was prostituting myself kept getting in the way and my hard-on was fading fast.

"How much did you drink?" she huffed, rubbing my soft cock over the material of my briefs.

Humiliation and anger made me push her away.

Not enough for this, I thought.

I forced my mind past my problems and remembered the ultra-hot fuck I'd had with Yveta the night before. That worked, and my cock started to stiffen. I cupped myself over my briefs and stared at Melissa.

She licked her lips and walked toward me as I shrugged out of my shirt and kicked off the pants that were pooled around my feet. When she was near enough, I unhooked her bra and tossed it to the floor and played with her tits which were real enough and heavy in my hands.

I fucked her on the bed, my eyes closed the whole time, trying to keep the picture of Yveta in my mind, her long muscled legs wrapped around my waist as I'd plowed into her backstage at the theater after everyone had left.

I had just enough awareness to make sure that Melissa came before I did something stupid like call her by the wrong name.

Her nails dragged down my spine as her back arched and she quivered around me.

I pulled out immediately, although I hadn't come. I don't think she noticed.

She smiled at me sleepily, her skin flushed, her eyes sated.

"You can see yourself out," she yawned. "There's money on the table."

I bowed my head and dressed hurriedly.

There was a small pile of money on the table. I scooped it up and left the room as quickly as possible.

Outside the hotel, I paused to count the money: $145. Plus five one-dollar bills.

I'm surviving. That's what I told myself.

After that first time, it became easier. I was better at picking my targets and charged more.

Three or four times a week, I'd head out and find a woman to pick me up.

My mistake tonight had been to get lost in the dance. I'd been so focused on the music, on the rhythm, that I'd missed the obvious fact that my dance partner was struggling, unable to keep up.

And then that girl, the one with the sad eyes—God, I'd wanted to dance with her, to feel like myself again, to dance with a woman because I could. It had been a shock when I saw her wheelchair. I was really off my game tonight.

I thought of Sergei, his notes and growing impatience, and even though the night was warm enough to send a trickle of sweat down my back, I shivered.

I knew what he really wanted: he wasn't going to get it. Ever.

Sighing, I slipped out of the hotel and made my way along the Strip. I needed to find another woman. The thought turned my stomach.

As I strode down the street, dodging the wide-eyed tourists, my mood darkened further.

And I hadn't been able to find out anything else about the girl. No one had seen her. No one knew anything. Even Yveta and Galina had refused point blank to talk about her. Marta wasn't mentioned.

After the evening with Volkov, they'd kept a wary distance from me for a couple of days, but soon they were back to their usual behavior with Yveta hitting on me. She was hot and I needed what she was offering—which led to the backstage sex. Galina was persuaded to disappear for the rest of the evening so we could use their room to fuck some more. And for a few hours, I was able to forget. When Yveta came, it felt like validation—I was a man and needed to feel like one. How fucking pathetic was that? But so much was out of my control.

I needed Yveta right now, and the way she clung to me, her breath hot on my neck, told me that she needed me ... this ... too.

But Sergei's notes and little 'gifts' had started to arrive more frequently—sometimes several times a day—hints that I could escape his debt by attending a 'private party' or 'dancing for friends'. I'd ignored them all. Then the threats had started.

Which is your favorite finger?

That's what yesterday's note said.

Strangely enough, Gary had become the one person I could talk to, but even he refused to help me speak to the police or find the girl.

And so I fucked tourists for a few hundred dollars.

A wash of shame settled in the pit of my stomach. *So fucking cheap.* That's how I'd felt, but then I did it again and again.

Gary suspected, but said nothing. Yveta was oblivious, talking about 'going on a date' and happily making plans.

I glanced up at the flashing neon lights, the gaudy welcome that Vegas offered every tourist.

I was in the middle of a crowded American city, and I'd never felt more alone.

To the people passing by, I was just another guy out on the streets looking for a good time. But there was a dark underbelly to Las Vegas, and it had me by the balls. Any day, I could wind up dead ... or wishing I was.

And then I saw a face in the crowd.

"Marta!"

She blinked, confused, then an expression of shock, hope, and fear brightened her dull eyes.

I saw her glance around, her face tight, then duck into an alley between an adult video store and a fancy boutique.

"Marta?"

She blended into the darkness, and the only thing that stood out was her pale face, eyes heavily ringed with makeup.

"I remember you."

"Yes! The first night at the airport—you were with that young girl."

"Have you seen her?"

I nodded slowly. "Yes, once."

"Is she okay?"

"I don't know," I said, reluctantly lying through my teeth. "What about you?"

"I'm so scared," she said, her voice shaking. "I think I could die here and no one will know."

Her hand gripped my arm and her eyes were begging me to help.

"They give me drugs and make me sleep with their friends. They said I owed them the price of my plane ticket. They said if I tried to run away they'd catch me and kill me. I think they would—they all carry guns. Girls have disappeared. Two since I came here."

It was exactly what I'd thought—worse, maybe.

"Can you go to the police?"

I asked the question, already knowing what the answer would be.

She shook her head quickly, glancing over her shoulder at the bright lights behind us.

"I'm scared," she repeated.

I reached into my pocket. "I have $430. You could take this and…"

Marta shook her head again, her thin arms trembling and her teeth chattering as she continued to dig her nails into my skin.

"They'll catch me!"

The too familiar rage and frustration boiled inside. I stared at the happy tourists streaming past, seeing only the light ignoring the shadows. I imagined their appalled expressions if I ran out and begged them for help. I knew what they'd say. I could almost smell their fear and confusion, their compassion fatigue, their reluctance to be involved. So much easier to walk on by.

And that's what sickened me the most—I was just like them.

But I also knew that if I'd tried to stop Oleg that night, I'd be dead now. Sergei would have pulled the trigger and I'd just be another immigrant who disappeared.

Marta shivered in the hot desert air and I realized that it wasn't just from fear. Her thin arms showed track marks on the inside of her elbow. The healthy dancer's body of just a few weeks ago had shrunk and decayed.

But her eyes were not quite hopeless, and they stared into mine, begging me to save her.

"Where are you staying?"

She bit her lip, her eyes darting restlessly toward the alley's entrance.

"They keep me at a trailer, about 30 minutes out of town. It's horrible. There are four of us. I'm supposed to meet men and take them to a hotel. I don't have long—they're watching."

"Give me the address and…"

And you'll what? What the fuck are you going to do to help her?

Marta's expression grew more desperate.

"You'll help me?"

"I'll try. Give me the address."

"The hotel is across the road there, but after the men … they take me back to this awful place. I'm not sure where it is. It's dry and dusty, very hot. It's near a ranch, I think. I can hear cows at night. And the road is close—maybe half a mile."

It wasn't much to go on, but I soaked up every detail.

"When they take me there, they head out of town in that direction," and she pointed west. "Toward the sunset, but a bit north. And they drive straight for 20 minutes."

She glanced out at the street again.

"Promise you'll help me. I can't take any more."

I grimaced as her nails bit into my forearm.

"I promise."

"*Please!*" she cried, her eyes glossing with tears. "*Please!*"

And then she darted out of the alley and disappeared into the crowds.

I leaned back, the rough texture of the wall digging through my shirt.

I couldn't stand by any longer. My heart began to race and my palms were sweating. I dragged them over my pants and took a deep breath. Then I stepped out into the stream of people sauntering along the Strip, my eyes searching for a police officer.

I began walking faster, dodging the dawdling tourists. Weeks ago, I'd memorized the location of the nearest police station, just over a mile away. Ready for this moment—the moment I dared to risk it.

I strode down the street, eyes darting left and right, my heart thudding.

I was close, so close, when a limousine with tinted windows pulled up next to me, and the window slid open with a soft hiss.

"There you are! I was beginning to think you didn't want to talk to me. You hurt my feelings."

Sergei was grinning at me and I could see Oleg sitting in the driver's seat.

"I have $430," I said, knowing it wasn't nearly enough.

"Oh, Aljaž!" he laughed. "I want so much more than that. Besides, you owe me $4,000."

"There's no way the clothes cost that much!" I snapped back furiously.

"Compound interest," he said mockingly. "And Daddy is tired of waiting."

"I'll have the rest tomorrow," I grit out.

I'd borrow it from Gary—I was out of choices, even though I didn't want to involve him.

Sergei sighed and drummed his fingers on the window's edge.

"Get in the car."

I swore in Slovenian and stuck up the middle finger from the hand that he'd broken.

Then I turned and started jogging in the opposite direction, knowing that I'd just pissed off a really fucking dangerous man.

I heard cars honking, and I glanced over my shoulder to see the limo forcing its way through a line of traffic as Oleg made a U-turn.

I broke into a run, weaving through the evening crowds. I was being herded away from the police station and back toward the hotel.

I calculated how long it would take me to change direction again and reach the police, but swore when I saw the limo wrench free of the traffic and start to speed up.

I was full out sprinting by the time I reached the hotel, racing up the fire escape stairs and slamming into my room.

Gary jumped, startled when he saw me.

"You just about scared me out of my skin, dreamboat!" Then he saw my expression. "What happened?"

"Sergei."

I only had to gasp out that one word for all the color to leech out of Gary's face.

"Now he's saying he wants $4,000. I tried to make it to the police station, but he blocked me off. What the fuck do I do now?"

I was pacing up and down the tiny room, fisting my hair, frustration and fear pouring out of me.

"God, don't go there!" Gary blanched even further.

"Then what? Wait here until he catches me and kills me? Fuck that! I'm going to get away—tonight. I have to. I'll … buy a bus ticket … hitch out of town … something."

Gary shook his head. "That won't work. But I'm going to call Elaine."

"Elaine?"

"Sure! She's busted her ass to get the new show off the ground—she won't stand for Sergei messing with her rising star."

"He won't listen to her—the guy is crazy," I protested.

"I know, but Elaine has Volkov's ear. He's sunk a lot of money into the theater and this show. Don't freak yet, Ash. Let me call her."

I nodded tersely but carried on pacing while Gary pulled out his phone.

I listened to the hurried conversation, my chest tightening with every second that passed, expecting Oleg to come busting down the door. Eventually, Gary ended the call.

"She's going to speak to Volkov now. She says to sit tight and don't leave the room again tonight."

"That's it? She'll *talk* to him?"

"What did you expect? You thought she'd put a gun to his head?"

"Someone should."

Gary sighed but didn't disagree.

Laney

The next morning, it took me nearly two hours to get ready and meet the others for breakfast in the hotel's restaurant. The first 45 minutes were spent uploading yesterday's photos to my Facebook page and checking emails while I sat in bed and waited for the meds to kick in.

When I judged that enough time had passed, I eased my stiff, aching body out of bed and into the wheelchair.

It really sucked waking up with a full bladder but having to wait forever to pee.

If Collin was here, he would have lifted me into my chair.

But my regret was short lived. If Collin had been here, he would have insisted that I go back to my room after dinner last night. And I would have missed seeing Vanessa and Jo dancing their asses off.

And meeting that gorgeous guy. What was his name? Ash?

He'd been so shocked when he saw my wheelchair. I had to admit that a part of me was pleased that he'd hit on me without knowing about the chair, even if he was one of *those* men. It had been a long time since something like that had happened.

Even Collin hadn't really flirted with me. We'd met in college and been in the same study group. Having coffee together turned into having dinner together, and before I realized what was happening, everyone assumed that we were a couple—including Collin.

He was a good man. He could be incredibly thoughtful, but at the same time he could be totally inconsiderate, talking about my job as if it was a hobby, just because I worked from home. And he always had to be right. Which meant that I was inevitably always wrong. Which meant another fight.

And when I had a flare-up, he was suffocating. I hadn't realized how much, but being in Vegas without him, it put a few things in perspective.

Living with chronic pain is a study in acceptance, but of understanding, too. What is too little, what is too much or too often. What is necessary, what should be forgotten. And I gradually learned to forgive my body for being flawed, for being imperfect. Ultimately, I had to forgive myself, although sometimes I struggled with that part.

Collin hadn't texted back so I guessed we really had broken up.

The thought made me sad—we'd been friends for nearly 10 years. At one time, I thought we'd marry, but Collin had never asked, and I'd stopped wishing that he would.

I made my way down to breakfast and saw Vanessa flirting with the server in the restaurant. He was cute and definitely interested. I smiled to myself and raised my eyebrows at Jo who was watching with amusement.

The waiter suddenly noticed my arrival and his eyes widened.

I caught the tail end of Vanessa's conversation.

"So, you and your friends and me and my friends? Sounds good to me."

But the server was shaking his head, his eyes darting away from me.

"Ah, you know what? I forgot that we have a thing and I can't get out of it. Sorry." He smiled weakly at me. "What beverage can I get you, ma'am?"

Whatever plans had been in the works, it was obvious that they didn't include a woman in a wheelchair.

My throat tightened, but I held my head up and ordered coffee while the server slunk away.

"Asshole!" Vanessa said loudly. "You okay?"

"Sure. Don't worry about it."

"So," said Jo, deliberately changing the subject. "I'm thinking spa day, lounging by the pool, hitting on cabana boys, dinner and a show. I've scored us tickets to the theater here—half price if you're staying at the hotel, and front row as we have a wheelchair user," and she winked at me. "Sounds like it'll be amazing. Real Las Vegas showgirls. We might pick up some useful tips."

I laughed. "I am *not* wearing tassels on my nipples!"

"Me either," groaned Vanessa. "Last time I tried it, I had to peel off the glue. I had sore nips for days!"

"Ouch!"

"You said it, sista!"

Ash

I was a mess. Completely wired and I'd hardly slept. After we'd had a full rehearsal, I was sitting in a chair while Yveta applied a fake tan to my face and chest, turning the palms of her hands orange.

I could tell that she was annoyed with me because I wasn't returning her flirting and I hadn't agreed to meet her after the show.

Elaine had pleaded my case with Volkov and got the boss-man to agree that I was off limits. I hoped that was enough to keep Sergei away. I'd also swallowed my pride and arranged to borrow the money from Gary.

Fuck, I hoped that Volkov's word could be trusted. Elaine said he was going to be in the audience tonight—that was the rumor. I was holding onto that. With the big boss around, Sergei wouldn't try anything.

My nerves were kicking into overdrive. I always got a little angsty before a performance—those were good nerves, adrenaline that gave me an edge. But tonight, my stomach felt like it was trying to climb through my throat.

Yveta added some rouge, a little eyeliner, and then dusted my face and chest with shimmery powder.

"Are we done?" I ground out, knowing I sounded like an ungrateful prick.

Yveta stalked away to finish her own makeup.

The changing room was tiny, and there was nowhere separate for me and Gary. We were crammed into a corner and told not to look when the girls were naked. Not that Gary cared, and I'd seen more tits in changing rooms than most men ever saw in a lifetime. I wasn't immune, but tonight I couldn't give a rat's ass if they glued rhinestones onto their bare pussies.

My nerves were jumping all over the place and my fingers drummed on my thighs restlessly.

"Oh my God, calm the freak down, will you?" Gary hissed. "You're making me nervous. Crapaloosa! Do I shift weight on the one?"

"What?"

"In the contra botafogo—do I shift weight on the one?"

I gave a distracted nod. "Yes, two changes of weight in one beat of music."

Gary sighed. "Did you hear that Elaine is talking about including a West Coast Swing number?" He paused then tossed a feather boa at my head. "Are you listening to me?"

My eyes flashed with anger and Gary jerked back.

"Sorry," I muttered.

"Jee-zus! Just chill, will you? Do some stretches or something!"

It was good advice and I knew that I was too close to doing something stupid like running. But maybe Elaine was right. Maybe the worst was over.

I started stretching out my body, working through the warm-ups that we all used.

"You have really good extension," Gary said, gazing critically.

I grunted, trying to tune out all the static in my brain and get into the zone while I loosened my shoulders and back muscles.

"Five minutes, people!" Neal yelled.

There was a rush of activity and the sharp smell of fake tan, sweat and perfume thickened as the girls lined up. With their headdresses of ostrich feathers, they towered over us—all fake lashes, sequins and thousands of crystals glued to their skimpy costumes.

Yveta still looked pissed and it was my fault.

"You're beautiful," I said honestly.

She beamed at me.

The music started and something inside ignited even as the pulsing beat calmed me. And then I was there, strutting onto the stage, owning it, lighting up from the inside as the audience clapped and cheered. I presented girl after girl until the dance-off with Yveta as my partner, and Gary and Galina as our competition.

The audience lifted us, made us fly.

This was my moment!

Laney

I gasped. "It's him!"

"Him who?" Vanessa asked, peering up at the dancers cavorting on the stage in front of us.

"The guy from last night—at the club. Wow! He's just … wow!"

"I think you're right," Jo said excitedly. "I guess he wasn't lying when he said he wanted to dance. He's h-o-t!"

He wasn't lying. The thought brought a warm pulse of pleasure to my chest. He really was a dancer, not a gigolo. So if he hadn't lied about that, maybe he really thought that I was pretty.

He was even dressed similarly to last night in tight black pants and black shirt, except that this one was slashed to his waist and glittered under the stage lights with sequins sewn onto the silky material.

I smiled happily and sat back to enjoy the show.

His name was Ash.

When he was on stage, the lights seemed brighter, the dancing hotter, the atmosphere electric. The dance-off with the other guy had been phenomenal, each of them trying to one-up the other. But there had never been any competition, not in my mind. Ash oozed sexiness, his muscled chest gleaming under the spotlights, testosterone pumping through him, obvious in the swagger of his hips and caress of his fingers along the arms of the dancers.

A twinge of jealousy surprised me. Why on earth did I feel possessive about a man I'd spoken to once?

Looking around covertly, I pulled out my phone, turned off the flash, and snapped a photograph. Something to remember him by—the hottest guy who'd ever hit on me.

The thought made me smile.

When the two men left the stage and the girls formed a chorus line for the can-can, I lost interest. My bladder reminded me of the three Mimosas that I'd had earlier.

"I have to go to the bathroom," I whispered in Jo's ear.

"Want me to take you?"

I winced internally. I hated to feel like a kindergartener, but I just smiled at Jo—it wasn't her fault.

"No, that's okay. You enjoy the show. I want a full report if that guy comes back on stage."

Jo waggled her eyebrows.

"Maybe I should get closer for a hands on approach."

I nodded at the stage which was just a few feet away.

"Any closer and you'd be sitting in his lap."

"I wish," sighed Jo. "See you in a few."

I didn't want to miss the show, but I didn't know where the bathrooms were and experience told me that waiting until it was urgent would be a mistake.

The usher pointed to a door by the fire exit and I pushed myself forward. From the sound of the bass pumping through the walls, I guessed that I was close to the backstage area.

The corridor was badly lit and very long. My arm muscles began to ache and I wondered if the usher had sent me the wrong way.

But then, with a sigh of relief, I spotted the sign for the bathroom right at the end of the corridor. At least it would be emptier now than during the intermission.

Cursing at the sweat trickling down my back and armpits, I nudged the door open.

"You think you can hide from me, you piece of shit!" screamed a man's voice. "I'm going to fuck your ass so hard you'll shit your own eyeballs!"

CHAPTER 7

Laney

A choked gasp escaped, and immediately four of the five men in the room turned around to glare, the ice in their eyes shocking me.

I was frozen, unable to move, and in that brief, horrifying moment, I stared at the scene in front of me.

One man was suspended between two others, his arms trapped brutally, his head hanging down. He was naked and his ripped clothes were scattered across the floor, a tattered shirt still hanging from one shoulder. Red marks marred his smooth skin where the fourth man had rained down fists across his ribs.

Worse still, the man's back and ass cheeks were lacerated where he'd been flogged with a leather belt, still clutched in the hands of the thug doling out the brutal and humiliating punishment.

The thug lowered his arm and glanced at the fifth man, as if seeking orders.

I had to swallow back bile when the small man in the suit tucked his erect penis back in his pants, a coldly furious expression on his face.

I'd interrupted something bad, something so horrific no one was supposed to see.

The naked man's head came up and he stared over his shoulder with bloodshot eyes.

Horrified recognition flared.

"Ash!"

The words ripped out of me. That beautiful man, the dancer … the sexy, confident guy was gone. In his place was a beaten, shredded ghost. His eyes were glazed and he seemed unable to focus.

"Get out!" he croaked. Then more loudly, "Get out of here!"

My mouth dropped open … and I moved.

The small man shouted an order as I rammed the bathroom door open with my wheelchair and propelled myself back along the corridor as fast as I could, my heart hammering, breath coming in gasps.

I heard footsteps running behind me and I started to pray.

Please, God! Help me!

Closer, closer, and the man shouted something.

I prayed harder, my eyes wide with fear, the muscles in my arms burning as I pushed the chair faster, harder, my legs useless beneath me.

I think God listened, because my prayers were answered when I saw two people walking along the corridor towards me, their steps leisurely and unworried in the gloom.

"Well, there you are! It's like a maze down here," said Vanessa. "I thought I'd better come and find ... Oh my God! What happened? Are you okay?"

"Do you need a doctor, ma'am?" asked the concerned usher who was with Vanessa.

"Help!" I screamed, my heart tripping as my lungs fought to suck in oxygen. "Those men!"

Vanessa and the usher looked up and the man who'd been sent after me hesitated.

"He's got a gun!" Vanessa screeched. "Shit, call the police!" and with shaking hands she pulled out her phone.

The man turned and ran back in the direction of the bathroom.

"Shit! Shit! Shit!" Vanessa hissed. "I can't get a signal. Let's get the fuck out of here!"

The usher clearly agreed, already running back to the auditorium, leaving us to fend for ourselves.

Vanessa tossed her phone into my lap and grabbed the handles of the wheelchair.

"No!" I shouted desperately. "He's hurt! We have to help him!"

"Who's hurt?" Vanessa shouted, pushing the chair faster and faster.

"Stop!" I screamed again, but Vanessa was too scared to listen. "Stop!"

I lurched forward, throwing myself out of the wheelchair, feeling every burning joint in my body catch fire as I landed heavily on the cheap carpet.

Pain caused tears to stream down my face.

"Laney! Oh my God, Laney!"

Vanessa tried to heave me up but my dead weight was too much for her.

"Go get help," I stuttered. "Ness! Go get help!"

Vanessa was torn, desperate to help me, desperate to get away.

"I can't leave you!" she cried out, her voice pleading. "Help me get you up, Laney! Help me!"

My voice was sharp with pain. "No! Find someone! Quickly!"

Her face stricken, Vanessa turned and ran.

"I'm coming back!" she yelled over her shoulder.

I lay on the floor, the carpet rough against my cheek. Flashes of the horror that I'd seen made me shudder uncontrollably.

What I saw! Oh my God!

Ash's beaten body, the thugs, the man with his cock in his hand, not a breath of sanity in his eyes, screaming at Ash.

They were going to rape him.

The ugly truth squeezed my heart and I started to cry in heaving sobs. Rage and shock and fear and pain—it was too much.

Every breath tore at my body, burning, tortured with fear and sorrow and hopelessness.

I was gasping, fighting for air as anxiety threatened to overwhelm me.

And then I felt gentle hands on my arms, on my shoulders, carefully lifting me into a sitting position.

"Are you okay?"

Ash.

His voice was hoarse and cracked, but his gaze was steady as he examined my face, his worried eyes darting to mine, along the corridor behind us, then back to me.

"Are you okay?" he asked again. "Should I help you get back in your wheelchair?"

I hiccupped, wiping the tears from my eyes and the snot from my nose as I nodded wordlessly.

Ash grunted as he took my full weight in his arms, lifting me smoothly and seating me in the chair.

I saw him wince as he moved, and I knew that helping me had caused him great pain.

I rested my shaking hand on his arm, my fingers catching in the ripped fabric of his shirt.

"Are *you* okay?" I stammered.

He swallowed and glanced over his shoulder nervously.

"We have to go. It's not safe."

Ash

Moving as fast as I could, ignoring the pain that sliced through me with every step, I gripped the handles of her wheelchair and ran along the corridor. I could feel the fragments of torn material pulling at the broken skin on my back and ass, blood soaking into what was left of my clothes. I was afraid to jostle the girl, aware that she was already hurting, but I had no choice. I didn't know how long we had before Oleg came after us.

Her interruption had saved me.

I knew that if she hadn't opened the door to that bathroom, Sergei would have plowed my ass until my backside was nothing but raw meat. He'd promised exactly that after he'd tried to fuck my mouth and I'd threatened to throw up on him again.

When Oleg had returned to say that more witnesses had arrived, Sergei had held the gun to my head, frothing with rage. But Oleg had yelled at his boss, and forced him out of the bathroom.

I couldn't believe they'd left me alive.

Crawling on hands and knees, skin on fire, I'd pulled my torn clothes together and forced them onto my mutilated body, the pain intense.

I'd already puked once from shock, but now I had a deeper fear. This girl had seen their faces, seen what they'd done to me—which meant she was in danger.

"Where's your room?" I hissed out, my mouth close to her hair, catching the scent of coconut.

"Go left. Room 113."

People stared as we crossed the hotel lobby, but I ignored them all. At the girl's door, I gently pried her purse from her shaking hands and searched through it until I found her keycard.

Once we were inside, her cell phone started to ring furiously and that seemed to shock her out of her daze. She spoke into the phone, her eyes fixed on me as I stood gazing at her warily, my breath still coming in heavy pants.

A few seconds later, I heard voices outside her room.

I peered through the peephole, hoping like fuck that it wasn't the evil bastard.

But I recognized them from the night before.

"It's your friends," I whispered, the relief in my voice obvious.

"Let them in, please," she begged, her voice breaking.

I opened the door and the two women almost fell into the room.

"Laney! Laney! Oh my God! Are you alright?"

"I'm okay," she said, tears making a lie of her words. "I'm okay."

Laney. That was her name

"Give me my phone," ordered the taller one, the brunette. "I'm calling the police."

"No!" I barked, grabbing the phone from her.

They all turned to stare at me, fear as well as anger on their faces.

"You can't call the police," I repeated, my voice harsh. "It's not safe."

The brunette shook her head furiously.

"That guy had a gun! My friend was nearly assaulted and…"

"So was Ash," said the girl quietly.

The brunette's head whipped around so fast, she almost sprained her neck.

"What?"

"That's what I saw in the bathroom," Laney said, her voice soft. "Four men were … assaulting him."

"Then we have to call the police!" the brunette cried out with frustration.

"I can't trust the police."

They all turned to stare at me again.

Laney bristled. "My father is a police officer! He's the most honest man I know! How dare you…"

I interrupted angrily. "I can't trust the police *here!* I can't trust anyone!" Then I walked to the door, fixing Laney with a hard stare. "He's seen you. You have to get out. Go to your policeman father. *Don't stay here tonight!*"

I was going to run. I'd take my chances on the road, not stuck here like a rat in a trap.

"Wait!"

Frustrated, I turned to Laney again.

"You're hurt," she said, her voice softening. "We can help you."

"Laney, we can't get mixed up in this," the brunette protested.

Laney stared at her friend.

"You weren't there. You didn't see what they were doing … what they were going to do. We *have* to help him." She paused, swallowing down her fear. "Besides, I'm already mixed up in this. I saw them—like he said. And they saw me."

The blonde frowned as she looked at me. "You've got blood on you," she said, standing up and approaching. "Your clothes are soaked with blood!"

"I have to go," I grit out. "I have to get away!"

The blonde ignored me and tugged apart the ripped shirt. All three of them gasped when they saw the bloody welts on my body.

"You're not going anywhere like that," the blonde said flatly. "Vanessa, get my first aid kit from our room and…"

"If he finds me, he'll kill me!" I growled, pushing her hands away. "I have to go *now.*"

Laney shook her head.

"No one knows you're here. You'll be safe…"

"He *saw* you!" I shouted, frustrated that she didn't understand the danger she was in. "He saw a girl in a wheelchair! How long do you think it will take before he finds you?"

Her eyes were wide with fear, but she shook her head.

"We have a few minutes. He doesn't know I'm in this hotel."

A wave of nausea made me dizzy and I had to grab the door handle to stop from falling over.

The blonde snapped her fingers.

"Vanessa, go pack up our room. Bring the bags here and hurry! Laney, do as much as you can here. And you," she said, pointing at me, "take off the rest of your clothes."

My face flushed with anger, but when I hesitated, she reached for the button on my pants.

I leapt back as if I'd been burned, the horrific images of Sergei doing exactly the same thing assaulting my mind.

I saw the sudden pity in the blonde's eyes and knew that she understood. Humiliation flooded through me and I had to close my eyes.

"I'll take care of you," she said calmly. "I'm a registered nurse. You can use the bathroom."

I nodded, knowing that I needed her help. I slipped inside the bathroom, blinking at the bright lights.

Laney

Jo disappeared into the bathroom with Ash, and I could hear the shower running. My stomach lurched as I imagined the water turning red with Ash's blood, lazily swirling down the drain.

I sat in my stupid chair, useless and terrified, unable to help.

Four minutes later, Vanessa tapped on the door. When I opened it, she was already wearing jeans and flat shoes; two wheeled cases bulging with badly packed clothes trailed behind her.

Vanessa whirled around the room, heaping all my things onto the bed.

"Ash needs something to wear," I said suddenly, realizing that his own clothes were past saving.

"Is that his name, Ash? He doesn't sound American," Vanessa said distractedly, as she shoved clothes into my suitcase.

"I don't know where he's from. Ness, you're the tallest—have you got some sweatpants, a t-shirt, something he could wear."

Vanessa frowned then dug out a wrinkled oversized t-shirt and gray sweatpants from her suitcase.

"I don't know—he's pretty tall."

"I don't think he'll care," I grimaced.

"No, probably not."

She placed the clothes for Ash outside the bathroom door so Jo could grab them.

"Who are these guys?" she asked. "What did they do to him?"

I didn't know who the men were—but I knew *what* they were.

"I think they used a belt on him," I said in a hushed voice.

Vanessa sucked in a shocked breath and I couldn't bring myself to tell her the rest. And I didn't know how Ash would feel—it wasn't my story to tell. He must be traumatized by what had happened. I blanched at the scene playing over and over in my mind—had the thugs continued what they'd started before he escaped?

Jo appeared from the bathroom, snapping off a pair of bloody latex gloves.

"I've done the best I can," she said, her professional voice edged with anger, "but he's taken quite a beating, and the belt buckle … it caused some damage. He needs proper treatment and rest."

"He needs to get out of here," I said adamantly.

"I still think we should call the police," Vanessa disagreed. "We don't know anything about this guy. He could be a criminal for all we know."

"Open your eyes, Ness!" I cried out. "He's a dancer! A *dancer!* I don't care if he's got gambling debts or … or a drug addiction … or anything! He needs us!"

Vanessa stared, biting her lip.

"If it helps," Jo said calmly, "I saw no sign of drug addiction. And if he's a criminal, well, you're the one with the police connections. Speak to your dad. In fact, call him now. He could…"

"If I do that, he'll tell me to go the police here—you know he will."

We were all silent, staring at each other.

"And what about Ash?" I asked desperately. "We can't leave him!"

At that moment, Ash opened the bathroom door, clouds of steam swirling behind him. He was dressed in Vanessa's sweatpants which were too short and hovered above his shiny patent shoes as if waiting for an invitation to join the party.

His movements were stiff, lacking the fluid grace that had first entranced me. His dark eyes met my gray ones.

"You should listen to your friends. Get out of Las Vegas. It's not safe for you now."

"What about you?"

He shrugged and then winced. "I'll hitch a ride."

"You're in no state to do that," I said decisively. "I'll buy you a plane ticket. Where do you want to go?"

Ash frowned.

"I can't catch a flight," he said flatly. "They stole my ID, but the airports aren't safe either."

I ground my teeth with frustration.

"What about a bus?"

"They watch the bus station," Ash shook his head. "He'll be looking for me now."

"We'll have to drive," I said quickly. "Can you drive?"

Ash nodded but looked worried. "Sure, but I have no money, no ID."

"I do."

"You're in no fit state," said Jo, seriously alarmed.

"I know that," I argued earnestly. "I'll rent the car and Ash will drive."

"To Chicago? You're crazy! That'll take three, maybe four days!"

"It's the only way to get him out of town," I said, determined. "And we don't have time to stand around here arguing."

That was one thing we could all agree on.

Jo took charge of checking us out and Vanessa called a cab.

As we piled into the waiting taxi, a police car was idling at the curb outside the hotel, and I knew that there would be trouble if we were caught. Fleeing the scene of a crime and failing to give a witness statement about a man with a gun in public—it wouldn't go well.

At the airport, I said goodbye to my friends, promising to stay in touch. Vanessa's plane to Seattle would board in less than an hour, and Jo was catching the red-eye to Boston. She'd also rented a car on her credit card for me and Ash, hoping it would throw anyone looking for a woman in a wheelchair off the scent.

Just thirty minutes later, I was sitting in the passenger seat of a Chrysler 200 while Ash guided the car through the flat darkness of the desert. Tiredness washed through me, but fear kept my brain fizzing and firing, making sleep impossible.

Ash's shoulders were hunched and his jaw was locked with tension.

"I'll understand if you don't want to talk about it," I said carefully, glancing at his profile, "but why did those men want to hurt you?"

He was silent for so long that I was certain he wouldn't answer.

When he did, his voice was low and quiet, but throbbing with suppressed anger.

"I came to Las Vegas to dance," he said. "I thought it was my big break," and he laughed harshly. "But I soon realized that I was working for Bratva."

"Who?"

"Russian mafia."

"Oh God!"

Mafia. The word alone conjured ugly images, and after what I'd seen…

"I've been here almost six weeks," Ash continued, his voice strained. "They took my passport and phone the first night. They told me that the airport and bus station were watched. They told me that the police couldn't be trusted." He glanced sideways. "Your father is a policeman?"

"Yes, he's a captain at the 13th district in Chicago. You'll be safe there."

Ash stared at me incredulously.

"Nowhere is safe!"

Ash swore loudly, his knuckles turning white as he gripped the steering wheel, and I cowered back from his anger.

Awareness of our situation settled over me.

I didn't know this man, although instinct told me to help him. But right now he was scaring me.

"He'll know what to do," I whispered. "You'll just have to trust me."

He was silent for a moment before glancing at me quickly.

"You know my name."

I smiled weakly. "You told me last night when we met."

He nodded once. "I remember."

But from his dark expression, it didn't seem like a happy memory.

"And you are Laney. I heard your friends call you that."

Ash tapped the steering wheel and I couldn't help staring at his hands. Everything about the man was beautiful. At least those thugs hadn't hit him in the face. I wondered about that.

I tried to force myself to stare out of the window into the empty night, but my gaze kept being drawn back to Ash. His eyes were narrowed in concentration and pain, and a muscle jumped in his cheek.

It occurred to me that staring like that was probably making him uncomfortable. I tried to think of a way to break the tension, but it was Ash who spoke first.

"Do you mind if I turn on the radio?"

"Sure! What sort of music do you like?"

"I like most music," he said, some of the tension loosening in his body. "Anything I can dance to."

"Oh, of course," I murmured.

Ash glanced at me for a second before he turned the radio on, passing over several Country music stations until he found a late night rock station.

"From 'Copacabana' to 'Hotel California'?"

Ash shrugged, and a tiny hint of the beautiful smile that lit up the stage tugged at his lips. "I guess. I listened to a lot of American music growing up."

I was relieved by the relative normalcy of the conversation after the horrors of the past hour.

"Where are you from?"

"Slovenia."

He glanced at me to see if I'd heard of his country. I was mortified that it didn't even sound familiar, but I guess he was used to that because when he saw me looking confused, he continued.

"Part of the old Yugoslavia. We gained our independence in 1991."

"Sounds like you've had to say that a few times."

He nodded. "Yeah, a few."

"Wow, somewhere younger than America," I teased.

"The Carmine Rotunda church was built in the eleven hundreds," Ash countered, raising his eyebrows.

"Oh," I said, feeling ignorant.

Ash shrugged.

"We're a small country. Only two million people."

There was an uncomfortable pause while we each thought what to say next. Inevitably we started speaking at the same time.

"Oh, you first," I said awkwardly.

Ash's eyes flickered to me and he licked his lips, shifting uncomfortably in his seat.

"There's a girl…"

Of course there is, I thought sadly.

"Okay?"

"She's in trouble," Ash said quickly, as if the faster he spoke, the easier it would be.

I frowned, not sure what to make of his words. "Pregnant?"

Ash seemed puzzled. "I don't think so. It's possible, I don't know, but she's in trouble. She's being used to … sleep with men, you know?"

"She's a … prostitute?"

"No. Yes, but she doesn't want to be. She's a dancer, like me. I met her the day I arrived here and only once more until last night. They're holding her at a place out of the city. I don't know where exactly."

His voice was frustrated, becoming desperate, almost pleading with me.

"It's a farm, I think. She said they had guns, that they were watching her. I have a car now—maybe we could find her?"

So many emotions tumbled through me. I felt horrible for being jealous when I thought that Ash had a girlfriend; then shocked by what he said had happened to the poor girl; then horrified that Ash could think we should take on the Russian mafia *who had guns*.

It was all such a nightmare. More than ever, I wanted to call Dad. I needed to hear his calm advice when I was so scared and my nerves jangled. I needed his clear-headed judgment. I surreptitiously checked my phone while I replied.

"Um, Ash, that doesn't sound like a great idea. I mean, you said they have guns and they're watching her. I've seen one gun already this evening, and I'm still shaking. I'm not sure what we could do. But she's being held against her will, so we should definitely tell the police."

Dammit! No signal.

"What's her name?"

Ash shook his head helplessly.

"Marta. I don't know the rest! I don't know anything! I promised I'd help her!"

And he slammed his hand on the steering wheel making me jump, so I dropped my phone into the car's footwell.

Ash glanced at me again before fixing his eyes back on the road. "I'm sorry. I just … can … will your father … can he help her?"

I touched his arm gently.

"When you meet him, tell him everything. He'll help you. That's *my* promise."

Ash frowned and nodded jerkily.

The road unfolded black and velvety in the night. The stars were bright pinpoints of light far away, so very far away. The car's headlights were consumed by the night and it felt as if we were alone in the universe.

There was a long silence before either of us spoke again.

"Thank you," said Ash.

When I woke up, it wasn't a slow, groggy coming to the surface of a misty dream, but a sudden, sharp intake of breath, feeling like my body was on fire. The sudden swell of pain startled me instantly and fully awake.

My eyes watered and I had to breathe slowly and deeply. When I felt sufficiently able to control the pain, I cautiously opened my eyes. I was alone in the car and thin fingers of gray light filtered through the window.

I turned my head carefully and saw Ash some distance away, standing at the side of the road. He bent over suddenly and was violently sick.

My instinct was to go to him, but my body fought me, confining me to the car seat. Instead, I reached into my purse and retrieved my meds, gulping them down with a bottle of water that I'd bought at the airport. It wasn't ideal taking them on an empty stomach, but I couldn't face a Snickers bar, which was the only food I had with me.

I tried to sit up straighter, but my body protested, locking me into a painful, lopsided position. The minutes ticked past and Ash was still standing by the road, but now his head was tipped back and he was staring up at the sky.

The early morning mist cleared and the sun painted the landscape in grays and browns that slowly turned to reds and golds as the sun rose higher. I was horrified to see that the back of Ash's t-shirt was stained—dark patches that could only be dried blood.

Finally, he turned and walked back to the car, his face shifting as he realized that I was awake and watching him.

We stared at each other awkwardly.

"I'm sorry I woke you," he said at last.

"You didn't."

He shrugged then winced.

"The road ahead divides so I didn't know which way to go."

If there was another reason he'd stopped, he wasn't admitting to it.

I pulled out my phone, then grimaced. Dead as a dodo. The battery must have died during the night and I could picture the place in my hotel room where I'd left the charger.

Sighing, I shoved it back in my purse and went through the glove box to find the rental agency's road map.

"From here, we get on the I-70. That takes us to Denver."

"Den-ver." Ash rolled the word around on his tongue and looked at me blankly. "Okay."

"Are you alright to drive? You look ... tired."

"I can drive."

I nodded although his reply hadn't convinced me.

"I, uh, I need to find a bathroom," I said uncomfortably.

Ash's forehead creased with concern. "Of course. I'm sorry."

"No, no, that's fine. I just ... I can't ... out here, you know?"

Ash gave me a thin smile. "Much easier for a man."

"Yes, just point and aim."

I'd spoken without thinking, but the realization that Ash had probably done exactly that, touching himself, made my cheeks burn with embarrassment.

"I'm sorry!"

But Ash smiled, one corner of his mouth turning up briefly.

"We have seen too much, I think, to be embarrassed with each other."

I didn't know what to say to that, but my memory flashed to Ash's naked body suspended between the two thugs, his blood dripping onto the floor.

"I should call Dad," I said, blinking rapidly.

"It's very early," Ash commented.

I looked at the car's dashboard clock. It was 5:47AM.

"He'll be awake now. Chicago is in a different time zone. I need to get to a phone—mine is dead."

"What will you tell him?"

I looked up and met Ash's eyes. I realized that they were lighter than I'd thought, hazel rather than chocolate—and very beautiful. I stuttered out my reply.

"Everything."

Ash nodded but didn't speak. He winced slightly as he climbed into the driver's seat and turned the key to start the engine.

As we pulled out onto the road again, I glanced at him.

"You got sick."

Ash's shoulders stiffened. "Yes."

He didn't want to talk about whatever had caused it. I didn't mention it again.

We drove another forty minutes and my bathroom needs became pressing. My bladder was so distended, I'd crossed my arms, legs and eyes. Luckily, my meds had kicked in and moving wasn't quite so painful. When we approached a diner, Ash pulled over and parked.

Without being reminded, he lifted my wheelchair from the trunk and brought it to the door. Slowly, I eased myself into the chair, flopping down with a sigh as Ash bent down to fold out the footplates.

Something so simple took so much effort.

But I couldn't help smiling as I saw Ash tugging the borrowed sweatpants lower on his hips, trying to make it so they weren't flapping around his ankles. He glanced up and caught the amusement in my expression.

"I look ridiculous," he pouted. "Like a clown."

I laughed my first real laugh in what seemed like a lifetime.

He certainly wasn't as put-together as usual. Dark scruff lined his cheeks and chin, giving him a rougher appearance, very different from his usual suave self.

His smile was reluctant, but it was there.

Then he shivered, and I wished I'd thought to get him something warmer to wear other than a thin t-shirt. We'd have to find a store soon.

He pushed me into the diner, and I watched the server's hard expression soften as she took in the wheelchair. Yep, there was the look: pity.

Ash took me as far as the bathroom door, then hesitated.

"Can you...?"

"Yes, I'll be fine," I said quickly, pushing the door open with my chair.

God, the relief when I was finally able to let go. I decided the pleasure of peeing in a toilet that flushed was seriously underrated. People should write poems about it.

Ash was still waiting for me when I came out. I'd expected him to be sitting with a coffee in his hand by now, but instead he pushed me to a table in the corner, then slid into the seat catty-corner to me.

He toyed with the greasy menu and shot an embarrassed look in my direction, although he didn't meet my eyes.

"Order whatever you want," I said quickly, as if it was nothing.

Ash closed the menu and crossed his arms, staring out the window. "I'm not hungry. Thank you."

"Listen," I said, leaning forward in my chair and resting my hand on his elbow so he would look at me. "It's a long way to Chicago and I'm counting on you. I can't drive when I'm like this. I need you, so please eat. Okay?"

He looked up, his eyes roving across my face, then he nodded once.

His agreement might have been reluctant, but when the server brought the plate of bacon, eggs and pancakes that I ordered for him, Ash ate hungrily.

My stomach felt tender—too many drugs on an empty stomach. I ate as much as I could, then pushed my plate away.

Ash's eyes followed it, but he didn't say anything.

"Perhaps you can finish it?" I suggested. "It's a shame to waste it."

Ash seemed torn, but then gave in to his hunger and pushed the leftover food onto his plate and finished every bite.

I wondered how he stayed so fit if he ate like that all of the time. If I so much as looked at a pancake, I wound up seeing it and its twin on my hips the next day. It wasn't fair.

Then I thought of what Ash had been through. No, life definitely wasn't fair.

Ash drove for the next eight hours. The road began to climb and the sky became a crystalline blue, the temperature dropping with every mile we traveled.

We didn't talk much, just listening to the radio, letting the miles flow past, each minute taking us further away from those vile people. I began to feel safer, maybe feel a little hopeful for Ash who was largely silent. Even though I dozed in a haze of meds and tiredness, I would have killed for the chance to lie on a soft bed.

We finally pulled in at a Super 8 not far from Denver.

Ash was almost sleepwalking and I was, well, whatever the equivalent is when you're in a wheelchair.

Like two zombies, only recently reanimated, Ash trudged into the motel, pushing me slowly. The good news was that they had a room free; the bad news, there was only one, so we'd have to share.

I was so tired, I was beyond caring, and Ash didn't look as if he could have walked another step.

He opened the door to our room and we stared at the comfortable king size. There was no couch.

Ash opened his mouth to speak, but I waved away any objection he might throw at me.

"I don't care. I just want to sleep."

Ash nodded wearily in agreement and tossed my bag onto one side of the bed and collapsed face down on the other.

Seconds later, his breathing evened out, and his soft lips parted, relaxed in a deep sleep. He hadn't even taken off his shoes.

I hesitated, then wheeled myself forward, carefully untying his laces and gently easing off first one shoe, then the other. Ash murmured something I couldn't understand, his long fingers twitching restlessly, then finally lay still.

Relieved that I hadn't woken him, I made my way to the bathroom. A shower would be wonderful, but too difficult. Instead, I made do with washing my face and brushing my teeth.

As I wheeled myself back to the bedroom, I gazed down at Ash's sleeping body. He looked younger, despite the dark scruff on his face. Something about his peacefulness seemed young. Maybe sleep erased all the ugly things he'd suffered, if only for a few hours.

Then I noticed goosebumps pebbling his arms. I would never be able to pull the quilt from under his heavy body without waking him, so instead I wheeled myself to the closet, sighing as I saw the spare blanket I wanted, folded out of reach.

Instead, I shrugged out of my jacket and laid it over his shoulders. It was the best I could do.

With some difficulty, I shed my jeans and fished around under my t-shirt to unhook my bra. Everything else stayed on.

Then I eased myself into the bed and tried to relax with a strange man next to me. But Ash's solid warmth was comforting and I drifted into a pain-free sleep.

CHAPTER 8

Ash

My pulse skyrocketed, startling me awake. Instantly alert, I looked for the threat, but the space around me was quiet. As my heart rate gradually slowed, I felt my body shaking from cold and the violent images of my latest nightmare.

My heart tripped again when I realized that I wasn't alone in the bed, but then I saw honey-blonde hair on the pillow and her—the pretty girl—the girl in the wheelchair.

I was clutching her denim jacket tightly, still draped over my shoulders. It smelled like her—coconut and something flowery. It was delicate, like her.

The perfect stillness curled through me until the ball of tension in the center of my chest began to loosen.

The nightmare faded slowly and the clarity of daylight highlighted better memories instead. I looked at the girl, woman, really looked at her.

I studied the freckles across her nose and cheeks that she'd hidden with makeup yesterday. Faint lines fanned out from her eyes and bracketed her mouth. Her wrists were narrow, and bony shoulders poked through the material of her t-shirt. But her arms looked strong—probably from pushing the wheelchair.

What had happened to her? An accident, maybe? But she could walk a little, I'd seen her, just very slowly and painfully.

Guilt made my headache worsen. I should have asked her. I'd been so absorbed with my own problems, I'd never tried to find out.

Something else to feel guilty about. Marta, the girl, maybe even Yveta and Gary. Anything could have happened to them by now.

I rubbed my temples, trying to push the throbbing headache away. I was dehydrated: too much coffee, not enough water.

I glanced again at the woman sleeping peacefully next to me.

Laney.

She was pretty. My memory hadn't been wrong about that. She wasn't beautiful, not the kind who stood out in a crowd, but now I'd seen her, I couldn't forget her. I'd known many beautiful women: dancers, friends, girlfriends. Ballroom is a glamorous world—beauty is something you work at. Beautiful lines, great frame, soft hands, flowing movement, whatever the effort. All the glamor is on the outside—inside is hard, hard work.

Most of my girlfriends had been dancers. I'd tried regular girls, but they always got jealous of the amount of time I spent training with my partner; resented the physical closeness and hated watching the sensual dances, especially the rumba.

But dating dancers is hard, too. If the relationship doesn't work out, the dance partnership usually breaks up, with months or even years of training wasted. That had happened with Jana, my last partner—she was pushing to take it further. From casual dating, she'd jumped to the conclusion that living together was the next step—things I didn't want. So she dumped me for a guy who was a former world champion twice her age.

It was one of the reasons I'd applied for the Vegas job.

But with Laney, it was her warmth that attracted me, her softness and her strength.

She'd seen me, too. *Really* seen me—at my worst, at my weakest—and she'd helped me. Saved me.

She was still helping me now.

So brave. So fucking brave.

I sat up cautiously. The skin on my back and ass was blazing with pain—like knives slashing me over and over. I really wanted to shower, but the other woman, the nurse, she'd put bandages on the worst lacerations and I couldn't reach them.

I grit my teeth, remembering the lashes of the belt, the buckle biting into my flesh, Sergei's grunts as he jerked off at the same time.

I swallowed back the nausea and the shame. I never wanted to think about it again. Ever. I'd leave it to my nightmares.

Laney had been so brave when it all happened. Jesus, was that only two nights ago? She hadn't fainted or screamed; she'd planned, made decisions—she'd helped me to escape.

I felt a warm rush of gratitude.

Moving stiffly, I made it to the bathroom for a satisfying piss.

I stared longingly at Laney's toothbrush but that felt wrong. Instead, I used my finger to clean my teeth, using some of her toothpaste.

God, I really needed to shower, but it would be humiliating having to ask Laney to take off the bandages. I didn't want to remind her how she'd found me—helpless, destroyed.

But when I walked back into the bedroom, she was sitting up and wiping sleep from her eyes.

"Hi," I said.

Her eyes widened and she anxiously pulled the sheet higher, but not before I saw the outline of her breasts and hard nipples pressing through her t-shirt. I felt a flare of heat and I had to look away.

"Hi," she replied quietly, tugging on the sheet again.

I tried to think of something to break the awkward silence, but nothing seemed right. What was I supposed to say to the woman who'd saved my life, a woman I barely knew but had shared my bed?

"I…" Nothing came out. I shrugged. "Thank you," I said at last.

Laney frowned slightly. "What for?"

For saving my life. For saving me from everything that fucked up sadist wanted to do to me. Thank you for trusting me.

But I didn't say any of that. Instead I nodded at her denim jacket, folded on the corner of the bed where I'd left it.

"Thank you for your jacket."

She smiled softly. "You're welcome."

We continued to stare at each other until I gestured toward Laney's wheelchair.

"Do you need help?"

"No, I can manage, thank you," she said. "I actually feel better today, so that should make things easier—a bit quicker, too."

She laughed, but it sounded forced.

It was my turn to frown. "You don't use it always?"

"No. Not that often really. Just when I have a bad flare-up."

"What's wrong with you?"

It was a full five seconds before I realized how bad that sounded.

Laney arched one eyebrow.

"My boyfriend says that liking 'Buffy the Vampire Slayer' is wrong because it's a show made for adolescents and I'm 29. I disagree—Buffy kicks ass. Is that what you meant, about what's wrong with me?"

I winced and ducked my head.

"I'm sorry. I just meant…"

Laney gave a thin smile. "I know what you meant. And the answer is Rheumatoid Arthritis."

I knew the second word.

"I thought it was something old people get?" I said, my words hesitant.

I must have still looked clueless because Laney quickly explained.

"You're thinking of osteoarthritis. Everyone gets it confused. That's the wear and tear arthritis. Mine, you can get at any age, from birth if you're unlucky—or special, you might say," and she laughed sadly. "It means my joints can become swollen and painful, among other things. Bad days, I need the wheelchair; most times, I'm well enough. Luck of the draw."

"There are no medicines?"

"Yes and no. It can be controlled, to an extent, but it's pretty much guess work. There's no cure." Laney gave a small smile. "Sometimes the best medicine is to do the things that make you happy, things that remind you that life is good and being alive is the best gift."

She smiled like she meant it and waved a hand at me.

"Ask: I can see that you have more questions."

I sat on the edge of the bed and stared at the empty wheelchair.

"Have you always had it?"

"RA? Since I was seven. Please don't say you're sorry."

I gave her a quick glance. "You hate that, don't you?"

"You noticed?" Laney laughed wryly.

I nodded.

"The way you looked at the woman in the diner yesterday—it was a very strong look."

"Oh dear! I try not to do that," Laney laughed, her nose crinkling. "Sometimes it just slips out."

I grinned.

"I know! My father's friends always look sorry for him, having a dancer for a son. They think it's…" I struggled to think of the word in English. "Effeminate," I said at last, my smile fading.

I looked at her intently, demanding that she understood.

"I'm not gay."

Laney's snorting laugh surprised us both.

"I'm not!" I said defensively. "I tell people that I dance ballroom style and they think I must be gay. Every time!"

"People believe stereotypes because they're predictable," she said, shaking her head. "But why ballroom? What first attracted you to it?"

"The Paso," I said with certainty. "So strong, so masculine—the man versus his own demons, his own weakness, fighting to be brave."

Laney's eyebrows shot up. I could see that she'd never thought about it like that, but I think she understood. Not with the same intensity, but she understood.

"Any woman would know from a thousand yards that you're not gay. You're just so…"

She stopped suddenly and I cocked my head to one side, wanting her to finish the sentence.

"I'm so what?"

"Um, I was going to say, so masculine," Laney muttered, clearing her throat.

"Gay men are masculine."

"I know. I meant, well, just that it's *obvious* you're not gay. Oh God, I'm saying this all wrong!"

Her cheeks flushed and her gaze darted to my body. My shoulders relaxed and I grinned at her, leaning in closer, my eyes still fixed on hers.

"You think it's obvious that I'm not gay? I could make it more obvious ... but you have a boyfriend."

I smiled triumphantly then moved away from her.

Her eyes narrowed. Then she surprised the hell out of me by grabbing a pillow and tossing it at my head.

I raised my hands reflexively and just missed getting hit.

Once my surprise melted away, I gave her an evil smile. She squealed as I started to swing the pillow at her. But then I remembered that she was disabled—it was hardly a fair fight. I dropped the pillow back on the bed, shrugging sheepishly.

"Sorry."

Her expression was something between annoyance and sadness, and I knew that I'd done the wrong thing.

"I have to go to the bathroom," she muttered.

She was upset, and I could have cheerfully kicked myself in the balls. I'd never known a disabled person before—I didn't know how to behave and the fact that I kept forgetting she used a wheelchair caught me off-guard.

"Could you just look the other way?" Laney said quickly. "I'm a little underdressed here."

I shot her a look. "You could pretend I'm gay."

"Turn around!"

I turned, standing with my back facing her, hands on hips.

There was a sudden silence.

"How are you?" she asked tentatively. "How's your back?"

I stiffened immediately.

"Okay," I lied.

"I doubt it," she said gently. "Ash, I'm the last person you need to hide pain from."

My head drooped to my chest at her words, and I threw a quick look over my shoulder to see her staring at me, her eyes flitting over my back, compassion on her face. And I knew she could see the fresh blood that had seeped through my borrowed t-shirt.

"It's sore," I admitted. "I'd really like to shower. I need ... could you help me take off the bandages?"

Laney nodded.

"Of course. Let me just ... give me a minute, okay?"

She slid into her wheelchair, trying to hide her underwear, but at least she seemed to be moving more easily.

I couldn't hear the shower running and wondered how she managed things like that, especially when she had … what did she call it? A flare-up?

I tugged off my shirt, frowning at the patches of blood. It was worse than I'd thought.

A few minutes later, Laney wheeled herself out again. She took one look at my body and her eyes glazed with tears. I didn't want her crying over what those bastards had done to me. But she forced herself to speak evenly.

"Okay, let me take a look."

One by one, she eased the bandages from my skin. I already knew that bruises were coming through as well, and the mirror told me that I was a kaleidoscope of black and purple.

"Can you kneel down so I can reach your shoulders?"

I knelt in front of her, my feet beneath her wheelchair and the backs of my thighs pressed against her knees. Her hands trembled slightly while she worked, but even though her touch was gentle, I couldn't help hissing with pain, and my muscles twitched under her fingers.

I knew that I'd be permanently marked, carrying the scars forever. I'd never outrun Oleg's handiwork. Or the sickening memories. If it looked really bad, I might have trouble getting theater work again. People go to see dance to feel good, not to have their stomachs turned by Quasimodo.

There'd be few Paso vests in my future.

Anger and frustration surged inside me: I'd *never* outrun the Bratva.

I felt Laney's cool hands on my burning skin. I liked the way she touched me—gentle but not hesitant. She understood pain and wasn't cowed by it. She didn't let illness beat her. It didn't own her. I gritted my teeth: I might be marked, but Sergei was *not* going to win.

My mind twisted with bitter thoughts of revenge. I'd never held a gun in my life, but I wanted to, very badly.

If the monster was standing in front of me right now, I'd pull the trigger. I could, I knew I could. And I'd feel … nothing.

It was as if the intensity of the last few weeks had left my emotional reservoir dry. I felt empty, with nothing inside.

Perhaps I should be worried? Dance was my passion, but it came from inside me. If my passion was gone, what was left?

Even that thought seemed distant and unimportant, as if a pane of glass separated me from viewing this fucked up life.

Then Laney touched a particularly tender spot, and I shuddered, sucking in a breath to keep the pain inside.

"Sorry," she murmured.

I tensed as she slid the waistband of my sweatpants lower, uncovering the upper curve of my ass as she tried to ease off another bandage. But a very different sensation rushed through my body.

Shit! Not now!

I cupped my hands over my dick, trying to hide the sudden tenting in my pants. Laney didn't need to see that. She'd think I was some kind of freak who got off on pain.

Then I started to wonder if she could have sex. Would it hurt her? Had she ever?

She had a boyfriend, but that didn't mean…

I pushed the thought away, instead concentrating on counting ceiling tiles.

Thankfully, my erection was mostly gone by the time she finished. Even so, I caught the flush in her cheeks as I turned around. Had she seen?

"I'll go shower now," I said, jerking my thumb at the bathroom.

"Wait! I should…" Laney stammered helplessly. "I should take a photograph. For evidence."

My face went blank. "Your friend took a picture. And your phone is dead."

Then I turned and walked into the bathroom.

I was just a charity case—I wasn't a man to her.

Laney

I heard the water in the shower and gave myself a mental ticking off.

He'd been brutalized and traumatized. He could be a rape survivor for all I knew.

And not only that, it was hard being near him, touching him intimately. Ash was just so…

Then I felt guilty about Collin. Sort of. We were broken up, weren't we? He'd never replied to my last text—well, not that I knew of.

My feelings for Ash were confusing. I wanted to help him, to take care of him, save him even. But I was attracted to him, as well. Those feelings weren't wrong … unless I acted on them.

I sighed.

Note to self: only rescue ugly guys next time.

Ash was in the bathroom for so long that I started to wonder what he was doing. But when he emerged wearing just a towel, he explained quickly, as if he was trying to reassure me that he wasn't walking around half naked for the hell of it.

"I washed my clothes. To get the blood out. I've hung them on the towel rack. They should be dry enough to wear soon. Or not."

And he gave me a small smile, because damp clothes were the least of his worries.

I returned his smile as best I could.

"I saw a Walmart next door," I said, striving for a conversational tone. "I'll go see if I can buy you some jeans and a few t-shirts or…"

Ash held up his hand, halting my teetering words.

"No. You've done enough. I can't take…"

"Ash," I said, gently interrupting. "It's not taking—it's me giving. And we're in this together."

He closed his eyes and muttered something in his own language.

"I'll pay you back. Everything."

"How about this," I said carefully. "It's a simple idea—I'm sure you know it: pay it forward."

Ash stared at me blankly. "I don't understand."

"I helped you because I could, because I wanted to. Maybe one day you'll see someone who needs help, so you'll help them just because you can. And they do the same. Paying it forward, you see?"

Ash swallowed and I watched the subtly erotic movement of his throat.

"You are a good person," he said.

Was I? Was I a good person? Lusting after this damaged man while my boyfriend/unboyfriend stayed at home?

Ash was still watching me.

"What's your name? Your family name, I mean."

I smiled. Getting-to-know-you talk—yes, I could do that.

"Hennessey. Laney Hennessey. Irish American for five generations. What about you?"

"Aljaž Novak. My father is Jure. Like how you say 'George'."

I waited for more, but that was all he said.

"That's your whole family?"

Ash nodded.

No mother? No brothers and sisters? I found that unbearably sad. I forced myself to keep the tone cheerful.

"Well, if we're doing my family, we'll be here forever."

The corner of Ash's mouth lifted in a smile.

"My clothes are drying—and I'm not going anywhere in a towel."

Yep, I was an altruist—saving women the world over from a gorgeous man with abs I could count, wearing nothing but a towel.

"Hmm, a captive audience!" I teased him. "You asked for it. My father is Brian, he's a police captain, like I said. My mother is Bridget, she's a homemaker; and I have three sisters, Bernice, Linda and Sylvia; they're married to Al, Joe and Mario, with seven kids between them. My Uncle Donald is in the fire department and he's married to Carmen. They've got four children—my cousins, Stephen, Paddy, Eric and Michael. My mom's sister, Lydia, is married to Uncle Paul, and they have two children, Trisha and Amelia. Heard enough yet? Because there's a ton of second cousins and family friends who are nearly family, too."

"Wow!" Ash blinked, shaking his head. "That's a lot of people."

"They're great, most of the time," I smiled. "But having a big family, well ... I'm the youngest of the first cousins, so it's like I have six moms and dads and a dozen brothers and sisters, and they're all up in my business the whole time."

I shook my head.

"You should see our house at Thanksgiving—crazy."

I waited for Ash to say something else about his family, but a distant expression clouded his face. I already knew he wasn't close to his father, and he hadn't mentioned his mother. Perhaps she wasn't in his life? Or perhaps it was none of my business.

I cleared my throat.

"Why don't you order from one of these takeout menus, and while we're waiting, I'll go see what delights Walmart has to offer?"

Ash fiddled with the edge of his towel, a frown on his face, and I sighed.

"We talked about this," I reminded him gently. "You pay it forward when you have the chance. Now what shoe size are you?"

"Forty-six," he muttered after a short pause.

I raised my eyebrows in confusion. "Excuse me?"

Ash looked up at the surprise in my voice then shook his head as if to clear it.

"Twelve in US sizes. Sorry."

"You had me worried there for a minute," I laughed.

I glanced down at his bare feet, suddenly reminded that there was a lot of naked male flesh on view. Even sitting on the edge of a motel bed he looked elegant, his muscled calves leading to thick, strong thighs, and his stomach was a flat slab of muscle above the towel, his ridged abdominals moving with each breath, the planes of his chest defined but not bulging. But the bruises...

I tore my gaze away before I met his eyes. I didn't want him to see my thoughts.

"What size pants?" I asked quickly.

"Thirty waist, 34 inseam."

"Right, I'll be back," I said, my voice too bright, over compensating. "Order whatever you want—I'm starving!" And I placed some bills on the small table.

"You don't have your shoes," Ash commented, his voice serious.

"I don't need them," I said, not wanting to mention that I couldn't face forcing my feet into the Louboutins again.

"It's cold out there, Laney."

God help me, but I loved the way he said my name.

I felt as though every time I looked into his eyes or let my gaze linger on his hard, beautiful body, my IQ dropped another few points.

"Your shoes?" he prompted.

My sneakers were in my suitcase, but I couldn't reach my feet to put socks on or to tie laces. I wasn't going to bother with shoes today.

"I don't need them," I argued, unwilling to admit there was something I couldn't do, especially in front of him.

"You're stubborn!"

His voice was quietly amused, but it was true. And sometimes stubborn was useful. Stubborn was refusing to give into pain. Stubborn was getting out of bed when my body was screaming not to be moved. Yes, I was stubborn.

"I…"

My voice caught as Ash didn't wait for my reply but rifled through my suitcase and pulled out a pair of red socks.

"Okay?" he asked, his voice edged with uncertainty.

I nodded wordlessly, and then he knelt in front of me again, carefully easing the bright cotton over my feet. He did it all so instinctively with no fuss, no drama.

Tears rose in my eyes as I studied his dark head bent over me, his hair still wet.

He eased my swollen feet into the sneakers and tied them loosely, then handed me my jacket and purse.

"You won't get cold now."

"Thank you," I said weakly.

He opened the door and I wheeled myself out, welcoming the chilly slap of air as I left the building.

Ash's gentle thoughtfulness moved me more than I wanted to admit, and I wasn't sure why.

Ash

After she'd gone, I paced the small room.

My thoughts tormented me. I wanted to gouge out my brain so I wouldn't remember anymore. But I couldn't. Instead, they preyed on my mind. And I started to think about what would happen when we reached Chicago, whether she would still want to know me. I'd have to tell her father *everything* if Sergei and Oleg were going to be caught and punished, if Volkov was going to be stopped.

But then I'd have to admit how stupid and weak I'd been, how they'd played me. I'd have to admit that I watched helplessly while Oleg murdered the girl, beat the Korean cook to death, and while Marta had been forced into prostitution. I'd watched and known and done nothing.

I'd have to admit what Sergei had done to me, not once, but twice.

The thick, choking memory made me gag and I ran to the bathroom to throw up. My knees hit the floor and the cold porcelain pressed against my bare chest. Hot, furious tears burned behind my eyes and I wiped them away angrily.

But then I slammed my hands on the basin. The bastards didn't get to win this one.

I rinsed my mouth and then went to sit on the bed to order breakfast.

I'd force myself to eat. I'd force myself to stay strong.

Laney

As I made my way around Walmart, I wasn't surprised that people stared. Most tried not to get caught, but one or two did it openly. If I was being charitable, I'd say they were concerned, but no—they were just staring.

I did my best to pick out some clothes for Ash. I'd been in too much of a hurry to leave that claustrophobic hotel room. Ash's presence filled the space. He brimmed with masculinity, testosterone flowing from him in heady waves; and I don't think he knew he was doing it, but I saw him checking out my boobs when I woke up. It was just a quick glance—well, two quick glances—but it was definitely there. It was a mystery to me how anyone could ever think he was gay, although it obviously bothered him a lot.

I suppose assuming a male dancer must always be gay was like assuming a woman in a wheelchair always needed an aide. We'd be fighting stereotypes our whole lives. After our conversation, I was okay with that comparison.

As well as two pairs of jeans, shirts and a coat, I bought Ash toiletries and more Advil, plus boxer-briefs and socks. It felt a little awkward buying underwear for a man I hardly knew, but compared to what we'd been through together, that small discomfort wasn't important.

Luckily, I was able to buy a phone charger, as well. It would be a relief to be in touch with the world again. I wondered how much trouble I was in with Vanessa and Jo.

I made my way back to the hotel, so loaded up with bags on my lap that I could hardly see over the top. This could be tricky. At any moment, they could all go sliding off, and then I really would be reliant on the kindness of strangers. Again.

But I made it back in one piece, and Ash opened the door as soon as he heard me outside.

"Clothes and a phone charger," I said, pointing my chin at the mountain of plastic bags.

I caught the scent of food, happy that it had arrived. We were both too hungry to wait and unpack what I'd bought for him, so I plugged in my phone while we sat on the bed, Ash wrapped in a blanket, as we fueled up for the day ahead.

Every few seconds my phone buzzed with another message or missed call.

"I guess people are worried about you," he said.

I nodded, my mouth full of eggs and bacon.

"I bet Jo and Vanessa have been blowing up my phone with messages. I'll call them as soon as we get in the car."

Ash glanced up at me. "Not your boyfriend?"

I pulled a face. "I don't know. Maybe. We kind of broke up. He didn't want me to go to Vegas." Then I gave an awkward laugh. "Looks like he was right, even if it was for the wrong reason."

Ash looked down at his half empty plate. "I will always be grateful that you came."

I was silent, and slowly Ash's eyes rose to meet mine. There was a connection there, I could feel it. Then he looked down again and resumed eating. The moment had passed, but I knew I hadn't imagined it—I just didn't know what it meant.

It was strangely personal, sitting side by side on a bed, eating breakfast. It was the kind of thing you did when you were dating not ... whatever we were. It was too early to call ourselves friends. I hardly knew him, and Ash certainly didn't know me.

After we'd drained the coffee pot, I handed over the bags stuffed with clothes.

"I forgot to ask your shirt size, so look forward to more clown clothes," I said with a smile that I hope softened my words.

Ash pulled out a three-pack of dark gray briefs. He didn't seem to know how to feel about them either, his dark eyes flashing with some quick emotion. But while I kept my back to him, he pulled on a pair without comment.

The jeans weren't a bad fit—slightly too loose on the waist—but the long-sleeved Henley fit better. And there were two more in the bags: one navy and one pale blue.

I'd also bought him a heavy peacoat in black, with matching gloves and wool hat necessary for Chicago. And sneakers. With socks. And, a toothbrush. I'd forgotten to buy a razor. Oh well.

Ash finished dressing and turned to face me.

"How do I look?"

I withheld a sigh. *Heartbreakingly handsome.* That was the truth, but it wasn't what I said.

"Not bad, although the towel made a statement."

"You think?" he asked, going along with my teasing. "What did the towel say?"

There was no way I could tell him what that small towel around his waist had me thinking. I improvised quickly.

"Um, rule breaker, loafer…"

"A loaf? Like bread?"

I smiled. His English was so good, it was too easy to forget that there were some phrases that he didn't always get.

"It means someone who's lazy … a loser, I guess."

Ash's eyes flashed with anger.

"I didn't mean it like that," I said quickly. "It was a dumb joke. I'm sorry."

He nodded stiffly but wouldn't meet my gaze again. Instead he packed up my belongings silently, his face rigid in its blankness.

Kicking myself mentally, I watched him pace around the room, deliberately avoiding me. I deserved that: what a stupid thing to say.

Sighing, I picked up my phone and scrolled through the long list of texts and missed calls. I tapped out two quick messages to Jo and Vanessa to let them know that I was fine and would be home tonight. Well, very early tomorrow morning, even if Ash could keep going for the next 15 hours. I hoped that I'd be well enough to take a turn at driving later on.

I was surprised to see a number of texts from Collin that had started last night. He wanted to know if I was okay, but he didn't comment on whether or not we were still a couple.

I sent a short message reassuring him that I was alright and that I'd be home after midnight.

Ash was still silent when he helped me into the car. Despite the fact that he was upset with me, the gentle, unobtrusive way he handled me hadn't changed.

I wanted to apologize again for my clumsy remark, but I didn't. It seemed best just to try and move past it.

Instead, I plugged in the phone and flipped through my contacts list to make the next call.

"Dad, it's me."

CHAPTER 9

Laney

With a frustrated growl, I tossed my cell phone down and closed my eyes. The conversation with Dad had been difficult to say the least. According to him, I deserved to be arrested for fleeing the scene of a crime, was completely irresponsible, with a flagrant disregard for my civic duty etc. etc. I began to think that he'd arrest me himself when I arrived in Chicago.

And he wouldn't listen when I said I'd come to the station with Ash tomorrow. He was going to send a cruiser to wait for us.

"That sounded hard."

I glanced over at Ash and gave him a tired smile.

"You could say that. Dad's going to meet us at my apartment tonight. I tried to put him off until tomorrow, but well, you know what parents are like."

"Does he know what the police in Las Vegas are saying?" Ash asked cautiously.

I winced.

"Uh well, they wanted to question us," I said carefully. "The theater usher reported seeing a man with a gun.

Ash's eyes widened and he glanced away from the road to stare at me.

"They think that was me?"

"No! No, but they're not happy we left the scene."

Ash's hands gripped the steering wheel until his knuckles were white, and his skin looked pale beneath his tan.

"If your dad sends me back there, they'll kill me."

I rested my hand on his bicep, hoping my touch would reassure him.

"That won't happen. I promise."

The look he gave me seemed to say he didn't believe I had the power to keep my promise.

I was horribly afraid he might be right. But I'd do everything I could.

It was frustrating. Dad hadn't listened to a word I'd said, which didn't bode well. But I had an idea of how to handle my father: I'd been watching my mother do it for years, and I'd learned from the best. So instead of trying to change his mind while he ranted at me, I picked up my phone again and started typing out everything that I'd seen and heard, from arriving in Las Vegas to this moment. I asked Jo to send me the photo she'd taken of Ash's back, and added it to my file. Then I emailed everything to Dad. Hopefully, given time, he'd see how wrong he was.

Ash was driving across the undulating foothills of Nebraska before we spoke again.

"I was wondering about your tattoo," I began.

Out of the corner of my eye, I saw Ash twitch, as if he'd been so lost in thought that he'd forgotten I was there.

"Does it mean anything?"

Ash looked affronted. "Of course! Why would I mark my body without meaning?"

My thoughts flew to his scarred back.

Ash sighed. "I'm sorry. I'm just..."

His sentence trailed off and I shook my head.

"It's okay. But people do get tattoos because they like the picture or the words. After all, you can go into a tattoo parlor and choose one out of a book."

"Have you got a tattoo?" Ash asked, raising one eyebrow, a mischievous glint in his eyes. "Because it's not on your legs or your arms. It's not on your neck. Where would Laney put a tattoo?"

I threw him a warning look, but Ash just grinned. I liked this Ash: playful, sexy.

"Nope, no tattoos," I answered. "I never found anything that meant so much that I'd want to get the ink. What's yours about?"

Ash frowned, the playful expression disappearing.

"It's a ... map," he said hesitantly, struggling to express his thoughts. "A map of my life. Things that happened, important things. When I have a new part of the story, I add to it."

He shrugged.

"I got my first when I was 16 after my mama died."

I kept the questions light after that. We talked about music and about dancing. Endlessly about dancing. I was fascinated by this brave new world that I'd never entered before. Ash's eyes glowed, and I saw again the man who'd claimed his place center stage in Vegas.

We talked about my work, writing student guides for school texts, and we talked about Chicago. It was a little bit like a first date; one of those tell-me-about-yourself' conversations. And unlike a lot of guys I'd met, Ash was as interested in finding out about me as I was about him.

He was eager to see the city too, but edged with nerves because the end of the journey meant … neither of us knew what it meant.

As dusk fell, we stopped somewhere in the middle of Iowa. Ash could barely keep his eyes open and we were both hungry.

He climbed wearily out of the driver's door, stretching his tall frame with a grimace. As he went around to the trunk to get my wheelchair, I called out to him.

"I think I can manage. If you'll help me."

"Sure," he said, changing direction, walking around to my door and opening it.

Collin would have argued. He would have insisted on a complete and exhaustive questioning of my physical capacity, and then he'd have gotten the wheelchair for me anyway. Because he knew best.

I used to think of that as him caring, and it was, but it was controlling, too. Ash simply believed me when I said that I could walk.

His arm was warm as I held onto it. He steadied my elbow with his hand, and the distance between us was only a few inches. I could feel the heat of his body in the cool air.

Once I was standing upright, Ash slid his arm around my waist, and together, we walked toward the diner.

It occurred to me that we probably looked like a couple, so much in love we couldn't bear to be apart for even a second.

I wondered again what would happen to us when we arrived in Chicago.

Ash

"We're here."

I felt Laney's small hand on my thigh, shaking me awake.

"We're here," she said again.

My whole body felt drugged with sleep, but then a sharp shot of adrenaline made me sit up straighter.

Chicago!

We'd made it.

I glanced out of the window at the wide city street and the first thing I saw was a police car. The headlights flashed once, and I saw the strain on Laney's face.

"It's my dad."

Her tone wasn't reassuring.

Laney's door was ripped open and a cold gust of wind wound around us, whipping her long hair into her face. It was forty-five degrees cooler than the heat of the desert, but I liked it. I didn't ever want to spend time in parched, arid air again.

Laney was already in her father's arms while he looked her up and down, as if checking that each arm and leg was still attached.

I climbed out of the car stiffly and pushed my hands into my pockets, watching Laney and her father.

He didn't look anything like her. He was tall and heavy, with a thick neck like a bull, bright red hair and rugged skin; not small and pale like his daughter. His eyes turned to me.

"Is that him?"

His tone was less than friendly, and Laney whispered something angrily that made him scowl. Then he jerked his head at another police officer who stepped forward abruptly, making me jerk back, slamming my back against the car door.

My vision dipped with the pain, and I guess my sudden movement freaked him out, because a second later, I was face down on the hood of the car, my cheekbone pressed painfully against the freezing metal. I swore, but couldn't move as pain radiated across my stretched skin.

"Stop that right now, Billy Jenkins!" Laney shouted.

"It's okay, Billy," said Laney's dad, "he won't be so stupid as to try anything."

My arm was released as suddenly as it had been grabbed. I stood up slowly, my heart pounding in reaction. I was tired and pissed, but Laney made me want to smile. She was facing down two big policemen, her small hands balled into fists.

"I can't believe you two," Laney glared, her voice furious. "He is *not* a criminal!"

Then she grabbed hold of my hand and marched us toward a tall brownstone building.

"Just for that you can carry our bags *and* my wheelchair, Billy Jenkins," she shouted over her shoulder. "And then you can take the car back to Hertz."

She didn't wait for a reply, but allowed me to help her into the building, slowing only slightly as she used the handrail to pull herself up the six steps at the front.

I couldn't help wondering how she managed them on her flare-up days.

I glanced over my shoulder, but her father didn't try to stop us. He looked annoyed and a little confused, but he wasn't going to argue with her either. Shaking his head, he fixed me with a hard stare. It was clear what he meant: *Fuck with my daughter and I'll fuck with you.*

"I'm sorry about that," Laney said tightly as we waited for the elevator, ignoring her father's angry snort. "Are you okay?"

I nodded, my eyes darting back to our police bodyguard.

"Have you been taking your meds?" Laney's father asked gruffly.

"Yes, Dad," she said with a soft sigh.

We rode the elevator in silence, but I was surprised when Laney continued to hold my hand. Her father didn't miss that detail either.

"Did you read my email?" she asked pointedly.

"Yes."

"And?"

"We'll talk inside."

I glanced at Laney, wondering what was in the email, but she gave a small shake of her head.

Her apartment was small but not cluttered. A couch took up most of the room, although there was still enough space to navigate the area with a wheelchair. A heavy bookshelf was the other piece of furniture, lined with hardbacks and paperbacks, shot glasses and several framed photographs. I recognized a younger Laney with her two girlfriends; pictures that were probably of her family; and a heavy guy with his arm around her. I wondered why she kept a photo of her ex.

I turned toward the European-style French doors that led to a tiny balcony. The drapes were open, and the whole room was lit with the soft, orange glow of street lights below. But if you looked up, you could still see a patch of sky and a few scattered stars between the towering skyscrapers.

I understood about wanting to see more of life, wanting to see over the horizon.

Laney sank into an overstuffed easy chair, leaving me and her father to share the couch.

Instead, Laney's father carried a hardback chair from the kitchen and placed it directly in front of me.

"Dad," Laney said, her voice level and controlled. "He's not a suspect, he's my friend."

I looked up quickly, meeting her eyes, and she gave me a conspiratorial smile that caused a vein to stand out on her father's forehead.

"You don't even know this man," he objected strenuously.

"We've spent the last fifty-plus hours together in a very stressful situation," Laney argued. "You've always said that you learn a lot about a person in extreme circumstances."

Laney's father looked annoyed to hear his own words thrown back at him. But he wasn't giving up. In fact, I was certain he was only just starting.

"According to Immigration records, Aljaž Novak left the country a month ago. You have no idea who this man really is."

"They took my passport," I growled, starting to stand.

"Sit down!"

Laney's dad barked out the command, but Laney stared angrily.

"Dad," she said in a warning voice.

I glanced at her again before sitting on the edge of the couch, hot blood hammering through my body. Those fucking bastards! God knows who was using my passport. Hell, it could be anything, drugs, guns, people smuggling. I felt sick at the thought.

"He can't prove who he is," Laney's father snapped.

"I can!" I spat out. "Go to the Slovene Dancesport Federation website—they'll have my picture."

Laney pulled out her phone and did a quick search, smiling when she immediately found my photograph, showing it to her father.

"Well," he coughed. "That's something. We can check the rest with your Embassy."

"I'm not a liar," I said angrily, staring right back at him.

Suddenly the front door swung open, making everyone jump.

The newcomer was the guy from the photograph. He was bigger than me, but whatever muscle he'd had was now lost in a large gut and two chins.

"Collin!" Laney's mouth dropped open. "What are you doing here?"

He froze mid-step and glared at her.

"Are you serious?"

"I asked him to come," said Laney's father, a puzzled look on his face as he studied his daughter's anger.

"I came because I care about you," Collin said stiffly, his gaze shifting to me.

I tried to keep a neutral expression, but hell, after three seconds I could tell that the guy was a first class prick. Any man worthy of the name would have been on his knees with relief, telling Laney that he loved her and would kill anyone who hurt her, then move heaven and earth to be with her. Not standing there like he had a stick up his ass. *Douche.*

I liked swearing in American, and my vocabulary had grown since I'd roomed with Gary.

Assface. Dickwad. Douche canoe.

I leaned back and folded my arms, staring at Laney's tool of a boyfriend, or ex-boyfriend, or whatever the fuck he was.

Collin turned to look at Laney. "I thought I should be here after what you've been through. You shouldn't be alone."

"I'm not," she said coolly. "I have Ash."

Laney's father and the prick started shouting while I looked at Laney in surprise. Again.

"Well, where did you think he was going to stay?" she asked impatiently when the yelling had calmed a bit. "He can't exactly check into a hotel." Then she pinned her father with a fierce stare. "And please don't tell me you were thinking of accommodating him in a cell for the night!"

"He's not staying here!"

"He most certainly is!"

"But…"

"I'm not arguing about this, Dad."

Her father jutted his chin out. "All the more reason for Collin to be here," he grunted. "You've no idea what this man might…"

"We've just spent the last two days together," Laney replied tersely. "Including sharing a hotel room last night. I think I know Ash pretty well by now."

Collin was silent but his face turned bright red.

"Oh for goodness sake," Laney sighed. "We didn't sleep together!"

I shifted uncomfortably on the couch, drawing all eyes to me.

"Fine, we shared a bed because that was all the hotel had," Laney confessed. "But that's all!"

"I'm not going anywhere," Collin ground out.

"Neither is Ash," Laney replied.

Her father coughed and looked at his watch.

"You both need to come in and make a statement about the gun incident…"

I felt a flare of anxiety. I still wasn't sure I trusted the police.

"And about what happened to Ash," Laney said quickly.

"Fine," said her father, narrowing his eyes at me. "Be at the station at oh-nine hundred and…"

"Dad! It's two in the morning! I'm going to sleep late, followed by a very long soak in the tub. Don't expect us until after lunch, and don't send anyone over because I won't be answering the door."

Her dad growled and huffed some more, but then he pulled her into a tight hug and muttered something in her ear that made Laney's eyes turn glassy with tears.

"Love you, too, Dad. And don't worry, I'm fine. I'll see you tomorrow."

Her father left, and the three of us were alone.

Laney held up her hand as Collin started to speak.

"Collin, I'm tired and kind of pissed at you right now. I'm fairly sure that the last thing you said to me before I went to Las Vegas was 'I'm done'."

Yep, proved what I thought: Collin was a douche.

"I was angry," Collin muttered.

"I already got the memo on that," Laney shot back. Then she relented, rubbing her eyes until they were red. "Look, we'll talk in the morning."

"I'm staying," he repeated, glaring at me.

"I'm too tired to argue with you. Fine, stay. You can help Ash make up the couch. You know where the clean sheets are."

She stomped off through another door which I guessed led to the bedroom.

As soon as the door closed, Collin scowled at me.

"If you lay a finger on my girlfriend, I'll…"

"She said you broke up."

He stopped mid-sentence, looking irritated and uneasy.

"It was a misunderstanding."

"She was very clear."

"Just stay away from her! Or else!"

And he glared threateningly. I shook my head with amusement and disbelief.

"Man, I've been beaten up by Bratva and had a gun pushed in my face. But you? Laney has more balls than you. Or maybe you gave her yours. If you find them, let me know."

Collin's face turned purple and his lips peeled back from his teeth. If he was trying to look intimidating, he was failing. He just looked like a balloon that was about to burst.

"You punk! You think I'm going to let a slick operator like you into her life? I think you're making it all up! There isn't a mark on you!"

I laughed. I couldn't help it. The prick was pretty damn funny. In fact, I was laughing so hard, I didn't hear Laney come back into the room.

"What's going on?"

"Your *friend*," Collin sneered. "He isn't right in the head."

My laugh died stone cold dead. "You're a fucking prick!"

"Boys!" Laney yelled, raising her arms between us. "Stop this! I'm tired and really, really past this juvenile macho posturing nonsense." She pointed a finger at Collin. "One more word, and you'll be out that door so fast you'll have rug burns on your ass. And you," she scowled at me, "just … stop."

She threw a pillow which I caught one-handed.

"The bathroom is through my bedroom, so if you want to wash up, go do it now or you can pee out the window for all I care!"

I tossed the pillow onto the couch and walked into Laney's bedroom. I frowned at the sight of her bed. I didn't like the idea of the prick sleeping with her. Especially not while I was on the couch next door.

I grabbed my toothbrush from our Vegas bag and washed up quickly. I peeled off my shirt and almost dropped it in the clothes hamper before I remembered that this was just a temporary stop. I wondered where I'd be sleeping tomorrow night. In a cell, if Laney's father had his way.

Then I ran a hand over the thick stubble covering my cheeks and chin that was starting to itch. I decided to go buy a razor in the morning…

Fuck! I'd have to ask Laney for the money to buy a fucking disposable razor until I could access my bank account and transfer some money. And I had no idea how that was going to work without ID, but I was too tired to worry about it now.

I walked out of the bathroom, glaring at Laney's bed again, then headed for the couch. I saw Collin's eyes widen and his cheeks flush as he took in the black, yellow and purple bruises covering my chest, stomach and arms.

I glanced at Laney and saw her watching me with concerned eyes.

"How's your back?"

I shrugged. "Okay, I think."

"Let me look. Sit on the couch—I've got some antiseptic cream to put on you."

"I'm fine."

"Shut up. Sit down. And stop pissing me off!"

I sat, ignoring the shocked gasp as Collin saw my back for the first time. I figured it must look pretty bad. I just knew that it hurt like a bitch.

Collin left the room, and I didn't know if it was because he was a pussy, or pissed to see his (maybe) girlfriend rubbing ointment onto another man's back.

Both, I hoped. But her kindness was fresh and unexpected. Touching. She was genuine, real.

"You're enjoying this, aren't you?" said Laney.

"What?"

"You're enjoying annoying Collin."

I didn't even bother trying to deny it. "He's a prick."

"He's not all bad…"

"You said you broke up with him."

"Technically, yes."

"Then tell him to leave."

"I can't do that."

"Why not? It's your apartment."

Laney sighed. "Well, for one thing, he'd call my dad…"

"Prick."

"And for another, we really should talk."

"He's still a prick."

"Ash! Stop it!"

I was silent. I could hear the tiredness and distress in her voice. After everything she'd done for me, I didn't want to hurt her. And I didn't know anything about their relationship except what she'd said and what I'd seen for myself.

But her hands were soft and soothing as she rubbed in the cream, and it took away some of the pain. I couldn't help leaning into her touch. She still smelled like coconut, although more faintly now. Her fingers drifted down my back, just above the waistband of my jeans, stroking, healing.

And then her hands were gone.

"I'll see you in the morning," she said. "Sleep well."

I nodded, and even though tiredness pulled at my body, I knew that the second I closed my eyes, I'd see the horror.

Laney hesitated, then leaned down and kissed me on the cheek.

"It's going to be okay."

I didn't believe her.

I sat on the couch with my head in my hands for a long time.

CHAPTER 10

Ash
If the night before had been awkward, the morning was worse.

The prick walked around the apartment like he owned it, completely ignoring my existence. I was half expecting him to piss on the walls to mark his territory.

He was built like a wrestler, but the muscles had turned soft and a gut hung over his pajama pants. Thick hair spread up from his chest to his shoulders and down to his stomach. The guy wasn't a friend of hot wax. Not that I cared one way or another: waxing was just part of the job because it showed off the pecs and abs. A lot of us did armpits, as well, because Paso outfits with armpit hair is kind of off-putting for an audience.

When Laney walked out of her bedroom, I had a hard time not smiling. She looked so cute in her Minions pajamas, mussed hair and sleepy face.

But she looked tired, too, and I wondered if she hadn't slept well. She gave short answers to all Collin's questions, and as he directed every remark to her alone, it was a stilted conversation. No one talked to me, except for Laney's mumbled 'Morning'. I sat in silence, mentally compiling a list of words to describe Collin. The list was alphabetical: I'd started with 'asshole', but was stuck on 'q'. There was no letter 'q' in my language.

Eventually, Collin left for work. That surprised me. If Laney had been my girlfriend, I'd have gone to the police station with her, just so I could hold her hand while she made a statement. The prick really was clueless. Now what the hell came after 'prick'?

As soon as the front door slammed shut, Laney glared at me.

"Stop it!"

"I didn't say anything!" I protested.

"I can hear you thinking!"

I held back the smile that was threatening to turn into a full laugh, leaned forward on the couch and raised my eyebrows.

"What am I thinking?"

Laney frowned and tugged her robe tighter.

"Collin cares about me," she stated firmly. "He's just trying to give me space."

I didn't reply. Getting into an argument with Laney was not on my list of priorities.

I closed my eyes, wondering what sort of fucked-up today would be. I ran a hand over my beard, scratching at my chin.

"Did you want to shave that off?" Laney asked. "I have disposable razors if you do."

Some good news. And I loved how intuitive she was.

"Thank you. It's starting to drive me crazy."

"Okay, well why don't you go do that now, because then I'm planning to spend at least an hour soaking in the tub."

"I could scrub your back," I said, only half-joking. "To thank you for taking care of mine."

"Hmm, very noble of you," Laney smiled, but I think I can manage. "Go. Shower!"

I smirked at her and sauntered into the bathroom. Teasing Laney was my new favorite hobby.

I showered, enjoying the hot water, despite the sharp stings all over my back and ass. Then I shaved off the stubble before dressing in another of the long-sleeve shirts that Laney had bought me. I wished like hell I could fast-forward 24 hours. Anxiety was beginning to wind cold spirals of fear through me, twisting my gut. What would happen this afternoon? What if the police didn't believe me? It would be hard enough going through everything that had happened, but if they didn't believe me after…

I scrunched my eyes shut, forcing myself to slow my breathing, then opened them and stared at my reflection, examining the smooth face that stared back blankly. The face other people said was handsome. I despised it.

I spat at the mirror, watching the gob of spittle slide down.

Laney tapped on the door.

"Ash! You've been forever and I'm bursting to pee! Hurry up!"

I took a deep breath, wiped the mirror clean and pushed the door open.

"Sorry," I muttered.

Laney's smile dropped when she saw me, so I guessed that I looked as bad as I felt.

"Are you okay?" Then she sighed. "Dumb question. I, um, I heard you in the middle of the night. Shouting. I was going to come, but by the time I'd got to the door, you were quiet again…"

"Sorry," I repeated, pushing past her.

I hated being so fucking weak. I'd hoped that no one had heard me last night.

"Ash," she said gently. "You've got nothing to be sorry for."

"Haven't I?"

My voice was bitter and I folded my arms across my chest, unable to look at her.

"No, you really don't."

I didn't answer.

Laney stood there, anxiously twisting the edge of her robe in her hands.

"There's something else I wanted to … you know you're not being accused of anything, right? You're not going to be arrested…"

I still didn't reply. What could I say? Admit I was freaking out?

"But I thought you should have a lawyer with you."

I stopped breathing.

"Her name is Angela, and she's a friend of mine from college. I called her first thing and she's going to meet us at the police station, okay? She's really nice."

I nodded but didn't speak. Couldn't.

With a sigh, Laney let me go.

In the living room, I paced up and down, feeling caged, but not sure where to go. Paranoia was making me tense, my skin itching and feeling like I'd explode. I loathed that I was too afraid to walk outside Laney's front door, seeing Bratva everywhere. My heart was racing, pulse jack-rabbiting.

One thing always calmed me. I needed to dance.

I found Laney's phone and scrolled through her play lists.

I didn't care that the space was small. I didn't care that audiences were a lifetime away. I danced because I had to, because right now, I'd lost everything but this.

It was jazz, it was ballroom, it was salsa and hip hop—it was everything and nothing and pure. I danced with no one watching. I danced because my body needed motion, like I needed it more than air to breathe.

Faster, spinning, bending, lunging for a future just out of reach.

Quiet applause broke the spell and I whipped around to see Laney watching me, admiration shining in her eyes.

"That was … I don't even know what that was," she said. "But it was amazing. Just … beautiful."

I dipped my head, resting my hands on my hips, breathing hard.

She wasn't supposed to see me, so I didn't answer and didn't look at her.

I think that made Laney feel awkward, like she'd spied on something private, because she changed the topic immediately.

"Are you nervous about this afternoon?"

I frowned and nodded slowly, still avoiding meeting her eyes.

"That's understandable," Laney said softly, patting my arm. "But remember—you're a survivor. You've been through worse than a police interview, okay?"

I grimaced and wanted to argue, but when I turned around, I realized that she was wearing just a thin robe. I saw her skin flush as my eyes trailed over her body. Even that faint contact of her hand on my arm sent a shiver through my body that wanted to settle in my cock, a low tug of arousal, heated by her closeness.

I stopped immediately, shrugging off her hand and cursing myself, turned to walk away and stare out the window.

"So," Laney said, her voice sounding tight. "Let's go out for brunch: breakfast pizza! That's a great Chicago tradition."

I forced a smile. "Sure, that sounds..." *Horrible.*

My stomach kept trying to climb into my throat, and the image of Sergei pointing a gun at me, those crazed eyes promising sudden death—it played like a horror movie in my head.

God, it made me want to claw my eyes out.

"Can I use your phone?" I asked abruptly. "I need to call ... home."

"Oh, of course! I'm so sorry! I should have thought of that before. Of course you can."

"Thank you."

"I'll go get dressed," Laney murmured, hurrying out of the room while I made my call.

It was mid-afternoon in Europe and the chances were that Luka would be busy, but he answered on the second ring.

"Damn, Ash! I've been getting ulcers wondering where the fuck you are! You didn't reply to my emails. How are you? Where are you?"

He was shocked when I filled him in, but relieved I'd got out of Las Vegas. It was a relief just to speak my own language, but after a few minutes I started to worry about how much the call was costing—and he asked too many questions about Laney. I ended the call, promising to keep in touch from now on.

When Laney walked back into the living room, she was dressed in jeans and a t-shirt and not wearing any makeup. It was strange to see her walking around. It made me feel even less of a man. At least when she was in her wheelchair, I could help her with getting around.

The thought made me feel like a jerk.

"Everything okay?" she asked, a worried look on her face.

I gave her a tight smile.

"I guess. It's going to be hard not having ID. Your dad said he'd call my Embassy, but..."

"Of course he will," she said sharply.

"Because he cares?" I asked bitterly. "Just more cheap Eastern European labor. I haven't met an American yet who'd even heard of Slovenia."

She looked away guiltily, and I sighed. I was insulting her father, her country, annoying Laney—and she was trying to help me.

I changed the subject.

"You're walking really well today."

Laney gave a bright smile that made her eyes crinkle.

"I know! What a relief. Flare-ups usually pass quite quickly for me, but sometimes it can take a couple of weeks."

I wanted to ask more about her illness, but Laney didn't give me the chance.

"Come on, let's go for breakfast—or brunch—whatever it is. My treat."

"I'll pay you back when I can," I muttered.

Laney sighed. "Ash, you tied my shoelaces."

I glanced at her, confused. "Your shoelaces?"

"You put socks on my feet and tied my shoelaces when I couldn't … because you didn't want me to go outside and have cold feet."

"Well, yeah?"

"Thank you."

"For … socks?"

"For noticing that I needed them."

She'd lost me. "I don't understand."

Laney gave a small smile. "I know. But you helped me when I needed it, and now I'm doing the same."

I didn't eat much of my breakfast pizza. My anxiety was contagious and Laney ended up asking the server to wrap the food to go.

By the time we reached the car, I must have looked as if I was about to bolt because Laney took my hand and squeezed my fingers.

Christ, that hurt!

I grunted and yanked my hand free.

"Sorry!" Laney gasped, wide-eyed.

I shook my head and held my hand tightly against my chest, willing the pain away.

"W-what did I do?"

I grimaced. "I broke my fingers a while ago. They're still sore sometimes."

"How did you do that?"

I didn't answer, and Laney paled as realization swamped her.

"Oh," she said softly, her expression wounded.

We rode to the police station in silence. I felt shitty that I'd hurt her—again. All she'd wanted was to give me comfort. I couldn't even get that right.

When I saw the police station, an involuntary shudder ran through me. It was an ugly concrete bunker, squat and low with small, featureless windows, and I was already fighting back the idea that I'd be locked up in there. I'd never liked small spaces but since being trapped in the back of Sergei's car, dislike had turned to panic.

My hands started to shake and I swallowed several times, trying not to throw up.

"It's going to be alright," Laney said, as she pulled into the parking lot.

I stared at her, wanting to believe it badly.

"Ash," she said softly, stroking my cheek. "It's going to be alright."

I blinked, then took a trembling breath and leaned into her hand.

We stayed there, touching, eyes closed. And when we walked into the building, she gently took hold of my other hand.

Laney's father came as soon as the desk sergeant informed him that we'd arrived.

"Hey, pumpkin!"

When he noticed that we were holding hands, he frowned, and his voice immediately became all business.

"We're ready for you now. Laney, you're in with Mark and Luis; Mr. Novak, you'll be with Detectives Petronelli and Ramos. And this is Angela Pinto—she's your legal counsel."

A tall, curvy blonde woman smiled at Laney and they hugged quickly.

"Angie! Thank you so much for doing this."

"No problem, Laney. I'm happy to."

"This is my friend, Ash."

Angela glanced at Laney quizzically, then introduced herself to me as we shook hands. I muttered something unintelligible, and was led away. It felt like I was going to my execution. Laney gave me an encouraging smile.

I couldn't return it.

"Do you need an interpreter, Mr. Novak?"

"Ash?" Laney asked when I didn't answer.

"What? Uh, no. Thank you."

"Well, if you're sure…"

I nodded curtly. I couldn't imagine delaying this any longer, even though I wanted to puke. Or run.

The interview room was brightly lit and quite large, but there were no windows, and I felt an unexpected wave of panic start to choke me. My brain imagined that I was trapped in here with Oleg, and I gasped for air, feeling like I was drowning. I closed my eyes and fought to control my breathing.

I couldn't seem to stop my body reacting to a threat that probably wasn't even there. But bad things happened in police stations, didn't they? My body started to shake.

"Could we get Mr. Novak some water, please?"

I heard Angela's voice but it was several minutes before I got a grip, and then one of the police officers returned with a paper cup of water. I stared at it, wondering if I'd be able to pick it up without dropping it. I managed to take a sip before water slopped over the sides of the cup.

"We can do this another time," Angela said, earning an annoyed look from one of the detectives.

"No," I said hoarsely. "No, I need to get this done."

"Interview with Aljaž Novak. Detectives Derek Petronelli and Oscar Ramos and Mr. Novak's attorney Angela Pinto are present. So, Mr. Novak, for the record, could you give us your full name, date of birth and address."

"Aljaž Novak. March 15th 1992."

"And what is your address—for the record?"

"I was staying with my friend Luka Kokot back home. You want that address?"

Not that it would do them any good as he was on tour.

"Could you tell us where you met Miss Hennessey?"

"In Las Vegas. She was in a club at the hotel with her friends. We talked for two or three minutes."

"And?"

"She went back to her room," *and I went to look for a quick fuck.* "I didn't see her again until … when everything happened."

There was a short silence, and I looked up to see them exchanging glances heavy with meaning.

"Could you describe the circumstances leading up to your arrival in Las Vegas?"

I took a deep, calming breath.

"I was looking for a new partner on a website I use, and…"

"A sexual partner?" Detective Ramos interrupted quickly.

What? I looked up, confused. Then realized what he was suggesting.

"No, no, a dance partner. I'm a ballroom dancer. I split up with my last partner and I'd been looking for someone of competition standard—it's not so easy to be compatible. But then I clicked a link for dance opportunities, and it took me to a website about working in Las Vegas."

"And were you employed as a dancer in Slovenia at the time?"

"No, it's hard to make a living that way."

"So what did you do?"

I sighed and stared up at the ceiling. "I worked in construction." *And hated every fucking minute of it.*

"Okay, so what happened next?"

"I emailed them my résumé and they replied the next day. They said I was just what they were looking for and that they'd arrange a work visa. I just had to buy my airplane ticket. It all happened really quickly."

"Did that surprise you?"

I shrugged. "Not really. I'd gotten their name from the Dansesport site, so I thought it was okay."

"Go on."

"When I arrived, that's when I thought there was a problem."

"Why was that?"

"This guy, Oleg, picked me up at the airport and there was a minivan waiting. There were four girls there—they looked like dancers."

"What do you mean?"

"Slim, good muscle tone and posture, hot, you know?"

Derek Petronelli was a huge guy who looked like he'd never met a donut he didn't like. But if the look on his face was anything to go by, he'd really like to know a bunch of hot women who were dancers.

"And what happened then?"

I rubbed my eyes. It seemed impossible now. I was so fucking naïve, but I'd been full of hope that evening.

"There was Yveta and her friend Galina—they were Russian. Marta was from the Ukraine—that's what Yveta said. I never knew the other girl's name. We didn't think she spoke English ... or Russian. She was young. I don't know, maybe 16? Oleg took our passports. I wasn't happy, but I didn't want to make trouble the first night with my new boss.

"When we got to the hotel, they told us to tell our families that we were fine, then they took our phones. I had a bad feeling, but I didn't know what to do. Then the next day I met Sergei."

"What's his last name?"

I shook my head. "I don't know. He was just Sergei. The only last name was the big boss, Volkov."

Petronelli looked at his partner, then back at me. "Would you be able to identify these people if we showed you some photographs?"

I grit my teeth and nodded. "I'll never forget their faces."

"Okay, we'll get to that. What happened after your phone was taken?"

I continued the story, describing the Korean and my belief that he was beaten to death.

"But you don't know for sure?"

The policemen shared another look and I started to sweat. They didn't believe me—I had no evidence. And I was getting to the part where I had to tell them about the girl ... and what had been done to me. When I described the end of the shopping trip, my pulse started to race.

"Sergei got in the limo and he said, 'Daddy wants to play'. I knew what he meant. I told him to..."

I glanced at Angela and she nodded at me to continue, her expression serious.

"I told him to fuck off. He just laughed and said that was the general idea. Then Oleg punched me from behind and I fell into the car. That's when Sergei pulled a gun. He held it to the back of my head. I could feel the metal pressing into my neck. I remember thinking, 'If he kills me now, the stupid bastard will shoot off his own dick'."

I took a sip of water, trying to ignore my shaking hands.

"He kept telling me to blow him, but I wouldn't. I'm not gay!" I stared up at the detectives, but their faces gave nothing away. "I'm not," I said again, banging my fist down on the table.

"It's okay. Take a moment," Angela said calmly.

I gripped the edge of the table and forced myself to go on. If I stopped now, I didn't think I'd ever be able to say it again.

"He forced my hand against the door and slammed the gun into it. He broke this finger. I still wouldn't do it, so he broke another finger the same way. I was afraid I'd pass out, but I didn't. I was so angry, almost more angry than scared. He asked me how many bones there were in my foot, because he'd break them all. I said, 'I'll bite off your fucking dick and spit it at you'."

The humiliation was fresh all over again, and I couldn't look at anyone in the room.

"Then he pressed a button, and the panel between the front seat and back seat slid down. Oleg ... he had the girl ... the young one. She was crying and she'd been beaten. Oleg started to squeeze her neck. I've never seen anyone's eyes bulge before. They went red—all the white parts went red—and I thought, *Oh my God, all the veins in her eyes are breaking!* She was looking at me the whole time. She just kept looking at me. Her lips were blue and she was scratching at Oleg's hands, but he just laughed. And Sergei ... he was laughing, too. He said, 'She won't last much longer'. And then ... and ... I didn't want her to die. Then she wasn't moving anymore. And I knew he wanted to kill her. He was *enjoying* it. They both were! Those sick bastards..."

I covered my face with my hands.

"So I did it. I did what he said. Oleg kept laughing and Sergei..."

I heaved, but managed not puke, swallowing back the vomit that threatened to humiliate me again.

"It made me sick. When he ... finished, I threw up all over him. He was so angry, screaming at me. He slammed the gun against my head, here, and I thought he'd shoot me, but he opened the car door and pushed me out. He held the gun and pointed it at me. I thought he'd kill me. I didn't even care anymore." I glanced up, but it wasn't the police station I was seeing. "The girl ... I think he killed her in front of me and I did *nothing!*"

I shouted out the last word and Angela rested her hand on my arm lightly. Her sudden touch made me lash out, overturning the chair as I leapt backwards.

There was an appalled silence while Angela stared at me fearfully.

"I think we should take a break now," said Petronelli.

Angela nodded and closed her notebook.

"Interview suspended at 15:24."

"I'm sorry."

But I wasn't sure who I was saying it to.

Three hours later, I sat alone in the interview room. I was wrung out, utterly devoid of any feeling other than the dull ache of shame, too exhausted to care any longer.

The questions had gone on and on: who had I seen, what had been said, who was the biker, had I seen drugs, had I been given drugs, what had Volkov said, where was Marta when I saw her, what had she said, where was the brothel where she was being kept, where was I going to get the money to pay Sergei, how many times had I sold myself to women, why hadn't I gone to the police when I had the chance? And then reliving the horror of the night they'd caught me and the evil bastard Oleg had flogged me with his own belt while Sergei jerked off.

Then the policemen had photographed my back and ass, commenting quietly to themselves on the marks.

Somehow it was worse that all of this was in front of Laney's friend. It was a mistake having her there. She'd been professional, kind even, but now she *knew* things about me. She knew and she judged me, whether she meant to or not.

But I guess Laney would find out one way or another. If not from Angela, then from her father.

Angela walked back into the room, pushing a cup of black coffee in front of me as she sat opposite. I couldn't drink it without cream and sugar, but I enjoyed holding the warm cup.

"How are you doing?"

I almost laughed and Angela gave me a rueful smile.

"That's understandable, but you did well. They've got a lot of information to work with and pass on to the Las Vegas police."

I raised my eyebrows.

"I know what you were told, but there *are* good officers there who will investigate. This won't be swept under the carpet."

I was silent. I'd wanted justice for the girl, for Marta and the others. But the justice Sergei and Oleg deserved was at the end of a gun or a rope, not through Courtrooms and police and polite pieces of paper.

"Your Embassy has been contacted and they're going to expedite a new passport, but it could take a while, bearing in mind that the current one has been used illegally. They're prepared to issue temporary ID so you can access your bank account in Slovenia and have your credit cards re-issued. But don't be surprised if it takes a couple of weeks. I'll do my best to hurry them along … unfortunately this means that they won't be able to arrange a flight home for you just yet, and with the ongoing police investigation, well, they'd like you to be around for the time being. However, your Embassy has authorized me to issue you $200 hardship money and arrange a hotel for you." She smiled at me. "But Laney says you're welcome to stay with her."

I looked up, stunned.

"She'll let me stay?"

"Yes."

I met Angela's eyes, reading the unspoken message.

Then I shook my head. "Her father won't let that happen."

Angela laughed lightly. "If you think her father could stop Laney when she's made up her mind, you don't know her very well."

"What about the pri— what about her boyfriend?"

"Same answer," Angela smiled at me, not missing my near slip, as she pulled out some dollar bills and handed them to me. "She's outside now."

I stood up slowly. Laney was waiting for me. Until that moment, I'd had no clue how much I needed to hear those words—just knowing that someone was here for me, that I wasn't alone.

I pulled the door open and she saw me immediately, throwing herself into my arms.

The surprise attack made me stagger, my back thudding painfully against the wall as Laney hugged the ever-living crap out of me.

As the surprise seeped out of me, I allowed myself to enjoy the warmth and softness of her small body pressed against mine. I wrapped my arms around her, holding her carefully as my head sank forwards, burying my face in her hair as if I'd been doing it my whole life.

Laney's face was pink when she pulled away. I thought she'd start asking questions, but she didn't. Thank God, she didn't.

"Come on," she said. "Let's get out of here."

I nodded my agreement as Laney tugged on my arm.

"I know the perfect place to celebrate."

I frowned at her.

"What are we celebrating?"

Laney threw her hands in the air.

"Life. We're celebrating life."

CHAPTER 11

Laney
Angela joined us for drinks at a bar I knew, half a block from the police station.

Ash insisted on paying since he had money, although neither of us wanted him to, but arguing about it would only have made things more awkward.

It was a muted celebration with a silent Ash, speaking only when I asked him a direct question.

I knew it must have been traumatic reliving everything that happened to him, but I'd meant it when I said we should be celebrating life. And he had so much to live for.

It didn't help that Angela seemed on edge, too, throwing worried glances at Ash while he was engrossed by his beer, staring unseeingly as he shred the label.

"Well," said Angela, "I really need to get going. Laney, walk me out, hon?"

Ash stood politely as we left the table, nodding once at Angela and muttering a curt 'thank you'. He couldn't meet her eyes, and I wondered if they'd had some sort of fight.

"Laney," said Angela when we were outside in the chilly air, "I love you like a sister so I'm going to be totally unprofessional and tell you that guy worries me."

"Ash? Why?"

"Look, you know I can't tell you, I'm just saying … stay away from him. I mean it. The packaging is gorgeous, I admit, but he's damaged. You get any more involved with a guy like that, and he'll drag you down with him. I've seen it happen. I know you have this thing about 'saving' people, but you have to let this one go."

"What do you mean, I have a thing about 'saving' people?" I bristled.

"Come on, Laney! You know you do. You've been trying to save Collin from being a boring asshole for ten years, and look how well that's gone."

"You don't understand!" I said, frustration sharpening my voice.

"Then explain it to me. *Make* me understand! Because what you're doing is way beyond what anyone else would do."

I wanted to be angry, but I saw only concern in Angie's face.

"I … it's hard to explain. But if you'd been there … when you walk into that kind of scene, it's just something you can't help. He was so broken—there was no other choice."

I could tell that I hadn't convinced her. Maybe because she was a lawyer and dealt in facts and what could be proved. Or maybe because we'd been friends for ten years and she'd never seen me like this before.

She sighed then swept me into a hug.

"Just think about it, okay?"

And she vanished into the night before I could reply.

I was irritated on so many levels. Her assumption that there was something going on with Ash was *way* off. And Collin had apologized for his behavior before I went to Vegas.

I think that knowing how close I'd come to getting hurt or even killed had been a wake-up call for both of us. We weren't going to throw away ten years on a single argument.

He wasn't happy that Ash would be sleeping on my couch for the foreseeable future, but that wasn't negotiable. I wasn't trying to *save* Ash, whatever Angela thought. He was a man who'd been through something traumatic, but I'd already seen flashes of the sweet, funny, sexy guy he'd been before.

In a couple of weeks, he'd get his passport and he could go home. I wasn't going to make him stay in some anonymous hotel where he didn't know anyone.

I turned to walk back inside, but I was surprised to see that Ash had followed me out and was leaning against the wall smoking a cigarette.

I hated smoking. I'd made Collin quit on our second date, although I'm not sure I'd have that sort of influence now.

"How can you smoke?" I glared at him. "You're a dancer for God's sake!"

He shrugged and winked at me.

"Isn't there anything you like that isn't good for you?"

Playful Ash was back in the building. I was happy to see him, but he wasn't getting off the hook that easily.

"Where did you get it?" I frowned.

"Some woman," he mumbled around the cigarette, sucking hard then blowing a long plume of smoke into the night air.

"Of course," I said, rolling my eyes.

"Why 'of course'?" he asked, grinning at me.

"Like you don't know!" I scoffed. "One smile and I bet she was putty in your hands."

He smiled and leaned closer, holding the cigarette away from me.

"Does it work on you?"

Oh boy, did it ever!

"I'm immune," I said, lifting my chin. "I have a boyfriend."

Ash scowled. "You're back with the prick."

"Stop calling him that!"

"Douche? Asshole? Fucktard? Hey, do you know any words starting with 'q'?"

He danced away as I tried to punch his shoulder.

"Stop being a jerk!"

"I already did 'j'," he grinned at me.

Happy Ash was adorable, even if he was being a pain in the butt.

I put my hands on my hips.

"Apologize! Right now!"

Ash put his hands together in a prayer, the cigarette dangling from his pouty lips.

"Sorry," he grinned.

I stomped inside and took a much needed drink of beer, letting it cool me down. Ash stopped to talk to a woman with dyed red hair. He seemed to be thanking her, so I guessed that she was the one who'd given him the cigarette.

I really didn't need to worry about him—he could probably get everything he needed from random women. But then I remembered the broken look on his face, blood on his back, when he'd yelled at me to get out of that bathroom in Vegas. The dread on his face as we drove up to the police station, the despair and exhaustion when he'd finished.

Ash caught up with me and grabbed my hand.

"Dance with me, Laney."

"What? Here?"

I glanced around, panicked, and noticed that two couples had edged onto the tiny dance floor and were gyrating to the fast music.

"I can't."

"Why not?" he asked, hauling me toward the dance floor.

"I ... I ... I don't like dancing."

Ash stared at me.

"But ... everyone likes to dance."

I chuckled at his shocked expression. "Um, nope. Not me."

He gave me a knowing look and pulled both my hands around his neck until our bodies were pressing together. He pushed one firm thigh between my legs, then leaned down, his smoky breath warm against my cheek.

"Don't worry. Even if you can't dance, when you're with me, you won't look bad."

Conceited ass! He'd totally called me on my complete inability to clap my hands in rhythm, let alone dance.

His wrists rested on my hips, and he used his whole body to control my movements. The beat of the music pulled me under, the warmth of his hands, the glow of contentment in his eyes as we moved together. For the first time in my life, I was dancing and enjoying it.

"Relax," he whispered. "You're dancing like you have a broom up your ass."

A laugh exploded out of me. "You're so rude!"

He grinned. "Yeah? But it worked, see?" And he rotated his hips, forcing me to move with him.

I glanced down at our joined bodies and saw the crotch of his pants jump—just enough that I noticed.

My cheeks heated up and I couldn't look him in the face, but I danced. I danced my uptight little ass off. And I loved it.

But then I thought of Collin and what he'd say if he saw us like this, my breasts pushing in Ash's chest, his hands low on my hips. My movements slowed and I rubbed my forehead: it was going to be a long few weeks.

Ash pushed my hands from my head and started massaging my temples, his long fingers sweeping gentle circles over my flushed skin. Then he spun me around so my back was pressed against his hard chest, and his hands slid down my neck, his strong thumbs digging into tight muscles, making me groan.

"Oh my God! You have great hands."

The words were out of my mouth before I realized what I'd said. I thought Ash would make some joke, saying he already knew, but when I squinted up at him, his face was serious, a small crease between his eyebrows as he concentrated on his work.

"Your muscles are really tight," he said, a chastising tone in his voice. "You should get a massage. I think it would help you."

I sighed as his thumbs dug in deeper, just this side of painful.

"I do sometimes, but I can't as often as I'd like on my income."

Ash pulled out all the money Angela had given him and tucked it into my purse.

"Enough for a massage," he murmured.

"Ash, no!"

He pretended not to hear me, so I pulled the money out of my purse and stuffed it into his hands, stepping back so he had to accept it.

"That's emergency money for you! Not so I can schlep off and get massages!"

"Then I'll do it," he offered. "I've learned a lot about sore muscles over the years," and he laughed lightly. "More than I want."

It sounded wonderful, but...

"Let me, Laney," he said, his voice low and full of emotion. "I have nothing else to give you."

"Ash..."

"Please."

I couldn't say no to him.

I'd drunk more than I realized, probably trying to make up for the edge of anxiety that had been there with Angela's presence, because when I moved away from him, I wobbled. Ash helped me into my coat, draped his arm around my shoulders, and we walked home like that.

It was nice. I felt safe.

But back at the apartment, it was more awkward.

Ash went to the fridge to get two bottles of water, his jeans tightening over his gorgeous ass. I shook my head. The man couldn't even bend over to look in my refrigerator without me molesting him with my eyes. How on earth was I going to live with him?

He passed me the bottle, then shooed me into my room and told me to wear pajamas and lie on my stomach.

When I was ready, he opened the door and walked in. I was somewhat taken aback when he climbed up onto the bed and straddled me, his thighs pressing against my hips.

Then he leaned forward and I felt his warm breath on my neck as he reached across my bedside table and squirted body lotion onto his hands.

With the scent of *Wild Hyacinth* in the air, his fingers dug into my muscles. Damn, that felt good! He really knew what he was doing.

I kept telling myself that it wasn't erotic—but the hell it was! His hands slid under my pajama top, massaging my bare skin. I was totally turned on, but forced myself to ignore such inappropriate feelings. *I have a boyfriend*, I chanted silently. *I have a boyfriend.*

For half an hour, he massaged my neck, shoulders, back, arms and legs, until I was a pile of mush beneath his clever fingers.

I vaguely felt his lips brush against my hair as he covered me with my quilt. I was asleep in seconds.

I woke with a raging thirst shortly after midnight. I'd only had a few beers, not enough to give a normal person a hangover, but my body didn't seem to respond to anything normally.

I tiptoed into the living room to get a couple of cookies from the kitchen, so I didn't have to take ibuprofen on an empty stomach. I noticed that Ash had left the drapes open and it gave me a chance to study his beautiful face, younger and softer in sleep.

But he wasn't asleep, and I froze.

He was stretched out on the couch, his bare chest almost luminous in the glow of the street lamps.

One hand rested on his chest, but the other...

The thin sheet was pushed down to his thighs and he was stroking himself. His long fingers that had massaged me so thoroughly earlier in the evening were firmly grasping his hard dick and working it up and down, his thumb sweeping over the wide head. His eyes were closed, his mouth slightly open, and his breaths were quick and shallow.

I knew I should turn around and go, leaving him alone in this very private moment, not watching like some creepy voyeur. But I couldn't. I was mesmerized by the sight of him pleasuring himself, his hand moving faster, his firm chest rising and falling rapidly.

He muttered something in his own language, and I could tell by the tightness in his face that he was close. And God, if it wasn't the hottest thing I'd ever seen. I could feel my own arousal as I watched, drinking it all in, imagining far more than I should—imagining him with me. In me.

His hips started to jerk and then he came, pearly liquid coating his stomach.

And he called out my name, his eyes open, fixed on mine.

Embarrassed, humiliated at being caught ogling, I gasped an apology and ran back to my room, forgetting my thirst and pounding head.

The last sight I had was of his intense eyes following me, his dick still dark in color, resting against his hard stomach.

Ash

She ran from the room like a frightened rabbit. She'd been watching me, I know she had. If she was so shocked that I was jerking off, why hadn't she left the room right away?

I grabbed the shirt I'd been wearing and cleaned myself off, tucking my spent dick away.

Part of me was glad she'd seen—seen me as a man, not just as some fucking victim that she had to feel sorry for, but another part of me regretted it. There was a good chance she'd kick me out in the morning.

It took a while to fall asleep after that, but when I did, instead of nightmares, I heard music in my head and dreamed of Laney.

In the morning, I knew she was still embarrassed because she took forever to leave her room. I was desperate for a piss, and seriously considering using the kitchen sink if she didn't hurry up.

But she finally shuffled into the living room, muttered 'Morning' and refused to catch my eye.

After I'd showered, she was still acting weird.

"I'm sorry about last night…" I began.

"Oh no, you, um, I'm sorry," she stuttered.

"Do you want me to go?"

Finally, she looked at me.

"No! Why would you say that?"

I shrugged. "I make you uncomfortable."

"No, you don't," she lied, tugging her robe tighter around her body.

I raised an eyebrow and she blushed a deep red.

"Honestly, you don't have to leave," she said. "I just forgot that the living room is your bedroom at night. I should have knocked or something."

"I don't think I would have answered."

Her face was so red now, I couldn't help wondering how far her blush went.

"Let's just forget about it," she mumbled, turning away and sticking her head in the fridge. "Do you want waffles?"

"No, thanks. I'm going to go now."

She whipped around, a look of distress on her face.

"You don't have to go! I said you don't, and I meant it."

"Hey, no! I'd like to stay until…" *Until what?* "A bit longer. I just meant I'm going to see if I can earn some money."

Her eyebrows shot up. "Doing what?"

I frowned at her. "I can do a lot of things. I can bartend, retail work, construction…"

She rested her hand on my arm. "I meant, because you don't have ID, a visa."

"Oh." I shrugged. "There's always someone who'll pay cash in hand. You worry too much, Laney. I'll see you later."

"Wait!" she called after me, fiddling around in her purse. "This is my address if you get lost, and take this."

She held out a twenty-dollar bill.

"I can't keep taking your money," I said sharply.

She sighed, stepping forward and tucking it into the front pocket of my jeans.

"It's *yours*. I know you put all the emergency money in my purse. You need lunch money and a bus fare. Please, just take it. I'd feel a lot better."

"Saving me again, Laney?" I whispered as I walked out the door.

It wasn't as easy as I'd hoped. After the fifth construction site asked to see my union card, I was close to giving up. I didn't even like construction work.

But as I was walking away, a guy in a hardhat jerked his head at me, showing that he wanted to talk.

I followed him until we were out of sight of the foreman.

"Russian? Polish?"

I shook my head. "Slovenian."

"You have any experience?"

"Yeah, I can do carpentry, plasterboarding, painting, brick-laying, basic plumbing."

"Yeah, yeah, good. Go to the building site at West Washburne and South Racine—it's in University Village. Ask for Viktor."

"Thanks, man!"

"Tell him he owes Bruno twenty bucks as a finder's fee."

I nodded, memorized the address, and set off again.

The site was an older building that had been a school and was being turned into apartments.

I was given a hardhat and a sledgehammer, told not to drop it on my sneakers because there would be no comp, then pointed toward some selective demolition.

It was boring, tiring and dirty. Clouds of dust rose up from demolished plasterboard, although the other men called it Sheetrock. The dust got in my eyes, my nose, my hair and my clothes. But it felt good to do something that used my muscles. I'd stiffened up after days of sitting and driving. My ribs still hurt from where Oleg had used his fists and the skin on my back burned, but it was better than sitting in Laney's apartment, letting her spend more money on me.

As I swung the sledgehammer, I wondered if Gary and Yveta were okay. I hoped that they hadn't gotten into trouble because of me. There was no reason why they should: it was Laney that Sergei's men would be looking for. I frowned at the thought.

I wished I had a way of contacting my friends, but it would be too dangerous—for them and me.

I swung the sledgehammer, feeling the tug in lazy muscles, and imagined it was Oleg's ugly face. I imagined his teeth splintering and flying into the air with his blood.

I swung the sledgehammer and imagined it was Sergei that I was turning into dust, like the fucking vampire he was, sucking the life out of everyone around him.

"Dude! Take it easy!"

I lowered the sledgehammer to the ground, breathing hard, and glanced around to see three men watching me with startled expressions.

"That's some serious aggression you're working out there, man," said a short guy with muscles like a bodybuilder.

"Just hoping to get rehired tomorrow," I said, which wasn't a total lie.

He raised his eyebrows, told me it was time for lunch break, and they walked off.

Five hours later, my eyebrows white from drywall dust, my face gray, I headed back to Laney's. I looked like shit and my muscles were screaming, but I had fifty dollars in my pocket and I felt like a king.

When Laney buzzed me up and opened the apartment's front door, her mouth fell open.

"What happened? You look like you've been rolling in flour!"

"Got a job. Just as a laborer, but they want me back tomorrow."

I pulled out the money and tucked it into her jeans pocket, just like she'd done with me this morning.

Laney laughed and pretended to slap my shoulder as I danced out of the way.

Then her face fell as she pulled out the five ten-dollar bills.

"Oh my God! Fifty dollars for working all day! That's slave labor!"

Anger roared hot and sudden inside me.

"Yes, I'm a slave!" I yelled at her. "I was a slave in Las Vegas and I'm a slave now. People don't care how their houses are built, and wives don't care who cleans their homes, or that girls are bought to sleep with their husbands, and no one cares that men like Volkov are businessmen in the daylight. We come here and we fall into the darkness. What happens in Vegas stays in Vegas, right? Nothing is mine! Not even my name. I am nothing! No one!"

I grabbed the money from her and tossed it into the air before I stormed out, slamming the door so hard that the whole building shook.

I heard her calling after me, but I ran down the stairs, too angry to wait for the elevator.

I was fifty meters down the street, when I heard her cry out in pain.

Panicked, afraid of what I might see, I sprinted back, dodging evening commuters hurrying home in the icy air.

Laney was lying at the bottom of the steep stairs in front of her apartment, shivering in a thin t-shirt and holding her right leg with both hands.

I skidded to a halt and crouched down.

"My ankle," she cried, tears clinging to the corners of her eyes.

I lifted her into my arms and cradled her against my chest.

"I'm sorry! God, I'm so sorry."

She didn't answer, only nestled her head and wrapped her arms around my neck, shivering from cold and pain.

I carried her into the apartment and laid her on the couch. I started to push up her right pants leg, but she winced.

"Don't."

"Let me see, Laney."

"No, these jeans are too tight. You can't … just help me into the bedroom, please."

She started to stand, but cried out, and I picked her up again, carrying her to the bed, laying her down carefully.

"I … I need to take my jeans off."

"Okay."

I turned my back while she shuffled out of her jeans, whimpering softly.

Her ankle was swelling and guilt flooded me.

"I'll get ice," I muttered.

She didn't have any ice in the freezer, but she did have a bag of peas. I wrapped them in a towel, then placed them over her foot.

I sat next to her on the bed, wiping her tears with my thumbs.

"I wasn't trying to insult you," she hiccupped. "I'm sorry I upset you."

"Laney, don't. I was a prick—like your boyfriend."

That made her smile, tears caught on her lashes.

"What's going on?"

Neither of us had heard the front door open. Collin was standing in the doorway to the bedroom, glaring at us, while I sat thigh to thigh with his girlfriend.

"Collin. I wasn't expecting you," she murmured tiredly.

"Are you sleeping with him?" he shouted.

I stood up quickly, my hands curling into fists, but Laney interrupted whatever was going to happen.

"Don't be ridiculous! I've hurt my ankle, and Ash was helping me."

Collin's eyes narrowed, then he glanced down at Laney's foot.

"It looks like you've sprained it. What the hell happened?"

"I slipped on the front steps," she said quietly as I left the room.

"Jesus, Laney! You're so clumsy! I've told you again and again that you shouldn't be living in a place with stairs. This was bound to happen and totally avoidable. When will you learn?"

Listening to him tell her off was infuriating. Why couldn't he just take care of her? I stomped into the kitchen and filled the kettle, then rummaged through her cupboards. I'd only ever seen her drink coffee, but something soothing would be better.

I eventually found a box of chamomile teabags at the back. One of my ex-girlfriends had sworn by their calming properties. Hadn't stopped her throwing a mug of tea at me when I told her I was breaking up with her, but that's another story.

I left the bag in the hot water until it looked about right. It smelled a bit like hay—I hoped she'd like it.

I carried the tea into her room while Collin was still rambling on, this time about finding an adapted apartment.

Laney was staring at the wall, her face stiff.

"Tea," I said, placing the mug next to her. "Drink it while it's hot."

Collin's monologue dried and he tried to intimidate me with his scowl. I shrugged and headed for the shower.

Laney

Luckily, the sprain was a mild one. Once Ash had put the bag of frozen peas on my foot, the swelling started to go down quite quickly and Collin's ranting was white noise in the background.

After a while, he noticed that I'd tuned him out. I was prepared for a fight, but he started to be sweet instead, reminding me of why we were together. I was almost able to forget that he'd accused me of sleeping with Ash. Almost.

It was bound to be weird, for everyone. I was sharing my one-bed apartment with a guy I hardly knew. I'd dated Collin for ten years and we'd never lived together. Now I was living with Ash.

And to be honest, I wasn't finding it that easy to share my space, although Ash was helpful around the place, almost as if he was trying to be invisible. It didn't work, of course. Having 6' 2" of hunky dancer in my living room was not something I could even pretend to ignore. He was just so *there*, even when all he was doing was breathing.

I think Collin must have felt guilty about what he said, although it didn't slip my attention that he hadn't apologized.

He even managed to be pleasant to Ash while we shared Chinese takeout.

Ash was polite in return, but distant, answering any questions, but not initiating conversation.

After half a glass of wine, I was ready for bed, and Collin helped me into the bedroom. He made it clear that he wanted to make things better between us, and we ended up having sex, which was nice. It had been a while.

I remember hearing the front door slam and was distracted by the thought that I hadn't given Ash a key to my apartment. Had he taken mine?

I didn't hear him come back, but he must have because when Collin woke up in the morning to go to work, Ash was gone again, his blankets neatly folded beside the couch and a used coffee cup in the sink.

I worked all day on boring study guides, limping only a little, wondering the whole time if Ash was okay. Then Detective Petronelli called to speak to him, and I had to make an excuse that he'd gone for a walk.

"Well, when he comes back, could you ask him to come to the station—we've got a few more questions for him?"

"Sure," I sighed. "We'll drive over later. Have you notified his attorney?"

"I believe so." He cleared his throat. "There's no need for you to come, Miss Hennessey."

"We'll see you later," I repeated, and ended the call.

When Ash came home, the cool distance that had been present at dinner last night was still there. I was a little hurt that he'd be like that with me after everything we'd been through. But when he walked out of the shower, tugging on a t-shirt, he had fresh claw marks down his chest. I guess I knew how he'd spent last night.

His eyes widened when I told him that Detective Petronelli wanted to talk to him again. He wasn't happy about it, but didn't argue.

He pushed his hand into the front of his jeans and pulled out a bunch of folded notes.

"There's $100," he said. "I did a full day."

"Ash, I don't want your money."

"And I don't want yours," he snapped. "I'm paying you back for the clothes, the hotel, the car rental, my fucking food!"

And he stomped off to the laundry room, leaving me shocked and saddened. I didn't want him to feel like he owed me. Stupid male pride.

Twenty minutes later, he slid into the passenger seat of my Mini Cooper, folding his long legs into the small space.

"Sorry," he muttered.

"Okay."

We drove to the police station in silence until Ash asked if he could turn on the radio. I should have thought of that. Music calmed him.

Detective Petronelli came out immediately, casting an aggrieved stare that said he really didn't want me here.

"Thank you for coming in, Mr. Novak. We just have a few more questions for you. If you'd like to follow me to the interview room. Miss Hennessey, you can take a seat in the waiting room."

"No, that's okay, Derek," I said with a fake smile. "I'll stay with Ash."

Ash threw me a puzzled look, but didn't argue. The detective, however, wasn't happy.

"Miss Pinto is waiting in the interview room," he sighed. "But just so you know, your dad will have my ass when he finds out that I let you sit in."

The other detective, Oscar Ramos, was chatting with Angie as we arrived. When he saw me, he looked questioningly at Petronelli, who just shrugged.

Hi Angie, thanks for coming."

"Of course," she said, giving me a quick hug. "Hello, Ash."

He nodded, but didn't speak, then sat on the hard plastic chair, his legs bouncing with a jittery restlessness.

"Thank you for coming in, Mr. Novak. We have some additional questions for you, particularly about your associates in Las Vegas."

Angie frowned. "His associates?"

"Mr. Novak mentioned the woman Marta whom we've since identified as Marta Babiak." He turned to Ash. "Was she part of the prostitution ring you mentioned?"

Ash looked frustrated. "That's what she told me. You already know this."

"What about Yveta Kuznets and Galina Bely? Were they involved in prostitution with you?"

I gasped. Ash had been involved in the prostitution? He glanced at me then closed his eyes, his face scrunched up as if he was in pain.

Angie looked down, pretending to read her notes. *She already knew.*

Oh God. Ash had worked as a prostitute. It was what I'd thought the first night I met him, but it was horrible having my fears confirmed. How many more secrets did he have?

"No, they were working on the show," Ash said quietly, avoiding my shocked gaze. "They're dancers."

"According to the information held by the Immigration Service, Marta Babiak left the US three weeks ago."

Ash stared at Petronelli, a bitter expression on his face.

"Do you believe that?"

Petronelli ignored his question.

"We have some photographs that we'd like you to look at," he said, his gaze shifting to me and back again. "This morning, the body of a Caucasian female in her mid-twenties was recovered from the desert outside Las Vegas."

Oh no, I hadn't expected this.

"And you think it's Marta?" asked Ash, his voice strained.

"We'd like to eliminate that possibility if we can." Petronelli looked at me again. "You might want to look away, Miss Hennessey."

This time I took his advice willingly. I closed my eyes and leaned back in my chair.

After a moment, I heard Ash's choked voice. "It's not Marta."

"Are you sure, Mr. Novak?"

"I've never seen her before."

There was a heavy silence, and when I opened my eyes, Ash had his head in his hands.

"You're sure about that? Because according to your statement, you only saw her three times briefly, twice at night."

"My client has already answered that question."

"I'm sure." Ash spoke without looking up, and the two detectives exchanged a glance that told me they believed him.

When Petronelli slid the set of photographs back into a folder, I caught a glimpse of a woman's body, naked against the desert backdrop, limbs folded at odd angles. My stomach heaved.

"Interview terminated at…"

Ash's voice cut in, the words stretched and awkward as he spoke in a low monotone.

"Can you find out about Yveta and Gary? If they're still in the show, they're okay. And Galina. I'd like … I need to know."

"We'll make inquiries," Petronelli assured him.

Ash closed his eyes.

"Just one more thing, Mr. Novak, Detective Susan Watson would like to talk to you. She's worked with other rape victims and you could…"

Ash's head shot up, anger and frustration spilling from him.

"No! I wasn't … they didn't rape me!"

"But, it's not just…"

"NO! I am not a victim!"

He stood abruptly and stormed out.

I stared uneasily at Angie and the two detectives, then followed Ash.

He wasn't in the lobby, and I wondered for a moment if he'd left the building completely, but then I saw him outside the main door, pacing up and down as if he'd been chained in a cage.

When he turned his eyes toward me, I saw shame, guilt, fear, and his hands shook slightly as he ran his fingers through his short hair.

"They could be dead because of me. Like that girl. What they did to her…"

He shuddered and swallowed several times.

"You don't know that."

"I do. If I'd told someone…"

"You'd probably be dead. These people are evil. It's not your fault."

He didn't bother to disagree again, but I could see that he didn't believe me either.

As soon as we got back to the apartment, Ash said he was going for a walk. I didn't try to stop him. Instead I gave him a door key and a twenty from the pile of bills he'd given me earlier.

This time he didn't argue, but nodded, opened his mouth to say something, then closed it again, shaking his head. I watched him striding down the street until he was out of sight.

We stumbled on, an awkward ménage: Ash silent and distant, Collin loud and patronizing.

It was tiring. The easiest thing would be to tell Ash to go, but I just couldn't do it.

Then one day, Dad asked to meet for lunch at an Italian restaurant near the police station. It wasn't something we did often, so I guessed it had something to do with Ash.

I hadn't even chewed my first breadstick when he started the interrogation.

"How's Collin?"

"Fine, thanks. Busy. Same ole."

"And how's your houseguest?"

"Fine."

"No problems?"

"Such as?"

He eyed me wearily.

"How's Collin taking it having another man living with you?"

"He's not a fan, but it's not his decision. What's this really about?"

"I worry about you being alone with him. You don't know this man."

"He wouldn't hurt me, Dad. He couldn't."

"You don't know what he's capable of."

"I know him better than you."

"Laney! Wake up! He's involved with some very dangerous people."

"That wasn't his fault! He was in the wrong place at the wrong time. Ash is a good person."

"Why are you helping him? Letting him live with you? Do you feel responsible for him? Because you're not! You've done more than enough."

Dad was partly right. I *did* feel responsible for Ash. I'd brought him to Chicago and involved him in my life. It had started with me simply wanting to help him—charity, I guess. But charity is usually faceless, impersonal—you make a donation, write a check, and that's it. But with Ash, I'd seen his face and I'd seen the abuse firsthand. That made it personal.

And as we'd shared my apartment, shared time together, I'd come to appreciate him for the man he was, or the man he was trying to be.

He was kind and thoughtful. He helped me but he let me breathe. He was decent and honorable. And I hated to see him crushed, so every smile of his felt like an achievement.

I took a breath and tried to explain as rationally as I could—which wasn't easy, because when it came to Ash, I wasn't sure that reason and logic could be applied.

"Because someone should. Because I can. Because since he came to this country, his world has been shattered—in America—land of the free. In our country, he was made a slave! This is real, Dad. This is happening, and what Ash has told us is just the tip of the iceberg. I've been looking into it: do you know how many slaves there are here today? Right now, in Chicago? Hundreds! Thousands! Tens of thousands every year across the whole country. Drug trafficking, prostitution, forced labor. You're the police officer, Dad, you tell me."

His hard expression softened. "I know, Laney, love. What I'm asking is *why him?*"

"I've told you," I said as my cheeks turned red.

"That's what I thought," sighed Dad, shaking his head.

We ate the rest of our lunch without mentioning Ash's name again.

Ash was late getting home that night. And as soon as he was inside the apartment, he strode into the kitchen and started scrubbing at his hands. He'd been much moodier since the last police interview. Each day that went by without news of his friends, his spirits sank lower. He looked tired all the time, and I knew he wasn't sleeping well because I heard him at night. He'd changed physically in the last three weeks, as well. His lean body was even harder, his biceps bigger. I suppose it was inevitable, working in construction. I'd never seen a body as good as his except on TV.

When he'd washed his hands four times, he dried them carefully. I'd noticed that they'd become callused. It made me smile when I saw him pump some of my rose-scented lotion onto his hands.

"Ash is a gi-rll!" I sang, thoughtlessly teasing him into a lighter mood.

A strange expression shadowed his face and his eyes glittered dangerously. Then he shoved away from me and left the room.

Uh-oh.

I followed slowly and found him sitting on the couch with his head in his hands.

"Ash…"

"I'm not a girl," he growled. "But I cannot be a man to you!"

"What?"

"You feed me, give me a roof, a place to stay. But I can't pay you enough. I can't work without fear. I can't even dance. I am nothing!"

He strode out of the apartment, disappearing into the night.

Stupid, stupid Laney!

I was sitting on the edge of my bed, summoning up the nerve to push the short needle into my thigh. It wasn't particularly painful, but it did sting. I just hated, hated doing it.

Tears gathered in my eyes, and I cursed myself for weakness, for my stupid body that needed chemicals to keep it working, keep it moving. I hated to be so dependent.

I heard Ash arrive home, concentrating on the quiet sounds as he moved around the kitchen: the tap running, the coffee machine. Two soft thuds as he kicked off his heavy boots. The sounds were fainter now as he padded around in his socks. Then I heard music start—he'd found my iPhone and was listening to Bruno Mars.

He tapped on my door and poked his head around.

"Laney, can I…?"

His words cut off and he stared at me. I flushed, covering up my bare legs, even though it was nothing he hadn't seen before.

"What are you doing?" he asked, his voice pitched higher than usual.

"Drug addict, remember?" I laughed awkwardly.

His eyes widened and then he gave a short nod of understanding.

"Your medicine."

"Yes, I'm just trying to get up the nerve. I do it every week, but I just … I'm being stupid, I know."

He took a step closer, moving into the room.

"Does it hurt?"

"No, not really," I sighed. "It's more the idea of it. I told you it was stupid."

He sat down on the bed next to me, his large body radiating heat and comfort.

"I'll do it for you—if you want."

I think my eyes nearly jumped out of my head. If I waved a needle around Collin, he looked like he was going to faint.

I stared at him in disbelief.

Ash shrugged. "I've done it before. My mother was diabetic. I used to help her."

"I don't know…"

"I won't hurt you," he said, leaning in and gently taking the needle from my hands.

Before I could protest, he'd pressed the point into my skin, depressed the plunger, and it was all over.

He placed the plastic cap over the empty needle and left it on my bedside table without a word.

It was an oddly intimate moment.

CHAPTER 12

Laney
The front door crashed open, making me jump. I dropped the knife I'd been holding, glad I hadn't lost a finger while slicing onions. I looked over my shoulder, ready to hand Ash his ass, but the smile on his face stopped me in my tracks.

I'd become so used to seeing him devoid of expression, that my heart jolted with pleasure and a warm feeling filled me.

His dark eyes sparkled, and I saw the dimples in his cheeks for the first time in so long. Too long. He strode toward me, happiness flowing around him.

Without pausing, he yanked me into his arms and twirled me around, making me feel graceful and giddy all at the same time.

"What's going on?" I gasped, half laughing.

"We're celebrating!" he shouted, waltzing around the tiny kitchen as my feet dangled above the ground.

His joy was infectious and soon I was shrieking with laughter as we whirled in circles.

"W-what are we laughing about?" I hiccupped.

"I have an audition," he shouted happily. "A real audition in a real theater—to dance!"

"Oh my God! How did that happen? When? Where? How? Did I say when? What is it? Ash, put me down, I can't breathe!"

I slid down Ash's chest, my cheeks reddening as I felt every hard ridge and plane of his body, until my face was pressed against his heart, listening to the wild pounding begin to ease as he rocked me gently, his hips undulating in a slow rumba.

"This is what I've been waiting for," he whispered, his breath blowing across my neck as he buried his face in my hair. "Let's go out and celebrate—anything you want, anywhere you want to go."

I started to remind him that he was saving his money and couldn't afford to treat me, but I bit the words back. Ash was a proud man, and being reminded of how little he had would only annoy him. I wouldn't spoil this moment.

"That sounds wonderful!"

Ash grabbed my hand and started tugging me toward the door.

"Wait!" I laughed. "I need a few minutes to get changed and you're still in your work clothes."

Ash looked down at his filthy jeans and boots with steel toecaps, and gave a rueful smile.

"I guess I'd better shower."

He bent over to unlace his boots, and don't judge me, but I couldn't help checking out his ass. I knew I shouldn't, but he had such a great ass: tight and round and squeezable as he filled out his jeans deliciously.

I glanced away quickly as he stood up again.

"Oh, I forgot to tell you—you've got mail," and I pointed at the coffee table in the living room.

Ash frowned, glaring at the brown envelope as if it would bite him.

"It's from the Embassy," I said.

He ripped open the envelope, pulling out several pieces of paper, then swore in his own language.

"What's wrong?"

"They won't send me a passport yet. It's still being investigated."

My heart flip-flopped uncomfortably.

"I have temporary ID, but I don't know if that will be enough to get access to my bank account," and he scowled.

"We'll work on that tomorrow," I said quickly. "We're celebrating tonight, remember?"

Ash smiled, his good mood instantly restored. Then he headed toward the shower in my bedroom, shedding clothes as he went.

"You are so messy!" I yelled after him, not really caring. "And you're going to tell me everything about the audition!"

Happy laughter was his only reply and I found myself grinning inanely at the bedroom door. Happy Ash was a beautiful thing, and it had been so long.

We'd gotten a rhythm going when it came to sharing the small space of my apartment. Being in the bathroom meant you had run of the bedroom, too. It worked, kind of, avoiding embarrassing moments of nudity.

But because Ash was in a hurry to go out, while he showered I rifled through my closet to find something to wear.

I'd just pulled out a pair of skinny jeans and silky tank-top when the bathroom door opened, a cloud of steam following Ash as he stepped out buck naked, his towel still in his hand.

It was several seconds before my brain kicked into gear and I turned away, Ash winding the towel around his waist, hiding an endowment that was still generous, even in the resting position.

"Sorry," I muttered. "I just ... um, I'll be outside."

I hurried from the room, my cheeks glowing.

A moment later, my bedroom door opened and Ash walked out wearing a pair of clean jeans and tugging a plain black t-shirt over his head. He was head-to-toe in thrift store clothes and he looked like a million dollars.

I scuttled past him, ignoring the amused, questioning glance he sent my way.

"I'll be ten minutes."

I took twenty, taking the time to curl and style my boring straight hair, as well as recover from my embarrassment.

When I re-emerged, Ash had put away his dirty work clothes and cleaned up the kitchen, putting the half-chopped onion in some Tupperware. Someone had trained him well.

I was surprised by the pinprick of jealousy I felt at that thought.

"Let's go!" he said, tossing my heavy winter coat across the room.

He wore an old army surplus coat that reached down to his calves, and a woolen beanie pulled low over his forehead. I blinked at the transformation. He looked dangerous, like the kind of guy you wouldn't want to meet in a dark alley. Gorgeous, of course.

Bundled up against the cold, we slogged down the icy streets. It was just five weeks before Thanksgiving and the stores were brightly lit and jammed with shoppers.

The cold wind whipped my hair into my eyes and I slipped on the slick sidewalk. Ash put his arm around my shoulders and tugged me into his side.

My hand crept around his waist and I felt guilty for enjoying it too much. Was Collin right? Was it impossible for men and women to be just friends? Or just impossible for Ash and me to be friends?

Without needing to discuss it, we headed toward a small, family-run pub with an Irish theme near the lake. The food was cheapish, and it had a warm, laid back atmosphere.

It was packed, being a Friday night, but Ash found us a couple of low stools near the fire. I was sweating before I managed to take off my coat. So much for trying to look nice.

Ash shrugged out of his coat and immediately attracted the attention of several women and a couple of gay guys. If he noticed, he ignored them, and headed for the bar.

The waitress had already taken my order for two Shepherds Pies, something that I knew was Ash's favorite, before he returned with two pints of beer.

Collin would have bought champagne and insisted on a French restaurant for a celebration.

"Cheers!"

"*Na zdravje!*"

"Now will you tell me everything?" I asked impatiently as our glasses clinked against each other.

Ash's excitement was contagious, and by the end of his story, I was on the edge of my seat, my drink in danger of tipping over.

"Tomorrow?! The audition is tomorrow? Shouldn't you be, I don't know, preparing?"

Ash smiled. "I'm thinking about it all. I need to use your iPhone. Is that okay?"

"Of course you can. What song are you going to use?"

"I'm not sure. Can I borrow it tonight, to listen while I sleep?"

Ash

I'd miss work for the audition, and I knew it meant that I'd be fired. And I got the impression that Viktor knew a lot of people, so it might not be easy getting hired on another construction job. I didn't care. I fucking hated it, and every day I was reminded that my dad's blood ran in my veins was a fucking miserable one.

I passed this old theater on my way home … I mean to Laney's home. It was usually closed, but tonight it had been brightly lit and a poster outside said 'open auditions'. I nearly walked past, assuming it was for actors, when I saw a girl with a huge bag over one shoulder and a pair of salsa shoes in her hand.

It was like seeing a rainbow, or drinking freshly ground coffee. It was seeing a beautiful woman, smelling a favorite perfume and following the scent because even if you tried not to, you couldn't help yourself.

I walked close behind the dancer, following her inside and scaring the woman checking names at the door.

"Can I help you?" she sniffed, looking me up and down.

I must have seemed ridiculous in my Army surplus coat, steel toecap boots and baggy jeans covered in demolition dust. I'd never looked less like a dancer.

"The open audition is for dancers?" I asked politely.

"Yes, and we're very busy," she huffed, trying to shoo me away with her hands.

I doubt if she was a day under 80, stood five-foot nothing, and weighed less than half my body weight. But she wasn't intimidated, just annoyed. It was kind of funny.

"Guys, or just girls?"

"Really, young man! I'm very busy!"

"I'm a dancer," I said, giving her my best smile, the one that usually worked on women.

"This isn't some Hip Hop club," she snapped. "This is for *trained* dancers."

"Yes, ma'am. I am two time finalist in All-Stars International Ten Dance … in my own country."

She blinked, then tapped her pen against the thick pad of paper, narrowing her eyes at me.

"Hmm, very well. Then tell me, in which dance would you see a syncopated separation?"

I smiled.

"Paso Doble—my favorite dance."

Her eyebrows shot up and I grinned at her as she thought of another question.

"Well, well indeed! And what is an *ocho*?"

"It's a tango step—the Argentine tango—the name coming from the figure eights women tango dancers make."

And I demonstrated for her, which wasn't easy in heavy work boots.

A thin smile passed her lips.

"Name?"

"Ash Novak."

"Well, Mr. Novak, all our auditions slots are filled for tonight…"

My face must have shown how I felt, because her own expression softened.

"However, I will put you down for 10AM tomorrow. Come with your music and a prepared piece of dance for us. And please, don't wear those monstrosities on your feet."

I leaned forward and kissed her papery cheek.

"No, ma'am!"

I'd run the rest of the way home. Home to Laney.

I spent most of the night listening to music and planning a routine. I tossed out several ideas before I was passably happy with the result, then slept for two restless hours until I heard Laney moving around in her bedroom.

She opened the door slowly, and peered cautiously into the living room. She'd been doing that ever since she saw me jerking off.

"Do you know what you're going to dance?" she asked.

Not 'good morning' as usual, or even 'hi'. She'd woken up thinking about my audition—same as me. I scooped her up and swung her around.

"Yes! I think so!"

She laughed, tugging on my t-shirt so I'd put her down.

"What music did you choose?"

"Either Raise Your Glass by Pink for a Cha-cha—Paso combo, or..."

"Or...?" she asked, her voice excited.

"Hunter by Pharrell Williams: a samba—hip hop mash up."

Her face fell slightly.

"What? You don't like that?"

I'd been so sure. Laney's lukewarm response affected me more than I wanted to think about.

"No, it sounds fine," she said, with a weak smile.

"Laney!" I gripped my hair. "Please, what is it?"

"I'm not the dance expert, Ash."

"But you have an opinion!"

"Okay, fine, but if it's a bad idea, promise me you won't do anything dumb."

I stared at her impatiently, and she sighed.

"You should do a rumba."

I didn't reply and she bit her lip.

"Why should I do rumba? It's ... not showy."

"That's exactly why!" she said, wringing her hands together. "Whenever I watch 'Dancing With the Stars', it's the one dance male celebrities *never* do well. But you're so..."

I wasn't following her thinking. What did a show about amateur dancers have to do with, well, anything?

"I'm so...?"

"Macho!" she said, her cheeks turning pink.

I broke into a smile at her answer.

"Thank you," and I winked at her.

"Stop it!" she laughed. "I'm being serious. A super-macho rumba would be ... sexy."

Her cheeks were glowing now, and I was sure that if I reached out and touched her, I'd feel the heat.

She snapped her fingers.

"James Bay, Let It Go."

"Play it for me," I said quickly.

She plugged in her iPhone and scrolled through while I waited impatiently. Then the first guitar chords flooded through the room and I knew she was right.

I will be me...

I could see it in my mind, how my body would move, the emotion I could show through my face, my arms, the tips of my fingers.

"It's perfect, Laney! Thank you!"

I cupped my hands around her soft cheeks and kissed her full on the lips.

She gasped slightly and wobbled.

"Okay?"

"Yup," she nodded breathlessly.

"I'll go shower," I said, jogging to the bathroom. "Then I need to practice."

"Ash!"

"Yeah?"

"Don't shave."

I turned to look at her.

"Just … the woman yesterday—she thought you were a construction worker, right?"

"Sure, I guess."

"Remember what we said about stereotypes? A construction worker who dances a rumba—they'll definitely remember you."

My eyebrows shot up and I grinned at her.

"No shaving."

I spent the next hour using Laney's living room as a rehearsal space. I even asked her to video me on her phone. I was used to rehearsing in dance studios that had mirrors so I could check my technique—it was frustrating not being able to see how I looked. The filming helped.

Itching to get to the theater, I ran through a checklist in my head: big bottle of water, check; towel, check; ballroom shoes, check; bananas—I'd buy some on the way. Laney had typed out a résumé for me and took a photo on her phone that she printed out. It looked professional by the time she finished. I didn't have kneepads or Latin shoes or any sheet music, so I had to hope they didn't penalize me for being unprepared. I'd just have to blow them away with my show piece.

But when I came out of the shower, Laney was sitting on the couch. Usually, she was in the kitchen making breakfast or already at her computer working.

"Are you okay?"

"Just a bit stiff. I'm fine."

I stared at her. She'd been well for weeks.

"Ash, I'm fine! Go! Or you'll be late."

She made shooing motions with her hands, so I grabbed one and kissed her knuckles.

"Wish me luck!"

"Luck!" She laughed. "But you don't need it. You're amazing!"

"*Moj sonček!*"

"What does that mean?" she called after me, as I jogged to the front door.

But I didn't answer. I knew it would frustrate the hell out of her—she was so cute when she was annoyed.

Her smile lit the dark corners inside me.

I'd been too wired to eat breakfast, even though that was a big no-no for auditions. It could be a long day, with maybe as many as four call backs.

I stopped at a convenience store and bought six tired-looking bananas: sugar and carbs. Can't beat it.

The line at the theater was as long as the day before, which was kind of depressing. Quite a few people were in pairs, and there was also a bunch of six guys who were practicing some street dance moves. They looked good, but unless they had technique to go with it, they probably wouldn't get through the audition. No technique usually means injuries, and no dance director will want that when you've got eight shows a week.

I'd worn a tight t-shirt to show off my pecs and abs—something working construction had actually helped.

The theater was heated, but I kept my sweatshirt on while I did warm-up exercises. They were taking people through in batches of 30 which meant for a fairly over-crowded stage. When my name was called, everyone in my group had the same idea—get to the front so you can see what's being taught by the choreographer, and the casting director can see you. Several short girls used their elbows to push past me. Yep, the dance world is competitive.

I hung at the back, knowing that they'd probably switch lines during the audition so everyone gets a chance to see and be seen. I was tall—it wasn't a problem.

I pulled off my sweatshirt and tossed it to the side. This was it. I needed to buckle up and focus. Pay attention, look, listen, learn—get the style, so the choreographer would know I could do the show, whatever it was going to be.

The run was a mash-up of various Latin styles with some jazz thrown in. It was immediately obvious who was trained and who wasn't, not that I spent a lot of time watching other people—that was a sure way to make a mistake.

And if you're not thinking about the music, about the dance, you'll end up with a blank expression.

Four of the street dance guys had no clue how to follow steps—the others weren't bad, but I didn't think they'd get called back. I was the only guy in my group who did the run all the way through. You don't stop in an audition, even if you're all over the place. What are you going to do in a live show? Walk off? No, you've got to keep going unless you're physically unable.

And then I remembered Gary telling me about dancing through the pain of a broken foot. I lost focus, wondering if he was okay, and earned a frown from the choreographer.

Even so, my name was called at the end of the round, so I got to stay.

For now.

I guessed there'd be maybe three more rounds. It was going to be tough.

I had 20 minutes to go eat my food and hydrate before round two. This time it was a rootsy, Hip Hop style and the guy next to me who'd nailed it in the first round was struggling. I guessed he was classically trained and couldn't connect with the earthy style and loose, bent knees. No matter what he tried, he was too upright, too straight-legged. He didn't make the cut.

By now I was sweating freely, and the remaining guys had taken off their shirts. I couldn't do that. The cuts on my back were healed, but the scars were fresh, and I didn't feel like answering questions. I wanted to forget.

When that woman I met in the pub had scratched down my chest, I almost knocked her over, pushing her away from me.

Too many bad memories to let anyone mark me again. She hadn't been happy. I wasn't all that into her anyway. I went back to the pub and stayed until it closed.

I'd started doing that every time the prick came over. I didn't want to hear him with Laney. At least it never lasted long. Why the hell did she put up with the one-minute wonder?

Round three was pair work and they tried us out with different partners. The music was salsa and we had to get up close and sexy with someone we'd just met. A tiny blonde girl was rubbing herself all over me.

Non-dance friends always ask if I get turned on by that, but if you're doing this all the time, there's not much risk of getting a hard-on unintentionally. Maybe for a while when I was a teenager, but mostly there isn't any energy left to think about anything apart from the dance. It's running a sprint followed by a marathon, while you're smiling and making it look effortless at the same time. Plus, she's sweaty, you're sweaty, so you've got two sweaty, stinky, slippery, grunting people, each depending on the other to do their job.

Yeah, it can happen, but usually with less experienced dancers or if you've got a brand new partner. Most pros can control themselves.

We switched again, and I got a tall Asian girl who was heavier than my last partner, but a way better dancer. If I'd been looking for a pro partner, I'd definitely be interested. If I got cut from the audition, I might ask her if she wanted to try out for some ballroom competitions.

But I didn't get cut. And it was time for my showdance.

I was tired and my body was aching.

But I thought of Laney.

The first time I saw her, sitting alone at that table, never guessing that she was in a wheelchair.

I'd wanted to dance with her then and God knows, I still did. But she was with the prick, so I was dancing solo.

Wanting to touch you.
Wanting to be with you.

It said everything I felt, and I was lost in the music. I was home.

Laney

I waited anxiously. I really hoped this audition was everything he'd hoped for. He was late, and I didn't know if that was good or bad. I didn't know the first thing about his world, except that when he'd left home this morning, he was happier than I'd ever seen him.

At six o'clock, hours later than I'd expected him, Ash walked through the door wearily.

"Well?" I asked anxiously.

His face broke into a huge smile. "I got it!" he yelled

"Oh my God! Oh my God!"

And he picked me up, hugging me tightly as I was spun around like a doll.

"It was brilliant!" he said, into my hair. "I mean, it was awesome."

He carried me over to the couch and we slumped down together, his arm automatically going around my shoulder as his head lolled back.

He told me about Rosa, the choreographer; Mark, the director; Dalano, the producer; and various members of the troupe and tech crew.

He was still talking happily when he leaned forward and unzipped the cheap gym bag that I'd loaned him, pulling out his dance shoes and sweaty rehearsal clothes.

"I'm going to put some laundry on," he said. "Do you have anything that needs washing?"

A large envelope fell to the floor, thickly stuffed with papers.

"What's that?"

Ash shrugged.

"Contract. I'm supposed to fill it in and take it back on Monday. Will you look through it for me? I hate reading that stuff, especially in English." Then he smiled. "But I got myself a new cell—you can message me now."

Then he disappeared toward the basement with his dance clothes and my weeks' worth of laundry.

I smiled to myself as I picked up the packet of papers and started reading his contract, impressed with the $850 per week wage. But I'd only got a few lines in before I realized that Ash had a serious problem. I'd gotten so carried away, little details like *work visa* and *social security* number had completely slipped my mind.

It was over before it had started: they would never allow Ash to dance. The foreman on a construction site might risk a day laborer, even in Chicago where the unions had things tied up tight, but the Steps Theater Group wouldn't.

Since he came home yesterday, Ash had been a different man: happy, confident, so much fun to be around.

But Ash had gotten a temporary work visa before—why couldn't he get another? This wasn't mission impossible.

I flipped open my laptop and started frantically typing questions into search engines. *What sort of visa did he need? How could he get one? How quickly?* But the answers were unambiguous.

Ash was a visa-overstayer, and therefore an illegal immigrant. But because someone had traveled out of the US on his passport, he was technically not in the U.S. either.

My mind whirred. There must be a way to help him, some sort of special dispensation. Did the Pope intervene on work visas? Probably not.

But God forgive me—that was what gave me the idea.

Because then I saw the words that stopped me in my tracks:

It is possible to obtain a green card based on marriage to a U.S. citizen even if you have overstayed your visa.

A shiver ran through me, a spark of possibility.

No, that was a really dumb idea. Just, no.

I read through the whole website, certain that there must be another way.

All of this depends on your ability to prove that you entered the U.S. legally, which he had.

You will also need to show that your marriage was entered into in good faith and not to take advantage of U.S. immigration benefits. You can do so by providing evidence such as photographs, a marriage certificate, utility bills, bank statements, and a lease or insurance policies in your name as well as your U.S. citizen spouse's name.

After everything that Ash had been through, after everything my beautiful country had done to him, didn't he deserve his chance?

I could help him.

All I had to do was marry Ash.

CHAPTER 13

Laney

I began to sweat. What the hell was I thinking? I was a police officer's daughter and I was planning to break the law. What would Collin say? He was already jealous of Ash. Maybe if I explained, he'd understand? Yeah, right.

Ash's voice made me jump.

"What do you think, Laylay? Pretty good money, eh? You've got to come to the premiere. I'll buy you a new dress, something upmarket, uh, upscale, you know? Michigan Avenue."

Ash was panting slightly, having run up four flights of stairs from the basement, but still grinning from ear to ear.

I gave him a weak smile.

He picked up on my mood immediately.

"What's wrong? You look sick," he said bluntly.

"Look ... just sit down for a moment. I've got something to tell you."

"You're pregnant."

"No! Just ... no!"

"You want me to leave?"

"No! Ugh! Will you listen for a moment!"

We stared at each other, Ash's lips tightening with annoyance.

"I'm not pregnant, God no! And I'm not asking you to leave." I took a deep breath. "There's a problem with your contract."

His shoulders dropped a fraction, but his eyebrows drew together in a worried frown.

"What problem?"

I sighed. "You don't have a visa."

He shrugged, unimpressed. "I'll get one. I got one before."

"It's not that easy. Technically, without your passport you're a nonperson. And even when that's sorted out, which could still take weeks, there's no guarantee that you'll get the new visa. They'll see you as an overstayer."

"An over— what?"

"An illegal immigrant."

"But..."

"I'm sorry."

"Weeks? You think it could take weeks?"

No, I think it'll be never.

Ash stood up and started pacing the floor. Then he strode to the balcony, flinging open the doors and letting in a freezing blast of icy air.

His fingers gripped the metal, and he leaned over the balcony, dangerously far.

"Ash!"

At my panicked shriek, he looked over his shoulder toward me, his eyes bleak. With a shake of his head, he walked back inside and closed the doors behind him, leaving the room chilled. Then he slumped onto the couch and his head thudded against the wall.

"It's over, isn't it? The Bratva have won. I'll have to go home with my tail curled."

"You'll ... what?"

He waved his hand impatiently. "Like a dog. With my tail between my legs. What else can I do?"

"You could marry me."

I mumbled the words so quietly, I wasn't sure if I'd meant for him to hear them.

But he did.

His expression froze in shock.

"Forget it. It's a stupid idea."

I stood up and walked into the kitchen to hide my embarrassment.

Ash followed, leaning against the wall as I rummaged in the fridge for juice. *Pineapple. Why did he always buy pineapple?*

The silence was painful. I could hear blood pounding in my ears, a loud roar of humiliation.

"You'd marry me?"

His words were as quiet as mine, but I heard him with perfect clarity.

Would I?

I closed the fridge door and turned to him. His beautiful face held no expression, and his voice was flat.

"Then you could get your green card."

"What about Collin?"

"After two years, we'd get divorced."

His face shifted marginally and I couldn't tell what he was thinking.

"A pretend marriage?"

"Well ... yes." *Had he thought I meant something else?*

"You'd do that? For me?"

I shrugged, uncomfortable under his burning gaze.

"We're friends. I want to help you. But, uh, we probably shouldn't tell anyone."

His forehead wrinkled in a deep frown.

"You're ashamed of me?"

"Ash, no! Of course not. It's just, well, marrying to get a green card is illegal."

He sighed and closed his eyes.

"I don't want you to get into trouble, Laney."

"I won't. Just as long as we keep quiet."

Ash

I couldn't sleep. No matter how many times I shifted on the uncomfortable couch, or tried to empty my mind. I kept thinking about Laney.

When she'd first suggested marriage, I think I stopped breathing. I'd never met a woman who'd even made me want to consider it. The only commitment I'd ever needed was to my art, to dance.

But marrying Laney ... I wasn't hating the idea. I couldn't believe she'd do this for me, basically putting her life on hold—again—so I had my shot.

The woman was so selfless. But...

I couldn't do it to her. It was illegal, she said, but it would also fuck up her relationship with the prick. Not that I gave a shit about him, but I didn't want Laney to get hurt. She didn't deserve that.

I'd said we should both sleep on her idea, because saying anything else seemed impossible.

I soon got bored of thrashing around alone in what passed for my bed.

I made sure Laney's bedroom door was shut, then padded around the small living room, moving back the few pieces of furniture to create a dance space. Tonight I needed something to calm and focus me.

People think rumba is the dance of love, but to me it's the dance of passion. It can be angry, sad, selfish, dramatic, jealous, cathartic and loving—all the passionate emotions. Besides, I preferred Rumba Flamenco to its safer cousin, ballroom rumba. This dance was part rumba, part Paso, part Flamenco—full of intensity. You needed focus to dance it well, full concentration. It suited me right now. I needed it.

Laney had left her iPhone in the kitchen, so I plugged it into the docking station and turned the volume down low as Hozier's Take me to Church flowed softly through the speakers.

My body understood this: music, movement, the single-minded focus that comes from being carried by the sounds, the lyrics, that crazy synergy of a perfect moment of dance and song.

I danced until sweat poured from my body and my muscles ached for relief. But it was my mind that needed the escape from the thoughts that hummed like angry bees, the stings of honesty the sharpest and deepest.

You can't let her do this.

She wants to help.

It's a mistake. You know it. Don't let it happen.

Shut up! Leave me alone!

It means nothing. You can never have her. She's with another man.

He's a prick.

She loves him.

I don't think so.

It doesn't matter what you think—she's not yours.

"Stop!"

"Ash? What's wrong?"

Laney stood blinking in the doorway, rubbing sleep from her eyes.

I turned around, wishing I hadn't woken her raving like a lunatic.

"I'm sorry."

I shut off the music.

"You don't have to do that," she said. "I know music helps you, dancing helps you."

I gave her a frustrated grimace. "Not tonight."

She nodded her head slowly. "You're thinking about it, aren't you? About marrying me."

"I am. It's the most anyone has ever…"

"Ash, don't say no. Let me do this for you."

"You've done so much for me already. I can't let you break the law." I gave a humorless laugh. "Your father would kill me."

"Ash, I want to see you succeed. You've been so happy since the audition. Seeing you like this … it's what you should be doing. You'll be giving pleasure to so many people. It might be the wrong thing to do in some people's eyes, but not mine. There's too much grimness and disappointment in the world—I don't want that for you."

"But marriage…"

She smiled suddenly. "And maybe I'm feeling a little rebellious."

I looked at her curiously. "What are you rebelling against?"

She sighed, her smile dipping.

"The RA mostly. People think when you have an illness, a disability, that you're automatically some sort of paragon; 'Look how good she is, putting up with that pain. So young and in a wheelchair', blah blah. I'm just me, and I'm not always good. Maybe I'm rebelling against expectations. Does that make any sense?"

I sagged down on the couch. I understood that, rejecting the road laid out for you, pulling to go in another direction. I understood that only too well.

She sat down next to me, close, but not touching. Then she reached over and took my hand in hers, the small fingers stroking over my knuckles.

"Maybe one day I'll see you dance on Broadway."

"It's insane," I laughed quietly, watching her fingers drawing lazy letters across the back of my hand, a shiver rippling under my skin.

"Ash! This could be your big chance!"

She was so passionate, so full of life. I admired everything about her. Except her two left feet. She couldn't dance—probably not even to save her life. She made me smile.

"What do you get out of this?"

She blinked, confusion and irritation at war in her expression.

"Me? I ... well..."

"You get nothing out of this, Laney. It doesn't make any sense."

She shook her head.

"You're wrong. I get to see you live your dream. And that ... that means a lot to me."

But why? "I already owe you so much."

"No, you don't, because you're going to..."

"...pay it forward. I know."

She sighed. "Ash, everyone always says, 'you can achieve anything if you want it hard enough'. Well, we both know that's bullshit. I can dream about being an Olympic gymnast for the rest of my life, but it isn't going to happen. And even though I kick and scream about not letting disability rule my life, there is definitely some dream adjustment involved. But you, you have the chance to catch that shooting star. You should do it for everyone who'll stare at the stars, but can never be one of them."

I shook my head.

"You make it sound selfless, but if I do this, it's for me. And it will be the most selfish thing I've ever done."

Laney smiled. "Now you're getting it!"

"You are a crazy woman. I love that about you!"

Her lips popped open and I wished I could swallow back the words, but she just smiled.

"So we'll do it?"

I rolled off the couch and onto my knees, catching her hand as I stared into her eyes.

"Laney Kathleen Hennessey, will you do me the extreme honor of becoming my wife?"

She laughed as I kissed her hand.

"Yes, my secret husband! I agree to be your secret wife, for the period of no more than two years."

I stood up, feeling foolish, and Laney's gaze softened.

"I'm sorry. I didn't expect you to do that."

"How does this work?"

Suddenly, Laney was all business.

"They do the quick marriages at the Marriage and Civil Union Court. We get our license at the clerk's office the day before, pay a fee and then sign the paperwork. Just forget to take in your contract to the theater for a few days."

"That simple?"

"Let's hope so!"

Of course it wasn't that simple. Because right after we'd agreed to marry, she got sick.

"Ash! Ash! ASH!"

I jolted awake, my heart pounding as I almost fell off the couch. But this time it wasn't my usual nightmares.

"Ash!"

Laney was calling for me, screaming, her cries raw.

I ran to the bedroom, throwing the door open so hard that it crashed into the wall. My eyes darted around wildly, expecting to see Sergei, or Oleg, some threat. But she was alone, splayed out on the bed at an awkward angle, one arm trapped under her body as if she'd tried to get up and couldn't make it. Her face was wet with tears and sobbing gasps made her body shudder painfully.

"Laney! What's wrong? Where does it hurt?"

"Ev-everywhere!" she cried out.

I half-knelt on the bed trying to put my arms around her but she screamed in agony.

"Don't touch me!"

I felt her pulse hammering under my hand, her heart beating so wildly I was afraid she'd have a heart attack. I'd never felt anything like it, and my own anxiety went into overdrive.

"I'm calling an ambulance," I shouted as I leapt off the bed.

"No! Drugs! I n-need my drugs!"

Sranje! Which drugs? Where were they?

I tried to speak calmly.

"Okay, I'll get them. Where?"

Her sobbing was so uncontrolled, her gasps so fast, it was impossible to understand her. And even when I made out the words, the long, medical name meant nothing to me.

"Yellow ones!" she begged. "Bathroom!"

I ransacked her bathroom cabinet until I found some that were a pale yellow color—her anti-inflammatory drugs.

"These?"

"Y-yes!"

I needed to get her upright so she could drink some water with them, but every time I tried to touch her or move her, she screamed.

"It burns!" she cried out, sobbing, her chest heaving.

I didn't know what to do. We needed help, but she begged me not to call an ambulance. I even thought about calling the prick—he must have seen this before so he'd know how to help her. But if I moved an inch from Laney she cried out.

"Don't leave me! Ash! Ash!"

I lay on the bed next to her, trying to wedge my body under hers so she could sit up. That didn't work, so in the end, I wrapped my arms around her and pulled her up, wincing as her piercing shrieks knifed through me.

I popped out one of the large pills, and pushed into Laney's mouth. She nearly bit my finger and I had to pull free quickly.

Trying to hold a glass of water to her mouth caused most of it to go over her and the bed, her hands shook and she gasped and coughed, retching as water went down the wrong way. After three tries, she managed to swallow the pill and I laid her down, her crying almost as wild as before.

Fifteen long and terrifying minutes later, her breaths began to slow, and her panic began to ease. Another half-an-hour, and she was able to rest in a normal position, instead of twisted and contorted as if she'd been dropped from a great height.

I rubbed her arm softly, trying to give comfort because there was nothing else I could do.

"Don't leave me," she begged, her voice shaking.

My chest ached at the desperation and fear I heard in her voice.

"I won't. I promise."

"Stay with me. Don't go."

"I'm not leaving you, Laney."

Moving slowly and carefully so I didn't jostle her, I eased myself into the bed next to her, covering us both with the quilt.

She gripped my hand and pulled it against her stomach.

"Don't leave me."

When I woke the next morning, I was confused. It was darker than I was used to. I never closed the drapes in the living room, so I should be seeing either daylight or street lamps. I rolled over and heard a soft, female gasp.

Memory came flooding back.

"Laney! Are you … how are you? Did I hurt you?"

Her head turned slowly to look in my direction. "I'm okay. Sorry about last night."

I sat up cautiously, staring down at her.

"That was scary. Are you really okay?"

Her lips turned upward in a sad smile. "I can't move, but I'm okay."

"You ... you can't move?!"

"Well, a little, but it hurts. Could you get me another of those pills, please?"

I rolled out of bed and quickly moved to the bathroom, stopping a second to yank the curtains open, then bringing her another of the yellow pills.

She gave a small giggle, her gaze dipping to my briefs. I was too worried to be embarrassed that my dick was saluting the morning, right at Laney's eye level.

"Can you sit up?"

"No. If you could just get me a little upright, I'll be able to take the pill."

She wrapped her arms around my neck, grimacing as I pulled her up, giving small gasps as if she was trying to keep her breaths as shallow as possible.

She took the pill, washing it down with several mouthfuls of water.

"You can put me back now," she said softly.

Her face scrunched even though I was moving as slowly as I could. And I watched her for several seconds until it smoothed out again.

"Does that happen often?" I asked at last.

Her expression was exasperated.

"No, hardly ever. Only once before. Why it had to happen now..." and her voice trailed off.

"You had a panic attack," I said flatly.

"I know," and she closed her eyes. "The pain was so intense. It feels like every part of your body is on fire. It was so sudden, waking up like that—it's what made me panic."

She turned her head to smile at me.

"You were great. Thank you."

I flopped back on the bed next to her.

"I was so scared, I nearly called the pr— Collin."

She poked me in the side, making me jump.

"Don't call him that. He can't help being..."

"...an asshole?"

"Ash!" She paused. "Anyway, I'm glad you didn't call him, or I'd be waking up in hospital right now." Then she gave me a big smile. "It's much nicer waking up next to you. Don't tell Collin," and she laughed happily.

I shook my head, awed by this amazing woman. The only parts of her that she could move without pain were her head and her arms, and here she was teasing me, joking with me.

Then she frowned. "You look very serious. What are you thinking?"

I chose to lie.

"I was thinking that I should probably go shower in case Collin decides on a Sunday morning visit and finds us in bed together."

"Good point. But at least the monster in your pants has gone back to his cave."

I nearly choked on a laugh.

"Monster?"

Her cheeks bloomed pink.

"Go. Shower."

Laughing loudly, I headed for the bathroom.

"I can't believe I said that," she muttered.

In the shower, my mood sobered. I worried that stress had caused this flare-up and the scary as hell panic attack. Maybe she'd reconsidered the whole marriage idea. I still didn't believe that she'd be getting anything out of it, no matter which way she argued it. All the benefit was on my side, and I'd be a selfish douche to let her do this.

Sighing, I dried myself with a towel, determined to persuade Laney to change her mind. But when I walked out into the bedroom, she was working her cell, still flat on her back.

She beamed up at me.

"Locked and loaded!"

"Excuse me?"

"All the paperwork is fairly straightforward. Your Consular ID will be sufficient, but I'll need to get a copy of your entry visa. Then we have to go to the clerk's office, take a number and wait. We could drop by one morning before you go to the theater. So … how do you feel about getting married on Friday afternoon?"

"Laney, I don't know…"

"Ash, stop. I can guess what you're going to say, but don't."

"We agree this crazy scheme and then you get sick with a panic attack and … this!" I said roughly, jerking a thumb at her prone body.

Her expression softened fractionally.

"It's not related."

"It must be!"

"I know my own body better than you."

I ran my hands over my wet hair in frustration.

"Don't you want this?" she asked.

"Not if it makes you ill!"

"Is that your only concern?"

"Not really. What would happen if your family or the prick find out, or if someone realizes it's a fake marriage? How much trouble will you be in? I figure I'll just be deported."

"Oh, is that all?" she laughed. "You should live a little, Ash."

Laney

By Thursday, I still hadn't gotten over my flare-up, which was annoying. God, the stares when I explained that we were there for a marriage license. I breezed through that on a wave of indignation. I'm not sure Ash noticed—he was too busy trying to talk himself into doing it. I wished I could convince him that it was the only solution.

But on Friday afternoon, waiting to get married, I was nervous and starting to fidget. It had suddenly occurred to me that I might run into someone I knew who might understandably be curious. After all, I was wearing a dress instead of my usual jeans and sitting with my so-called roommate, a seriously hot guy that other women definitely noticed, in the anteroom to where the wedding ceremonies took place.

Ash had been full of confidence first thing this morning, dismissing my concerns.

"You can't spend your life worrying *what if*. We all die and feed the chickens."

"You mean worms?"

"Chickens, worms, we all end up in the dirt, yeah? 'What if it rains?' I'll get you an umbrella."

But now, he looked like he was about to be sick.

It was warm inside, the old heating system cranking out plenty of hot air, and the press of bodies was making me feel sweaty and uncomfortable.

Despite the heat, Ash looked unwrinkled and chic in a pair of black chinos, crisp white shirt that he'd ironed himself this morning, and a dark navy tie, all found in thrift stores. Although his usually golden complexion was verging on green. I hoped he made it to the end of the ceremony before puking. But then I figured lots of grooms get nervous.

As he'd insisted we dress up, I'd wanted to buy him something new, but he refused. Did I mention he was stubborn?

I'd planned to wear a cute little black dress that had been hanging in my closet for such an occasion. Well, not a secret marriage, obviously, but something that required being fancy.

But Ash said we looked as if we were going to a funeral not a wedding and no one would believe it, so at the last minute I changed into a pale lemon sundress that got Ash's nod of approval. It was completely inappropriate for October in Chicago, but he liked it.

When our names were called, Ash made everyone clear out of the way as he eased my wheelchair through the door, ignoring the pitying glances of the happy and loud *real* wedding party.

I could tell that they felt sorry for Ash—sorry because he was marrying a woman in a wheelchair, who was obviously no prize.

No matter how many times I told myself that I didn't care what strangers thought, I did care—just a little. Ash said nothing.

It wasn't how I'd imagined my wedding day. Not that I was one of those women who planned everything from the dress to the food to the guests, impatient only to meet a man who would complete the picture. But I had imagined that my family would be with me.

And it was all a lie—we weren't passionately in love, we hadn't declared our need to live together for the rest of our lives, I'd never said I loved him.

But now ... I swear it had started with wanting to help, but his quiet kindness, his sensitivity, his potential for sheer joy, all those emotions had tunneled toward my heart. And against all reason, all reality, I was falling for this frustrating, flawed, broken, battered and beautiful man. Why was I so careful with my health ... and so reckless with my heart?

The ceremony was short, and Ash surprised me with a simple gold ring that must have cost him every penny of the money he'd saved from his hated construction job. Then we heard the words, "You may kiss the bride," and I offered him my cheek.

But instead he kneeled in front of the wheelchair and carefully held my face between his hands, as if he was holding a precious jewel, and his lips came down on mine, soft at first, and then increasingly passionate until I gasped and felt my face heat up.

A camera flash surprised us both, and the wedding officiant smiled.

"Perhaps not one to show the grandkids," she chuckled.

With a photo on my phone showing us in a very steamy embrace, we tumbled from the building into bright Fall sunshine.

"What was that?" I demanded, as soon as we were out of earshot.

Ash laughed, far more relaxed than I'd seen him in days.

"What was what?" he asked slyly, knowing exactly what I was talking about.

"That ... that kiss!"

"Had to make it look real," he said off-handedly.

Which was the right answer, but now it felt so wrong.

He'd slipped away early from rehearsals today, telling the director that he had a prior appointment.

Now the short ceremony was over, we had our first evening as man and wife.

"Where should we go to celebrate, Mrs. Novak?"

"Don't call me that," I laughed, shaking my head.

"Why not? I have a piece of paper that says you are my wife," he teased.

"Yes, very funny."

"There is nothing funny about the sanctity of marriage," he said, leaning over and kissing the top of my head.

"You definitely shouldn't joke about that with a good Catholic girl."

"But I'm a good Catholic boy."

"Really?"

"Yes, why are you surprised?"

"I don't know, I just am. Do you ever go to church?"

"I used to go with Mama, at all the big festivals, Easter, Christmas. She gave me a St. Christopher for my 8th birthday. I used to wear it for her." He frowned. "I don't have it anymore."

I was surprised to hear him mention his mother—he so rarely did.

"Are you close to her?"

"I was." His voice hardened. "She died when I was 15."

"Oh, Ash."

He didn't offer anything else and I didn't want to push him, but it broke my heart a little.

"Hey, we're not far from the theater," he said, his voice lightening. "There's a Dutch pancake house that looks good. Do you want to try it?"

"I thought all you dancers lived on water and bananas and ate super-healthy, protein-rich, sugar-free food."

He bent low over the wheelchair so his warm breath washed over my cold cheeks.

"I'm craving pancakes and syrup and those chocolate sprinkles the Dutch put on bread. Come and be bad with me, Mrs. Novak."

"You really shouldn't call me that," I said seriously. "Or you'll get used to it and say it at the wrong time."

"I like the sound of it," he said, making my poor heart stutter.

I couldn't help thinking about that kiss. It hadn't just looked real, it had *felt* real as well. Was he really that good an actor?

The truth was, I'd liked it, which could lead me to very dangerous territory if I let it. I tried telling myself that the attraction was superficial, brought about by his undeniable exotic good looks.

Then I told myself it was the intensity of our meeting, the shared danger, surviving together. And I told myself that even if I was attracted to him, it was a one-way street.

I'd changed my mind about Ash so often that I might as well be a weather vane. But that kiss had gotten me hotter than anything Collin had ever done, either in or out of the bedroom. At least now I knew how I felt about that relationship.

"Here we are," said Ash, reaching down to squeeze my shoulder. "We should order champagne."

"Um, Ash, I don't know what sort of pancake houses you're used to, but this one doesn't have a license to sell alcohol."

He looked shocked, as if he couldn't imagine such a thing.

"If you want to have a drink, we'd be better off going to that Italian place next door."

He sighed.

"No chocolate sprinkles?"

"How about a pound of pasta and tiramisu instead?"

"Deal!"

He maneuvered my wheelchair through the narrow doorway of the small Italian restaurant, ignoring the server's forced smile as she contemplated having to ask a dozen diners to move their chairs so I could get through.

I hated this part, and almost asked Ash to go somewhere else, when I heard his name being called.

"Ash! Hey, over here!"

A group of skinny women were waving at him, their eyes bouncing back and forth between us.

Ash swore under his breath.

"They're from the show," he muttered.

"We should leave."

Ash grunted his agreement, then said, "I should go say hi first."

But one of the women was already on her feet, pushing her way through the Friday evening crowds.

"Ash, darling!" she said, her voice very loud and very English. "You've been a naughty boy, sloping off early, while we've all been sweating our bollocks off. Hello, I'm Sarah. You must be Ash's girlfriend…"

Then she spotted the gold ring on my finger that I hadn't had a chance to remove.

"Oh! Ash didn't tell us he was married—sneaky sod!"

Shit! Shit! Shit!

For a moment I saw a flash of panic in Ash's eyes, but then he shrugged.

"Yes, this is my beautiful wife Laney."

"You lucky cow," Sarah grinned, leaning down to press her cheek to mine. "We've all been lusting after your husband, but don't worry, he hasn't laid a finger on any of us, except when the Führer is barking orders at us. More's the pity."

Then she yelled at the top of her voice for everyone to move out of the way, grabbed the handles of my wheelchair and shoved her way back through the crowd.

Ash followed grinning.

"Everyone, this is the gorgeous bird who's married to Ash. You can call her Laney; I'm going to call her lucky bitch."

So much for being low key. I gave a limp wave while Ash squeezed a chair into the space next to me.

"How come you're all dressed up and looking swanky?" the curious and loud Sarah asked, as everyone turned to stare at us.

Ash held my hand and smiled at me.

"It was a special occasion."

"Oh God, he's disgustingly romantic, too," Sarah moaned. "I need another bottle of lager."

I couldn't help laughing. She reminded me of Vanessa, not giving a damn what people thought of her, taking my wheelchair in her stride.

"So, what do you do, Laney? I doubt you're a dancer?"

I blinked, taken off guard, and Ash frowned at her, throwing his arm across my shoulders.

"Oh," Sarah said, contrite. "That sounded rude. Sorry, Mum's always saying that I'm too blunt. But, whatever, it saves time."

"No, I'm definitely not a dancer—I'm a writer."

"Yeah? Cool! So how did you two meet?"

We hadn't had time to concoct a cover story, but Ash just smiled at her.

"We were in a club and I asked her to dance."

"What?"

"I didn't notice the wheelchair."

"Aw, you were blinded by her beauty. Sigh. You can stop talking now, Ash. You're too good to be true. No, wait! Laney, tell me something totally gross about him so I can sleep tonight."

I laughed at her serious expression.

"Um, I don't think ... well, it's not gross but it is annoying ... he calls my boyf— my best friend Collin a prick," I finished lamely.

"Is he a prick?" Sarah asked, stuffing an enormous forkful of pasta in her mouth.

"Yes," said Ash as I said, "No."

Sarah laughed, and pieces of pasta sprayed over the table, causing the other women to jerk back and throw disgusted looks.

"He probably doesn't like competition," Sarah said knowingly, giving Ash a sharp look. "Even from pricks. But yeah, that's not gross."

"The way you eat pasta is," one of the women muttered.

Sarah ignored her, and the server arrived, smiling brightly at Ash.

"Does she want a menu?" she asked, not even glancing at me.

"Why don't you ask her?" he said coldly.

The waitress looked flustered, so I quietly asked for a menu while she hurried away.

Everyone stared. They always did.

Ash's new colleagues were friendly, talking excitedly about rehearsals.

But I can't pretend it wasn't painful to be surrounded by women who were all tens.

And able-bodied.

Ash

What a seriously weird day.

I was so certain I was going to get arrested and kicked out of the country that I nearly puked. Added to the fact I was getting fucking married.

To a woman who liked me but didn't love me, so I could stay in a country that had sent me to Hell and back, to dance in a show that I was beginning to have serious doubts about. And now, my secret wife wasn't a secret to the other dancers in the show.

That was enough to make anyone's head spin. I had another drink, feeling the warm fingers of alcohol trickle through my bloodstream.

Laney's face was flushed from the heat in the crowded restaurant and from the glass of champagne that she'd drunk.

She was laughing at something Sarah had said. Her head was thrown back and her eyes sparkling. She looked happy. Then she caught my eye and her smile softened as she leaned toward me.

"It'll be okay," she whispered.

I wanted to kiss her again. Well, I wanted to do a lot more than kiss her, but I couldn't. She wouldn't want that. I'd taken a risk during the ceremony, but it had felt like the right thing to do. And then, when she'd responded, I wanted her. Badly.

She was my friend. The best friend I'd ever had.

Maybe I was reading it wrong, but it felt like there was something more between us.

It was confusing.

But then the memories slammed back, reminding me that she was too good for a man who would never feel clean again.

Laney

I'd nearly had a heart attack when Sarah saw my wedding ring. But it hadn't turned out as badly as I'd expected.

Ash's co-workers were really friendly and accepting. They admitted openly that they thought he was gorgeous, but none of them gave me a vibe that they wanted more than friendship.

Ash seemed to enjoy himself, but then his expression had darkened and I wondered what he was thinking. He'd made an effort to be light hearted again, but I could tell the difference between his real smile and the one he put on for a performance.

We stayed long enough to enjoy gorging on pannacotta, then Ash told the others we were leaving.

He'd wheeled me home, made some chamomile tea for me, and brought my meds.

And then he'd taken me into my room and left me there.

My wedding night was spent alone in my bed, wondering if Ash would open the door and walk inside, hoping he would.

I knew one thing for certain—I had to break things off with Collin. I wasn't being fair to either of us.

Unfortunately, Collin had left for a two week business trip. I wasn't going to end a ten year relationship over the phone. But it was frustrating.

So for the next two weeks, we continued on as roommates, our marriage certificate hidden in my bedroom drawer while various photocopies were sent off to facilitate Ash's green card, my wedding ring unworn.

Ash didn't try to kiss me again, but I saw him watching me sometimes. I knew that I wanted him to, but he had to want it as well, and right now, his expression was quizzical, uncertain. When our eyes met, he'd smile quickly and look away.

I heard him at night, almost every night. It would start with short, muttered sentences, always in Slovenian, the couch creaking as he moved restlessly. The whispers would get louder and suddenly he'd shout out. That woke him, and then I'd hear him padding into the kitchen to get a drink. Sometimes that would follow by music playing softly and I knew that he was dancing.

I wanted to go to him, to stop those nightmares, or at least let him know that he wasn't alone, but uncertainty stopped me every time. And this dancing, this nighttime dancing, that was private.

He spent every day of the following two weeks at the theater, coming home too tired to do more than slump in front of the TV. Twice, he asked me to come out with the other dancers after work again, but I always said no.

And then the unthinkable happened.

Collin asked me to marry him.

The day he came back to Chicago, he surprised me by showing up at the apartment with a bunch of flowers.

And he made his proposal while I was laying on the couch watching TV and Ash was pretending to wrestle with the coffee machine in the kitchen.

My nerves were shredded and I wished Ash would take the hint and go out. But he ignored all my signals, staying stubbornly put.

Out of the corner of my eye, I watched him slamming drawers and doors in the kitchen, thinking that Collin would sense something was up, but he was so used to pretending Ash didn't exist, that I don't think he even noticed.

I kept wondering if I was doing the right thing, and whether my infatuation with Ash was pushing me to make a big mistake. I didn't think so, but ten years is a lot to throw away.

When I say Collin asked me to marry him, it wasn't a big romantic proposal—that wasn't his style. First of all he asked me to move in with him.

"Collin, I need to talk to you about…"

"I know—me, too. I've been doing a lot of thinking while I was away. We could save money if we live together," he encouraged me. "And this apartment has never been practical for you, but you're just too stubborn to admit it."

I gave him a sour look as he blundered on.

"My place is far more suitable, and it means we'll be able to save to buy sooner rather than later."

"Collin, I don't think…"

"Then we'll get married, Laney," Collin said enthusiastically. "Well, we'll get a specially adapted apartment, everything you'll need. I know, I know, you don't need one now, but you will. One of us needs to plan ahead. When we have kids we can…"

His words jolted me out of my shocked stupor.

"No."

He looked irritated by the interruption.

"No? What do you mean no? No what?"

"I don't want kids," I said.

"I know you don't now, but…"

"Not ever."

Collin looked confused. "But you love kids?"

I swallowed and looked down.

"I'm not ruling out adopting a child one day…"

Collin's face turned red.

"Why the hell would we adopt?"

I met his angry gaze stoically. "Because of me."

His expression smoothed out.

"Honey, if you get sick or you can't manage, we'll hire help. Get a nanny or a nurse—whatever you need."

I closed my eyes. He could be so kind. So darned oblivious and so kind. But his kindness bulldozed through my own wants and needs. It always had and I'd always let him. Until now.

"No, Collin. I don't want children of my own, because I don't want to pass on my genes. I couldn't bear to see a child of mine suffer, knowing that I'd caused it. There are plenty of children out there who need to be loved, who need a family. I can adopt."

Collin's face went very still.

"And what about what I want? Suppose I don't want some other man's child. I want our child. That's the whole fucking point!"

Collin never swore. He said it showed a lack of vocabulary, so hearing him now, I realized how upset he was.

"This shouldn't be a surprise to you," I said gently. "You've known all along that I don't want children."

"I didn't know you meant not ever!" he shouted.

"Then you should have listened better!" I yelled back, my own anger and frustration igniting. "I told you I didn't want kids on our third date!"

"Every woman says that!" he roared. "Nobody ever thinks they mean it!"

I lowered my voice.

"I meant it then and I still do."

Collin rubbed his hands over his face.

"Laney, honey, they're making great medical strides all the time. Your illness is kept in check."

"Yes!" I interrupted angrily. "Because of the drugs I take—the toxic drugs that I'd have to give up before getting pregnant. I could lose the mobility that I have now. Permanently."

He backtracked immediately.

"That's not what I meant. You're twisting everything. You always do that."

I tried to swallow my anger, knowing that everything I said was hurting him.

"Then I'll be really clear, so there's no misunderstanding. I don't want to get pregnant. Ever. I don't want to have my own children. Ever. I can't risk it."

Collin leaned back in his seat.

"And I don't get any say in this?"

I shook my head, knowing this was final. Even if I'd chosen Collin, he wouldn't have chosen me—not in the long run. The threat of tears made my throat close up.

"No, you don't."

"Wow." Collin massaged his temples. "Wow," he said again. "That's it? No discussion? No compromise? Laney has spoken, so that's it?"

"I can't compromise on this," I whispered. "And I can't marry you."

He stood slowly, his chest rising and falling rapidly.

"I could have had anyone," he said, his voice tight. "But I wanted you. And even when you told me that you were … what you are … I didn't care. I would have gotten you the best doctors, the best therapists…"

"I don't need a nurse," I said softly.

"You might! One day you might!" he shouted, his voice rising again.

"Collin," I sighed, my voice cracking. "All you see when you look at me is someone you want to make well. I'll never be well: this is as good as it gets."

"You don't know that!"

"I do. I do know that. I can't be with someone who wants to change me."

"I don't want to change you! I just want you to be…"

"Better."

I finished the sentence for him.

He closed his eyes, his head hanging, and my heart jolted at the pain and defeat I saw when he opened his eyes again.

He walked around the table and hovered, as if he was going to lean down and kiss me on the cheek. He caught himself at the last moment and stood upright.

"Bye, Laney. Look after yourself."

"I'm sorry," I said softly, my voice hoarse.

He nodded and a moment later, he was gone.

I leaned back in my seat and let hot tears spill from my eyes.

Collin was a good man and I hated hurting him.

"Laney, are you okay?"

Ash's soft voice broke into my unhappy thoughts.

"No."

He sat down opposite me in the seat Collin had just left, then reached across and held my hand, not speaking.

I felt the warmth from his fingers press against the palm of my hand until our fingers were twined together and his thumb stroked across my skin.

"Did you hear?" I asked, a sickening numb feeling creeping through me.

"Yes," he said simply, his dark eyes giving nothing away.

"Did I do the right thing?"

The pressure on my fingers increased.

"A bird in a cage is safe from the eagle, but she cannot fly very far."

I gave an unattractive snort. "Is that a Slovenian saying?"

Ash smiled at me. "No, it's an Aljaž saying."

"I don't think it will catch on."

"No? I liked it."

"Me, too," I sighed, my sadness taking over again.

Then I started to cry in earnest: for me, for Collin, for ten years of friendship lost. Ash moved closer, wrapping his arms around me and pulling me against his firm chest, rocking us gently.

We stayed like that for a long time.

When I thought about it later, Collin never once said that he loved me. And really, that said it all.

CHAPTER 14

Ash

Lies on lies on top of more lies, and it was hard keeping track of them all. Laney and I pretended that we were friends and then had to act married the one time that she met the other dancers.

At the theater, I had to answer questions about her, about us, when there was no 'us'. We were friends and I respected her: the way she dealt with her illness was humbling to see. But it wasn't just that: she worked hard at her job and was unfailingly loyal to the people she loved.

I pretended that my green card would arrive any day, when the truth was I didn't know for sure if it would happen.

The prick was out of the picture, but Laney didn't seem any happier, and I wondered if she regretted breaking up with him and the fake marriage to me.

The police had no news about the Bratva, and all their promises about justice seemed hollow. Nobody would tell me if they'd identified the girl they'd found. I saw her dead eyes in my nightmares each night, and the numbness spread through me.

There was still no news about Yveta or Gary, and I'd been told that the Las Vegas police hadn't been able to find the place that Marta described. Another dead end, a fog of defeat.

Rosa, the choreographer was frustrated, pulling me aside and saying that my work lacked passion. I was losing the one thing that I'd thought would always anchor me. Rehearsals were going to shit, and not just because of me, but I couldn't talk to Laney about it, not after everything she'd given up already. So when she asked me, I was always okay.

Dancing and the time I spent in the theater shouldn't feel fucked up. But then Rosa quit after several loud arguments with the producer. Dalano's ideas were stale and old-fashioned, and I don't think he'd had a new idea since *42nd Street*. Mark, the director, was Dalano's boyfriend, so he did whatever he was told. After Rosa left, every bit of originality and creativity was stripped out of the show. I didn't need passion now: all Mark wanted was cardboard cutouts of the dancer he'd been thirty years ago.

The show was due to open the first week of December and we were getting called into costume fittings. I stared at the gold lamé pants, tail-coat and matching top hat and groaned.

It was going to be a fucking disaster.

Laney knew that something was wrong, but she'd married me so I could have this chance. How the hell could I tell her the truth?

Like storm clouds on the horizon, pressure dropping like a stone, something was going to break.

We were opening the first weekend of December, and I guessed that the show would close by New Year. After that, I didn't know what I was going to do.

"What's wrong?" Laney asked for the hundredth time.

"Noth—"

"Nothing, right? You're fine. You're okay. There's no problem. That's what you always say these days. I don't know why I bother asking."

She scoffed loudly and walked into the kitchen. Almost immediately, I heard the sound of the coffee machine.

I slumped back on the couch and closed my eyes. The constant small arguments were wearing. Sometimes I really felt married. Except my wife didn't sleep with me. Well, from what other guys said, that wasn't unusual either.

I was 23 and hadn't been laid since … not since Yveta.

My mood darkened even more. The police hadn't been able to find her. I don't know how hard they'd tried, or even whether they'd tried at all. Not knowing was like a constant dull ache. I could ignore it most of the time, but every now and then…

I felt the couch dip next to me and I cracked an eye to find Laney holding a cup of coffee for me.

"Peace offering," she said simply.

I nodded and took the cup.

"You can talk to me, you know. You can tell me anything, Ash. Something is bothering you. I wish you'd just tell me. I hate guessing. We're friends, aren't we?"

"Laney, please…"

"No, Ash. Not this time. You're going to tell me what's got you all wound up." Her lips pressed together in a thin line. "Is it me?"

I sighed and looked down. "No, it's not you."

"Then what? Please don't make me ask twenty questions."

I put the coffee down on the table.

"It's the show," I said at last. "It's bad."

Laney frowned. "What do you mean?"

"Bad as in shit. Bad as in boring. Bad as in no one in their right minds would want to see it. If it lasts a month, I'll be amazed. All the dancers know it. But since Rosa quit, there's been no one to stand up to Dalano. We've all tried to say something but he just says if we don't like it, we can leave." I grimaced. "None of us can afford to do that."

"This is what you've been worrying about?"

Laney's voice sounded almost relieved, which really made me pissed.

"Yes!" I yelled. "This is what I've been worrying about! You've sacrificed everything for me, for a shitty show that won't last a month. So forgive me if I'm a bit fucking upset about it!"

"Don't yell at me!" she shouted, her face turning red and her eyes flashing.

Silenced rushed between us and I swear I could hear her heart beating.

She glared, her gray eyes darkening dangerously, and I was sure she was going to slap me. My muscles tensed, but then she laughed.

"At least you're not saying 'fine' anymore," she smiled, prodding my chest with her finger.

"I totally get why you didn't want to say anything to me, and I'm sorry this show hasn't worked out for you, but I'm not a shrinking violet—I can take the truth."

"I don't know about any shrinking flowers, but you are quite short."

"Watch it, mister!"

I grabbed her hand as she tried to prod me again.

"I'm sorry," I said seriously. "You are strong. I know this."

She smiled at me, her eyes sparkling. I had a sudden urge to kiss her and my gaze dropped to her lips.

She cleared her throat and moved away, her cheeks pink.

"So, you know it's Thanksgiving this weekend, right?"

I rolled my eyes.

"Yeah, I think I've noticed."

Even a blind, deaf dog would have noticed that Americans were entering the holiday season. I didn't quite understand it—it all seemed like a rehearsal for Christmas. But if it meant I got an extra couple of days off from rehearsals, that was fine by me.

"Well, I always have a family thing—it's at my aunt's house this year…"

"Laney, I'll be fine. I'll probably just sleep, do laundry, watch some TV."

It was her turn to roll her eyes.

"You're invited, you dope. Besides, my family is dying to meet you, especially my mom."

I frowned at her, confused. "She is?"

"Of course! The mysterious Slovenian roommate."

"What about your father?"

"He'll be there, but he doesn't have any say in who gets invited for Thanksgiving—the wives are in charge of that."

I looked at her skeptically.

"Honestly, it'll be fine. There'll be a ton of people there and…" she gave me a sly look. "There'll be loads of food. Aunt Lydia is a really great cook: turkey with stuffing and cranberry sauce, mashed potatoes, pumpkin pie. I always eat so much that I have to undo the button on my pants at the dinner table. What's not to like?"

My stomach growled appreciatively, and Laney laughed.

"At least part of you agrees. Good, that's decided."

I guess I was going to meet the in-laws.

Laney

I'd arranged to meet Ash right from the theater, and then we were driving out to my Uncle Paul and Aunt Lydia's, an hour outside the city.

Even though most places let people leave early on the Wednesday before Thanksgiving, the rehearsal schedule hadn't stopped, and from what Ash said, the director begrudged everyone their long weekend.

The area near the theater was busy and I'd had to park a few blocks away. People were already getting into a holiday mood, and the shops were as full as the bars with people rushing around for last minute shopping.

Ash had told me the entry code for the artists' entrance at the side of the theater, but I hesitated, feeling awkward encroaching on his work space.

My breath misted in the frigid air as I tried to decide what to do. The alley was a little creepy and that made up my mind.

Just as I started to tap in the number, the door flew open and Sarah breezed out, followed by several of the other dancers.

"Laney! Where the bloody hell have you been hiding?" she yelled at full volume. "I must have asked Ash a gazillion times for you to meet us … oh my God!"

"What?"

Her stunned expression made me check over my shoulder, but no—her wide-eyed stare was pinned to me.

"You're walking!"

"Oh, yeah," I laughed self-consciously. "I only use the chair on bad days. I'm mostly pretty mobile."

She stared, then blinked and seemed to come back to herself.

"Wow! I mean, wow!"

Sarah was still staring when Ash walked out of the theater. His hesitation was brief as he saw us together, but then he wrapped his arms around my waist and pulled me into a kiss that warmed me to the tips of my toes.

I don't think friends kiss with tongues, but I guess he was putting on a good show for his work colleagues.

I could smell mint shower gel that he used at the theater, along with a hint of cigarette smoke that I'd definitely be asking him about later.

"Hello, my wife," he said with a wide grin as I slid down his hard body.

"Hi," I squeaked back.

"God, you guys," Sarah snorted, shaking her head. "Laney, you and I are totally doing drinks next week. Don't blow me off, luv!"

She marched away, waving her hand in the air.

"Is she always like that?"

Ash shrugged. "Yeah. I like her."

"Me, too."

I paused, noticing for the first time that he was dressed in the chinos he'd gotten married in, with his heavy army coat hanging open.

"Ready to meet your in-laws?" I teased.

His eyes crinkled in a smile. "Mothers love me," he said with a wink.

"Have you met many of them?"

He shrugged carelessly.

"All my partners' parents." Then he glanced at me, still smiling. "Dance partners."

"So, you never took a girlfriend home to meet your parents? I mean, your father?"

His face turned grim. "No."

Yep, there I went again—turning his good mood to bad in less than ten seconds.

We were nearly run off the sidewalk by three men who were staggering and reeked of alcohol.

Ash dropped his gym bag and caught me as I teetered. He opened his mouth to yell at them, but something distracted him.

I did the yelling for him. "Hey!"

The men turned and one of them pointed at me laughingly.

"Sorry, shorty. Didn't see ya standing there."

"Jerk," I muttered.

Ash still hadn't said anything, but seemed to be gazing right at them.

"What are you looking at, pretty boy?"

Ash didn't speak, but he didn't stop staring, and I was afraid it would turn into something if we didn't leave. I tugged on his sleeve and whispered his name.

He seemed in a daze, but then he shook his head quickly and picked up his gym bag, ignoring the men.

"Faggot!"

Another of them shouted at Ash, and they all laughed. I felt him stiffen at my side, but he kept walking and didn't turn around.

"What a pussy."

Ash rolled his eyes and muttered something I couldn't hear. I hoped that we were far enough away from them that there wouldn't be any trouble.

But then the leader yelled again.

"Yeah, he can suck my dick!"

I saw the change in Ash instantly: the light went out and a darkness filled him. He dropped the gym bag again and ran toward the men.

They seemed taken aback but were too drunk to move.

I watched in horror as Ash skidded up to the first man and punched him in the face without saying a word. *Bam! Bam! Bam!*

Blood spurted from the man's nose and his arms windmilled as he fell in slow motion.

The yellow street threw weird shadows over the ugly scene. Ash's face seemed demonic as he swung three more times. It all happened so quickly, only the second man tried to hit back, his fist tangling in Ash's coat.

Then two of them were laying on the cold sidewalk, their breath steaming like horses, surprise and pain on their faces.

The third man stared in disbelief, his alcohol soaked brain trying to work out what had just happened.

I was so shocked, I hadn't moved a muscle, but when I saw Ash grab him even though the guy wasn't putting up a fight, punching him over and over again until the man puked and collapsed in his own vomit, I cried out.

"Ash, no!"

I swear I heard the snap of breaking ribs as Ash stamped down hard. Then he hesitated and turned slowly to look at me. Across the street, people were shouting, and I could see two of them on their cell phones, probably calling the police. We had to get out of here or Ash would be spending Thanksgiving in a jail cell. And this time I was certain my dad wouldn't help him.

Ash lowered his foot and seemed to come back to himself. He jogged toward me, scooped up the gym bag and grabbed my hand, tugging me down the street, until we turned the corner and the men were out of sight.

My frozen fingers fumbled as we reached my car, and Ash calmly took the keys from my shaking hand, opened the passenger door and helped me inside.

Then he jumped into the driver's seat and pulled away from the curb, his face tense, his hands gripping the wheel tightly. I'd never seen anything so ... so *vicious* before. Those drunk guys hadn't stood a chance, and I'm not sure Ash would have stopped before he'd done even more serious damage. What the hell had happened? We'd been walking away? What had set him off? I tried to think back, but my mind had gone blank.

"Did you see him?" Ash asked suddenly.

"Yes! I ... my God, Ash! Those men! That was..." *Insane. Horrifying.*

Ash threw me a confused look, then his face settled into a hard mask. "They were assholes."

"Yes, but..."

He sighed out a long breath. "Are you mad at me?"

The hot and cold emotions running through me couldn't be summed up in one word or even one sentence, so I didn't try.

"You have blood on your shirt."

His lips tightened again. "You're mad at me."

"You could have been arrested for assault."

He shook his head. "I can go home—back to the apartment—if you don't want me to be with your nice happy family."

His tone was sarcastic, but there was a vulnerability that made me want to protect him, to make it okay. Which seeing as he'd just taken on three guys—drunken guys I'll grant you, but three guys all the same—he definitely didn't need my protection.

"No, it's over now. Just ... I can't believe ... so ruthless."

We didn't speak again, except for me to give him directions as we left the city and headed south.

It felt a lot like our escape from Vegas. There was the same tension in the air and uncertainty between us as Ash drove into the night. Finally, I remembered the trick that always worked with him: I turned on the radio. We listened to a mournful Country song before Ash hit the button and found a Chicago jazz station.

As we drove south, we passed through the quaint community of Canaryville where I'd grown up. Each street had a memory, with the landscaped yards, sprawling old trees and a cultural life that centered on St. Gabriel's. Mom was going to love the fact that Ash was Catholic. I knew that come Christmas, she'd be dragging us off to Midnight Mass.

As soon as I had the thought, I paused. Ash wasn't my family, no matter what a piece of paper said, and for all I knew, now that he had money, and his passport and green card were on the way, he'd be flying home for Christmas, especially if the show was going to close like he thought.

A sharp ache made me press my fingers to my chest. And it wasn't the cold November night that made me shiver.

But then my phone rang, and my cousin Paddy's name flashed up.

"Hi, Paddy!"

"Hey, kid! You on your way?"

"Yes, another 10 or 15 minutes. Why?"

"Well, don't freak, but Collin's here."

"Collin?"

Ash threw me a questioning look.

"Yeah. He's been drinking…"

"Collin never drinks."

"Well, he is now, Laney, so you'd better get over here. And, um, he's been saying things."

"What sort of things? What's he been saying, Paddy?"

There was a sigh. *"Just get here, Laney,"* and then he hung up.

"That was weird."

"Everything okay?" asked Ash.

"I don't know. Apparently Collin showed up. Oh God, that's going to be awkward! What on earth is he doing at my aunt's place?"

Ash tapped a long finger on the steering wheel.

"He wants you back."

"No, not after how things ended. You *heard* what he said."

Ash didn't answer, and I was left stewing in questions for the next ten minutes.

Just before we arrived at Kankakee, I told him where to turn and we drove down increasingly narrow roads until we stopped outside a large two-story building, with split rail fences and a white porch. It had a southern feel about the place, even though the air was crisp enough to promise snow.

I unclipped my seatbelt but before I could climb out, Ash grabbed my hand.

"Are we okay, Laney?"

I knew what he was asking, but I found it hard to meet his eyes. The sudden violence had shocked me. The fact that he wouldn't stop hitting that man. And it made me wonder how well I really knew Ash. My father's words flashed through my mind.

"Yes," I said slowly. "But please don't do anything like that again."

He shook his head. "I can't promise."

What was going on? Why was his expression so bleak? I wished he'd talk to me, but now wasn't the time.

"Just … fine … but leave Collin to me. In fact, let me do *all* the talking, okay?"

Again, he shook his head.

Hell, this was going to be a messed up Thanksgiving.

I didn't want to be here. To keep myself from going completely crazy, I spent a moment ticking off a list of grim and tragic places where I'd rather be, then ran out of fingers. I wished I could take off my shoes to continue my new hobby.

Ash unloaded the trunk, taking out our luggage and the bags of food that we'd brought with us. I hoped he'd have time to change his shirt before he met my parents.

Squaring my shoulders, I walked up the steps to the front door, but before I could press the bell, the door flew open and a red-faced Collin teetered in front of me.

"There she is," he sneered. "The blushing bride."

Oh no!

A hand came from behind, and I saw Paddy grab a fistful of Collin's shirt and drag him back inside.

I glanced over my shoulder, certain that the shock I saw on Ash's face was reflected in my own. But then my mother and aunt were standing on the doorstep and pulling me into the hallway, smothering me with hugs and questions.

Ash followed more slowly and I heard him drop the bags onto the wooden floor.

"Laney, what is this nonsense?" asked Mom before I'd had a chance to take a breath. "Is it true?"

"Let her through the door, why don't you?" huffed Aunt Lydia. "We're all in the kitchen."

Mom glared and stomped through to the large farmhouse kitchen in the back.

I stared at Ash and he shrugged his shoulders. Then he reached for my hand, and after a short hesitation, I took it.

The air was warm and spicy, the delicious aroma of hot cider and cinnamon filling Aunt Lydia's kitchen. I breathed deeply, letting the familiar scent of childhood soak in.

Dad was already sitting at the heavy wooden table with Uncle Paul, each nursing a glass of beer. Collin slumped down, his threatening smile loose, his eyes hard and hurt and accusing.

"Are you going to deny that you married *him?*"

"Ash is my husband."

Everyone looked stunned, including Ash but he recovered before anyone noticed and smiled proudly, slipping his arm around my shoulders.

"I'm a very lucky man," he said like he meant it.

I sat on the hard chair opposite Collin as my knees gave way, and Ash slid into the seat next to me. As everyone stared, I suddenly felt stifling hot in the room. I loosened a couple of buttons on my coat, wondering if we'd be better off turning around and heading back to Chicago.

Under the table, Ash grabbed my hand again. I threw him a quick look, but he was staring coldly at my ex-boyfriend.

Collin raised a glass and saluted me as beer slopped over the rim.

"To the happy couple!"

Paddy took the glass out of his hands and tipped the beer into the sink.

"You've had enough to drink, buddy."

Collin wasn't drunk enough to argue with Paddy, who was a big guy, like all the men in my family, and worked for the Fire Department.

"Laney?" My mom's eyes were wide as she stared at me.

"Um, well…" I cleared my throat nervously, feeling as if I was 13 years old, not a few months from thirty.

Collin laughed loudly. "He married her for a green card. Why else?"

My face flushed red.

Ash's hand tightened over mine and he looked questioningly, waiting for me to answer. But I had nothing. I'd told him I'd do the talking, but I just couldn't find the words.

Ash raised my hand to his lips and placed a soft kiss across the knuckles.

"Laney is my sunshine," he said simply, then he smiled his breathtaking smile.

I was willing to bet that smile had won over most of the women in the room, but not Dad. Of course.

"Laney, what the hell were you thinking? Immigration fraud is serious."

Ash's hand tightened compulsively and my mouth dried as I stared at my father's disappointed face.

"I…"

The words still wouldn't come.

"I know you don't want me for a son-in-law," Ash broke in, his face hard, "but I care about Laney and I will always protect her."

Dad's glare was furious, the cop gone, the angry father very present. His gaze flickered, then he looked away, his expression defeated.

"I should have guessed," he muttered.

"When … how long … are you really married?" asked Mom, still looking stunned and hurt.

I nodded.

"Father Patrick didn't say a word!"

"We had a civil ceremony, Mom."

She shook her head and pressed her lips together.

"When?" Dad echoed.

I licked my lips and glanced at Collin. "Three weeks ago."

The pain on his face was awful.

"Three weeks ago? *Two* weeks ago I was asking you to marry *me!* You didn't say anything! Why? Why?!"

"I'm sorry."

God, that sounded so inadequate.

"Were you fucking him all this time?"

The room exploded. Ash's chair crashed to the floor as he rounded the table to get to Collin. Paddy was there first, hauling Collin up by his collar, which tore free with a loud ripping sound. Collin bounced back against the table, sending glasses and plates flying. Aunt Lydia screamed and Dad was shouting, the room in uproar. Paddy's brothers Stephen and Eric were pulling Ash's arms behind his back as he bucked and fought them, shouting in his own language, words that sounded like curses. Uncle Donald ran into the kitchen to help Dad and Uncle Paul manhandle Collin from the room, although he wasn't putting up much of a fight.

Ash was still swearing up a storm as Collin was dragged away.

"Ash, no!"

For the second time this evening, I was trying to talk Ash down. The rage in his eyes still glowed, but I could see him slowly regain control. He wrenched his arms free and stalked out of the room.

Paddy grinned at me. "That went well."

"Shut up."

"Seriously, Laney. You're married to that guy?"

"Seriously—yes."

Paddy shrugged. "At least you didn't marry the prick."

"Why does everyone call him that? Collin is *not* a prick. He's just…"

"A prick," said Stephen and Eric together.

I sighed. "He's hurt and angry. I can't blame him."

"Did he really ask you to marry him?"

"Yes, he did. Oh God, I'm such a horrible person!"

Paddy slung his arm around my shoulders.

"Nah, you're not so bad. Sure made the party start with a bang though. Well, come on. I want to meet the man who finally put a ring on it."

"You make me sound like an old maid."

Paddy winked at me. "If the ring fits."

I gave him a different finger, but he just laughed.

Ash was sitting on the front porch, staring up at the stars as cigarette smoke hung in lazy swirls around him.

"Laylay, I'm so sorry…"

But when he saw my cousins flanking me, his words dried and he stood abruptly, grinding the cigarette butt under his boot, his stance defensive.

"Welcome to the family," smiled Paddy, slapping Ash on the shoulder. "That's quite a temper you've got on you. Any Irish blood in there?"

Ash shook his head, his eyes darting to mine.

I poked Paddy in the arm and made the introductions as we all trooped back into the house.

"Well," said Aunt Lydia, venturing out to the hallway again, "Collin is sleeping it off in the other guestroom, so … since you're a married couple, this way."

She led us to one of the smaller bedrooms.

"Sorry, Laney," she said apologetically as we squeezed in, eyeing the narrow twin bed. "I thought you'd be in here by yourself. I was going to put Ash in the guestroom, but…"

"That's fine, Aunt Lydia," I said weakly.

"I'll leave you to get settled in," she said, glancing at Ash. "And then I think we'd all like to meet your new husband properly."

She closed the door behind her and I collapsed onto the bed.

"This is a total nightmare," I groaned.

I felt the small mattress dip as Ash sat next to me.

"Maybe it's better this way."

I sat up and glared at him. "How on earth is it better?"

"We don't have to lie anymore."

"Are you kidding me? Of *course* we'll have to lie. You don't know my family! The questions will be endless. Mom will be pushing for a church blessing, and we'll be everyone's favorite topic of conversation for the next decade!"

Ash shrugged. "They'll soon forget about it."

My eyes bulged.

"Two years from now we'll be divorced, right? Old news."

He looked away as I studied him.

"Right."

He gave a humorless laugh and sat with his back toward me.

I unbuttoned my coat and tossed it onto the tiny bed.

"I'm going to go downstairs and … I don't know … try and calm things down. Just be prepared for a *lot* of questions." I reached down to touch his cheek. "I'm sorry about this."

He surprised me by leaning into my hand, his eyes closed.

"I should be apologizing to you. I do, Laney. I'm sorry … for everything."

I sighed, feeling the soft prickle of five o'clock shadow against my palm. Then the moment passed and he pulled away.

As I turned to walk out of the room, I paused by the door.

"Don't forget to change your shirt."

Ash glanced at the blood spattered across the white cotton and nodded.

CHAPTER 15

Ash

I couldn't believe how badly that had gone.

Parents usually liked me once they met me: mothers loved that I danced, and fathers appreciated that I worked in construction—steady job, macho bullshit. Laney's family must have hated me for putting her in danger before they even met me. God knows what they thought now. The prick was going to have some questions to answer when he sobered up.

But that wasn't what bothered me the most. Twice tonight, I'd completely lost it. I used to be a nice guy. I was competitive, I wanted to win, but I'd never been violent. But all that had changed. I'd wanted to hurt those men in the street, really hurt them. End them.

I stared at my swollen knuckles, rubbing at a smear of blood. Christ, I nearly killed that one guy. If Laney hadn't stopped me, I could have.

When he told me to suck his dick, I'd heard Sergei's voice, seen Sergei's face, and I couldn't stop hitting him. In my mind, I was hitting Sergei—seeing his leering face as he pointed a gun at me, as he jerked off, as he fucked my mouth. I wanted to puke.

I tore off my coat and strode down the hallway until I found a small bathroom. I retched into the toilet, nearly turning my stomach inside out. I'd probably never stop feeling like that when I thought about the evil bastard still walking, still stealing air, ruining lives.

Wiping my face with my sleeve, I pulled my shirt over my head and used it as a towel. There had been a guest towel in our bedroom but I couldn't be bothered to go back for it.

I looked around, giving my stomach time to stop trying to climb up my throat.

The bathroom was nice, homey, with an old fashioned claw-foot tub and pine cabinets. I didn't belong here.

When I walked back out, a kid of 13 or 14 was waiting outside, leaning against the wall and playing on his phone.

He didn't speak as he sidled past me into the bathroom, and in return I just nodded at him. But then he called after me.

"Dude! What happened to your back?"

I hung my shirt over my shoulder, covering up some of the scars.

"Accident."

"Woah! That's totally messed up. Cool!" He paused, squinting at me. "Kind of looks like you got stabbed like a hundred times."

"Something like that."

He nodded sagely. "Awesome. You're Aunt Laney's husband. Everyone's talking about you."

He closed the door and I heard the lock click.

"Awesome," I agreed.

I found my way back to the tiny bedroom and pulled a clean t-shirt out of my gym bag. I only had one more button-up shirt to wear and I was saving that for tomorrow. Then I saw beer stains on my chinos, probably from the prick flailing around.

I changed into my jeans then went back to the empty bathroom to try and scrub the stain off of my pants. It reminded me of being away for the competition circuit and staying in cheap hotels—you managed with very little.

Taking a deep breath, I headed back down the stairs: showtime.

The house was crammed with people. It was hard to find Laney over the heads of all the tall red-haired men who were obviously related to her dad. It wasn't just the hair that gave them away, but the way they watched me as if I was a suspect. Laney had said they were in the Fire Department, but they looked like cops to me. I wondered how much they'd been told— Christ, maybe they all knew everything.

I finally found Laney in a room next to the kitchen. She was chopping vegetables, but it looked more like an interrogation as the women sitting with her questioned her about me. I rested my hands on her shoulders and kissed the top of her head. It was more than just for show; it was an apology, too.

"*Moj sonček*," I whispered as she smiled up at me.

"Are you ever going to tell me what that means?"

"No."

I realized that the room had gone silent and everyone was staring at us. Laney gave me a conspiratorial smile, then returned to chopping vegetables.

The kid I'd met earlier got yelled at for trying to steal one of the freshly-baked cookies. If I thought I could have gotten away with it, I'd have done the same.

"I'm bored," the kid complained. "No one wants to play *Black Ops III*."

"Nolan, no one wants to play those horrible games. Go watch TV or something."

"I'll play you."

Laney gave me a look.

"What?"

"I just didn't know you liked that nerdy stuff."

Nolan huffed. "It's not nerdy! It's cool."

I winked at her and stood up straight to follow the boy, who was staring at the cookies again.

Laney took pity on him, handing us two each and waving away the irritated huffing of the other women.

"Go shoot stuff," she laughed.

For a moment, my thoughts darkened. If I'd had a gun around Sergei…

Her mom stopped me as I took my first bite of cookie.

"Laney tells us you're a dancer, Ash."

I chewed and swallowed quickly. "Yeah. Yes, ma'am."

"I imagine that's not a very secure profession."

"No, ma'am."

"So how do you propose to support my daughter?"

"Mom!" Laney snapped. "I support myself. I always have."

"Good Heavens, Laney! There's no need to bite my head off! I'm just trying to get to know your new husband."

"You can ask me anything, Mrs. Hennessey."

"No you can't, Mom," Laney said flatly.

There was an uncomfortable silence, then I followed Nolan out of the room.

Laney

"He plays video games? How old is he?" Aunt Lydia asked, raising her eyebrows.

"Lots of people like those, but since you asked, he's 23."

"He looks younger."

Sometimes he did, especially when he was freshly shaved, but his eyes were old. They'd seen too much and experienced all the wrong things.

"Laney looks younger than her age, too," my sister Bernice said with a wink. "And I've gotta say, that's a fine-looking man. Nice going, sis."

"Really, Bernie! This isn't a laughing matter," Mom complained. Then she turned her attention back to me. "And what about his family? I presume he does have a family? What do they think of this secret marriage? Or maybe you told *them*."

Mom was being very waspish. She was hurt, I knew that, so I bit my tongue and tried to answer calmly and comprehensively.

"His mother died when he was 15 and he's not close to his father. Ash left home when he was 18 and has supported himself working in construction."

"Well, I suppose that's something," Mom huffed, not very sincerely.

"But his passion is dancing. He's a champion in his own country, but wanted to broaden his horizons."

"And he got mixed up in all that unpleasant business in Las Vegas," Mom added. "Some people just attract trouble."

I slammed down my knife and stood abruptly.

"Since he's been in this country, he's been victimized and abused. I'd hoped that my own family would treat *my husband* better."

And I stormed out of the kitchen.

As a rule, I wasn't someone who stormed out of places, but Mom was dig, dig, digging, trying to get under my skin. Well, she succeeded, and I wasn't going to have her do the same to Ash.

My uncles and cousins were all crammed into the family room watching an action movie with my dad. Kids were running around the house, high on sugar and excitement. I helped Lottie braid her hair, and broke up a fight between James and Kevin. A series of gunshots and explosions eventually drew me to Uncle Paul's study where I found Ash sitting with Nolan, frowning in concentration. I stood and watched for a while before Ash glanced up and saw me.

"Everything okay, Laney?"

That made me laugh. "Of course. What could possibly be wrong?"

His lips twisted in a wry smile, but it was Nolan who answered.

"Granddad and Grandma are mad because they think he married you to stay in Chicago. Uncle Paddy says it's no one's business, and Aunt Carmen says that you should have married Collin. But I don't like him—he never talks to me. I wish I'd seen you fight him. Trisha and Amelia said he's cute, but they're totally lame."

Nolan's verbal vomit left Ash looking bemused. Nolan was on the autism spectrum and didn't always pick up on social cues. But at least now we knew what everyone was thinking.

"Okaaaay then," I smiled. "Ash, I'm going to lie down for a bit. Come find me when you're finished."

He nodded as something exploded on the screen and I left him to it.

I'd hoped to escape everyone, but I'd barely sat on the bed in the guestroom when Mom knocked and walked in immediately after.

"Mom, I…"

"You will listen to me, Laney Kathleen Hennessey!"

"Why?" I said sharply. "You've already made up your mind, so why should I listen to you?"

She only hesitated for a second. "Because I'm your mother."

"And Ash is my husband, so be *very* careful what you say."

Her eyes widened, then she did pause. "Do you love this boy?" she asked quietly.

"He's not a boy." I closed my eyes and breathed deeply. "He's amazing, Mom, if you could just give him a chance. He's kind and sweet, really funny. He works hard and he's so talented. I'm really proud of him."

She sat on the bed next to me and wrapped her arm around my shoulders.

"Do you love him?"

Ash had come into my world through rage and violence, but every time I saw him, I smiled; when he walked into a room, he lit it up. The way he'd kissed me, twice, my skin sizzled under his touch.

But I couldn't lie to my mom. I tried to find the right words and swallowed nervously.

Mom studied my face, then kissed me on the cheek.

"That's all I needed to know."

What?

After she'd gone, I lay on the bed, replaying our conversation, wondering what she meant. What had she seen in my face that had made her smile like that?

I woke when the door opened and light from the hallway streamed into the bedroom.

"Laylay?"

"I'm awake," I coughed, my voice hoarse.

Ash sat on the bed, his thigh pressed against my back, his hand rubbing my shoulder gently.

"They're getting ready to eat."

"Already?"

I glanced at my watch, surprised to see that I'd napped for over an hour.

"Oh, wow, I didn't mean to sleep for so long. I'm sorry I left you alone. Was it okay?"

He laughed quietly.

"Your family is nice. They're not monsters, Laney. I'm fine."

"I know, but they can be full on sometimes."

We walked down the stairs together and at the bottom Ash took my hand and kissed it. I glanced around expecting to see someone watching us, but it was just us.

My bewildered heart gave a happy jolt and I threw him a questioning look, but the only answer was a slight curve to his full lips. I wanted to ask him what it meant. Everyone was being so confusing this evening.

But voices were calling us, and we headed into the lion's den.

It wasn't as bad as I'd thought. I guess my earlier hissy fit had gotten the desired result. Either that or Mom had laid down the law. Everyone was friendly, although Dad was still throwing loaded glances at Ash.

But they stared. They kept on staring at Ash, stealing furtive glances, as if he was a flamingo who'd accidentally landed on a duck pond, foreign, fascinating, but in the wrong place.

He looked so different from the men in my family, darker, more exotic. His accent had a strange slur to it so the words rolled into each other, especially when he talked quickly.

But they were trying. We were all trying.

I was surprised when Eric and Ash struck up a conversation about soccer, and Ash revealed that he was a supporter of the Spanish team Barcelona. I asked if there were any famous soccer teams in Slovenia, but he and Eric laughed at my ignorance, so I butted out. Ash was doing fine without me.

I started to relax for the first time since Collin had opened his big mouth. I think I knew how he'd found out: one of his college friends worked at the clerk's office where we were married. I didn't know they were close friends, but I suppose the circumstances were unusual enough for Andy to get in touch with Collin. Not that it made a difference now.

Ash was right about one thing: it was more of a relief than I'd expected now that my family knew. I watched him talking with animation, energy pouring from him; so different from the angry, volatile man he'd been earlier. It reminded me that I didn't know him, *my husband*, that well. I had time to find out—except that our marriage had a two-year expiration date.

After more food and more drink, Ash's cheeks were flushed and his eyes bright. He grinned at me, leaning in to kiss my neck. And despite the warmth of the crowded kitchen, a small shiver raced under my skin.

How good of an actor was he? It felt real, but was it?

Then from the living room, the sound of cèilidh music floated into the kitchen.

"Come on," Paddy laughed. "Let's show Ash some real dancing!"

My family was so Irish it was almost cliché: music, dancing, Guinness. I really thought I must be a throwback because I was the only person in my family who hadn't inherited the tall, red-haired genes; the only one who couldn't dance or carry a tune; and I never drank Guinness.

Ash followed the stampede next door, then suddenly realized I wasn't with him, turned back and pulled me up from the table.

"Come!"

"Ash, no!" I wailed. "Everyone knows I can't dance!"

"Yes, you can," he laughed happily.

He dragged me into the living room, ignoring the smirks. My whole family knew I was hopeless—totally rhythm-proof. But Ash simply lifted me up and whirled me around so my feet didn't even touch the floor. I locked my arms around his neck, laughing at his mischievous smile as we danced around the room, my feet swinging somewhere around his shins.

We were dancing, together, our rhythm matching perfectly, because I was moving to *his* rhythm. His strong arms were wrapped around my waist, and my cheek rested softly against his. With Ash, I could dance.

We spent the rest of the evening with my family, and it felt good. I could see the questions in their eyes, but they let us just ... be.

It was only slightly awkward when we went to bed. After all, it wasn't the first time Ash and I had shared a bed, only this one didn't leave much space between us. I was hanging onto the edge, trying not to fall off, but however I angled myself, some part of me was touching Ash. In the end, after several minutes of both of us failing to get comfortable, he grunted with frustration, rolled me onto my side, and wound his long body behind me, so his chest was pressed against my back.

"Sleep," he said, his warm breath blowing across the back of my neck.

I jerked awake as Ash's elbow crashed into my ribs and he cried out. Then some garbled words in a long moan as his body thrashed around.

I struggled to free myself from his arms and roll over, but when I did, I saw that his eyes were tightly shut and a thin layer of sweat made his skin glisten in the scattered moonlight.

"Ash, wake up!"

He yelled again, then sat bolt upright, his eyes wild, panic turning them into black pools.

He reacted suddenly, but it wasn't what I expected.

His lips crashed down on mine with bruising force and I gasped as his heavy body pressed me into the mattress. Shocked, I pushed hard on his shoulders, but he lifted only slightly, moving his mouth to my neck, his hands tightly gripping my waist.

"Laney," he muttered hoarsely. "My wife."

Was it a statement, a question, an invitation? I couldn't tell, but I did hear the need in his voice, and as one hand brushed against my hip and squeezed hard, my body leapt.

This was weeks of pretending I didn't want him. This was two months of ignoring our mutual attraction. This was the man who had crashed into my life and painted it with color.

This was the missing piece.

"Ash, I want..."

"Laney, I need..."

We spoke at the same time, but his mouth slid to my throat, to my breastbone, and whatever words he was going to say were lost. Then his teeth bit through the material of my pajamas, fastening around the hard nipple, and I gasped.

He knelt up, ripping his sweat soaked t-shirt from his body while my hungry hands pushed the waistband of his shorts over his hips and the curve of his ass. He kicked them off impatiently and his whole long, lean body was revealed briefly, his thighs solid, his cock rigid. He braced himself over me, then his head dipped and he dragged my shirt up with his teeth and ripped my pajama pants from my legs with one hand.

A second later he was inside me, my body barely prepared.

I cried out as he pushed my knees up, sinking deeper, and this time a zing of pleasure ran up my spine, then settled low in my belly.

Ash's eyes were closed, his forehead lined with a deep frown, his dark head bent.

Then he buried his face in my neck, pumping so hard the bed shook and creaked. I was right: he fucked like he danced—intense and full of passion, utterly focused.

I felt wanted, needed, all woman, desirable and desired.

It was so sudden and furious, so urgent, answering a craving I hadn't acknowledged, so surprising, so shocking, so intoxicating. One hit and I was hooked.

I hung onto his shoulders as he pounded into me, trying to lock my legs around his waist, but the chaotic, thrusting force of his dick ramming into me shook me loose. All I could do was hold him against me.

Sweat slicked our chests together, my breasts flattened almost painfully.

He came suddenly with a growl and I felt the pulse of hot cum inside me, making me cry out.

"Ash!"

Hearing my voice, he froze, then lifted his head slowly, a sort of wide-eyed wonder on his face.

"Laney?"

He stared at me, shock and disbelief clear on his beautiful face. I gasped, my clit shooting bolts of pleasure through my body.

"I was dreaming," he whispered. "I thought I was dreaming."

"Feels real to me," I whispered, loosening my fierce grip on his shoulders.

He pulled out abruptly, making me wince, and as his cum leaked out of me, the level of embarrassment for both of us was painful.

He swung his long legs so he was sitting on the edge of the bed, his head in his hands.

"God, I'm so sorry, Laylay," he said, his body trembling. "*Moj sonček*, I'm so sorry."

I didn't know how to respond. My body was warm and satiated, but my mind was traveling a million miles an hour.

"I ... um ... I'd better go clean up," I muttered.

I grabbed my robe from the floor and hurried to the bathroom, feeling moist and uncomfortable as semen continued to trickle down my thighs.

I cleaned up quickly then took a deep breath, trying to process what had happened, or rather, what it meant for me, for Ash, for us.

He so obviously regretted what had happened. I ought to—God, he hadn't even known it was me, had he? But somehow, I couldn't regret it. I wanted him. From the first time I'd seen him, the attraction had been intense, but so much had come between us. Life had been cruel.

When I opened the bedroom door, he looked up. He was in the same position, still sitting on the edge of the bed.

"I hurt you."

His sharp cheekbones threw shadows across his face, and his eyes were clouded.

"I was surprised," I said quietly, sitting next to him.

He searched my face for any trace of a lie, or pain, or fear, but seemed satisfied as I watched him steadily.

"I'm sorry," he said softly, his eyes dropping to his empty hands.

"For what?"

His gaze shot up to meet mine, questions in his dark eyes.

"I think I went a little crazy," he said, his words bumping together as his body worked through a long shudder.

"I think we both did," I said, taking one of his hands in mine.

Our fingers wove together and he studied our joined hands before speaking again.

"You're really okay?"

"Ash, if you buy me daisies instead of tulips, I will lie and say I love them; if you eat the last cookie and leave the jar empty, I'll lie and say I wasn't hungry; if you wear socks with sandals, I'll lie and say I don't care—but I promise, I'm not lying about this."

I leaned forward and kissed his bare shoulder, his skin cool and satin smooth.

"You're cold. Come back to bed."

He sighed and his shoulders lifted a little as if a great weight had been released.

He was still naked, but unembarrassed by his body. Unlike me. Despite what we'd just done, I slipped my pajamas back on before sliding into bed.

He pulled me against him immediately, shivering only slightly when our legs tangled and my cold feet pressed against his calves.

He shifted, his body tense.

"Laney," he said, his voice still uncertain. "I didn't use a condom."

"It's fine," I said calmly. "I have an IUD. I can't get pregnant."

There was a long pause, the night drawing out the moment.

Then his arms tightened around me again. "Laney, I…"

I stroked his strong forearms as they held me.

"No, not now. In the daylight—that's when we'll work things out. Now, in the darkness, we'll just hold each other. Tonight, let's believe the fairytale."

His arms relaxed a fraction and I felt his soft lips in my hair.

All the worries, all the fears were silenced within that deep quiet of my aunt's bedroom, one cold Chicago night.

Light was filtering through the thin curtains when I woke up. I was immediately aware of the large solid body behind me, not least because Ash was holding my boob and his erection was pressing into my ass.

What had happened last night, now, in the daylight, it felt awkward.

I was about to try and slide out of the bed without waking him, when Ash's long fingers flexed as he swam toward wakefulness, squeezing my breast gently. I gasped, and he stroked my hard nipple, moving his hips in a rocking motion.

I turned in his arms, and for a moment his eyelids drooped and he let out a long sigh. He looked up again, watching me carefully as his fingers slid under my shirt, stroking the soft skin between my small breasts, then closing his hand over the warm flesh.

A sigh of pleasure turned into a moan of arousal and that sparked a fire in Ash.

"Last night was too fast," he murmured, his voice husky in my ear. "I want to make love to my wife."

Ash

I'd never used a woman the way I'd used Laney last night, and I was ashamed. It had just been fucking, proving to myself that I wasn't what the bastard had tried to make me. I was no one's bitch. I'd rather die. And I mean that in the literal put-a-gun-to-my-head-and-pull-the-fucking-trigger way.

But even in my half-waking, half-dreaming state, it wasn't the violent crash of urgent, thoughtless physical release that I'd had with Yveta: it was more. I just wasn't sure why or how much more. It didn't make sense, but it did. We weren't a match, but we were. We weren't in love, but we were married.

I respected her, admired her, and she deserved more than heated rutting at the dark end of a nightmare. And if all I had to give her was a warm body with a frozen heart, then I'd make it the best I could.

I kissed down her shoulder and arm, turning her so she was on her back, staring up at me. Surprise became desire, turning her eyes smoky, and she took my hand and pressed it between her legs. Her gray eyes held mine as my hand slipped from the waistband of her pajamas. My fingers met the soft cotton between her thighs, already damp.

"Please," she whispered, her voice soft and aching.

"Beautiful wife, what do you like?" I asked, kissing down her neck as her back arched, pressing her covered breasts against my bare chest.

I paused, meeting her eyes, seeing a faint flush of embarrassment.

She laughed awkwardly. "Just the usual stuff, you know?"

"Hmm, well, this morning I will make your body our playground, yes? Stop me if there's something you don't like." I was serious for a moment. "I don't have anything. All I have is my body. I like fucking. I'm good at it. Last night wasn't … I want to make you feel good."

And it's all I have to offer. Because sex makes you feel alive. Because you're so fucking sexy and you don't even know it, because you're stunning, so brave, and because I know we'll be amazing together.

"This is for you, Laney."

"I liked the massage you gave me," she said, smiling up at me, her cheeks pink.

"But that sent you to sleep," I argued, puzzled.

"Not before it turned me on," she grinned with a glint in her eye.

I remembered how that night had ended, with her watching me jerk off.

Smiling, I undressed her slowly—far too many clothes for what I wanted to do. Then I rolled her onto her stomach, pouring her favorite body lotion onto my hands, warming it before I placed a dot on every freckle across her back.

"What are you doing?" she asked, trying to see over her shoulder.

"Playing," I answered. "Joining the dots. I wonder what picture this will make. Hmm, looks like a sexy woman."

She gave a husky laugh that made my cock twitch. Greedy bastard would have to wait—this was about Laney.

Although, childish as it sounds, I couldn't resist using the warmed lotion to write *Mrs. Novak* across her back. Then I started at her shoulders, smoothing out the tight muscles as she moaned and groaned. My dick was making it hard to concentrate, a third guest at the party, rubbing down her spine, dragging through the lotion as I worked her muscles.

I took the easy way out and headed down to her feet, pressing my thumbs into her soles. But even there, the noises she made, the warm scent of her skin, it was driving me to a new level of madness. I glanced down at my dick, unsurprised to see the head leaking. I closed my eyes, trying to ignore the way my balls were tightening and begging for release.

My thumbs dug into the back of her calves. She moaned again and my dick jerked in sympathy.

Her pert little ass made me lose it. Those two soft globes were more than a flesh and blood man could stand.

I pulled her hips upward, forgetting to warn her, so she face-planted in her pillow. Her muffled words barely made me pause as I pushed the tip of my pinkie finger into her little puckered hole.

"I don't do that!" she snorted, her cheeks flaming as she pulled the pillow from her face and glared at me.

I slid my finger in and out slowly, raising an eyebrow as her mouth dropped open and a soft "Oh!" rounded her lips.

"Just playing, my wife," I said, leaning forward to kiss the back of her neck.

I couldn't help wanting to say that again: *my wife*. The words intrigued me, like a new toy that came without instructions.

"Well, *my husband*," she said, a hint of steel in her voice, "you're not getting anal: exit only! We clear?"

I laughed, easing my finger in a little deeper while circling her clit at the same time.

My husband—even more intriguing.

"Very clear, my love. I'm just playing. Doesn't that feel good?"

"Yes, very," she sighed. "But, I'm not..."

I slid my index finger into her wet pussy and her words faded away. Her back arched and she shook her honey-colored hair over her shoulders, pushing her ass against my hand so my finger sunk in further.

I could smell the musk in the air as her arousal, my arousal raised the temperature in the chilled room.

There was so much more I wanted to do, to please her, pleasure her.

I slid flat on the bed and tongued her from behind. A sharp gasp outlined her surprise, and I tasted her sweet little pussy for the first time, dipping my tongue inside, circling her clit.

She surprised us both by coming immediately, her small body shaking, eyes squeezed tightly shut.

She collapsed onto her stomach, breathing heavily, then she giggled—such a beautiful sound.

"That was ... unexpected!"

I stretched out next to her, pulling her heated body against mine, and letting my lips drift up behind her ear.

Even though my cock had been stiff for the last 30 minutes, I was content to rest next to her, pulling the quilt over our cooling bodies.

I was almost asleep when I felt her warm, wet lips close over the head of my cock.

"No!"

I pushed her shoulders roughly, knocking her backward.

From peaceful bliss, I was suddenly back in that Las Vegas bathroom,

Sergei on his knees trying to arouse my flaccid dick, Oleg gripping my arms.

I pushed away the darkness, pulling myself toward the light—and turned to see Laney's frightened face.

"Laylay, I…"

Horror, the horror at what I'd done, nearly done, what had been done to me—I retched. Laney shot out of bed, managing to grab a small trashcan just in time. I gripped the cold metal and emptied my stomach. Again and again.

I was only vaguely aware that she'd left the room, but then I felt a cool washcloth against my feverish forehead, my cheeks, my mouth.

"It's okay," she whispered. "I'm sorry. I'm so sorry."

I tried to shake my head because she had nothing to be sorry for. It was all me—I was the fucked up one. Not her. Never her.

I lay back on the bed, exhausted and depressed. I'd just wanted to please her, to feel normal, and now everything was a thousand times worse.

But she didn't leave in silent disgust as I expected. Instead, she pulled the quilt over both of us, resting her head on my arm and gently stroking my chest.

"No, it's my fault," she said quietly. "I should have known better than to take you by surprise. I *do* know better—it won't happen again, Ash."

I sunk further into the black cloud that always hovered nearby. A man should be able to have a beautiful woman give him head without freaking out. I threw my arm over my face, humiliated again.

The torture in my mind was far worse than the physical pain had been. My armor was gone, my nerve endings exposed, skin raw.

I felt Laney's soft fingers tugging at my wrist.

"I know what you're doing," she said. "You're beating yourself up about this. Don't. We just have to work on our communication." She paused. "Now that we're married."

I let her tug my arm to my side and saw her smiling at me carefully.

I couldn't summon up the energy to smile back. Instead, I closed my eyes, letting the frustration wash over me.

"Why are you doing this, Laney? Since you met me, everything has gone wrong for you."

She paused, perhaps thinking, turning it over like a stone as she looked for the truth.

"No, it's just life," she said simply. "And having you in my life—it makes it better. I know that's not part of the plan, but I can't help it."

The plan. The great plan. Married for a piece of paper, living together for convenience. God, I was a fool.

I sighed, caught by the great lie.

"My body knew I wanted you before my brain did. I was numb for so long—you've brought me back to life. You've saved me over and over."

She smiled.

"We've done everything backward: we met, we married, we had sex. That's our story, Ash. I've given up trying to understand it."

She kissed my chest, her lips soft and warm, and my shameful body reacted again. And this time I had to have her. That's when any semblance of gentleness, of finesse, fled.

Our eyes locked and then she launched herself at me, kissing me hard.

For a half a second I was too stunned to react. And then I did.

I'd thought about kissing her every hour of every day since our wedding nearly three weeks ago. That was a fucking hot kiss, I'd felt the passion inside her, but I didn't think she really wanted me. I'd seen her looking, but that's all she'd ever done. And after rehearsals the other day, with the excuse that Sarah and the girls were watching, I'd done what I'd been wanting to ever since; taken what I'd needed.

Even as her nails dug into my scalp and my dick hardened, I kept thinking, *This is my wife! I'm kissing my wife!*

It was hard, but not fast. It was intense, but not fevered. It was my balls slapping against her ass as she clung to my body, her legs clamped to my waist. It was me inside her, and her all around me.

And when we came, it felt like it meant something.

We lay on our backs breathing hard, her chest pink from arousal, her neck and chin red from my stubble.

Then she turned on her side to look at me.

"Ash," she said softly, stroking her fingers down my chest.

I knew she could feel my heart pounding, and not from the sex we'd just shared. She'd caught me off guard, and she knew it.

"It's okay. You're safe." She paused. "Can you tell me what you were dreaming about last night ... and earlier?"

I threw her a dark look, refusing to give in.

"Why do you want to know?"

"Because I want to know you—everything about you—good and bad."

I shook my head. "No."

"Why not?"

I sighed and stared at the ceiling, hoping that the right words would magically appear. I glanced across, meeting her eyes.

"You'll look at me differently."

"I won't," she said softly.

"You will. Of course you will. You should. I don't like to think about it—ever. I don't want you to have that shit inside your head."

I sprang to my feet and started pacing up and down in the tiny space, feeling caged.

That was how I coped when I was upset or angry—my body needed movement. But showing her how twisted up inside I really was ... she looked like I was breaking her heart.

"Hey," she called quietly, holding out her hand to me.

I halted my pacing and turned to stare at her, hoping she wouldn't see the dark despair, the grief, the disgust.

I took her hand, holding it gently within my own. Her finger joints were a little inflamed today and her skin felt hot to the touch. Despite the sex we'd had earlier, I felt the need to handle her as if she was delicate, precious ... and when I looked at her, I wanted her to see that she was beautiful and desirable.

Her face flushed.

"You are the strongest person I've ever met," she said, staring into my eyes. "You are," she continued as I shook my head. "You've survived so much and you never stopped fighting." She sat up straighter. "Whatever you did, it was because you had to."

I couldn't look at her.

And I turned away, ashamed.

Slowly, she brought her hand to my cheek, bringing my face toward hers, willing me to see in her eyes the trust she felt.

It was a moment suspended in time.

I was surprised when she ducked down and scrabbled under the bed, looking for something. Then she placed a small jewelry box on the quilt next to me.

"Happy Thanksgiving," she said softly.

"Oh, shit. You swap presents at Thanksgiving? I'm sorry, I didn't know."

"Not usually, but ... well, you bought me my ring so I thought, well, I hope you like it."

I opened the box and stared down at the silver St. Christopher, similar to the one I'd lost.

"Patron saint of travelers," she said, lifting it from the box and fastening it around my neck. "And you've traveled so far, Ash."

I didn't have the words, so I kissed her, showing her with my hands and with my body how much that meant to me.

My hands cupped her cheeks then slid to her neck, her pulse trembling under my fingers. I let my hands move down to her shoulders, arms, waist, hips, tugging her against my new erection.

She laughed softly against my skin, her lips warm on my chest, gently pushing me away, pink, breathless.

Reluctantly, I lay back and she began tracing her fingers around my tattoos.

"You never did tell me what all these meant. What does this say?"

I didn't need to look at the one she was talking about.

"It's Serbo-Croat, written in Cyrillic. My grandfather was Serbian. It says 'born to dance'."

She laughed softly.

"Of course it does. When did you get it?"

"I was 16. It was my first—and illegal if you're under 18. But Mom had died a few months before and I'd been bugging the guy at the tattoo shop to do it for me. When he saw I wasn't going away, he gave in."

She nodded her understanding and let her fingers drift over my shoulder and the rest of the ink.

"And your dad hated it."

"Yes."

She hesitated over the next question.

"Have you spoken to him since … since everything?"

I shook my head.

"No, and I'm not going to."

She frowned. "But family is important."

"My mama was important. I don't give a shit about him."

"Why? What did he do?"

I sighed. "I hate talking about him."

"Ash, after everything we've been through, you can't tell me?"

She sounded hurt.

"It's not that."

"Then what?"

"He's just an asshole. He never wanted me around. My parents married six months before I was born."

"Oh."

"Yeah. He made it obvious that I was a mistake. I have no memories of him smiling or laughing with us. When he was out with his friends, yes, but not with us. I don't think he wanted to be a father."

"And your dancing?"

"It was Mama's idea. She loved to dance, so she sent me to classes when I was small. My father was angry when he learned what she'd done. He thought I'd grow out of it." I gave Laney a small smile. "He's still waiting."

"Surely he was proud when you did so well in competitions?"

"No, it was embarrassing to him when my name was in the newspaper. His friends told him I was gay. It was just another reason for him to hate me. It wasn't too bad when Mama was alive, but after…"

I stretched back on the bed and closed my eyes, smiling as I felt Laney's soft kiss on my bare chest.

"He thought he could make me stop and he sent me to work for his construction business. 'You live in this house and eat my food', that's what he said. When I couldn't stand it anymore, I moved out."

Laney's fingers stroked across my stomach.

"It's his loss," she said softly.

But by now, I could hear the sounds of voices and knew that everyone was awake. That meant our moment in this cocoon of feeling was over.

Laney knew it too and sat up.

"You can tell me about the rest another time," she smiled. "Right now, I'll check if the shower is empty. I'd say come with me, but Aunt Lydia's guest bathroom is too small, unfortunately."

She grinned at me and padded out of the room.

My head swam with new thoughts.

The urgent, necessary drive of the night before and just now. This, with Laney, had left me a different man since I walked into our borrowed bedroom.

I was 23 and I'd lived three lifetimes: the time before, Las Vegas, and then my life beginning again with Laney. Each one had sculpted me, and each one had changed me.

I just wasn't sure it was for the better.

Laney

Each new piece of the jigsaw was building a clearer picture.

Whatever had happened to Ash in Las Vegas was more than I knew. But with what I saw, I'd have to guess at sexual assault alongside the beating, although he'd denied being raped. Thank the Lord. It would explain why both Angie and my father had alluded to Ash being 'damaged'. His reaction, the epic fail when I'd tried to give him a blow job was evidence of that. But thinking back, the way he'd decimated those men outside the theater, the catalyst was one of them yelling at Ash, "Suck my dick."

It scared me seeing him so, so *inhuman*, for want of a better word.

Part of me needed to know the truth because forewarned is forearmed, but another part of me didn't want to live with the horror inside me. Maybe that made me a coward, I don't know. But Ash didn't want to tell me either, or rather, he didn't want me to know. It would also explain why he was so off-hand with Angie, why he was reluctant to be friendly with her. *She knew.*

I'd have to say that the last 24 hours had been an eye-opener.

And Collin, who'd never shown anything approaching passion in the ten years we'd been together, had driven an hour out of the city to confront me with the truth. The guilt from that was strong. We should have ended things years ago.

And now there was Ash. Confusing as it was, I knew there was no way to predict the future, and I still hadn't dealt with my past—I had to speak to Collin.

I kept my shower short, aware that there was a line of people waiting to use it, and trotted back to the bedroom, wishing this old farmhouse had better heating. Although Ash was doing a good job of keeping me warm.

He'd pulled the quilt up so high, all I could see was a tuft of his dark hair poking out the top.

I decided to let him sleep. With rehearsals six days a week for *Broadway Revisited*, he only got the chance of a sleeping late on Sundays, and that wasn't easy when his bed was in my living room. Not that he slept well anyway. And he'd been looking tired before yesterday's debacle and this morning's revelations.

I slipped into a pair of jeans and a tank top, glad I'd brought the novelty sweater that Mom made for me three years ago, smiling at the knitted turkey's startled expression.

Thick socks and a pair of Aunt Lydia's slippers completed my stylish ensemble. My family didn't dress up for Thanksgiving—that was saved for Midnight Mass at Christmas.

I clomped down the stairs, meeting my sister Bernice, her toddler clinging to her like a baby bear.

"Happy Thanksgiving, sis. Marie, say hello to Aunt Laney!"

The little girl squirmed, then squealed like a siren going off when she saw Mittens the cat. Bernice put her down with a grimace, then smiled as she watched my niece's chubby legs chase after the poor beast.

"Sorry about that," she said. "We're working on her 'inside voice' but it's a work in progress—obviously."

"Obviously," I laughed.

"You look happy," she said, raising one eyebrow. "Nothing to do with that incredibly hot mystery husband you've been humping all morning."

My mouth opened automatically to deny it as blood rushed to my cheeks.

Bernice laughed out loud. "You should see your face. I'm jealous, of course. A toddler in the room definitely cramps our style. But here's a tip, sister to sister: for the sake of my sanity and marriage, please move your headboard away from the wall."

She winked at me while I looked for a convenient hole to crawl into.

I should be used to this by now—there was rarely any privacy in a large family. It was one of the reasons I'd gotten my own apartment as soon as I could afford it. But because everything with Ash was so new, so unformed, it was embarrassing to think that we'd been overheard.

The kitchen was wonderfully warm and full of delicious aromas, with the enormous turkey already in the oven.

And lucky me, the full set of my parents, aunts and uncles were sitting around the table. It was obvious they were talking about me because the conversation dropped away as soon as I walked in.

I grabbed a piece of toast from a stack and started spreading it with thick, creamy, country butter. I was 29 years old and I earned my own living—I didn't need their approval.

"Happy Thanksgiving!" I said brightly.

"Happy Thanksgiving, pumpkin," said Dad affectionately.

"Where's your, um, husband?" Mom asked. "Oh goodness, it feels so strange to say that!"

You and me both, Mom.

"He's sleeping in. He's been at rehearsals Mondays through Saturdays for a month, and long hours, too. The premiere is in just over a week."

"Are we invited *this* time?" Mom asked coolly. "Or is it a *secret* premiere?"

I loved my mom, but she had the ability to make me feel wretched without saying a single word. Except this time, she had plenty to say.

"Well," I said carefully, "Ash will be given four free tickets for family and friends, but he's a bit disappointed in the show." I sighed. "He doesn't think it will do well, so you might not want to…"

"We're going!" Mom said emphatically. "I've sat through 22 years of school plays and concerts—I'm certainly not going to miss this. If I'm invited, of course."

I withheld a sigh.

"You're invited. You too, Dad. Anyone else want to go?"

Eventually, the spare ticket was allotted to Bernice, although Mom declared that all my sisters would want to go, as well. I didn't know how Ash would feel about that, but there wasn't much I could do. And I kinda loved that my family was trying to find a way to support him—us.

"Good, that's decided," said Mom. "Now, I need to call Father Michael about arranging … well, I don't know what it would be called … some sort of blessing. What faith does Ash follow, if any?"

"Bridget," Dad chided gently.

"No, Brian, this is important. I don't know why Laney chose to sneak off to have a secret marriage, but as her mother, the least I can do is ensure that she stands in good grace, whatever husband she is married to."

Everyone winced, but I glared at my mother.

"Mom, just stop! We're happy as we are. We don't want any fuss—that's why we did it this way."

Which wasn't a complete lie.

She changed tack abruptly.

"Father Michael will be so disappointed, I won't know what to say to the poor man. He officiated at your Christening and your Confirmation; all your sisters' weddings. He was good enough for them. Just because you chose to marry outside the faith, I don't see why…"

"I didn't."

I knew I shouldn't have said that, but Mom brightened immediately.

"Ash is Catholic?"

"Yes," I sighed, "but that still doesn't mean that we…"

Over Dad's shoulder, I saw Collin walk into the room, looking tired with red eyes, and blotchy skin beneath his pale stubble.

Everyone stopped talking, even Mom, and the day was officially the worst start to Thanksgiving ever.

"Hello, Collin," I said quietly. "Would you like some coffee?"

He nodded then cleared his throat.

"Coffee sounds great. Thank you."

I poured him a cup then suggested he drink it out on the covered porch. It was cold out there, but at least we'd have some privacy.

I passed him one of my uncle's coats, and I wrapped myself in a thick quilt.

"How are you feeling?" I asked, as he nursed his coffee.

He thought about that for a few moments.

"I don't know, Laney. Confused, I guess. Why did you do it? Why did you marry him and not me?"

I decided to go for full disclosure. I owed him that.

"I gave up thinking that we'd get married a long time ago, Collin. I just assumed it wasn't what you wanted and I was happy living in my apartment. You'd never mentioned marriage."

"After ten years, I would have thought that it went without saying!"

"No, it didn't."

"But you married *him*. Behind my back. When we were still dating!"

He shook his head in disbelief and I felt ashamed.

"It happened suddenly," I tried to explain. "He needed a green card to be able to keep his job. Dancing is important to him, and after everything he's been through, I wanted to help."

"What about everything *we've* been through?" he said, his voice rising. "Ten years, Laney! Ten years! Ten years of managing your flare-ups and…"

"Collin," I sighed. "You always saw me as a problem to be solved, you still do—and it doesn't work like that. This isn't something I'll recover from. This is something I live with. Each flare-up will go, eventually, but there will be others. I can't focus on what the pain is taking from me—I have to focus on what I can do, what I will do. And … I don't want to be your duty."

He was silent for a moment.

"But you admit he married you to get a green card?"

"Ash is my friend. I care about him—deeply. But when I suggested that he marry me…"

Collin looked stunned. "It was *your* idea?"

"Well, yes," I admitted weakly.

"Wow," he said. "I can't believe this."

"You and I were already on the edge," I said carefully. "We'd broken up once and it would have happened again."

"Because of him!"

"No," I said quietly. "Because of us."

He thought about this for a moment and he didn't argue.

"Were you going to tell me?"

I hesitated. "No, not about the marriage," I admitted. "We weren't going to tell anyone. But about you and me, yes—as soon as I got the chance to talk to you face to face, which is what happened."

He winced when I said 'we', referring to me and Ash, but still looked angry. Not that I blamed him.

"Your family seems to think this sham marriage is real," he said bitterly.

I stared out at the frost coating the fields and barns; it all looked so pure, so simple.

"Well," I said carefully. "I've come to have feelings for Ash, and I believe he feels the same."

Collin laughed angrily. "Are you really that naïve? He's telling you exactly what you want to hear. As soon as he's got his green card, he'll be gone."

"That's your opinion," I said stiffly. "I'm sorry you had to find out the way you did. You didn't deserve that."

"No, I didn't."

We sat in silence while he drank his coffee.

"I have one more question," he said, frowning into his cup.

"Go ahead."

"Are you sleeping with him?"

I looked him in the eye as I answered.

"I promise, I never cheated on you."

I could tell that he didn't believe me, but there was nothing I could do about that. I'd done enough.

The door behind us swung open and Ash was there, standing with his arms folded across his chest, frowning at us.

Collin stood abruptly and tried to body check Ash as he walked back into the kitchen.

"Asshole," Collin muttered as he walked past.

"Prick," Ash replied, without missing a beat.

The strong scent of testosterone hung in the air.

CHAPTER 16

Laney

We drove back to the city after supper. My parents were disappointed that we weren't staying longer, but Ash and I really needed some privacy to talk about what had happened last night.

And besides, I wasn't comfortable with the idea of having sex with him again while my family was in the house. I didn't even know if that was something that was going to happen.

And wouldn't it be a crying shame if that was it? Because that had been the best sex of my entire life.

As I drove through the darkened streets toward the highway, questions crowded my mind. Were we together or not? Should we go back to him sleeping on the couch? Was he expecting to sleep in my bed? Did I want him to?

Well, at least I knew the answer to that last one.

When we finally closed the front door of my … of *our* apartment … my head was pounding and it was a relief to be home.

I flopped onto the couch, happy to leave Ash to carry up our luggage and load the fridge with all the leftover food that Mom insisted we take with us.

He stole my iPhone from my purse, and the soft sounds of the new Adele album poured from the speakers.

I listened to Ash moving around in the kitchen, filling the kettle with water, setting it to boil, and soon the aroma of chamomile tea filled the room.

I cracked one eye as he pulled off my boots and started to massage my aching feet.

"That feels good," I groaned, as he dug his thumbs into the arch of my left foot.

He didn't answer, humming along with the music, his lips moving wordlessly.

His fingers slid up to my ankles, massaging thoroughly. He couldn't go any higher because I was wearing skinny jeans. I should really wear more skirts.

I blurted out the thoughts that were on my mind.

"What happens next, Ash?"

He raised his eyebrows and looked up at me, his hands still moving rhythmically.

"Whatever you want, Laney."

I frowned, frustrated that he hadn't given me a real answer.

"I just want to know where we stand."

He sighed and sat back on his heels.

"I don't know," he said simply.

I was going to have to spell it out. I steeled myself for the conversation.

"Are we together, Ash?"

His forehead puckered. "We're married," he said, as if that explained everything.

For other people, perhaps, but not for us.

"We married to get you a green card," I said, as patiently as I could. "But ... last night and, um, this morning, we had sex."

He grinned at me, his eyes glittering with carnal thoughts.

"Yeah."

I shook my head in frustration. "I don't just sleep with people!"

His sudden, irritated expression matched mine. "I'm your husband!"

"On paper!" I snapped. "It's not real."

He stood abruptly, his nostrils flaring with anger. "I don't know what you want!"

I took a deep breath, forcing myself to keep calm.

"We need to work out some rules," I said, my voice tight and clipped.

He swept his hand in front of him theatrically.

"What are these rules?" he asked, his voice full of disdain.

"Well," I replied, thinking on my feet, "will you ... are we going to have sex again?"

He blinked, surprise replacing anger. "Of course." Then his face clouded. "You don't want to?"

I almost laughed. What a comedy of errors. I had to try and wrestle my turbulent emotions into some semblance of order and tranquility, or we'd never get anywhere. Least of all the bedroom.

"Ash, come sit next to me," I said calmly, patting the couch.

He sat stiffly, oozing reluctance.

"What I'm saying is ... if your dick is in some sort of popularity contest, I'm not interested in competing. Or sharing at all."

Ash reared back in shock.

Oops, that might have been a little more brutal than necessary.

"There is no one else!"

"Not even the woman you spend your nights with? Or was it women?"

Ash was stunned. "What woman? There is no woman!"

"Ash, I saw you! With nail marks down your chest … and all those nights you weren't home."

His lips twisted.

"I should have stayed to listen to you fucking the prick?"

Oh, this wasn't going well.

"No, of course not. I…"

"Hearing you with him—it made me sick to my stomach," he said angrily. "I couldn't stay here anymore."

"So … where did you go?"

"The pub."

"Oh!"

He raised one eyebrow challengingly.

"Not … you weren't with … women."

"No."

"But your chest? I saw you!"

He sighed and looked down.

"I wanted to. You were with the prick, so I wanted to. I met a woman to fuck. But when she … marked me … I couldn't do it. I didn't want her anyway."

The expression on his face was dark, and I realized how that must have affected him—being *marked* by someone else. My heart squeezed painfully.

I tried again.

"We're in a rather unique situation," I said, understating wildly. "And I'm not sure what's happening with us. But … I can't sleep with … I can't have sex with you if you're going to have sex with other people. I know we're not together in the traditional sense, or any sense at all in fact, but…"

His face relaxed and he pulled my hand between his own.

"You married me to help me, I know this. But I think there is something more, yes?"

"Well, yes."

He stroked my cheek with gentle fingers.

"I don't want anyone else, Laylay. My wife. Do you?"

"No, I really don't. Then … we're together? For real?"

I had a momentary qualm asking this question. Asking Ash to live with me in my world, I would be the never-ending burden. I wanted to take the words back and bury them somewhere deep.

But instead, Ash lifted my hand and held it against his chest.

"For real."

I studied his face, trying to read every thought he'd ever had. It was bittersweet. Ash had chosen me, closing down other possibilities.

"I hope you never regret your choice," I said, my voice breaking. "What if you stop wanting me because my body breaks?"

Anger flashed in his eyes.

"What if? That's all you say! You hide behind it like a shield. What if you are in a wheelchair! What if you walk like an old woman!"

"You bastard!"

"I'm a bastard because I make you look at the truth? I don't care about those things! You are my sunshine!"

My family and then Collin had shielded me from many of the highs and lows of life. But with Ash, each extreme would be part of our lives.

Together.

I sighed and leaned against him. "Take me to bed, Ash."

His eyes glowed, passion firing through them. Then he lowered his head and kissed the back of my hand.

It was a sweet, old fashioned gesture, totally at odds with the lust I saw as he let his eyes stroll across my body, seemingly unable to choose between my breasts or my lips.

I helped make up his mind by folding my arms around him and tugging his head down so I could press my lips against his.

He opened his mouth, then proceeded to give me the hottest, slowest, most tantalizing kiss I'd ever had. He was telling me that he was in control and he'd kiss me the way he damn well wanted.

Playful Ash, serious Ash, flirty Ash—I couldn't help thinking that sexy-as-sin Ash was proving to be my favorite.

His hips moved in a slow rhythm that may have been dancing or may have been back-to-basics grassroots grinding. I reached down for the heat between his legs, massaging the growing bulge at the front of his jeans.

A shudder ran through his body and he ground harder against my hand. I couldn't wait to be skin to skin.

I unbuttoned his shirt clumsily, fingers deft as sausages as I tried to get at his bare skin. He laughed against my lips and lifted his arms so I could pull the cotton over his head.

Skin like warm silk, smooth and soft, covering hard muscle, my fingers dragged across the planes and ripples of his chest and stomach, then fluttered over the welts and scarred flesh of his back.

He grunted with relief as I unzipped his pants. His cock was pressing so hard against the seam, I was worried it would have a permanent zipper imprint.

I eased his clothes down, wishing I could drop a kiss onto the glistening head as my hands slid downward. But I didn't. Maybe we'd get there one day, but we had all the time in the world. What a wonderful thought.

Ash kicked off his shoes, and rid himself of the rest of his clothes before prowling toward me. His eyes said, *naked now!* Mine replied, *make me.*

He swept me from my feet so swiftly, my stomach swooped, and he carried me to the bed, *our* bed, working my clothes from my body between slow, hot kisses.

I closed my eyes, needing some defense against his beautiful face and the sensations that threatened to overwhelm me. He was an ocean wave, the high tide, and I was drowning in happiness and physical pleasure.

I raised my knees, a thrill of anticipation lighting my body as he paused to kiss my thigh, breathing deeply as he nuzzled my mound. His warm, wet lips met mine, and he circled my clit with his tongue, tasting and touching, exploring intimately. Then a moment later, he pressed his hipbones against my inner thighs, and the heat of his beautiful, powerful flesh was inside me.

We both paused, our breath coming in short pants as we stared at each other, acknowledging together that this was real, that *we* were real.

And then he started to move, showing me exactly how much stamina a professional dancer had, so far above that of us ordinary folk. Twice. He really was an overachiever. And I enjoyed every second.

We fell asleep from sheer exhaustion, happily post-coital, Ash's arm curled around my left boob. It seemed to be his new favorite place, and I saw no reason to complain.

It was so wonderful to sleep in. And we finally woke at the crack of noon.

Telling the rest of my friends about our sudden marriage was awkward. I FaceTimed Vanessa, cringing as she reamed me out for not inviting her. She swore that she'd seen a connection between me and Ash—more than the threat of imminent death, apparently. I didn't argue. I had to promise that I'd visit as soon as possible, with Ash.

Jo took it better, claiming that I sounded happier with Ash than she'd ever heard me, and couldn't wait to see us both.

Then I told my closest work colleagues, but I guess the message got a little confused, because my boss sent me a card congratulating me and Collin. I'd sort that one out when I saw him in person at our monthly meeting.

Mom handled telling my extended family and they were all desperate to see Ash.

So was I.

For the last week, he'd hardly been in the apartment. He'd trail in the door after hours of rehearsals, shattered, with barely enough energy to eat before collapsing into bed and passing out.

But then the one time we actually had a whole evening free together, we ended up fighting.

The argument was over the stupidest thing. Well, I thought it was stupid, but Ash didn't.

We were watching re-runs of 'Dancing with the Stars'. When I'd first persuaded him to watch it, he'd been quite snooty, saying it was about amateurs and he wasn't interested. But it only took a couple of dances before he was hooked—and annoying—talking through the whole show, explaining what the pro-dancers were teaching. Well, until I offered to tape his mouth shut.

His eyes were hazy with tiredness, and we were watching the program cuddled up on the couch, a blanket thrown over us. He was tired and a bit moody. On the TV, they were showing some video tape where the actress was saying how much she missed her dad who'd died nine years ago, and this dance was for him. And then she got all weepy. I rolled my eyes.

"What?" Ash asked sharply.

"It's so manipulative! 'I'm sad because my daddy died. Vote for me!' It just bugs me, that's all."

Ash's jaw clamped shut and I could see a muscle ticking by his eye.

"It's not manipulation. When you dance, you have to feel the emotion. It's like a … a muscle memory, pulling the emotion into the dance."

"Oh, please! It's a cheap ploy to get votes. It's tacky and unpleasant."

He stood up suddenly, surprising me.

"You don't know what you're talking about!"

Then he stamped out of the living room and I heard the bedroom door slam behind him.

I blinked. What the hell had just happened? We were fighting over a TV show?

It was hard to dodge his emotional landmines when I didn't know where they were. It was tiring. I was tired.

He reappeared twenty minutes later, damp from the shower and apologetic.

His way of apologizing was to take me to bed for some more athletic sex. The man was a machine, and if he hadn't been so exhausted from long days of rehearsing, I'm not sure we'd have gotten to sleep at all. Although Ash rarely slept well. Most of his nights were disturbed. Demons still chased him through the darkness of his dreams.

When the day of the first performance finally arrived, Ash was brimming with nervous energy, despite swearing that the show was going to be a disaster. He'd left the apartment after delivering a searing kiss that heated me from tip to toe, with a promise of more.

I met my mom and sisters for cocktails at a bar that was stumbling distance to the theater, even in the fierce freeze that clawed the city.

A decent crowd gathered at the theater, and I was hoping that Ash was wrong about it being a disaster. He was probably just being too hard on himself.

Unwrapping my coat, scarf, hat and gloves, I settled into my seat—really good ones in the third row—between Mom and Bernice. Dad had planned to come but pulled a sudden shift, or so he said. But I was glad it was just a small part of my family.

I drummed my fingers restlessly until Mom took my hand in hers and gave my fingers a reassuring squeeze.

"Thank you for coming, Mom," I whispered.

"I wouldn't have missed it," she smiled.

I wondered how Ash was feeling backstage, waiting in the wings. And I sent up a quick prayer that it would go well.

When the lights dimmed and the pre-recorded music started, my hopes were high. I felt a rush of adrenaline, and I realized that was just a faint reflection of how Ash would be feeling. But despite everything, it was exciting—I was going to see my *husband* on stage, performing for the first time since Las Vegas. It *had* to be special.

I was squirming with anticipation and nerves as the dancers ran and leapt onto the stage, but drop by drop, my happiness drained away.

I didn't want to believe it, but Ash was right. *Broadway Revisited* was awful. It was a trite mishmash with no coherent theme or storyline. I felt bad for the cast—they'd all worked so hard. The director and producer still seemed to believe that they'd pulled off the show of the century, but they were the only ones. The reviews were going to be brutal.

Muted applause greeted the dancers as they took their bows. There was no encore request, and the half full theater emptied quickly. We were supposed to go for drinks 'to celebrate'. I wasn't sure anyone would feel like it.

"Ash was good though," Bernice said kindly. "And that blonde girl he danced with."

"That's Sarah," I sighed. "She's really nice."

"Yeah, they look good together .They should have let them do more than that one tango. That was hot."

Yes, that was my husband—a man who looked hot when he was dancing. Or standing, or sitting. And very hot laying in my bed.

A warm glow of possession made me smile. Bernice caught my expression and raised her eyebrows in amusement. I didn't care.

We headed out to the nearest pub, but it was twenty minutes before I saw Ash making his way toward us, freshly showered, his fake tan orange under the unsympathetic lighting.

A hot blast of jealousy shot through me when I saw that he had his arm around Sarah, his head down, talking to her. But it dissipated quickly when I saw that she'd been crying, her pretty blue eyes bloodshot and puffy.

I moved across the booth to make room for her and she plopped down next to me.

Ash gave me a thin smile, nodded at my family while Sarah got acquainted with them, then headed to the bar, soon returning with a bottle Hennessy's whiskey and six shot glasses.

We clinked them together and downed them in one.

"God, I needed that," muttered Sarah. "I swear, Laney, if it wasn't for your fella, I'd have gone off the deep end long ago. He's always so friggin' calm. I don't know how he does it."

Neither did I. My enduring opinion of Ash was that he was a hothead. It was intriguing hearing this about him, and another flutter of jealousy stung me.

We stayed for a few drinks and some of the other dancers joined us, but no one was in the mood to party and we left soon after.

It was a relief to tumble into our apartment and regain feeling in my fingers and toes. Ash was flexing his right hand and wincing. The fingers that had been broken often ached, but it was worse in the cold.

I was going to suggest making some hot chocolate, but Ash surprised me by pulling me into his arms and kissing me hungrily. He tasted of whiskey and cigarettes, but I was too turned on to take issue with that right now.

He shoved both hands into my jeans and squeezed my ass.

"Aaagh! Your hands are freezing! There'll be payback, mister!"

He laughed against my lips and I tugged at his belt as we reeled across the apartment, shedding clothes and sharing whispers—all the hot and dirty things we were going to do to each other.

I shuddered slightly as Ash pulled me under the chilly sheets, but then shuddered with pleasure as he warmed me in a wonderfully old fashioned way.

Ash was awake early the next day, throwing on his jeans and coat to run out and buy the early editions of the newspapers.

We'd expected bad news, but hoped for good.

Ash paced up and down the room as I found the entertainment section and scanned through the reviews.

I winced when I read the headline.

This Christmas turkey is one to avoid.

Ouch.

"Read it to me," Ash asked quietly.

> 'Broadway Revisited' is the type of show that should have stayed a bad idea and never reached the stage. Mark Rumans made his career as a dancer in 'Forty Second Street' on Broadway but doesn't seem to have had an original idea since. Rumor has it of backstage fights with respected choreographer Rosa Hart, who left the production a month ago.
>
> The only bright spot is newcomers Sarah Lintort and Ash Novak. Their Argentine tango from 'Evita' was a masterclass in sexual tension, musicality and suppressed longing, as the toothsome twosome dueled their way through the only interesting moment of a long, dreary evening.
>
> One star for Lintort and Novak, but otherwise one to avoid.

"He liked your tango," I said lamely.

Ash nodded and walked into the kitchen.

He was leaning by the sink, staring out into the gray, overcast morning. Wrapping my arms around his waist, I rested my head on his back. I felt his warm hands cover mine and heard his heavy sigh.

"I'll be out of a job by Christmas. I'm sorry."

"You have nothing to be sorry for—you were wonderful—even that reviewer thought so. You'll find another job, I know you will."

He didn't reply.

When he left for the theater that evening, my heart ached for him. It had been a difficult day and he hadn't spoken much. I could see how hard it was to have to do it all over again, knowing that it wasn't good, despite the small ray of sunshine the reviewer had shined on him.

Given our unusual circumstances and our original agreement that we'd divorce after two years, despite our ongoing sexual shenanigans, I had an odd sense of wanting to stand by my husband.

"Oh God! Don't stop, Ash! Don't stop!"

He thrust harder, less than a minute from his climax, although mine was much closer.

At first I thought the knocking was the headboard slamming against the wall. Ash had moved it away twice, but somehow the bed always crept back, and now there was a dent in the dry walling that Ash had promised to fix.

The day had started so well and my orgasm was beginning to fizz, hot tingles shooting up and down my pelvis. Then I heard it again.

"Ash!"

"Yes, my love!" he gasped, his teeth gritted, hips pistoning against me.

His thumb pressed down on my clit, and despite my distraction, an explosion rushed through me, urgent and relentless, lights exploding behind my eyes as my lids tightly squeezed shut.

Then I heard it for a third time.

Ash was fast approaching loss of control, his movements wilder, sloppier, that perfect rhythm more desperate.

"There's someone ... at the door!" I gasped.

Ash growled something that was probably very rude, but as it was in Slovenian, I couldn't be sure.

KNOCK! KNOCK! KNOCK!

"Mr. Novak! Mrs. Novak! This is Ralph Phillips with the U.S. Citizenship and Immigration Service. Please open the door."

"Oh, my God! Ash! Stop! We have to ... have to..."

With another curse, Ash put his head down and headed for the home straight. It was good ole fucking, hard.

"This is Ralph Phillips with the U.S. Citizenship and Immigration Service. I must insist that you open the door."

Ash swore and pulled out suddenly, stomping toward the front door, his face stormy.

I watched his retreating back and delicious butt stalking away, stopping only to scoop up a towel—a small piece of material that did nothing to hide the fact that he was still hard.

I pulled on a robe and peeped into the living room. Ash's chest was rising and falling rapidly, his face flushed as he flung open the door to the apartment.

A tall, thin man with round spectacles took a step back, as 170 pounds of angry Slovenian glowered at him.

"Ah, Mr. Aljaž Novak?"

"What?"

"I wonder if we might talk to you and Mrs. Novak. I am Ralph Phillips with the U.S. Citizenship and Immigration Service and this is my colleague Moira Walsh."

"We're busy!" Ash snarled.

I saw the man glance down at Ash's towel and his face turned red.

"Even so," he said, obviously flustered, "I must insist."

I thought Ash was about to slam the door in their faces, so I hurried out.

"Sorry," I said, smoothing down my hair. "We, um, I was just about to shower."

"I do apologize. Mrs. Novak, I'm assuming."

"Of course," I said snippily.

He looked a little abashed, and withholding a grimace, I let him in.

Ash was still irritated, and his dick was in danger of trying to shake hands with our visitors. I sent him to shower while I made coffee, and Lord knows, I needed some, too. I caught a glimpse of my reflection in the kitchen window, horrified by the red patches on my cheeks, chin, neck and chest—and wild, wild sex hair.

My heart was thumping, and not just from the last half an hour. The Immigration Service only made impromptu house calls when they suspected a sham marriage. I wondered who had reported us. Would Collin have been so vindictive? Even though things had ended badly between us, I didn't want to believe that.

The man, Phillips, eyed me suspiciously, but his colleague seemed more sympathetic. Maybe it was a version of good cop/bad cop, or maybe her mood had been improved by seeing a mostly naked Ash first thing in the morning—it always worked for me. But I wished that Ash and I had thought to discuss what to say if this happened. I'd been such a fool.

I served up the coffee, taking several gulps of the steaming brew, then turned to head for the shower, but Moira, as she asked me to call her, was admiring some artwork in the living room. Too late, I realized that she'd delayed me just long enough that Ash was already dressed and out, giving us no time to confer. She smiled benignly as he passed.

I sighed, taking myself off to shower and dress, quickly returning to the living room where Ash sat looking surly and on edge.

"And we'll want to interview you separately," concluded Mr. Phillips, after explaining the process.

Ash shot me a quick look, but what could I say?

Ms. Walsh accompanied me into the bedroom, and Ash was left with Phillips.

"Oh, what a pretty room," she exclaimed as I hurried to straighten the sheets and smooth out the quilt. "You do have some lovely views."

"Yes, thank you. It's why I chose this apartment."

"And you didn't know Ash then?"

"No."

"How long have you lived here?"

"Six years."

"And how long have you known your husband?"

"Three months." *Nearly.*

She tapped her pen against her notepad. "That was a short engagement."

I didn't reply.

"What does your family think?"

I was cautious, wondering how much to say.

"They like Ash, but they would have preferred a big, family wedding."

"But you didn't do that?"

"No."

"May I ask why not?"

"I have three older sisters. For each of their weddings, my Mom went completely over the top. That's not me. Or Ash."

"And how did you meet?"

I took a deep breath and launched in. By the time I finished, Ms. Walsh's eyebrows had disappeared beneath her bangs.

"Extraordinary!" she muttered. "Just extraordinary."

She was right about that.

I thought maybe the questions were at an end, but I was wrong.

"Does he have a pet name for you?"

I blinked, surprised.

"Well, yes. It sounds like 'moy suncheck' but I don't know what it means. He won't tell me."

She frowned at that, but wrote it down anyway.

The interview gradually became more personal: what color toothbrush did Ash use; what side of the bed did he sleep on; did he like the light on or off during sex; what position did he prefer.

Anger at the intrusive nature of the questions began to build inside me. And it felt like punishment. My government really wanted to know this?

"Mrs. Novak, if you could answer, please?" Ms. Walsh asked gently but firmly.

"He sleeps on the left," I said tightly. "Sometimes we keep the light on, sometimes we don't. And we enjoy a variety of positions."

My cheeks were scarlet. I felt violated and dirty as she noted down every word.

Ash

The questions were weird. He wanted to know who took out the trash and who bought the groceries, who cleaned the apartment, who did the vacuuming. He started to get annoyed when I answered almost everything, "We both do," but it was true.

"Do you have lamps in the bedroom?"

"Laney has one on the bedside table."

"But you don't."

"No."

"Why is that?"

"I don't read much." *And reading English was hard work.*

He gave a dry laugh. "You don't read much, although she writes for a living; and she doesn't dance, although that's your profession. Exactly what do you and your wife have in common, Mr. Novak?"

I didn't know how to answer that. On paper, we had nothing in common. But we never ran out of things to say to each other. There were no uncomfortable silences with Laney—just silence, and that was peaceful.

"She likes listening to music, too," I said weakly.

"Hmm. And which side of the bed does your wife sleep on?"

What the fuck? I took a deep breath. "The right."

He wrote something on his form.

"When you are intimate with your wife, does she like to have the light on or off?"

I folded my arms across my chest.

"None of your business!"

He peered over his glasses at me.

"You do realize, Mr. Novak, that we have every reason to believe that your marriage to Miss Hennessey was to obtain U.S. citizenship? The odd circumstances that you yourself have described, the haste with which you married: these questions are valid. If you cannot answer them, we will be forced to draw our own conclusions. It is in your best interests—and hers—to answer plainly."

I stared up at the ceiling, furious and impotent. He was just like Sergei, but without the psychopathic violent streak. And he wore glasses.

"Lights off."

Laney didn't like her body. She thought she was too thin, too shapeless. But she was all woman to me.

"And what position does she prefer?"

I clenched my teeth and refused to answer.

He sighed. "This is my last question, Mr. Novak."

"All of them!" I grit out.

I stood up and walked into the kitchen. I couldn't stare at his smug face for a second longer without wanting to punch it.

At that moment, Laney walked out of the bedroom, looking pale and upset. I wrapped my arms around her in silence as her small hands gripped my t-shirt tightly and she rested her head against my chest.

"We'll be in touch," said Phillips as they left.

I swore loudly and Laney turned away to fall onto the couch, her hands covering her eyes.

For the next few days, we were both on edge, expecting a phone call, letter, or another personal visit from the Immigration goons (my new favorite word that I learned after watching re-runs of 'Breaking Bad'). And each evening I had to go to the theater and do my best to entertain an audience that seemed to be shrinking fast.

We were all waiting for the axe to fall, so when Dalano and Mark asked everyone to come in ten minutes early, I had a good idea what they were going to say.

We gathered in a circle on the empty stage, Sarah leaning against my shoulder while Dalano hushed everyone then cleared his throat.

"Thank you all for coming in early. I have some bad news. Ticket sales have not been going great. Those asshat reviewers don't know class when they see it. Mark has done an amazing job of choreographing you," and he turned to smile sadly at his boyfriend, "but launching just before Christmas—which was the theater's choice—has worked against us. We're going to have to take a break, so our final show for now will be Christmas Eve. I know this will be a shock to all of you, and we hate having to say it, but I promise you all from the bottom of my heart that this is *not* the end of *Broadway Revisited* and we will rise like a phoenix from the ashes."

He took a deep breath while we all stared at him stonily.

"I feel so much love in this room tonight, and I'd like to thank you for all for being a part of this amazing vision. We're ahead of our time," and he gave a small laugh. "I'm expecting you all to dance your asses off and prove the critics wrong. Break a leg."

Nobody clapped, but Dalano and Mark didn't seem to notice as they stared into each other's eyes.

We all headed for the dressing room and after I'd shaved, I sat next to Sarah while we started on makeup. I could do mine in three minutes: gel eye liner, foundation, bronzer topped with powder, finish with mascara and lip gloss. It wasn't my favorite part of being a dancer, but I'd been doing it for years and it didn't bother me. Although if you'd asked me when I was 14, you'd have gotten a different answer.

"I booked my flight back to London a week ago," Sarah said while she dotted concealer under her eyes.

"Yeah? Are you coming back to Chicago after?"

"I doubt it. Well, I'll go wherever I get hired. A friend of mine from RADA works at the Sydney Opera House, and she's always trying to get me to visit. Maybe I will—some winter sun would be fab. What about you?"

I shrugged. "Look for another job, I guess."

"You should give London a try, Ash," she said, smearing foundation across her smooth skin. "My friend Paula told me that there's a couple of shows that are hiring in the New Year. You wouldn't even need a work visa as Slovenia is part of the EU. Laney could come with you. She usually works from home, right?"

I couldn't help laughing, and Sarah gave me a confused look. Wouldn't it be ironic that I'd married Laney for a green card, but if I worked in Europe it would be the other way around—she'd be able to work in Britain because we were married.

"You're a weirdo," Sarah said, throwing a powder puff at my head.

She was probably right. But what she'd said gave me a few things to think about. It made a change from worrying about whether or not I'd get kicked out of the U.S.

The show stumbled on with an audience of fewer than fifty people in a theater that held 500. There was nothing worse than dancing until your heart was ready to burst, and hearing only thin and scattered applause. But we kept smiling. We painted on our fucking smiles every night and danced until our feet bled.

I woke up on Christmas Eve with a strange feeling, ominous like a storm brewing, like someone had stolen my breath. My heart thumped wildly, but nothing seemed out of place and Laney was sleeping silently beside me.

I slipped out of bed as quietly as possible and headed to the bathroom. I stared in the mirror, wondering what life was going to throw at me next.

I'd tried to compartmentalize everything, trying to forget about what had happened in Vegas, about Sergei, even about my friends. Sometimes it worked, but sometimes I felt like I'd go crazy with all the fractured parts of me falling apart like broken glass.

The woman I'd left in bed had helped me in so many ways. I'd be grateful to her forever. She held me together and stopped me from shattering—I didn't even know why.

I'd wanted to buy her a really great Christmas present, and I had thought about getting her an engagement ring to go with her wedding band, but that didn't feel right and I wasn't sure she'd want it.

Instead, I'd bought 100 of my favorite songs and secretly downloaded them to her phone. They all meant something to me—and I hoped they'd mean something to her.

I splashed cold water on my face but avoided looking in the mirror. It was easier that way.

Laney was still sleeping when I walked back into the bedroom. I stared down at her, a small frown on her face. She'd been limping for two days now and we both knew she had a flare-up coming, she just didn't want to admit it. Or rather, she wouldn't let it stop her from going on with her life.

She lived with restrictions and limitations; there were things she couldn't do, shouldn't try, would never do, but she had the biggest, most open heart of anyone I'd ever met. She was remarkable in so many ways, but she didn't see that about herself.

She'd opened her home to me when she barely knew me. But she always trusted me and looked out for me when I knew that everyone was telling her to stay back, be wary.

In a world where it was easier to look the other way, she actually gave a shit about something other than herself.

She'd saved me, and I'd repaid her by turning my back on my friends and trying to carry on with my life. I'd done nothing for Yveta, or Marta, Galina, or Gary. And the girl—that nameless kid who haunted my dreams and was forgotten in daylight—I hadn't saved her either. I could pretend all I liked, but the only person I'd saved was myself.

I was making coffee, when I heard someone knocking at the door. My first thought was that those fucking government goons were back with their snooping, spying questions.

That's what I thought—but I was wrong. The Fates hated me. And this was much worse.

I pulled on a pair of jeans and yanked the door open.

A uniformed cop was standing in front of me.

"Mr. Novak, I'm Officer Jenkins."

"Yeah, I remember you."

The asshole had pushed me face down onto the hood of his squad car the night I'd arrived in Chicago. I wasn't planning on forgetting that.

"We'd like you to come to the station for questioning."

I felt Laney's presence behind me, and her hand rested on my shoulder: a warning as well as reassurance.

"*More* questions, Billy? Do I need to call Angela?"

The guy turned pink and swallowed nervously.

"Your dad, um, Captain Hennessey just told me to bring him in. He's not under arrest."

"I should think not!" she said firmly. "What's it about this time?"

"I don't know, at least, I'm not sure. And that's the truth, Laney."

He was practically pleading with her, which would have made me laugh if I wasn't already on edge.

Laney glanced across at me.

"We should probably go."

The police guy looked much happier after she said that. I can't say I did.

Grim faced, I finished dressing, collected my coat and followed them out the door.

The journey to the police station was quiet. I guess policemen weren't allowed to listen to *The Mix* or *Kiss FM*.

Instinctively, I reached out to hold Laney's hand. If this was it, if I was being sent home, I needed to spend every last second letting her know that I'd always be her friend, that...

Her gray eyes turned to mine, full of compassion, full of love.

A shockwave of realization overwhelmed me. I'd hardly seen it happening, hadn't known what it meant, had been denying it for so long—but somehow, somewhere, friendship and admiration had turned to love.

I was so fucking in love with her I didn't know where I ended and she began.

My lungs squeezed painfully and I sucked in air. I didn't know that love could make you forget how to breathe. Sex with Laney had been on my list of priorities for a while now, right under air, above food, and equal with dancing. No, not anymore. Laney was above the need for oxygen. *Moj sonček*—my sunshine.

"We're here," she said softly.

I hardly heard her as I leaned across, pressing my lips against hers, holding her face to mine, then kissing her like it was the first time or the last time.

"I love you," I said, my breath whispering across her skin. "You are my sunshine, Laney Novak. I love you so much."

She blinked, startled, and then her beautiful smile spread across her face, lighting her like the sunshine she was.

"Took you long enough," she said. "I've loved you since the first day I saw you."

I laughed in surprise, and we sat there, grinning like two love-blasted fools, until Officer Dickwad jerked the car door open.

Laney's smile fell.

"Whatever happens, Ash, we're in this together, right?"

She squeezed my hand again, and I nodded, my mouth dry.

Captain Hennessey was waiting, but this time he didn't try to separate us and he didn't comment on the way Laney clung to me. Or more truthfully, the way I clung to her like a drowning man clings to even a splinter of wood.

He led us to an interview room where Officers Petronelli and Ramos were already sitting, as well as Laney's friend Angela, and a man in a suit that I didn't know.

"Angie! "What's going on?" Laney asked, leaving my side to hug her friend.

"I'm still waiting to find out," she said frowning at me before shaking hands briefly. "But I hear congratulations are in order."

Laney nodded and smiled. "Thank you."

"You look happy," Angela said reluctantly.

"I am. We are," Laney said, reaching for my hand again.

Laney's father shut the door, signaling that it was time to get serious, and my heartrate jacked up. I hated being in enclosed spaces—it was too much like being trapped in that car with Sergei.

Sweat broke out over my body as I tried not to lose my mind.

Laney gripped my fingers too tightly and I winced.

"Sorry," she whispered, letting go immediately.

"Thank you for coming in, Ash," said Laney's dad. "We…"

"I'll take it from here, Captain Hennessey," said the suit without even looking at him.

Laney's dad bristled. "Ash is my son-in-law," he said, as my eyes snapped to his.

There was a pause.

"Of course," said the stranger calmly. "I'm Special Agent John Parker with the Bureau for Alcohol, Tobacco, Firearms and Explosives. My team has been investigating your friend Volkov and his connections with the Outlaws, a motorcycle gang that's responsible for 55% of criminal activity in Nevada, and that's just the things we know about."

He looked directly at me.

"Thanks to your information, we were able to locate the epicenter of their prostitution and human trafficking ring."

Laney's dad shot an irritated look at the man. "Ash, they've found your friends Yveta Kuznets and Gary Benson."

Laney's fingers tightened around my hand again. This time I welcomed the pain.

"Are they alright?"

He grimaced. "They will be."

I didn't know what that meant.

"Marta? Galina?"

"We haven't been able to trace Marta Babiak," Parker replied for him. "A woman with her passport left the U.S. over a month ago, but after that, the trail goes cold."

"Galina?" I asked, my voice cracking.

"We have reason to believe that Galina Bely was killed on or about December 15th."

While I was dancing in a stupid show. Oh God.

I closed my eyes, but couldn't stop tears burning behind my eyelids.

"Mr. Novak," said Parker, "following leads that started with your information, we have been able to rescue 137 women and 27 men from a dozen different locations across the country. And there'll be more." He cleared his throat. "We have also taken 33 of the Outlaws into custody, and we'd like you to try and identify the one that you saw. Volkov has severed ties with them, and he's lost a number of his own men in gun battles. We believe Volkov is cleaning house. He's shutting down operations. What you did, getting away, you've saved lives."

I felt Laney's cool hands on my cheeks and realized that she was wiping away tears.

"You did good, baby," she whispered. "I'm so proud of you."

I shook my head. I'd done nothing except run away, saving my own skin.

"There's one other thing," said Parker. "We've found the, um, the remains of a white male, aged between 30 and 50. We think it could be Oleg Ivanowski, Sergei Boykov's second in command. We'd like you to try and identify him."

"What do you mean by 'remains', Special Agent Parker?" asked Angela. "My client is not a forensic pathologist."

The man looked at her directly as he answered.

"We have a head, Ms. Pinto."

Laney's face was as white as paper, and her hand felt clammy in mine.

"Does he have to?" she whispered.

"It would really help us out, Mrs. Novak," replied Parker.

"I'll do it," I said, my voice as dry as dust.

He nodded, waiting until Laney was looking away, then laid a black and white photograph in front of me. It didn't look real, the bloated pumpkin-shape in the picture. The close-cropped hair looked like Oleg's, but it was hard to tell.

"I don't know, it could be. He … Oleg … had a long scar on his right cheek and his nose had been broken."

Parker seemed pleased with my answer.

It felt odd, staring down at a photograph of Oleg's head. It didn't match the menace, the pure evil that I'd always felt around him. Instead, he was nothing.

I hoped his body was feeding the worms.

I hoped he'd suffered when they killed him.

I hoped he felt every blade of every knife, every bullet of every gun.

I hoped he'd screamed in agony.

I hoped he'd taken a long time dying.

And I was glad he was dead. The world was a better place without him in it.

"What about Sergei?" I asked, almost choking on the name.

Parker shrugged.

"Volkov is very thorough. It's likely that Boykov is already dead or will be soon. We got lucky with Ivanowski. A rancher found the remains when he was riding his property-line. We think coyotes … well, it doesn't matter now."

My stomach quivered, but I wasn't sick. Laney gave a small gasp and I put my arm around her automatically.

"Are you going to arrest Volkov?"

"We're still gathering evidence. We don't just want Volkov, we want all his contacts, and we're working with Interpol. That's all I can tell you right now."

I didn't know how to feel. Was it all over, after all these months? I should have felt relief. I wanted to feel something, but I couldn't. The numbness crept over my whole body left me with a cold, floating sensation. Even Laney's small frame curled into my chest didn't move me.

Funny, this morning I'd felt like I was in love with her. Now, I felt nothing. I knew I still loved her, at least I thought so—I just couldn't feel it.

Her father was watching me with narrowed eyes. I stared back at him until he glanced away.

"Yveta and Gary?" I prompted, looking at Parker.

"They've been brought to Chicago. Mr. Benson has family in Kenosha. Ms Kuznets opted to come with him. He was very happy to hear that you're in the same city."

"Where did you find them?"

Parker looked at me thoughtfully before he answered.

"They were found at one of the Outlaws' hideouts near Boise. They'd been moved around several times before that."

"Can I see them?"

"That can be arranged. They're being looked after at Mercy."

His words confused me, but Laney explained. "It's the name of a hospital."

Her voice seemed to come from a long way away, as if the pane of glass between me and the world grew thicker, hazier every second. My head began to throb.

"Why are they in hospital?"

Parker's expression remained neutral, but I could see that there was something he wasn't telling me.

"Dehydration, mainly. When the Outlaws started getting hit by Volkov's men, they left your friends behind. We're not sure, but we'd guess they were without food and water for three or four days."

I rubbed my temples, willing the pounding in my head to lessen. Laney caught my fingers and held them gently.

"They wouldn't have let them travel if they were really unwell," she tried to reassure me quietly.

"Unless you have anything further, my client has had enough for today," Angela said firmly.

Parker shot her a look. "Just the photographs, and we'll be done."

One by one, he pulled out a set of photographs. Some of them were mug shots, others looked as if they'd been taken from a distance, probably surveillance cameras. I thought I recognized the biker, but I couldn't be sure. Parker didn't seem disappointed—the guy showed less emotion than a stone. I definitely knew that feeling.

Eventually he nodded at Angela.

"We're done here. Thank you, Ms. Pinto. Mr. Novak, Mrs. Novak."

They all stood up to leave, but I had to know.

"What if Volkov doesn't find Sergei?"

Parker pursed his lips, and I thought for a moment that he wasn't going to tell me. But then he shook his head.

"He crossed the border into Mexico. We think we know where he's going. It's just a matter of whether Volkov finds him first or us."

I hoped Volkov found him, castrated him and killed him.

In that order.

CHAPTER 17

Ash

I didn't want to face Gary, and when I walked into that brightly lit hospital room, I had no idea what I'd find or even if he'd want to see me. Everything that had happened to him—and I still wasn't sure what that was—it was because of me.

Gary sat in bed, the TV was on a low setting, but he was staring out the window, lost in thought. When he heard the door opening, he turned, frowning. But then his face lit up in a huge smile. I winced when I saw that several teeth were missing, and that yellow bruises were fading on his face.

"I look hideous, I know. You look gorgeous as ever. Give me a hug, showboat."

He grinned, waving his arms at me.

I leaned down to hug him and I felt a tremor run through his body, his arms squeezing tighter.

"I'm so fucking glad you made it," he whispered.

I jerked back, surprised. I was expecting blame, not ... this.

"God, it's good to see you. Not a cute doctor in sight," he said, half laughing, half crying as he wiped his eyes with his fingers. "How have you been?"

"I ... I don't know what to say. Why aren't you yelling at me?"

Gary looked surprised.

"Well, I'm happy to shriek in delight at seeing your pretty face, but why do I get the feeling that's not what you mean?"

"But this—it's all my fault!"

Gary shook his head emphatically.

"No. No. You're wrong. You tried to get me to do something, to tell someone, and I didn't want to know. Jesus, even when you were all beaten up and desperate ... I should have done something to help then. But I didn't."

He gestured to his own face and body.

"This is all on me. I'm just so happy that you got out. I have no idea how. I thought at first that they'd killed you, but when they kept asking me where you were, how you'd gotten away, I was happy. Well, I'd have been a lot happier if they'd stopped hitting me, but other than that, yeah…"

His words stuttered and stopped.

"They just beat you?" I asked doubtfully.

Gary glanced down at his hands, and then I saw the raw skin around his wrists. He'd been tied up or handcuffed.

He gave a fake laugh, his cheeks flushing.

"Well, I had to suck a few dicks, but that's nothing new."

And when he looked at me, I saw the darkness in his eyes that matched my own.

"You do what you've got to do to survive," I said.

His eyes widened in understanding. "You, too?"

I nodded.

"Sergei?"

"Yes."

"How did you get away from him? We never saw you again—you didn't come back for the second half of the show."

I grimaced and Gary was immediately apologetic.

"You don't have to tell me."

I shook my head. "Yes, I do."

He didn't speak as I stripped off my coat, sweater and shirt. Then I stood with my back to him. I let him look.

After a moment, I turned to face him. His expression was grave and he looked older.

"A woman found me before they did more," I said, my voice soft. "A tourist. She got away and it gave me the time I needed. That's when I ran. I'm sorry. I couldn't warn you."

He was thoughtful for a moment, simply watching as I dressed in silence.

"We all have our demons, Ash. I'll be okay. My parents have been to see me. They're upset, as you can imagine, but they came. So yeah, I'll be okay. Eventually. I'll just have to get some new teeth. I can't go around looking like a hillbilly forever. But how did you end up in Chicago? I couldn't believe it when they told me you were here."

I cleared my throat. Explaining about Laney wouldn't be easy.

His expression changed from surprise to disbelief to something more guarded as I spoke.

"I guess congratulations are in order," he said, throwing me a fake grin.

"Thank you."

His smile faded quickly.

"Have you seen Yveta yet?"

"No, I came to see you first."

"You know they killed Galina?"

I sucked in a breath.

"The police told me they thought she was dead, but…"

"They killed her in front of us. After Sergei let his biker friends have her. God, Ash. I've never seen…"

His voice shook and he swallowed several times before continuing.

"It was obvious we didn't know anything. Hell, I shit myself the moment they looked at me. I think that's why they left me alone mostly. I was too disgusting for them."

He closed his eyes and breathed deeply.

"Yveta had it worse. A lot worse. She … she's not doing so well, Ash."

I'd always thought of anger as hot and sudden, but what I felt now was ice filling my body. I could feel frost creeping through every vein, every artery, until my heart was frozen, too.

"You should go see her," he said, resting his hand on mine and squeezing gently. "Just don't expect too much. Try not to stare—she hates that. And, um, don't tell her about the wife. Not yet."

"But…"

"Seriously, Ash. One thing at a time."

With that cryptic warning ringing in my ears, I nodded and stood up.

"I'll come back."

"Thanks," said Gary, trying to smile. "I'd like that."

Laney was waiting for me, her expression anxious, but I had no words for her. I simply nodded at the policeman outside Yveta's room, and he let me through.

The only light came from the sinking sun, and deep shadows filled the room.

"Hey, it's Ash," I said quietly, not wanting to startle her.

Her head turned toward me slowly, but she didn't speak and her eyes were lifeless. The left side of her mouth was pulled up, deformed by a long, puckered scar—new and badly healed—that stretched all the way up to her hairline.

"Is it okay if I sit down?"

She didn't answer. Gingerly, I sat on the edge of the chair next to her bed. I couldn't tell if she recognized me or not. Maybe she was so drugged up she didn't know anything. I hoped so. I hoped like fuck that she was.

I didn't know what to say to her.

I reached out slowly and took her hand in mine. Her fingers were cold, so I stroked them gently. Speaking quietly, I told her everything—almost—that had happened to me, and that I was sorry. Over and over again, I told her that I was sorry.

When I'd finished, I looked up. Her eyes were closed, but tears tracked down her cheek. I didn't know if she was crying for herself or for me or for all of us. I wanted to cry, too, but my tears were frozen, locked away inside.

I wondered if I'd ever feel anything fully again.

I sat for an hour, holding her hand, saying nothing, until a nurse came to chase me out.

"I'll come back," I said, repeating the words I'd spoken to Gary.

I don't know if she understood.

Laney was still waiting outside, and for some reason that annoyed me. I wanted to be alone with my dark thoughts. Laney was the sunshine, but I couldn't stand her brightness right now.

She must have read my mood, because she didn't try to touch me, although I could tell she wanted to. But she had questions, and that was worse.

"Will you ever tell me? About Sergei, I mean? Why he was so relentless?"

I shrugged, uneasy, wariness darkening my eyes.

She took hold of my hand, and I walked slowly along the hospital corridor. I found myself rubbing my ribcage, as if touch alone could relieve a pain that came from inside.

I still hadn't answered her. My mind was trying to push away the panic and dread. I'd almost forgotten Laney was there, waiting to hear my story: sweet Laney, kind and good.

I looked up into her eyes.

"I can't tell you."

Her disappointment stabbed me in the gut and I had to look away.

"You can tell me anything. I love y—"

I snapped, all my rage and disgust and frustration aimed at Laney. I didn't want to think about all that shit. Why did she keep coming back to it? It was done! Finished! Why wouldn't she let it go?

"I survived!" I shouted.

Laney

I jumped as he slammed his fist into the wall, and then he ran. I could only listen to Ash's rapid footsteps pounding down the corridor.

Tears started in my eyes and I rubbed them away angrily.

"Stupid," I muttered aloud. "So stupid!"

Did I need to know every sordid, desperate thing that Ash had done? I'd seen what Sergei had been prepared to do to him—seen it with my own eyes. But some instinct still warned me that Ash was the one who needed to accept what had happened. If he couldn't talk about it with me, maybe he needed to talk to someone else. A therapist, perhaps? For both of us.

I knew that Ash had moments of being completely numb. He coped by compartmentalizing what had happened. But maybe after all, the best therapy was in each other's arms, clinging together, two shipwreck survivors.

I found him waiting outside the hospital entrance, smoking, his forehead furrowed in a deep frown.

"I've called a cab," I said. "It'll be here in a few minutes. We can go home…"

"I have a show to do."

"Ash, you don't have to…"

"Yes, I do!" he yelled. "Yes, I do! Why don't you understand that?"

A passing nurse gave me a worried look, trying to decide if she needed to intervene, but in the end she walked away, throwing concerned glances over her shoulder. The staff probably saw a lot of crazy people in their hospital.

The cab ride was silent until Ash suggested that I go back to the apartment.

"No, I'm staying with you."

His eyes narrowed and I felt another twinge in my chest, but I tried to ignore it.

The driver dropped us at the corner by the stage entrance, and I followed Ash inside. I could tell that he'd rather be alone, but the theater didn't open to the public for another hour and it was cold outside. Besides, I thought he needed me, even if he didn't seem to agree.

Ash was the last to arrive and the director didn't look pleased, but seeing as it was the closing night, he didn't say anything.

"Nice of you to turn up," snarked Sarah. "Oh hey, Laney! Come to see us waltz off into the sunset?"

"Something like that," I answered with a weak smile.

"What's up? You two look like you've been to a funeral. Oh my God, you haven't, have you?"

"Just a really, really bad day," I said quietly. "I'll tell you later."

"Okaay," Sarah said doubtfully. "Ash, do you want to get changed first or shall I do your makeup?"

"I can do it if you like," I offered.

Ash shook his head curtly. "No, you don't know what to do."

That hurt and he knew it. Sarah put her hands on her hips.

"You're kind of being a dick, you know?"

I found a quiet corner to sit in while Ash went to shave and change into his first costume.

I watched without speaking, but I could tell he was wishing me far away.

Once he finished, he joined a couple of the other dancers in the room they used to warm up, and I muttered that I'd see him later.

"You're being a real dickhead to Laney," I heard Sarah say, as they went through their stretching routine. "Did you have a fight or something?"

Ash

I almost laughed. Was that the worst thing she could think of?

But then as soon as I had that thought, I was disgusted with myself. Would I want someone like Sarah to know that the bogeyman is real because she'd been ruined by him, too? No.

Sexy, smiling, flirty Yveta had been turned into something lifeless and hopeless.

I felt a small piece of the ice in my heart shatter, and I blew out a long breath as I glanced at Sarah.

"No. Just a bad day. A really bad day."

She stared at me, her head on one side.

"We all have them," she said evenly.

I looked away, stretching out my hamstrings.

"I was at a hospital. I saw some friends. They ... they'd been hurt badly."

Sarah's hand covered her mouth.

"Oh my God, I'm so sorry. Was it a car accident? I'd hate to drive in Chicago, the traffic is just crazy and..."

"It wasn't a car accident. It was ... someone hurt them."

Sarah looked even more shocked, but we were interrupted by the AD who told us five minutes to showtime.

There'd been a sudden rush on tickets—nearly 70 sold. The biggest audience we'd had all week.

I stood in the wings, in the darkness, listening to the audience, hearing them breathe, whisper, rustle papers and sweet packets. I could smell the dust swirling under the stage lights, the greasepaint, the sweat from the dancers standing nearest to me. And when the music started, more of the ice dropped away.

My heart began to beat faster.

It was impossible to see beyond the footlights, but I pretended that the theater was full, and I told myself that this mattered—dancing, entertaining—it all mattered. Because living is hard and the world is cruel— and we all need a little sunshine in our lives.

Laney was *my* sunshine, so I would dance for her.

We moved onto the stage in unison, a shimmering chorus line, and the thin applause broke out, scattered and piecemeal, but it was there. I moved my body the way I'd been taught, and I smiled the way I'd been taught.

Sitting out there in the dark, she watched me. I knew because I felt it and a little warmth crept back into my numb body.

When I stepped onto the stage in the second half for my tango with

Sarah, it was Laney that I danced for. The tango is a love story and a hate story; it's two people fighting—two people at one with the music, at one with each other.

It's hard to explain with words—you have to *feel* it—the push and pull, the intensity of the emotions.

I lunged forward, my hand snapping sharply, finishing the move. A noise like the crack of a whip rang out above the music and searing heat shot through my fingers.

Astonished, I stared up at my hand, completely missing the next move as Sarah stumbled, my body not being where it should have been to support her. I was mesmerized by the blood pouring down my wrist.

Someone screamed and then chaos broke out.

I'd been fucking shot!

I stared at my hand in disbelief, the tip of my index finger completely missing.

Adrenaline made me move and I dropped to the stage's sprung floor, temporarily protected by the bank of footlights, clutching my hand to my chest, as screams rang through the air.

"He's got a gun!" someone shouted.

It all came pouring back: the pain, the fear, the complete certainty that Sergei was out there—and that I was going to die.

One crystal clear thought pierced the panic and the overwhelming pounding of my heart: *Laney!*

I half jumped, half fell off the stage and into the orchestra pit. It was still dark in the auditorium, but yellow gashes of light appeared at the exits as people streamed out, panicked and desperate. I prayed that Laney was with them, but I instinctively knew that she wasn't.

The night before Thanksgiving, I'd seen Sergei's face. I'd thought it was part of my waking nightmares, but it had been real.

I knew that now. Just before I'd fought those men, I'd *seen* him, watching me, watching us. He knew about Laney. And he hadn't been taken out by Volkov, he wasn't in Mexico—he was real and he was here, hunting me, hunting Laney.

I felt hot and feverish at the thought of him getting his sick hands on her.

The sound system cut out suddenly and all that was left were terrified screams. Another shot rang out, and this time I was closer to the source.

"Come out, come out, wherever you are, Aljaž!" Sergei sang. "I've got your little wifey! Daddy's waiting, and you've been a bad, bad boy!"

I saw the dark, bulky shape two rows in front of me, and my stomach lurched.

He had Laney.

And a gun to her head.

Laney

I saw Ash fall from the stage and I cried out. A desperate, intense fear filled me. Ash! My love, my husband, my life. My world had ended just as it was beginning. Hope and joy and every pure, human pleasure had been killed.

My knees gave way and the creep struggled to hold me up. The powerful smell of his aftershave combined with body odor made me want to puke.

I guessed who he was as soon as he'd slid into the empty seat next to me just as Ash's tango started. And I also guessed that the cold metal pressing into my stomach was the barrel of a gun.

"I've been watching you," he whispered, his rancid breath making me gag. "Mrs. Novak. Ha! The boy is cleverer than I thought, marrying a scared little mouse for a green card. Well, he owes me, and I *always* collect."

Then he lowered the tinted glasses that he was wearing and peered at me with one empty eye socket.

"An eye for an eye, that's fair, isn't it? A wolf took mine, so I think I'll take *his*. It's almost a shame—he has pretty eyes, doesn't he? Such a lovely color—almost amber when he's pissing himself with fear."

"My father is a police officer," I gasped out.

"I know," he whispered, stroking my cheek with a leather glove.

Then he slapped it across my face. It stung, but that was all.

"You're Sergei."

He smiled, his empty eye winking at me.

"Oh, so he has talked about me?"

"Yeah, he said you're a sick fuck!"

Incredibly, the man's ego inflated, obviously pleased.

"Hmm, that about sums it up," he laughed. "Although I seem to remember that he rather liked my sick fucking. Oh yes, my dear, I've had those sweet lips around my dick. He was very good at sucking me off. I enjoyed it very much."

His good eye glinted maliciously.

"You're lying!"

He actually laughed at me, then called out loudly in a sing-song voice.

"Come out, come out, wherever you are, Aljaž! I've got your little wifey! Daddy's waiting, and you've been a bad, bad boy!"

Then he turned back to me and spoke conversationally.

"Why would I lie? I'm going to kill you anyway, so what does it matter? I want you to die knowing that … but I think I've changed my mind. Maybe I'll let you watch while I fuck him up his pretty little ass—and then I'll kill you."

I couldn't help it. I puked on his shoe.

Revulsion rolled across his face and he raised the gun and crashed the barrel down. I threw my hands up over my face protectively and heard my wrist snap as pain sliced through me. I cried out and fell to the floor, slipping in my own vomit.

I rolled under the row of chairs and started crawling in the darkness, listening to his infuriated screams when he realized that he'd lost me.

I flinched as two gun shots whined overhead. I hoped Ash had enough sense to stay hidden, away from the bright lights of the stage where he'd be an easy target. If we could just hold on, the police would be here. I was certain that every single person who'd been in the audience would have dialed 911. We just had to hold on…

And then the house lights came up.

Sergei twisted around, searching for me, grinning from ear to ear as the gun barrel followed my crawling body. I would have screamed with frustration if there'd been any breath in my lungs.

I saw Ash lunge up, sprinting forward and throwing himself at Sergei. There was another gunshot and Sergei staggered into my row, but didn't fall. He watched my shock as Ash collapsed to his knees, holding a bleeding hand over his chest, and slowly sinking to the ground. Sergei grinned, aiming his gun at my head.

Ash! Oh God, no!

My world ended.

Ash

They say time slows down as you face your own death.

Sergei smiled when he pulled the trigger.

My body felt frozen as I stared down, the gun pointing at my heart. But Laney's shocked and terrified face jolted me into action, a primal urge to protect her, to hurt the thing that threatened her, and I started to move.

Even as my muscles tensed, ready to drive me forward, I felt the impact of the bullet, the air punched from my lungs. I saw muzzle flash and heard a popping sound. It was all in the wrong order, and that bothered me.

I tumbled over the edge of the stage, falling into the orchestra pit, a discordant jangle of noise as I crashed against the drum kit.

I lay winded on the floor, stunned, motionless, my lungs empty. I stared up at the ceiling, the spotlights from the stage painting a silhouette of evil as Sergei leered in triumph. But when he turned and pointed the gun at Laney, time stopped. It was seeing every future falling into black nothingness, and I didn't want to live like that anymore.

Breath surged back into my body and the torn edges of my vision crystalized.

But I was too slow. Even as I pushed myself upright, even as the air rushed past my face, even as I flew forward, I was too slow. Sergei fired the gun and this time it was Laney who fell to the floor.

My body smashed into his and we were wedged between two rows of theater seats, the flip-up section pressing into my screaming ribs.

"You really won't die, will you? Never mind, I've always wanted you on top of me, Aljaž," Sergei mumbled as I rained down punches.

My knuckles split and I could feel a finger sliced open against his teeth.

He spat out a gob of blood and started to speak. I didn't care what he was going to say. Every dark thought that evil bastard had ever had, every breath he'd ever taken had the stench of depravity. Laney was my sunshine, and now she was gone.

In the distance, I heard police sirens, then yells.

Sergei sighed theatrically then grinned at me through bloody teeth.

"I'll be out of jail before breakfast. Then I'll be coming for you."

I shook my head. "Not this time."

The Devil had come for his own.

I pulled the gun from his limp hand and kneeled up. In the distance I heard someone shouting at me to drop the gun. But I had something to do first. I pointed the gun at Sergei's face, ignoring his streaming nose and torn mouth. I pushed the barrel of the gun into his empty eye socket. He laughed.

And this time I pulled the trigger.

His body jerked once and I could smell the sharp stench of cordite.

Hands grabbed me from behind, twisting my arms, forcing me to drop the gun.

I stared down at the gory splatters on my chest: mine, his, I couldn't tell.

I stared in fascination as blood pooled around his head, and a thicker ooze of brain and splinters of bone.

I stared and felt nothing more than a butcher would feel looking at a side of beef. No emotion.

Satisfaction, yes. Relief, yes. Conscience, no. My conscience was quiet.

The pain in my chest shrieked through me as my hands were forced behind my back with a quiet *click*—the cold steel of handcuffs.

And then I saw Laney, still and silent, the side of her head sheeted in blood. Every emotion slammed back, a door opening with a flood of grief and terror and shock.

"Laney!"

I called out her name, trying to reach her, but I was held tightly.

"Laney!" I screamed.

I tried again to get to her, but my cuffed hands were yanked backwards and the pain in my chest was so intense, the light dimmed and I thought I was going to pass out.

"He's her husband! Let him go!"

And then Billy was there, yelling some more.

"Take the cuffs off *now!* Shit, he's been shot, you morons. Where are the paramedics? Ah, fuck, Laney!"

Laney

I was dreaming, floating in that happy place between two worlds.

We were lying in bed together. It was very soft, like resting on clouds, or the ocean on a summer's day. Yes, we were lying on a beach together, the water lapping at our feet.

"Do you dream, Laney? You must do. What do you dream about?"

Ash was bare chested, his skin a deep golden tan, his eyes the color of Irish whiskey. Dream Ash was impossibly beautiful, his long, lean, toned lines, his muscled thighs and sculpted torso. He glistened and glowed under the warm sun—so beautiful.

Dream Ash smiled at me, more relaxed and happy than I'd ever seen him, the tension in his eyes completely absent for once.

"My daytime dreams are different from my nighttime dreams," I smiled. "At night, I dream about flying, not in an airplane, just me, flying through the air." I laughed quietly. "It's pretty self-evident what that means. What do you dream about?"

"Daytime dreams? Those haven't changed. I dream about taking my dancing all over the world, telling stories through dance, making people happy. At night, I used to dream about standing in a spotlight, and if it was a good dream, the music would begin and I'd start to dance. It would start off real, but then the jumps would become bigger, until I was flying through the air—like you."

I smiled. "Do you still have that dream?"

"Not lately, I..."

"We don't have secrets from each other," I reminded him with a gentle nudge.

The sunlight was too bright, so I closed my eyes, listening to the soft slur of Ash's light accent.

"I still dream that I'm standing in the spotlight, but when the music starts, my body doesn't move. It's like I'm frozen. I'm trying to move, but I can't. And then ... then Sergei is there, sometimes Oleg too, and they're laughing and laughing. Once, the girl was there as well, and they pointed the gun at her and then at me, deciding who they'd shoot first."

I felt moisture in my eyes and I opened them to find Ash staring at me, tears running down his cheeks, as well.

"You mustn't give up on your dreams. Not because of those monsters. Never because of them."

And I wasn't sure which of us had spoken...

CHAPTER 18

Ash

I sat by Laney's bed, watching the steady rise and fall of her chest. I could see traces of dried blood in her hair. She'd hate that. A white bandage covered the left side of her head, one forearm heavy under a thick blue cast.

She'd been lucky, they said. The bullet had sliced across the surface of her skull and knocked her out. But he hadn't killed her. She'd wake up soon.

I was lucky, too. Luckier than I deserved. My St. Christopher had been folded in half by the impact of Sergei's bullet. X-rays confirmed that I had a cracked sternum which made it painful to breathe. Black and purple bruises were spreading across my chest, and they kept checking my EKG. Something to do with a trauma injury to the chest, I didn't care.

Up and down. Up and down.

For hours, I watched Laney breathing. I watched her living. And that was enough.

My left hand throbbed, wrapped in bandages. Sergei had shot off the tip of my index finger. They hadn't found it, so it was probably still at the theater. I felt sorry for the janitor. Sweeping up candy wrappers was one thing; blood and body parts probably wasn't in their contract.

Up and down. Up and down.

The police had talked to me while I was still being treated. I couldn't focus and didn't really understand their questions. I didn't care either. Laney's dad told me that Angela was helping. But nothing mattered—just Laney.

Her father was sitting on the other side of the bed, and he kept glancing toward the door, expecting Laney's mother at any moment. She'd been out of town with Laney's sisters, but now they were all on their way.

He cleared his throat.

"We have a witness—one of the ushers says you threw yourself at that piece of shit while you were unarmed."

My head jerked up, surprised that he'd spoken to me. I was still waiting for him to throw me in jail for getting Laney hurt.

His face reddened and his eyes watered as he stared at me.

"You saved her life."

I cocked my head to one side, weighing his words and finding them sincere, but so wrong.

"Sergei came to Chicago because of me. Laney would never have been in danger otherwise."

"Son, I can see that you're not the kind of man who goes looking for trouble. There are a lot of fucked up people in this world, and bad things happen to good people. I don't know why and neither does anyone else. My wife tells me that God knows. Well, good for Him, 'cause it sure as shit makes no sense to me." He paused. "But I know that my daughter is alive because of you."

Then he stood up to shake my hand.

"Welcome to the family, son."

It was so unexpected that I just stared at him like an idiot until I realized that I'd left him hanging. I stood painfully, trying not to breathe too much, and shook his hand.

A moment later, the door was flung open and Laney's mother and sisters poured in. Their questions rattled like rain on a tin roof and I couldn't concentrate.

Thankfully, her dad was used to it and worked his way through the questions one at a time, until they were all satisfied that Laney was in no immediate danger.

"But what about the big boss?" asked Bernice. "The mafia boss?"

Laney's dad grimaced.

"We think he's the reason Boykov was here in the first place. The big boss, Volkov, is cleaning house. It looks like he got tired of the mess his second-in-command was making. If Ash hadn't taken him out, Volkov would have."

Their wide eyes switched to me.

"The boy saved our Laney."

That was it—I was engulfed in hugs and kisses that made me groan with pain. Laney's dad peeled them off one by one, explaining that I was injured, too. Then they fluttered around and I wanted to wave my hands until they scattered like starlings. They meant well, but being surrounded by so many people made me twitchy.

I leaned forward, concentrating on Laney's face, and when I looked up again, much later, they'd all gone.

It was getting light. Morning had finally arrived. I knew that bogeymen didn't vanish at dawn—but something about sunlight made me happier.

The nurses had tried to make me leave, but after Laney's dad spoke to them, they left me alone. One of them returned later with a blanket, so I stayed in the chair next to Laney's bed, watching.

The door opened slowly and I saw Gary standing there, looking uncharacteristically nervous.

"Can I come in?" I nodded and he stepped inside. "Is this her?"

"My wife, yes."

He crept into the room and peered down.

"Man, I can't believe you're married."

My lips twitched with amusement.

"I fly 7,000 miles to get hijacked by Bratva, get whipped by a psycho who wants to fuck me up the ass, I drive across half of the USA to escape him, and then he follows me and tries to kill me … and the part you can't believe is that I'm married?"

He pushed my shoulder, making me wince.

"Sorry," he said. "But it is kind of crazy. She's cute though."

"No, she's the most beautiful, amazing woman I've ever met."

He looked at me sideways.

"I wish some guy would look at me like that."

"I think you're amazing, too," I said sincerely.

Gary grinned.

"Aw, honey! You say the sweetest things. But I'm not going to sleep with you—not even if you beg. Well, maybe if you beg."

Then his face fell and he looked serious.

"Um, just to warn you—Yveta hasn't taken it well."

I frowned, confused.

"Hasn't taken what well?"

Gary sighed. "You being married."

"But…"

I didn't know what I was going to say. I'd had sex with Yveta a few times. I'd never thought that it meant anything to either of us. Just something that we both needed at the time, temporary.

Gary waved a hand.

"I know, I know. But when we were in that place, she kept saying that if you had gotten out, we could, too. And when we did, she was going to look for you. You were a sort of good luck charm—the hope of better times." He sighed again. "She was really cut up when she found out about the wife thing—they had to sedate her."

Gary shook his head.

"I'm sorry, Ash."

He laid his hand on my shoulder for a moment, then bent down to kiss me on the cheek.

"Merry Christmas," he said quietly as he left.

Hope. Such a small word, in my language, too: *upanje*. A small word, but a big emotion—the biggest. But having too much will crush you when you're weighed down with the impossibility of your dreams.

Laney was the sun, my sun. She warmed me, she dazzled me. She lit the way like a beacon of hope.

But Yveta didn't have a Laney. And I didn't know what I could do that might help.

"Ash? Am I dreaming?"

Laney's eyes fluttered open and the stone I'd been carrying in my heart dissolved.

"No, my love. You're awake now."

Her forehead wrinkled.

"He killed you. I saw Sergei shoot you!"

I leaned down to kiss her cheek, nuzzling her neck.

"Sergei can't hurt us anymore. He's gone."

Her eyes drifted closed.

"Is he coming back?"

"Never."

She smiled and I held her small hand in mine as she drifted toward sleep.

"Merry Christmas, my love."

Gary's parents arrived to take him home—solemn and sincere, grateful to have him back in their lives, bemused to find him hand in hand with Yveta. They invited her to spend Christmas and New Year, and she gratefully accepted.

Gary said they were still holding out for a straight son, but I think he was joking.

Yveta made it clear that she didn't want to see me, which meant I had to explain it to Laney.

The stress of the last 24 hours had left us exhausted and we were both on pain meds. I could see the weary resignation on her face, but she tried to joke about it.

"I was hoping for hot sex under the Christmas tree but having you to myself is nice, too."

"I'll give you a raincheck," I promised.

Her parents wanted us to spend Christmas with them. I didn't say anything, but I couldn't stand the thought of being surrounded by people, so I was relieved when Laney insisted on going home instead. She compromised by saying that we'd visit soon.

A cab dropped us at the apartment and we climbed the six steps wearily, Laney leaning against me for support.

I picked up the mail, shocked to see a letter from the U.S. Immigration Service addressed to both of us.

Almost numb, I opened the envelope and pulled out a single sheet of paper. It still took me a while to read English, but three words stood out: *No further action.*

I took a deep breath. They couldn't send me away from Laney—and I had the paper to prove it.

Laney

I was so relieved to be home. Although I couldn't remember everything clearly, flashes of the horror inside the theater plagued my thoughts. Getting whacked on the head by a .32 bullet does that to a person, or so the doctors told me.

Ash was in pain, too. He was given some codeine tablets to take the edge off a cracked sternum, and I had my broken wrist which ached, and my head was throbbing dully.

We spent Christmas curled up on the couch under the quilt from the bedroom, slowly munching our way through frozen pizza, potato chips and everything unhealthy that we could find while watching silly holiday movies. Then we shuffled into the bedroom and fell asleep holding hands.

I was woken the next morning by my cell phone. Ash cursed sleepily as I picked it up to see who was calling so early, but the number was unknown. I pressed 'reject' and tossed it back onto the bedside table, but a moment later, it was ringing again.

If this was a telesales call, I was going to be pissed.

"Hello?"

"Mrs. Novak, good morning. My name is Phil Nickeas from the 'Chicago Tribune'. Is this a good time to talk?"

It took a few seconds for my brain to make a connection. For a start, I wasn't used to being called by my married name, and secondly, *what the hell?*

"How did you get this number?"

"From Angela Pinto. She's a friend of mine and we've worked together a couple of times. She thought if I talked to you it could really help your husband's case."

Case?

My brain was struggling to make sense of what he was saying.

The caller took my silence in his stride.

"I'd really like to get your side of the story before the investigation. Russian mafia—that's big news. I won't be the only journalist to call you, but I'm a crime reporter, not a sleaze-monger. Angie said she was going to call you about me." He paused. "Maybe you need a minute to talk to your husband ... okay, well you can call me back on this number. Any time."

I muttered something and hung up. Ash was sitting with a quizzical expression on his face.

"That was a reporter from the Tribune. He wants to talk to you—to us—about Sergei, I think."

Ash was already shaking his head.

"He said it would help your *case*. What does he mean?"

Ash shrugged and winced as he adjusted the pillow behind him. His chest was a rainbow of ugly black, purple and yellow bruises radiating out from the center.

"Ash, what *case*?"

"The murder case, I guess."

My heart skipped a beat. "What ... what *murder* case?"

His eyes shifted to mine before sliding away.

"Because I shot Sergei."

"You! I thought the police shot Sergei?"

His lips pulled to the side. "No-o. After he shot you, I fought with him. I took the gun and shot him."

A sigh of relief escaped me. "So, it was self-defense."

Ash nodded.

"Thank goodness for that. I thought for a moment ... I don't know what I thought. He made it sound like the police charged you."

"They talked to me at the hospital, but your dad said I didn't have to leave you."

A headache was starting behind my eyes.

"Ash, tell me *exactly* what the police said."

He frowned. "I have some papers they gave me."

He rolled out of bed, moving more stiffly than I was used to seeing. He was normally so graceful and fizzing with energy.

He dug around in his discarded jeans and tossed a packet of papers onto the quilt, then sat back on the bed, watching me.

I unfolded the top sheet and as I started reading, blood drained from my face.

"Ash, it says here that there's going to be an investigation. They'll be gathering evidence from witnesses and you'll be interviewed formally. We both will." I bit my lip. "I don't see how they can possibly charge you with anything—it's ridiculous."

Ash didn't seem the least concerned.

"Your friend Angie left a message on my cell—she wants to talk to me."

I nodded quickly. "Yes, that's good. I'll call her in a minute. But ... I don't know ... why did that reporter talk about a 'case'? There is no case."

"I killed him. I don't care what they call it," Ash snapped, his jaw tight. "We could hear the police sirens and their voices. Sergei laughed, saying he'd be out of jail by morning and then he'd come after us. So, I pushed the gun in his face and pulled the trigger. He wasn't laughing anymore. And I'd do it again. One of the policemen took the gun."

I thought I was going to pass out—this wasn't an open and shut case of self-defense. Could they call it murder? I didn't want to believe that was possible.

The police would investigate then bring it to the DA. He'd decide if there would be any charges.

Oh my God, surely not. It was self-defense.

"Ash, you need to speak to Angie as soon as possible. This is serious."

"I did what I had to!" he yelled.

He stormed into the bathroom, slamming the door, and a second later I heard the shower running. I hoped it was a cold one, because he had to cool down. He clearly had no idea how serious this was.

I called Angie immediately.

"Finally!" she said, answering on the first ring. "I've been calling and calling you! I've left messages!"

"I only just found out. Oh God, Angie. What are we going to do?"

"Firstly, don't panic. I need to talk to Ash, but this is it in a nutshell: armed officers entered the theater. Boykov was on the floor and Ash was hitting him with his bare hands. They couldn't see clearly because they were on the floor between two rows of seats. The next thing they heard was a gunshot. Boykov was dead and Ash was holding the gun. But the Russian had already fired at both of you. Personally, I don't think there's much chance that they'll file charges."

I was finding it hard to breathe.

"But there is chance?"

"Laney, calm down. We've got a few facts in our favor. One: even though two police officers shouted at Ash to drop the weapon, he didn't appear to hear them. You know the drill—people usually look in the direction of sudden noise. Ash didn't even flinch, which goes to suggest that he hadn't heard the orders. Two: no one else saw what happened."

"But..."

"Don't tell me anything I don't want to hear, Laney," she warned. "Thirdly, during prior police interviews with Ash, they'd suspected that he was suffering from a post-traumatic disorder. This is all in his favor."

"Okay," I said quietly, trying to take it in. "What about this reporter? Why did you give him my number?"

"He's a good guy, Laney. I've worked with him before—a real straight shooter. He's been working on several mafia-related and people-trafficking stories. He'll be fair, and Ash could use some good publicity—it'll get the community on his side. The fact that he's a foreigner and that he married you so quickly will look like all he's after is a green card. Hey, don't shoot the messenger!"

I huffed quietly, even though what she said wasn't untrue—except that now it was.

"He needs to make sure he charms the hell out of everyone he meets from now on." She paused. "Talk to Phil. I'll brief Ash about what he can and can't say. Okay?"

"Okay."

There was a long pause, then she spoke more quietly.

"I'll do everything I can."

We ended the call, and I promised to speak to her reporter friend.

But first I had to talk to Ash.

Ash finally reappeared looking calmer, although I could see the lingering tension in his expression.

"We have a few things to talk about."

For a moment I thought he was going to argue, but then his body sagged and he sat down on the bed.

I explained everything Angie had said and why she thought we should talk to the reporter. He wasn't keen at first, but eventually agreed.

I reminded him to call Angie to talk through his approach while I contacted the reporter. But Angie had already been in touch and Phil Nickeas was already on his way over.

It didn't give me much time to shower and dress, especially as I had a broken wrist.

Ash tidied the apartment, which didn't take long as neither of us were particularly messy, and he hadn't been around that much lately. Then I heard the coffee machine puttering in the kitchen. I hadn't even had my first gulp before Ash was buzzing in our visitor.

Phil Nickeas was a good looking guy with sandy hair in his mid-thirties. I don't know what I'd expected, maybe a grizzled older man.

"Thanks for taking the time to see me, Mrs. Novak, Mr. Novak."

"Well, Angie spoke very highly of you, so…"

He grinned, looking much younger.

"Smart woman, Ms. Pinto."

Oh, yeah. He was totally into my friend. Interesting.

I suddenly felt a lot better about the interview. Ash, on the other hand, was wary and uncomfortable, looking as if he was itching to pick a fight, or find a reason not to do the interview.

"Is it okay if I record this as well?" Phil asked as he placed his phone between us.

Ash glanced at me and I nodded.

"So, Mr. Novak, take me back to what brought you to the U.S. in the first place."

Ash's mouth twisted in distaste and I held his hand to reassure him. Or me. Probably both of us.

"It's hard to talk about all this," Ash said stiffly. "I keep trying to put it behind me."

"I understand, but with all due respect, that's not going to happen."

"I just want to live my life!" Ash growled. "Be with my wife, dance. It's not so much!"

His accent always became more pronounced when he was upset.

"Your best chance to make this go away is to give your side of the story now. Angie is a great criminal attorney and she wouldn't have suggested that you speak to me if she didn't think it would help your case."

Ash bowed his head, staring at our hands.

"Okay."

"If it helps any, I already spoke to Mr. Benson and Ms. Kuznets—they only have good things to say about you."

Ash looked up. "You've seen them? How are they?"

Phil's expression was sympathetic.

"You've all been through some bad stuff, and it'll take time. Bratva are ruthless, vicious. But they're clever, too. Good at covering their tracks—at least that's true of Volkov. This Sergei character, it looks like he'd been a loose cannon for a while and Volkov was itching to get rid of him. Hell, you probably did the guy a favor."

"He was evil. I'm glad I killed him."

I squeezed Ash's hand, warning him not to admit to anything. Yes, this reporter was on our side, but ultimately, he was here to sell newspapers—we had to be careful.

Ash took a deep breath before launching into his story, starting from seeing an advertisement for a job in Las Vegas. I chimed in with a few things about our escape: Ash's memory of that was hazy. I should have realized at the time that he was in shock, but I'd been too scared myself to fully understand.

Ash wouldn't look when I showed Phil the photograph of his lacerated back, although he did agree to let the reporter see how it had healed. My poor boy's scars were worse on the inside.

Ash stood in the center of our small living room and yanked his shirt over his head, breathing in humiliation as Phil took several photographs.

Then we talked about our relationship, and I even admitted that I'd been seeing someone else when I met Ash, but tried to downplay that as much as possible. I wasn't proud of the way I'd treated Collin.

And because Phil was good at his job, he also worked out that Ash had taken the theater job before his green card had come through.

I winced, knowing that the same information would come out in the event of a court case.

"Ash came into the U.S. on an H-1B Specialty Occupations work visa. That was legitimate and he believed it was still valid," I improvised. "We were already married when he realized that it was time-expired. It was a genuine mistake."

I'm not sure if he believed me, but he didn't challenge us on it either.

And then Ash was asked to describe what had happened in the theater. He started off calmly, but soon his voice rose and he started pacing the room, tugging on his short hair.

I threw him a warning look, but he was too locked in his memories.

"I saw Laney fall and my world ended," he cried out. "I wanted to die with her—but I wanted *him* to die first."

He took a deep, satisfying breath.

"So I killed him."

Oh, Ash.

Phil's eyebrows shot up. "Um, so you might want to practice that answer before the police interview you."

"Why should anyone care?" Ash yelled. "He was evil! He was a murderer! He liked to torture people—who cares that he's dead? He tried to kill Laney! I'd do it again!"

"Ash," I called, holding out my good arm to him.

He threw himself at my feet, wrapping his arms around my waist as his knees bumped against the couch. Shuddering breaths wracked his whole body.

"I love you," I whispered, tears pricking my eyes as I held him tightly. "I love you."

Out of the corner of my eye I saw Phil stand up.

"I'll see myself out," he said quietly.

Ash

I had no ego left, no arrogance. It had all been stripped away. Stolen. And I was naked before her. There was nothing left, just Laney and her arms around me.

We stayed that way for a long time, her gentle fingers stroking my back, running through my hair, soothing, wordless.

Eventually, my knees protested about the hard wooden floors and I stood clumsily, wiping my eyes, too exhausted to be embarrassed that I'd broken down in front of that reporter.

I'd lost everything else—the loss of dignity wasn't going to kill me. I wanted to laugh at the irony.

No, I was wrong. I hadn't lost anything, because my Laney was still here.

When I dared to look, her eyes were gentle, warm. It was one of those quiet, subtle moments, where words weren't needed to communicate the deepest feelings.

We were together, through the good times and the bad.

And I finally understood. Why have a beating heart if you don't know why it beats—or for whom.

"I love you, too," I said.

CHAPTER 19

Laney

Phil Nickeas' article came out on December 28th, the morning of our police interview. Angie had given me a heads up that it was going to be published. Ash volunteered to run out and buy the newspaper, and he needed to get out of the apartment. Despite the pain from his fractured sternum, he was going stir crazy with nothing to do. He didn't like reading in English and television bored him. He spent most of his time surfing the net and listening to music, exercising as much as he could—probably more than he should.

He returned ten minutes later, his cheeks flushed from the cold and snowflakes clinging to his long eyelashes.

He flung the paper onto my desk and stalked into the kitchen.

I was only four pages in when I found Phil's article:

SLAVES OF THE SYSTEM
Murder, rape, drugs trafficking, people trafficking, a guerilla war of attrition. And it's not a million miles away in some Middle Eastern caliphate; it's right here in the U.S.
It's right here in Chicago.

Crime reporter Phil Nickeas' met with three victims of the rise of the new mafia from Russia, three people who survived terrible oppression and modern-day slavery.

And there was a large black and white photograph of Ash mid dance, his intense gaze staring from the page, his powerful physique displayed. I recognized the costume—black pants and silver shirt slashed to the waist. It was from the tango he'd performed in *Broadway Revisited*. They'd cut Sarah from the photo—I bet she'd be mad about that. But then I remembered that she was 4,000 miles away in London.

The article was a powerful voice, crying out against organized crime and the way loopholes in the system were used and abused. From the general, it went to the specifics, telling Ash's story alongside Yveta's and Gary's.

My cell phone rang and Angie's name flashed up.

"Have you read it?"

"I'm reading it now. It's good, really good."

"Told you. I think this will really help the case. Phil wants to keep the pressure on the authorities both here and in Nevada. He's got evidence that other cases have been swept under the rug, and victims who survived are just sent back to Europe or Africa or wherever. But Ash is too public—it's just what was needed."

I bristled at her excited tone.

"Ash is a person, not a story!"

She was instantly contrite.

"I know, I'm sorry. But if Phil keeps Ash's case in the newspapers, it will help other people—you must see that."

I sighed. "Yes, I do. But I also see the stress it puts him under."

"Fair enough." She paused. "So, I'll see you both at the police station."

"Yes."

"It's going to be fine, Laney."

"Sure."

And so for the fourth time since I'd known Ash, we spent the afternoon at the police station being interviewed.

I wasn't allowed to sit in with Ash, or hear what he said, but Angie told me that he'd done well and hadn't allowed himself to become emotional.

Now, all we had to do was wait.

"My best advice is to try and put this behind you both," she said. "It's New Year's in a couple of days. You should go out—celebrate. After all, going into a new year you've got more to celebrate than most people."

I laughed dully.

"Well, that's definitely true. Actually, we're having lunch with Gary and Yveta at his parents' house on New Year's Day. They're up in Kenosha. We don't want to do anything much for the next few days, so we're staying in and keeping the TV company—low key is all either of us can take right now."

We parted with mutual promises to meet soon and discuss additional publicity strategies. *Would we ever put this behind us?*

As the sun sank behind the city, and the clouds turned from purple to an ominous gray heavy with snow, we watched the old year fade into the past. Alone, but together.

"It's been some year," I said thoughtfully.

Ash slipped his arm around my waist as we snuggled on the couch, my head on his shoulder.

He shifted slightly so he could look at me.

"Do you regret it?" he asked cautiously.

"Yes, lots of things," I said honestly. "I should never have let things go on so long with Collin. I hate the way he found out. He's a good man—he didn't deserve what happened. But you're a good man too, Ash. I regret the way we met. I hate what happened to you, but I will never regret that we did meet, and I will never regret marrying you. We don't make any sense, nothing about us fits, but we're real."

He smiled, his eyes the color of chocolate in the dim lighting, his sharp cheekbones casting stark shadows.

"You are the strongest person I have ever met, Laney. I am awed by you, my love."

I shook my head.

"No, don't give me false credit. But I will say one thing: I'm stronger with you. It's like..." and I struggled to find a word that conveyed everything I felt. "It's syzygy," I said, finally.

Ash's forehead creased.

"I don't know that word. Is it Polish?"

I smiled.

"No, it's from Ancient Greek. The psychoanalyst Carl Jung used it to mean 'a union of opposites'. In astronomy, it's an alignment of the sun, the earth and the moon—three celestial objects."

I could see that the idea appealed to him. He pulled me against him more tightly.

"My sunshine," he said.

I sighed. "I really want to make love to you right now, but I'm so tired and everything hurts."

He was silent for a moment.

"Maybe I could make you feel good without fucking?"

"Such sweet words. You're really turning me on," I said, deadpan.

Ash laughed ruefully, then kissed my neck.

"Does that mean yes?"

His fingers swept up my side, sending sparks shooting along my spine and settling low in my belly. I reached up to kiss him, but accidentally swatted his chest with my cast, making both of us flinch.

"Maybe not," I winced, holding my broken wrist.

His eyes flattened with disappointment, but he didn't argue.

Then he reached out to hold my hand and kissed it gently, his soft lips lingering.

"Happy New Year, my love."

New Year. I liked the sound of that.

Snow had fallen overnight, transforming the city into a winter wonderland. Only a few cars and trucks had driven along the powdery streets, and the sidewalks were still fresh and clean. The long decay into slush and dirt wasn't far away, but for now, I could stand on our balcony and breathe in the sharp, cold air and feel like everything was reborn.

Ash had been happy when Gary had invited us to his home, and I saw something spark inside him. Then he told me what he wanted to do, the thoughts and plans whirring through his incredible mind, I was awed. And so proud. But he needed Gary. And Yveta.

We arrived a little late, and Gary must have been watching for us, because the second we pulled up, he ran out of the house to meet us wearing ridiculous bunny slippers. He grinned broadly and I tried not to wince as I saw the gap on one side of his mouth where several teeth were missing.

He yanked open the driver's door and pulled Ash into a tight hug, whispering something that had Ash smiling at his friend.

"Welcome to my humble abode, lovely Novaks!" Gary sang. "Come in and meet the 'rents." He lowered his voice. "We saw the article in the newspaper."

"What did you think?"

"It was fair. I don't know if it will make any difference."

"How's Yveta?" asked Ash.

Gary sighed.

"Up and down. I think she needs some help, but no one wants to know. The Russian Embassy has offered to fly her home, but she doesn't have any family or close friends once she's there. I don't know how long they'll let her stay here…" He glanced at me. "Maybe I should marry her."

Ash punched him in the shoulder and Gary laughed. Then he walked around the car to help me out, sliding his arm through mine as we made our way up the path to the front door.

It was an older style wooden farmhouse, although there were several other new-builds near it now.

Gary's parents, Judith and Henry, were like something out of a Grant Wood painting, very upright, restrained, almost severe in their welcome. How they managed to have a son like Gary who was so flamboyant—that was anyone's guess. I knew that Ash harbored a lot of resentment because of his father who'd thought dancing was effeminate, and I tried to imagine how it must have been for Gary growing up here.

But when we walked into the house, it was filled with a wonderful aroma of baking bread, taking me back to a simpler, less complicated time in my life.

Yveta was curled up in an armchair in the living room, the curtains drawn, the lighting dim.

"Oh my Go— good grief!" snapped Gary. "This is all too American Gothic. Open the damn— dang drapes!"

He yanked back the curtains, making us all blink, and I saw Yveta for the first time. My eyes were instantly drawn to the ugly puckered scar on her cheek, making it seem as if she was sneering at the world, and maybe she was.

She was tall and very thin, with thick blonde hair that hung across her face unstyled.

Ash simply walked up to her and kissed her on both cheeks, smiling down at her as he held her hands.

Yveta's cold eyes turned glassy and she threw herself into his arms, her tears sudden and heart-breaking.

I watched in awkward silence, not knowing what to do or where to look, until Gary nudged my arm.

"Coffee?"

I nodded and followed him out to the kitchen where his parents stoically set the table with cloth napkins and silverware. They seemed to ignore his presence and he did the same.

"Yveta does that all the time," he said sadly. "She's better though, I think. Calmer. But long term…" he blew out a breath, then changed tack.

"So, tell me all about Mrs. Novak. I'm dying to hear about the woman who snapped up the hottest talent in town."

"I'm sure Ash has told you how we met."

Gary waved a hand.

"He's a guy. I need to hear some girl talk."

I smiled.

"You'd love my parents' house—four daughters. Dad is completely outnumbered."

"Sounds like heaven. Speaking of which, how have they taken to the exotic delights of your new hubby?"

"Surprised, but they're getting used to the idea." I shrugged. "My Dad is having a bromance with him ever since Ash saved my life."

Gary's face was serious.

"He must really love you."

"It's mutual."

Then we heard the front door slam and two seconds later, Ash and

Yveta were disappearing down the driveway, crunching through the snow, their heads bent low, his arm around her slim waist.

Gary threw me a quick look.

"They've been through a lot together."

"We all have," I said softly.

Ash

We walked slowly through the thick snow, our boots crunching and our breath misting around us. My hands hurt, the stump throbbing, the broken fingers aching.

I was comfortable with silence and despite everything, being out of the city felt good, like I could breathe.

"This reminds me of home," Yveta said after a few minutes. "Although it's warmer here," and she shot me a quick smile, her hair sliding across her scar. "I grew up in Siberia. Like Galina. I didn't know her then and we didn't meet until we both moved to St. Petersburg when we were 14. We didn't have much, it was hard, you know? Our apartment was an old Soviet concrete block with fifty other families. You found a way out by working hard: ballet, chess, math, gymnastics, dancing. I practiced every day for hours, before and after school. Dancing is all I've ever wanted."

She snorted in sour amusement.

"But who wants to see a scarred dancer? No one, I think."

I didn't disagree with her because I knew she was right. My own scars were less obvious.

"What about plastic surgery?"

"Maybe," she sighed. "If I had the money."

Then her eyes darted to mine.

"Do you love her? Or is it for a green card?"

I'd expected this question.

"At first. But now, yes, I love her very much."

She stared, as if she wasn't sure I was telling the truth.

"We should be getting back."

"To your wife?" she sneered.

I ignored her tone and turned around, retracing our steps.

After a while, she tugged on my sleeve, and I looked up to see her apologetic expression. I sighed and linked our arms together so we were walking side by side.

"I thought about you all the time we were in that terrible place," she said, her voice soft. "When those men … I shut my mind to it. Instead, I thought about dancing with you—how happy we were when we were allowed to duet: you and me, Gary and Galina. It seems a lifetime ago. It *was* a lifetime ago. I think I died in that place with Galina. She was my best friend. But Las Vegas was my idea. She'd still be alive if … I hate myself. I don't know who this ugly person is now."

"You're not ugly," I said sharply.

She gave a hollow laugh.

"Don't lie to me, Aljaž. I'm a monster. No one will want to look at me on a stage. No one will send their child to take lessons with me—they'd be terrified. My life is over."

I stopped walking and tugged her around to face me. Carefully, I drew my finger down her scar, then tipped her chin up as she tried to hide her face.

"You are scarred, but you're still you and you're still beautiful, Yveta."

Her eyes glossed with tears, but a smile trembled on her lips.

"There's something I wanted to talk to you about," I said, looking at Gary and Yveta in turn.

I held Laney's hand under the table, and she gave it an encouraging squeeze.

"After I talked to that reporter, I kept thinking that it wasn't enough. The FBI is breaking up Volkov's network, for now, at least. But, we can do more. I *have* to do more."

"Don't tell us you're joining the Marines," Gary deadpanned.

"I want to tell our story. I say we tell *our* story *our* way."

"And what way is that?" asked Gary skeptically.

I sat back and stared at him. "Through dance."

There was a long silence, then Gary shook his head.

"Nice idea, showboat, but it would never work."

"Why not?"

"Because people go to the theater to be entertained, not made miserable."

I raised my eyebrows. "I don't remember a lot of laughs in 'Romeo and Juliet' or 'La Traviata'."

Gary looked thoughtful, but didn't answer. I leaned forward, wanting … no, *needing* them to understand.

"We can do this! We tell our story, everyone's story: Galina, Marta, the girl. We show what happened to us, and we show that we survived."

I could see that even Yveta was intrigued, her eyes alive for the first time since…

Gary shook his head.

"We'd never get backing. All the money is in tried and tested shows—the freakin' hills are alive. Nothing like you're describing has ever been done before."

I grinned at him. "Yes and no. People go to the ballet, yes? Well, we'll take them to the ballroom instead. We just have to get someone interested—a backer. But guess what—we know a journalist who wants to help us."

"And what are you going to call this extravaganza of blood, sweat and dance?"

"*Slave—A Love Story.*"

Gary smiled and clapped his hands together.

"So we make them cry into their popcorn and candy because they get their happy ever after. Hmm, it's got legs, honey. But what about music? What about performers? Rehearsal space? A theater?"

"For music, we use a mix of classic ballroom numbers, rock and pop. The audience will know some of them, but not all. We get a group who can do covers…"

"Woah! Woah! Not recorded music?"

I shook my head.

"No, we want the 'wow' factor. It's got to be 100% live. I want people to *feel* the music, *feel* the dance. I want them to know what it's like."

Gary's face hardened. "You really want to put all our dirty linen out in public?"

"No, but I need to. This isn't just about Sergei or even Volkov. This is about dozens, maybe hundreds of girls like Galina, like Marta; thousands of people like the Unknown Girl. They had no voice, but we have a chance to speak for them—to tell *their* stories. If we do this, it means the Bratva haven't won."

Gary was silent, glancing at Yveta. But her eyes were fixed on the pitted and scarred kitchen table.

Laney nodded, her eyes glowing, giving me her silent approval.

Gary frowned. "You really think you can pull this off?"

"I don't know," I said honestly. "But I have to try."

Gary took a deep breath.

"I'm in. Yvie?"

She didn't look up. "I'm in."

CHAPTER 20

Laney

I was so proud of him. So damn proud. After everything he'd been through, his heart was so big, so full of love.

He was taking on a huge challenge, but I'd do everything I could to help him.

Yveta, Gary, Ash … me. Could all these broken people make something whole?

Phil loved the idea. He met us at our favorite coffee shop to listen to Ash's pitch.

"It's a great story," he said, twirling his pen between his fingers. "I'll get something in next week. I can mention that you're looking for backers, and I'll speak to Chris Jones, our theater reviewer. He might know some people. What do you need?"

Ash shrugged.

"Everything: a theater to take the show—maybe one outside the city, as well; dancers, singers and musicians, rehearsal space, costume and makeup, marketing, ticket sales, publicity, graphics, ads, backstage, front of house, lighting, audio, a producer…"

He sighed and glanced across at me, discouraged by the long list of things it would take to get this show on the road.

Phil was upbeat and took some photographs of Ash that were suitably dramatic, standing in the snow, his hands resting on his hips in a defiant stance, his bandaged hand stark against his dark coat.

When we made it back to the cozy warmth of the apartment, his energy levels were high, whereas I felt like wrapping myself in a quilt and eating pizza until I passed out.

I watched him pacing up and down, deep in thought. Then he pulled out the smart phone that I'd bought him for Christmas, and plugged in his earbuds. Lost in music, an intense frown of concentration on his face, I could tell that he was thinking about the new show. Every now and then, he'd make a dramatic sweeping gesture with his arms or suddenly slide into a lunge. Then he'd frown and nod, or frown and shake his head. It was fascinating to see him work, and soon I gave up any pretense of reading, preferring to watch him, so graceful, a dynamic presence.

Sometimes I could tell the style of the dance because of the very specific moves; other times it was looser, less pure ballroom and more pure Ash.

The afternoon passed and the sky darkened, the street lamps washing the world in a deceptive glow that promised warmth. But winter days were short and the nights long.

I must have fallen asleep eventually, because I woke when Ash sat down next to me, passing me a chamomile tea.

"Luka is in," he said excitedly.

"Who?"

"My friend Luka—he texted me. He's been on tour in Germany, but he finishes soon, so he's going to fly out here. Is it okay if he stays with us?"

I rubbed my forehead.

"Ash, did you offer him a job?"

"He's a great dancer," he said, defensively deflecting my question.

"I don't doubt that. But he doesn't have a work visa, we have no way of paying him, and we don't even know when or if the show will happen."

Anger flashed in his eyes and he leapt off the couch.

"You are always saying that we work and try and don't give up. And now you want to give up before we start."

"That's not what I said! I'm just pointing out…"

"What? That it's hard? That there are mountains to climb? My friends were raped, two girls were murdered, but this is too hard for you!"

"You're not being fair!"

"Life isn't fair!" he shouted.

"Stop yelling at me! I'm on your side!"

He stood in front of me, his fists clenched, his nostrils flaring.

"Ash," I said more calmly, "I'm just saying there's a lot of work to do before we're anywhere near offering Luka a job. I'm not an expert in this—I don't know if *I* can pull off helping you produce this show. And I don't want to let you down."

He sat heavily, his head thudding against the back of the couch.

"How much money do we need?" he asked, his eyes closed.

"Well," I said, swallowing. "I'm basing it roughly on what you were paid for *Broadway Revisited*. If we assume 20 dancers, 12 musicians, six lighting, audio and backstage, two admin at $800 a week, say … and you want a month of rehearsal?"

"Minimum."

"That's $128,000—plus a couple of thousand for renting rehearsal space. My best guess, $135,000 for the first four weeks of rehearsals."

"Fuck!"

"And if we assume a theater of 500 seats, $45 per head, 75% capacity—that works out at $16,875 per night. With the theater having 50% of the take and paying salaries for a three-week run..." I took a deep breath, wincing as I handed out the news. "We'd have to sell 10,500 tickets to break even."

Ash stared at me. He looked sick. "Ten *thousand?*"

I nodded.

He stood up, fisting his hair and pacing the room with long strides.

"*Ten thousand?*"

"Yes."

"*Pizda!*"

"Excuse me?"

"Fuck! *Fuck! FUCK!*"

Ash grabbed his coat and stormed out of the apartment.

The truth was, we needed the best part of a quarter of a million dollars to make the show viable.

Ash

I strode down the street, the heat of my anger warming me, even though I could feel the wind biting at my cheeks.

I wasn't angry with Laney. I saw now why she'd been so worried. I was a fool—an imbecilic naïve fool. How could I not have understood all this? I'd got everyone's hopes up for nothing.

And then I thought of Yveta's face—the flicker of life in her eyes when I'd talked about the show, about taking control of our lives, taking back what had been stolen.

Somehow, *somehow* I had to find the money.

My footsteps slowed as I squinted up at the sky, but the stars were hidden under heavy clouds that promised more snow, and I could feel the weight of what I was trying to do press down on me.

Laney

Ash returned half an hour later, looking frozen, apologetic, and he wasn't shouting at me anymore. But he was quiet, and I wondered what he was thinking.

His face had settled into a sort of grim determination.

"Laney, does Chicago have a mayor?"

"Yes, why?"

He nodded.

"Good, then we start at the top. Can you make a list of 100 of the most influential people in Chicago: politicians, business, media, Chief of Police—everyone you can think of. We'll contact them all."

I blinked, surprised by what he was suggesting. A slow smile crept across my face.

"You're not giving up."

He stared grimly. "I can't."

The next two weeks were a whirlwind. The article came out and we milked it for all it was worth. Ash turned out to be a natural at schmoozing when he needed to, and soon we had TV and radio stations asking for interviews. Of course, it helped enormously that he was handsome and charismatic.

Money was beginning to trickle in. Not from traditional routes—all those grant applications would take months to secure, and that was just filling in the reams of paperwork. No, the public was funding us directly. Our Go Fund Me account already had nearly $13,000. We had a long way to go, but we were getting there. Ash was making it happen.

One of Angie's colleagues agreed to donate time to prepare any contracts once we got to that stage, and Dad was setting up a press conference/photo opportunity with the Police Commissioner.

Best of all, my local gym offered Ash, Yveta and Gary free memberships, and use of the dance studio when it wasn't being used.

Ash said he needed to get in shape. Believe me, I'd been checking, and his shape looked darn good to me. But the offer was a godsend and he spent a lot of hours there doing a combination of yoga, swimming and even weight lifting. That surprised me—I didn't think dancers wanted bulky muscles.

"I don't," he said. "But I use light weights—the idea is to stretch and tone the muscles, not build bulk. For dancers, it's best to go for more reps and fewer pounds, to build endurance. It's not really necessary in traditional ballroom, but when you're training to lift a partner, yeah, it's useful."

"Will you be doing a lot of that, lifting, I mean?" I asked, puzzled.

Ash gave me a look I couldn't interpret and nodded.

Ash

I looked down at Laney, seeing the stress on her face, hating that I was the cause of it. She was in pain again, although she didn't say much. She'd met me at the dance studio today because I'd been working late with Gary and we were all going to eat after.

I hadn't shared my ideas for the show, and when we got to really rehearsing—if that ever happened—I'd have to ban her from coming, which would be hard because she wouldn't understand and I couldn't explain yet.

Laney was still watching me, her expressive face tired and worried. I leaned down to kiss her again, seeing in the studio's mirrors, over and over, the reflection of two lovers, traveling into infinity.

I kissed her once more, my lips lingering as ever. Then with a promise of more later, I headed for the showers. Gary was already dressing when I got there, discretely eyeing up some men I recognized from the weight room.

He grinned and winked as I walked past, and I raised my eyebrows.

"Hey, showboat! Your locker has been ringing for the last ten minutes. Laney must be missing you."

I frowned. "No, I just saw her in the studio. She's going to wait for us at the front."

"Well, someone wants to get their hands on your cute ass, not that I can blame them."

I sat down on the bench and pulled my phone out of the locker—there was a missed call from a local number and a voicemail alert.

I listened intently.

"Hello, Mr. Novak. My name is Selma Pasic and I'm Director of the Savannah Phillips Theater. I've been reading about you and your dance performance. Well, we have a two-week slot available for the last two weeks of March and we'd like to offer it to you. If you're interested, please call me as soon as possible to discuss terms."

I replayed the message for Gary. He stared at me in disbelief.

"Holy shit! We have a theater!"

I called back immediately but got voicemail, so I tossed my phone to Gary.

"I'm going to shower. If she calls back, set up a meeting. I don't care when. Now, if she wants."

Three minutes later I was trying to pull my clothes over a damp body and Gary was twitching excitedly.

"She sounded really nice," he gushed. "Totally in love with the concept. Oh, leave your shirt undone a bit more."

"What?"

"She's a woman. She has a pulse. Leave the shirt open."

"Fuck that. It's January and five below out there!"

"Listen, showboat! Right now the woman on the end of that phone is offering you everything you want. Work your freakin' strengths. Shirt. Open."

Muttering to myself, I did what he said. At least no one would see until I took my coat off. I felt like a douchebucket.

As soon as Gary saw Laney, he launched into an explanation, then grabbed the handles of her wheelchair and started to push.

I elbowed him out of the way.

"My job," I growled at him.

"Much as I adore your wife," he said pointedly, "I'm still gay. Stop being so territorial."

"My job!" I repeated.

Laney giggled, but Gary poked me in the ribs, making me squirm.

We skidded along the rain-soaked streets, Gary marching ahead and waving everyone out of our way as if we were royalty.

"Is he always like this?" Laney asked quietly.

"Worse," I snorted.

"I can totally hear you!" Gary snapped.

Laney buried her face in her scarf to stop herself from laughing.

God, every day I fall deeper in love.

It was a slow falling, like floating through clouds, my body weightless. It was a peaceful falling, with sun on my face, my heart warmed. Just ordinary things that nobody else would notice—the way she tapped her fingers out of time when a favorite song was playing, the way she looked at me when I walked through the door. Always the same: my eyes, my lips, my body, back to my eyes.

And she was so strong. I was in awe of her.

Also, sex with Laney was the best I'd ever had. I couldn't figure that out. She wasn't the most athletic, obviously; she wasn't the dirtiest and it took a while to persuade her to try new things. But every time, the woman rocked my world. I came so hard and so often, I sometimes couldn't believe I wouldn't shrivel up and die happily.

Maybe it was love that made the difference.

We skidded to a stop outside a slightly shabby theater with fresh posters of new plays. It might be small and older, but they were showing some interesting work.

"Uh, maybe I should wait at that coffee shop," Laney said hesitantly.

"What for, honey?" asked Gary, beating me to it.

"Well, she's expecting to see dancers, not me."

I yanked open the door, pushed her inside, then leaned down and whispered in her ear.

"Where would we be without our producer?"

"Besides," said Gary, arching one eyebrow. "Between us, we cover all the diversity groups: gay, foreign, less able." Then he frowned at Laney. "Can you pretend to be a black lesbian, too?"

"I can't believe you said that!" she snorted, trying not to laugh.

A striking looking woman with long brown hair and a nice set of tits came around the corner to greet us.

"Mr. Novak?" she asked, her eyes flicking from me to Gary and back again, then dipping to Laney.

"Yes," I said, holding out my hand and ignoring Gary's whisper to open another button on my shirt. "Ms. Pasic?"

"Call me Selma."

She looked at me expectantly.

"Ash," I smiled. "And this is my wife Laney Novak, also our producer; and my co-lead Gary Benson, also co-choreographer."

She led us to a small and cluttered office, pushing aside a prop of a horse's head to make room for Laney's wheelchair.

"So, we unexpectedly have a slot for the last two weeks of March. Since it's such short notice, we'll cut our commission to 40% of the box office takings, and provide all the front of house services, as well as our sound and lighting team. You'll be responsible for bringing the production to the stage: and that includes all the relevant permissions for music and insurances. We'll take care of ticket sales and marketing, but we'll need you to keep up some media presence. So, what do you say?"

I was nodding throughout her whole speech, amazed that finally things were going our way, but Laney rested her hand on my arm.

"It all sounds wonderful, Selma. If you could forward the contracts to me, I'll have our legal team go over it."

I grinned at her. We had a legal team now?

Thirty minutes later, we were out of the door with draft contracts in our pockets.

Laney

"I need a name for the company," he frowned.

"You could call it *Novak*," I suggested. "You told me your surname translates as 'new man'—it seems apt."

Ash shook his head. "It means something more like 'rookie'. Anyway, I need something that explains *us*."

I wasn't sure who he meant by 'us': the dancers, the story, or him and me, but I had an idea.

"How about *Syzygy*: a union of opposites, a mystical alignment?"

His face lit with a huge smile.

"Perfect, my clever wife," he said, kissing me soundly.

Later, I wondered if that's what love is—the never-ending conversation with a man who interests and excites you your whole life.

The next day, I sat down with a pad of paper and a calculator. After half an hour, I felt like crying. Whichever way I worked it, however much I tried to cut corners, the figures were stark.

We were $80,000 short.

But … if we sold half of the available seats for every single night, we'd break even. Anything above that, and we'd be in profit.

It was a risk.

But then again, life is a risk.

Isn't it.

I picked up the phone and called my bank.

"Hello, I'm calling to enquire about a loan, please."

Ash was furious when he found out what I'd done. He went on one of his famous, drama-filled rampages.

"We've overcome the biggest hurdle, finding a venue," I stated calmly. "And I know you can pull off the dance stuff, so what's the problem?"

His eyes flashed with fury.

"The problem!" he yelled. "I have eighty thousand problems. Holy fucking shit, Laney! Eighty thousand dollars!"

He prowled toward me, pushing his face into mine as he clamped his hands over the wheelchair's armrests.

"No! I won't allow it!"

"Too late. It's done."

"Send the money back! Say you changed your mind."

"I'm already paying interest on the loan, so I'm really not keen on that option. You'll just have to choreograph an amazing show and pay me back later. Do your dance thing."

"My dance thing? My dance *thing!* It's hours of fucking work, Laney! The music, the choreography, costumes. Shit, I don't know!"

"By the way, I spoke to Selma and sent the signed contracts back. She's also willing to hold open auditions at the theater on Saturday at no charge. I've placed an ad in several newspapers as well as online, and I've called half a dozen dance studios in the city to let them know. You should get a good selection of talent from that."

His mouth dropped open, his eyes wide with surprise.

And then he kissed me. He held my face between his hands and ravaged my mouth with such passion and intensity that I was breathless.

Later, as we lay in bed, warm and satiated, Ash absently stroking my thigh, he brought up the subject again.

"We are husband and wife, yes? A team?"

"Of course," I said, snuggling into his chest.

"But you made this big decision by yourself."

"Oh. Well, you'd have said no."

"Yes, I would."

"That's why I didn't tell you. We can totally do this. *You* can totally do this."

He pulled away slightly so he could see my face.

"Laylay, how mad would you have been if I made such a big decision and you had no say in it?"

"Pretty mad," I acknowledged. "But you would have said no for the wrong reasons. You think you'd be protecting me, but really you'd be taking away my chance to see you happy, to see you succeed—*our* future."

He rubbed his forehead tiredly.

"You're too clever with words for me."

I snuggled closer and kissed his chest again. "You're clever with words, but it's more fun when you're clever with your body."

I felt silent laughter shaking his chest.

"I do understand. You're right to be mad at me, but please trust me, Ash. This is the right thing to do."

"I trust you with my life," he said softly.

Two days later, Luka arrived. He looked like a dancer and had the same lean build as Ash, with a thick thatch of white blond hair sticking out from under a wool hat, his eyes a startling dark blue. He was very attractive, but he knew it. I could tell from the confidence in the way he held himself and the assessing look he gave me that women usually swooned at the sight of him.

"Luka, this is my wife Laney," Ash said proudly.

Luka took my hand, then pulled it to his lips and kissed the back.

"Enchanted, madame," he said smoothly, his accent stronger than Ash's.

"Nice to meet you, too," I said, carefully extracting my hand.

Luka gave me a wide grin, then slung his arm around Ash's shoulder and spoke rapidly in Slovenian, making Ash laugh.

But he wasted no time, barely letting Luka put his suitcase down before they were making plans. I reminded Ash that we'd arranged to meet Yveta and Gary for dinner in a small diner that I knew. Yveta was very self-conscious about going out in public, so she preferred quiet places.

I decided to take the wheelchair because although I felt reasonably well, I tired quickly. But the look on Luka' face as his eyes shuttled between me and Old Ironside ... and he said something in Slovenian.

Ash frowned, replying quickly. Then he looked at me, smiled and shrugged.

"I forgot to tell him."

He needed to be kissed for that, because my man, my *husband*, always saw me as a woman first, never as a problem to be taken care of.

When the kiss became a little more heated than was appropriate in company, Luka cleared his throat, an amused expression on his face, and he spoke in heavily accented English.

"Maybe I should go for dinner by myself, or is one minute still long enough for you, Aljaž?"

Ash cuffed him lightly around the ear and muttered something that sounded very rude.

Luka grinned.

"My friend is in love—I never thought I'd see it happen."

Ash grinned and winked at me, tightening his arm around my waist.

I loved the way he looked at me. I'd never get tired of that.

Then I remembered that Luka might not know about Yveta. Ash might have forgotten to tell him that, too.

"Uh, Luka, when you see Yveta, don't stare at her scar, okay?"

He gave me a serious look as Ash nodded his agreement. But when Yveta and Gary walked into the diner, Luka did stare. Ash kicked him under the table.

He said something in Russian to Yveta and she flushed but wouldn't meet his eyes.

"What did he say?" I hissed at Ash.

Ash gave me a small smile. "I think he told her she's beautiful."

"I did," Luka nodded. "I told her that I stare at all beautiful women."

Gary was still standing, hovering protectively next to Yveta. But hearing Luka's words, he rolled his eyes and sat down heavily.

"Another Slovenian hunk with more charm than is healthy—they must breed them specially. I think I'll plan a vacation there."

Luka gave him a flirtatious look and leaned in closer, resting his hand on Gary's thigh.

"I'm already on vacation."

I threw a questioning look at Ash while Gary fanned himself.

Ash shrugged. "Luka likes men and women."

"It's true!" Luka smiled, then said something that made Ash laugh.

Three voices at once yelled out, "What did he say?"

Ash held up his hands and shook his head.

"Excuse me," Luka said slyly, "my English is not always good. I said that I am equal opportunities in fucking."

I choked on a cough and Gary burst out laughing. Yveta looked as though she didn't know whether to laugh or cry, but instead she gave him a shy smile.

Luka's grin softened as he smiled back.

I relaxed in my seat and took a long sip of water. Things were going to get even more interesting—and by 'interesting' I meant complicated.

But what the hell. We'd survived worse, so bring it on.

The next day was auditions. Gary and Ash were running the show, but Yveta and Luka hovered in the background, making notes and whispering to each other.

Selma was there, too. I liked her and the way she got things done, but her personality was something of a freight train. In her enthusiasm, it was quite possible she'd run right over you.

"Are you liking being the producer?" she asked.

I gave her a quick look, knowing she didn't make small talk.

I shrugged. "I'm learning."

She gave me an appraising look.

"No offence, but this is a big job for someone who doesn't know what the heck they're doing."

"True. But we can't afford to pay anyone. We're barely scraping by as it is."

I didn't tell her about the massive loan that was giving me nightmares.

"I have a proposition for you," she said, leaning forward, her astonishing cleavage lending a playful tone to her serious and intense expression. "I'll take on producer duties—no fee necessary. I'll accept a percentage of the profits instead."

I sat back in my chair, my mind ticking over the possibilities.

"There might not be any profits," I pointed out.

Selma smiled. "I believe in this project. And if it goes as well as I think it will, I'll be amply reimbursed for my time."

I studied her thoughtfully.

"It's something I've wanted to do for a while," she said. "What your husband is doing, it's new and fresh. For now, I'd keep my job at the theater, but if *Slave* takes off—and I really believe it will—it'll be a huge stepping stone toward working as a theatrical producer full time. Everyone wins."

"Have you discussed this with Ash?"

"You're the producer, honey. He's just the talent."

I laughed as she winked at me.

"I'll get back to you," I said, and we shook hands.

Luka waved as soon as he saw me, and I sat next to him, trying to ignore the fact that Yveta seemed oblivious to my presence. Again.

"How's it going?"

"Good, very good," he said, leaning forward. "See that older guy, the small one at the left? That's Oliver—he'd make a great Sergei."

Hearing his name, I shuddered, and Luka threw me a sympathetic look.

"It was really good of you to come here," I said. "Especially when everything was on a wing and a prayer."

Luka seemed uncomfortable.

"It was the least I could do. I couldn't help him before, so…"

Then he turned back to the dancers on the stage.

Ash was there, wearing a black wife-beater, gray sweatpants and his ballroom shoes. He and Gary were working together to give the dancers the steps they wanted them to follow. His expression was focused and thoughtful, a small frown of concentration etched on his forehead.

I glanced across at Luka who was watching Ash carefully, his lips pursed in confusion.

"He's different, Aljaž, I mean. He was always such a kid. Not immature exactly, just … playful, always joking around, pulling pranks. But now…" he shook his head. "He's so serious."

My heart fractured for the loss of that Ash—playful, happy, carefree Ash.

"You're good for him," Luka said quietly. "I couldn't imagine him being with someone who isn't a dancer, but it works, doesn't it?"

I nodded stiffly, thrown off by his backhanded compliment.

"I think so."

At that moment, Yveta stood up and walked away, Luka's eyes following her.

"She doesn't like me."

Luka shrugged.

"She doesn't hate you. She'll get over it. Probably when she meets someone else."

I arched an eyebrow at him. "Are you talking about yourself by any chance?"

He shook his head, and for a second I saw flicker of some strong emotion, but then he grinned at me.

"I'm no one's dream."

Ash

I loved having Laney watching the auditions, loved having her see what I could really do.

By the end of the day, we had our full cast. It was scary, but exciting. The scary part was knowing that I'd be paying them a salary from Laney's loan soon. I was still kind of mad about the way she did that, but I'd also accepted that there was no going back—for any of us.

Laney walked across and gave me a much needed hug.

"Ugh," she said, as her arms tightened around me. "You're all sweaty."

"Want to get sweaty with me?" I asked, kissing down her neck.

"Yes, but not here," she laughed. "I loved that movement you got them to do with their arms. It somehow *made* the sequence of steps. I couldn't believe how that one small thing made such a difference. How did you come up with that?"

I shrugged. "I don't know. I just heard the accent in the music."

"Accent?"

"An emphasis, something louder or more dramatic, but it can be subtle."

"What goes through your mind when you're performing?"

That was easier to explain.

"The music—I'm always lost in the moment." And I leaned in closer so only Laney could hear. "That's why I made a very bad gigolo. When I danced with my partners, I would be lost in the music and forget I was supposed to seduce them. Bad for business."

Her face went red and she glanced around.

"You shouldn't say things like that," she hissed nervously.

"Laney," I said seriously, "it's part of my story."

She sucked in her cheeks, and I could tell she was thinking it over. She took a step away from me and folded her arms over her chest.

"Show me that thing with the arms again. I want to understand why it made a difference."

I studied her, my head cocked to one side. If she needed time to think about what I'd said, about what I *wasn't* saying, I'd give her that.

I demonstrated the sequence of steps that she'd asked about, watching her eyes the whole time.

"Accents like that are good staging and they help draw the audience in. but they need to be rehearsed, because if the person you're dancing with did them for real, impromptu, they'd surprise me, distract me. It's all pretend, Laney. Except when I dance with you."

I grabbed her and pulled her to my chest.

"I can't dance," she laughed.

"Yes, you can. I'll teach you." And I moved her hips against mine, then stepped back. "See, I invite you into my embrace, and I do that by leaving space. Now you follow me."

She stumbled after me for a few steps, nearly kneeing me in the balls as she trod on my feet. Maybe she was right—my wife really couldn't dance.

"Anyway," she laughed, "there's something I want to talk to you about."

"Sounds serious?"

"It kind of is, but in a good way. And I really enjoyed watching the auditions today. You were different."

I picked up my towel and draped it around my neck.

"Yeah? How?"

"You were the boss out there. I hadn't seen that before."

I threw her a shocked look. "I'm the boss in the bedroom always."

She flicked my stomach.

"I'm being serious! It's like … two different people."

I felt like that sometimes, like two different people. I got flashes of *before*-Ash, but mostly I was *now*-Ash. But I knew what she meant.

"I have two sides," I explained simply. "The public side, being the choreographer out there, or pleasing the audience—whichever is needed."

"And the other?"

I shrugged. "I'm not sure."

Was I lying? I didn't know anymore. But I didn't want to talk about the dark side, not to my sunshine.

"What's this thing you wanted to talk about?"

She looked at me as if she knew I was changing the subject—she just didn't know why, but she let me off the hook.

"Selma has come up with an interesting offer…"

Two days later, our first rehearsal with Gary, Luka and Oliver had been amazing. It was a bit freaky showing Oliver how to 'be' Sergei, but he was a nice guy, so I'd have to get over it, although my body was having a hard time understanding the difference.

And I was right about Sarah—she was going to be extraordinary. My mind exploded with the possibilities. Gary seemed equally excited.

"Oh my God!" he shrieked. "You are so right about her. Can the theater do wire work? We should use the harness to have her flying across the stage."

Sarah must have heard the comment, because she walked over, her eyes wide.

"Oh no fucking way! I'm not doing wire work, Mr. Tinsel Toes!"

Gary's eyes narrowed, and they were soon slugging it out. It was odds-even who'd win. At first, I thought they hated each other, but after a full day of rehearsals, it was just kind of how they were with each other. Whatever, it seemed to work for them, and they had a lot of amazing ideas sparking off each other.

It was the hardest I'd worked in my life, and because I was the lead and in every scene except one, my body took the brunt of it: strained muscles, bruises, taped up shoulders, ice baths and emergency stretching. All for the dizzying intoxication of hoping and praying for the standing ovation, the desperate need to avoid more scorn from the reviewers, the sucker punch of bad comments.

I felt broken, emotionally and physically, and everything hurt. Even after an ice bath and a deep tissue massage, I'd spend the rest of the evening walking like an old man. But the adrenaline, the rush—when I stood on that stage in front of Laney—that would be the second proudest moment of my life.

At least I didn't suffer the lacerated feet of the female dancers. Sure, blisters and sore feet were an occupational hazard, but I couldn't imagine what it was like dancing in high heels for hours a day. They all put white spirit on their feet to harden the skin.

It wasn't glamorous, but if we got it right, it was going to be amazing.

I hoped.

Laney

It was after 11PM when I arrived at the dance studio. The janitor raised his eyes and tapped his watch, telling me that Ash had ten minutes to get the hell out.

I could hear music playing, something with a tango beat. Ash was standing in the middle of the empty studio, his hair black with sweat.

I pushed open the door and his head jerked up. I think he tried to smile, but it came out as a grimace.

"Hi. It's late. Are you ready to come home yet?"

"Soon," he muttered, bending down to give me a quick kiss.

"Actually, now. The janitor is waiting to lock up. Anyway, you look like you're hurting."

He gave me a thin smile.

"I dance through the pain, that's what I do."

"Are you being dramatic, or do you mean that?"

"Both," he smiled, but I could see how tired he was. Then he sighed. "I've been lifting all day."

I was confused. "Weights?"

His eyes were closed but he smiled at that. "No, girls—dancers."

A burn of jealousy heated my blood to boiling point. Such a stupid, wasteful emotion—and so potent.

Then he held out his hand and kissed my wrist slowly.

"Let's go home, my love. Tomorrow is the first day where I'll have everyone together."

I tapped his forehead lightly.

"Then try and turn off that busy brain of yours."

His eyes darkened. "I can think of one thing that would do that."

Ash

The first day with all the dancers was hard. I couldn't tell if it was good. I needed it to be amazing, or Laney would be bankrupted.

I rubbed my forehead, feeling the pressure building again.

Then Gary walked up, an odd expression on his face. Without speaking, he pulled me into a tight hug. I was surprised to feel his body shudder. He was crying.

"Thank you," he gasped out.

That was all. The man whose mouth never stopped was silent. There were no words left.

And I understood, because I felt it too—it wasn't revenge for what had been done to us; it was a reckoning.

"Gary! You are such a tart!" yelled Sarah, breaking the moment. "Poor Ash—you're always trying to cop a feel. Have some dignity, why don't you?"

"Oh, look what the cat dragged in," snarked Gary. "Talk about a bitch in heat."

Sarah poked out her tongue, then pulled him into a tight hug, and I saw her wipe away his tears with her thumbs.

And then I felt Yveta's hand in mine and she met my surprised gaze. She never looked anyone in the eye anymore, but right now, that's exactly what she was doing.

"Luka is right," she said softly. "It is amazing. We will be amazing. Thank you."

CHAPTER 21

Laney

I sat in my specially designated disabled seat at the end of the front row, Mom gripping my hand tightly, me holding my breath. Dad sat next to her, then my sisters and their husbands, along with most of the cousins and second cousins. The Hennessey clan was out in force, my enormous firefighter cousins wedged into the small flip-up seats looking uncomfortable among the red velvet, rococo plasterwork and gilt chandeliers of the quaint theater. But they'd come—to support me, to support Ash.

Gary's parents were here too, silent and stoic in their Sunday best. Angie was with Phil as her date, and his reviewer friend from the Tribune had also showed up. We'd given out 35 press tickets and it seemed as though most of them had come, which was unheard of, apparently.

Vanessa and Jo had both flown in for the first night and were sitting directly behind me with several friends from work.

We also had a considerable police presence, bearing in mind what had happened last time Ash was on stage—that, and the fact that the Mayor and Police Commissioner were here with their wives.

With all the publicity that Ash's hard work had drummed up, the two weeks were almost sold out, and if the reviews were good, there were several theaters who'd expressed an interest in taking the show. I really hoped that was the case because Ash and I had put ourselves into debt to make up the funding gap. I cringed every time I thought of it.

I so desperately wanted tonight to be good, to be great. Since I'd been barred from rehearsals, I'd lost any sense of how things were going. I'd gratefully handed over the production duties to Selma, but now I felt even more adrift.

Ash had been coming home exhausted and largely silent. The only people he really talked to, and then only on his phone and in hushed tones, were the other dancers. Or to Luka, of course, in Slovenian. I was jealous of all of them—it seemed as if they were stealing Ash away from me.

But now, after all the heartache, after all the work—the blood, sweat and tears—we were here.

Mom gripped my hand as the house lights dimmed, and I saw her cross herself with her other hand. Soft rustlings died away as the audience waited, hushed and expectant. The theater itself seemed to tremble with anticipation and whispers slid into silence.

When the eerie sounds of a harpsichord rang from the orchestra pit, surprising me—as well as half the audience, if I could go by the mutters—the curtains opened to total darkness. Suddenly, the stage flashed, lights swirled and dipped in neon colors, bright searchlights crisscrossing the stage as 'Bad Romance' boomed out.

The ugly beauty of Las Vegas…

The backdrop was of a half-finished skyscraper in some unfamiliar European city that I guessed was Ljubljana, as a construction gang of six men strode onto the stage. In the lead was Ash, wearing boots, overalls, tool belt and hardhat—and looking super macho, his back arching, his arms whipping into the strong, masculine shapes of the Paso Doble, banderillas stamps and the exaggerated Flamenco taps with his feet, disdainful promenade and counter promenade.

Although the bib overalls covered his chest, his arms were bare, the spotlights catching the play of his toned biceps when he moved.

A tarpaulin became a matador's cape, as the men lunged and fought their way across the stage in a series of striking and scripted poses.

I doubt anyone had ever seen ballroom dancing that was so aggressive, so red blooded and muscular. And definitely not with hardhats.

"Oh my!" said Mom, her mouth dropping open.

And then I saw Luka slink onto the stage, shaggy hair and yellow contact lenses that gave him a feral intensity to match his wolfish prowl. This was Volkov, all his cruelty on display, and when he smiled, his lips pulled back in a sneer, his teeth appeared to be sharp and pointed.

I drew in a deep breath. I knew this was Luka, I knew he was acting, but it was chilling to watch him stalk Ash across the stage from the shadows.

Then the music switched, and I smiled to see Ash channeling his inner Elvis as his hips rolled to 'Bossa Nova Baby', integrated into a fast-paced jive as the other construction workers joined him then peeled off one by one.

We had a brief glimpse of an airplane against a backdrop of rolling clouds before the scene changed to Las Vegas in all its nighttime glory.

Ash tossed away his hardhat and tools, and dropped the bib from his overalls leaving him bare chested, his prominent abs on display. He had a huge, surprised grin on his face as eight Las Vegas showgirls strutted onto the stage to 'Hanky Panky', all towering headdresses and wide smiles, led by Yveta, thick makeup hiding her scar, but only as long as she kept smiling. The moment she stopped, the ridged scarring was obvious. How bitterly ironic.

Gary sashayed onto the floor, doing the gayest jive I'd ever seen, and the audience started to laugh.

Ash and Gary danced side-by-side, sharp kicks and flicks, moving so rapidly I was out of breath just watching.

Then Ash leap-frogged over Gary, achieving the full splits mid-air and landing perfectly in time. Gary did a slide through Ash's open legs, winking at the audience.

Two of the showgirls danced forward and the jive became increasingly athletic as the girls threw themselves at Ash and Gary in a series of stunning Lindy Hop inspired jumps and lifts. The audience clapped and cheered their appreciation.

I noticed that the wolf character was still in the background, watching silently as he prowled the edges of the stage, an ominous presence, occasionally licking his lips.

Creepy.

Mom squeezed my hand and I leaned my head toward her.

"Ash is amazing! This is fantastic!"

I threw her a wide grin.

"Told you so!" I whispered.

The jive continued with increasing craziness as Ash exited the stage for his first costume change.

Moments later, the backdrop became an opulent hotel room with two women dressed in a hooker's version of Catholic schoolgirls, perched on a couch.

I hoped there weren't any real schoolgirls in the audience.

Then Oliver swept onto the stage. Even though I knew he wasn't the real Sergei, it gave me chills to see the navy three-piece suit and neatly-combed gray wig. Volkov spun him around and they crossed the stage together in a slow foxtrot to the strains of Sam the Sham's 'Little Red Riding Hood'.

Yveta and Ash edged onto the stage looking lost and scared, hand in hand. Yveta wore a fifties-style prom dress in soft pink, and Ash had a scarlet silk shirt that clung to his chest and arms, disappearing into tight black pants that showcased his trim waist, narrow hips and beautifully toned butt.

The music was chilling, telling the story of these two innocents, babes in the wood, dancing with wolves.

A tasty treat for a big bad wolf…

The sinister music rose and fell as the creepiest American smooth that I'd ever seen flowed across the stage. Ash danced with Yveta and then was whisked away by Sergei. I choked as Oliver stroked Ash's chest and ass suggestively. I wondered how much this bothered Ash, how many bad memories it brought back.

I was shocked when Oliver/Sergei cupped Ash's genitals and smiled. A horrified gasp undercut the sensual music as the audience grasped the changing tone of the story.

The two Catholic schoolgirls danced together, their movements so sexual that I broke out into a sweat and saw Dad shifting uncomfortably in his seat. Never had ballroom dancing been so beautiful and so disturbing.

I nearly retched when Sergei pulled out a knife and drew it across one of the girls' throats, filled a wineglass with the 'blood' and then drank it as she slumped to the floor, her eyes lifeless.

It was so shocking, so unexpected, and a brilliant metaphor for everything that had happened.

"That's too much," Mom muttered, unable to look.

She wasn't the only one.

"It's real," I whispered back.

"Too real," she said, and I couldn't disagree as my stomach churned.

The lights dimmed and the music warped and changed again, this time to a nightclub beat.

The scenery was familiar…

Vanessa tapped me on the shoulder.

"Laney, is that *our* nightclub?"

She was right. Ash had recreated the club in Las Vegas where we'd met. And he was dancing suggestively with six women, seeming to promise them everything as they tucked dollar bills in the front of his pants.

Jealousy flared hot and deep inside me.

It's just dancing, I told myself. But it was more than that—it was Ash announcing to the world that he'd whored himself in Las Vegas—and I wasn't sure how I felt about that.

I asked him once if he would have tried to get money from me.

His answer was enigmatic.

"When I dance, I lose myself in the music—it isn't good for business."

What could I say to that?

One of the women ripped his shirt open and I wanted to break every finger on her manicured hand.

It's just dancing, I told myself.

And then the cute, poppy lyrics of *Little Mix*, but now with an uneasy undercurrent of sex for sale.

I could barely watch, until the artistry and sassiness of the sexy and seductive cha-cha with its Cuban breaks and vividness drew me in. It became a party, almost an orgy, as Ash danced with each of the women and all the backing dancers were on the stage, thrusting and grinding lewdly.

It was men with sleek stomachs, polished like Greek bronzes, tapered waists, strong thighs and tight asses.

It was women as voyeurs, window shopping for beautiful young men. I understood it, recognized it, but it made my blood boil when Ash's partner looked at him with lust in her beautiful eyes. And God, it looked as though Ash felt the same.

It's a performance, a beautiful goddamn performance.

But still, Volkov and Sergei lurked in the background, the evil puppeteers, glimpsed between the dancers so that you wondered if you'd really seen them or whether your paranoia was running overtime—and knowing that's how it had been for Ash.

Slowly the music faded away, leaving just the jagged sound of a heartbeat as two pure white spotlights lit the stage. Sarah sat alone at a table, wearing a simple yellow dress that caught the light, the bodice glittering with tiny crystals.

She looked so vulnerable, so beautiful, and Ash stared at her, mesmerized. Another hot bolt of jealousy made me clench my fists.

A slow pulse of music started, in time with the heartbeat, and I recognized one of Ash's favorite songs by Adele, but the lyrics were subtly altered as a man's voice poured out his longing for a lost love.

Ash held his hand out to her, as if asking her to dance, and I gasped. That was me! Sarah was me! He'd recreated the moment that we met. This was how he saw me, how he felt when he thought of me. Tears formed in my eyes and I rubbed them away impatiently.

When the table was rolled away, revealing Sarah sitting in a wheelchair, the audience inhaled sharply.

I saw Ash's shock. I saw the disbelief. I saw Sarah's pain. I saw her humiliation and defeat—*my* humiliation and defeat.

Mom gripped my hand tightly.

But then Ash scooped her from the wheelchair, carrying her in his arms, her bare feet moving in exquisite rumba shapes, although they never touched the ground.

I was awed by the beauty of the dance, amazed at the display of physical strength as Ash carried 110 pounds of dancer in a way that appeared effortless, but I knew wasn't.

And I finally understood why he had barred me from rehearsals.

Because this was his gift to me, the dance we would never have; the first dance as it should have been but could never happen.

And this time I couldn't hold back the tears. Every step, every look at *her*, every gesture he made to *her*, was to me. And he carried her for the entire dance.

And I forgave him for being stubborn and secretive. And I forgave him for being intense and driven. And I forgave him for shouting at me when he was stressed and tired. I forgave every time he'd closed me down or shut me out, because this was him telling me through every step, through every movement of his beautiful body, that I was loved, that I was desired, and that everything that had happened between us was real.

We were real.

When the dance ended, the audience stood on their feet and applauded. Except me, of course, because just like the night we met, I couldn't stand on my own two feet.

The house lights came on, but the applause didn't stop for several minutes.

All around me people were smiling and wiping their eyes; Angie's reporter friend was scribbling furiously in his notebook.

"Oh my God!" Vanessa said, stunned shock and awe in her voice. "That was *you!* That's your story. He danced that for you! With you!"

"Yes," I said, my voice lost and small.

Mom threw me a look of concern, then pushed my wheelchair up the slope to the tiny theater bar.

People pointed and whispered when they saw the chair, and a couple even blatantly took photographs of me. I was surprised and annoyed, but then two reporters came up to me, phones in hand, wanting impromptu interviews.

I steeled myself and smiled, answering their questions as well as I could.

So I was grateful when Selma arrived to help, agreeing to set up interviews with the principal dancers in the next few days.

"The reviews are going to be good, Laney," she said once we were alone, her tone serious.

I smiled sadly at her, already knowing where she was going with this.

"There'll be offers from theaters across the country. I'll be able to put together a national tour."

"I know."

Her expression shifted.

"You're not going to come, are you?"

I sighed and looked down.

"No. My body has been going through some changes, I know you've noticed. I've not been well ... as well as I should be. That happens sometimes with RA. You have months, years even, of being at a plateau, and for no reason that you can think of, the meds don't seem to hold it back anymore. My doctor wants me to try a higher dose of chemo, maybe even different drugs. And … I just feel I'd do better if I stayed in one place. At home."

She nodded slowly.

"Have you told Ash?"

I shook my head.

"No, not yet. I wanted him to have this … tonight."

"He'll be devastated."

"I know. But I'll never be part of his world like that. It's not possible for me. And I don't think he can live without it."

"Are you sure about this, Laney? Because I think it's *you* he can't live without."

I didn't know what to say to that, but I was saved trying to find a reply when the Mayor and his wife came to shake my hand and say how pleased they were that this 'phenomenal work' had premiered in Chicago. Then they had their photos taken by the Press as they stood with smiles next to the woman in the wheelchair.

The Police Commissioner came and said a few words to my mom and dad, smiled at me, and disappeared into the crowd.

There was a feverish excitement in the bar, everyone wondering how the rest of the show would play out, despite many of them having read about Ash's story in the newspapers.

"Did that really happen?" asked Vanessa avidly. "Did that Sergei guy really drink a woman's blood?"

I shivered at the mention of his name, and Jo elbowed her in the ribs.

"What?" Then she looked at me. "Oh, sorry."

"I think it's a metaphor," I said, my voice tight. *At least I hoped it was.*

My cousin Paddy strolled across, casting an appreciative eye over my friends.

"Some show," he said thoughtfully, handing me a glass of whiskey.

"What do you think of it?"

"Totally fucked up," he grinned, "but the dancing is fuck hot. Nice one, cuz," and he sauntered away, winking at Vanessa.

"Is he…?"

"Off limits," I said, as she pouted at me.

Jo laughed.

"Trust me. Paddy has slept with half of Chicago, and the other half is in his contacts list. Don't even think about it."

I groaned as I saw the light of challenge in Vanessa's eyes. Oh well, she'd been warned.

As everyone settled into their seats for the second half, my nerves were wearing a permanent groove. I *felt* the show was good; it *seemed* people were enjoying it. But my objectivity was long gone, so I couldn't be sure.

I had to smile when the stage burst to life in a blaze of color and light as the pulsing, happy beats of Viva Las Vegas erupted from the orchestra pit.

Ash swaggered onto the stage, dressed all in black, although sequins on his shirt caught the light and I think someone had dusted his chest with glittery powder. He was doing some sexy shimmy thing, followed by samba rolls, his crotch pressing into Yveta's ass. I winced, finding it hard to watch my husband getting so up close and personal with another woman, especially since I knew he'd slept with her before we'd met. I saw the way she watched him when she thought no one was looking and she totally ignored me.

Sergei and Volkov were haunting the stage again, and wherever they went, blood red spotlights followed them. There was something macabre about the way they moved, prowling, gliding—the ghosts at the feast.

I gasped when they suddenly descended on Ash, gripping his arms and tearing him out of the chorus lineup. None of the other dancers noticed and I wanted to scream at them to look, even though I knew it wasn't real.

While the dancers quickstepped in the background to 'Tu Vuo Fa L'Americano', their smiles transformed to clowns' grimaces, bathed in a ghoulish green light, Volkov dragged Ash across the floor in a parody of a Paso step.

Two of the backing dancers ran onto the stage, holding Ash's arms. Then Volkov ripped the shirt from Ash's back, and Sergei tore the pants, waist to ankle.

Ash stood with his back to the audience, seeming completely naked, although I knew, of course, that he'd be wearing an almost invisible dance belt.

Even so, seeing my husband stripped naked on a stage was horrible to watch. And when Volkov handed Sergei a whip, I couldn't look. Horrified gasps cut through the horribly upbeat music and I could hear the special effects sound of a whip cracking through the air as Sergei appeared to laugh, his free hand clamped over his own dick.

Behind me, I heard Vanessa swear as Ash collapsed to the floor.

The music died softly, and he was left in a pool of light, alone, beaten and naked—just the way I'd seen him that awful, terrible night. I clamped my hand over my mouth as tears burned my eyes.

For a heartbeat, there was silence, and then a sound like a soft breeze filled the small theater, and from up above, Sarah descended like an angel, still dressed in yellow, the light creating a halo around her.

As she reached the stage, the lights went out and a sudden thunderclap made everyone jump.

Yveta and Gary were dragged center stage while Volkov and Sergei waltzed together, an obscene duet to *A Kiss from a Rose*, Seal's haunting lyrics.

Was I his light in the darkness?

I watched between my fingers as they were repeatedly brutalized by a gang of backing dancers dressed as bikers. It was horrific, grotesque, and the moment that Yveta was slashed with a knife was almost unwatchable. And, against that ghastly backdrop, Ash waltzed onto the stage with Sarah in his arms, spinning round and around, a sweet, loving Viennese waltz. Ash was dressed in jeans and a loose white shirt, while Sarah was still in the yellow dress.

I felt a little sick. Was our love really at the cost of his friends? Or maybe that was how Ash felt about it. I didn't know, but I wanted it to stop.

It didn't. It went on and on, until Gary and Yveta were dragged away, bloodied and beaten. I'm sure I wasn't the only one who felt a huge sense of relief that I didn't have to watch their torture any longer, strongly laced with guilt at preferring not to see the truth.

It was too hard to watch.

The strains of a violin filtered softly through the air and I held my breath, wondering what was coming next.

Then I suddenly remembered what Sarah's costume reminded me of— the yellow sundress that I got married in.

A shiver went through me. And then I recognized the song: 'With You I'm Born Again'.

And it was her softness, his gentleness…

Ash placed her on a chair, then swept onto the floor alone. Slowly, her legs appearing to tremble, Sarah stood. And then she began to dance, echoing his steps until they were moving together in the most achingly beautiful waltz I had ever seen. I'd never known this side of Ash, never realized just how his dancing was so full of passion, of deep emotion. He said he'd felt numb for so long, but he was wrong. It was all there, a deep well of emotion that only dancing brought out. Dancing and, I hoped, me.

Tears trickled from my eyes, imagining for just a second what it would be like to dance with him like that, to be swept away, to float, to glide, to caress his skin, to move with him through the music, the music that enslaved him. Music was in his heart and in his soul, and in that moment, I knew I had to set him free.

This show was going to be a huge success. I'd hoped for it, wanted it, but I'd been afraid to believe it. But now I felt it, knew it in my bones. The two weeks in this small theater was not the end, but just the beginning. I had no doubt that offers would flood in. And when they did, I had to let him do the tour. Without me.

And I had comforted him through the madness…

I'd helped him and held him, and for the briefest of moments we'd held each other, but now, like a wild creature, I needed to let him go. And pray he'd come back to me.

With you I am reborn…

And tears trickled down my cheeks, because I was losing him, if he'd ever been mine at all, and it was the right thing to do, even if my heart was breaking.
And I cried, because it was true. Ash had made me brave and strong. In his arms, I could face anything—anything except the day he left me.
I was exhausted, emotionally wrung out, but it wasn't over yet.
Volkov and Sergei prowled onto the stage, hunting the two dancers who were spinning through the light, so in love they were blind to the danger surrounding them.
The music morphed into the harsh chords of 'El Tango De Roxanne', and the two loathsome beasts performed a breathtaking and disturbing Argentine tango, cheek to cheek. Sergei/Oliver, performing the most extraordinary assisted jumps in Volkov's/Luka's arms. Then the enganche: hooking, coupling, as the men took turns being the 'follower' wrapping their leg around the other, the 'leader' displacing the feet from inside.
Ash told me once that the Argentine tango had been a dance for men. The gauchos riding off the range, a dance of immigrants from the poor barrios, all needing a way to impress the few women they met. That's what he said.
"Jealousy!" yelled Volkov, and gripped Ash's hair, forcing him to his knees.
"Lust!" yelled Sergei, pulling out a gun and pointing it first at Volkov and then at Ash.
As Volkov slowly prowled away, disappearing into the shadows, I saw the gun in Sergei's hand, almost falling out of my wheelchair as the gunshot echoed across the stage, as he casually shot Sarah.
She collapsed to the ground, in a pool of yellow satin.
Mom's nails dug into my arm and she whispered something, but I couldn't reply, my voice strangled into silence.

The fight, the gun battle in a theater not unlike this one, was brutally painful to watch. It was a duet, it was a duel, and when Ash finally seized the gun and pushed into Sergei's face, his own twisted with hatred, I couldn't help letting out a hoarse cry.

Someone in the audience screamed, and I cringed. Mom gripped my hand even more tightly.

"It's okay," she whispered. "You're safe here."

Another gunshot cracked out and the music died away in a crash of discordant noise. Then lights and sirens and shouts filled the theater as the backing dancers were transformed into police officers.

Ash picked up Sarah from the floor, cradling her to his chest, the noise and chaos swirling around them.

She 'woke', if that's the right word, and the eerie, sudden silence made me feel as if I'd gone deaf.

A full moon lit the stage.

A beautiful, magical moondance…

It was a foxtrot American Smooth, danced with every bit of astonishing grace and flair, so lyrical, so touching. And so uncomfortable to watch Ash making love to someone else, no matter how beautiful the dance.

But then something unexpected happened. He pulled a small box out of his pocket, a ring box. But instead of offering it to Sarah, he walked to the front of the stage and jumped off.

The music died away, and from the way all the dancers gathered onto the stage, grins on their faces and barely suppressed excitement, I knew they'd been expecting this.

Voices hushed as Ash walked toward me, the ring box in his hand.

He stood in front of me, then slowly sank to one knee.

"Laney, you are my sunshine, *moj sonček*. I loved you before I knew it. And although you are my wife, today I kneel before you and ask you to take me as your husband forever, in this life and in the next. Never leave me again, my love. Be with me always."

He opened the box, presenting me with an engagement ring, a stunning yellow diamond that matched the little sundress I'd married him in.

I held out my hand, a glazed expression on my face.

"You shine so brightly," I whispered.

"You're the one who shines, *moj sonček*."

I laughed quietly. "At least I know what that means now. Sneak."

Ash smiled his beautiful smile, and slipped the ring onto my finger, then leaned forward to give me a searing kiss that broke a hundred hearts, including my own.

"You made me very proud last night," I said, cupping his cheeks with my hands. "Don't stop. Dance like the world is watching."

Mom coughed, and when I glanced at her, she was wiping her eyes.

Ash stood up straight, grinned and winked, then vaulted back onto the stage as the band broke into Beyoncé's 'Crazy', and the maddest, wildest, craziest, most over the top and life-affirming cha-cha that I'd ever seen. The entire cast was on the stage, giving it their all, saying that life goes on that love goes on and that evil will *never* win.

My feet burned with agony as I struggled to stand.

"What are you doing?" hissed Mom.

But I had to. My arms and legs shook with the effort, but I stood with the rest of the audience, clapping and cheering, our applause raising the roof of this tiny theater. And I sobbed wildly, damn sure that I was ruining my makeup.

Finally, the dancers stood at the front of the stage to take their bows, chests heaving with the strain, sweat glistening on their faces, on their arms, and the biggest smiles on their faces.

And there was my Ash, my love, my husband, shining so brightly.

"I love you," I whispered.

He saw my lips moving, and he raised his damaged hand to rest it over his heart.

I love you, too.

Tortured, Horrific, Terrific

I thought I'd seen it all, seen every kind of dramatic trick to manipulate an audience's emotions. I've seen real pigs eyes used during that scene in 'King Lear'. I've seen a version of 'Coriolanus' so bloody that the front row had to be given raincoats to wear, but last night every emotion was drawn out of me willingly in the freshest, most brutally honest performance it's been my privilege to experience.

Ash Novak's 'Slave—A Love Story' was not my first choice for a night of entertainment. Ballroom dancing is full of sequins and cheesy grins, or so I thought, but this talented dancer and choreographer suspended then dissolved every crumb of disbelief, in a magical, gut-wrenching, life-altering display of brilliance.

Every step was another piece in a horrific story of modern-day slavery, human trafficking and organized crime.

If this show doesn't break your heart, then you should see a doctor to check you still have one.

The charismatic lead never put a foot wrong, and was ably support by Sarah Lintort, Yveta Kuznets, Gary Benson and Luka Kokot.

Chicago's must-see show. Catch it while you can because it's going to be the hottest ticket in town.

EPILOGUE

Five months later...

I jumped when the apartment door swung open without warning.

My heart thudded in my chest as I saw Ash standing there, his suitcase at his feet, his key in his hand.

"What are you doing here?" I gasped, one arm in my coat sleeve.

"The tour finished and I caught a flight from Dallas."

"Yes, but what are you doing here *now?*"

He cocked his head to one side, staring at me, puzzled.

"I came home."

I stared back, transfixed. He looked the same, but different. The same long, lean build. The same mahogany hair and feline eyes the color of Irish whiskey. The same sharp cheekbones, the same strong, unshaven jaw.

But there was a new confidence in the way he held himself, a new certainty that he was doing what he needed, and standing where he belonged.

"I was supposed to meet you at the airport."

"You're not happy to see me," he said, his voice flat.

"Are you nuts?" I shrieked. "I've missed you so damn much!" And I threw myself at him.

Ash staggered, catching me before his back thudded against the wall. He grabbed me around the waist, his lips sucking on my neck as I tackled his belt buckle.

"We don't have time for this," I muttered, ripping open his shirt to expose his smooth chest, ignoring the buttons that ping-ponged across the wooden floor. "We're having dinner with my family."

"What sort of world is it where I don't have time to make love with my wife?" he asked, his words finishing with a groan as I wrapped my hands around his hot, hard dick.

What kind of world is it?

I didn't have an answer for that. The world spun around us at a dizzying pace, our lives a confusing mass of moments, colored by highs and lows, joys and sorrows.

He grabbed my grasping hands, laughing with the sheer pleasure of living in this moment. And then he carried me to our bedroom.

It was rough and messy, heated, hedonistic thrusting, gasping into each other's mouths as he pinned me to the bed and fucked me until my body shuddered with new pleasure. He trembled above me, and his eyes squeezed shut. Then with a satisfied grunt, he pulled out and rolled onto his side.

"Holy shit!"

I laughed a soft papery laugh that was part longing, part joy, part tears that threatened to fall, a pouring out of release that was too much to keep inside.

"We'll be so late," I whispered as his thumbs brushed tears from my eyes.

"I don't care."

"Me neither."

He gave me a huge, beautiful smile that I'd missed so much, and flung himself onto his back, pulling me against his chest, his gentle hands sweeping across my shoulders.

When we made love again, I kissed every scar on his back, soothing the scars on his soul and mine.

I kissed his fluttering eyelids and watched his lips curve upward in a smile.

"I'm not doing that again," he said, his eyes sliding open to gaze at me.

"What?!"

His chest rumbled as he laughed.

"Oh, I'm definitely doing *that* again," he chuckled. "I meant I'm not touring without you."

"Ash…"

"No, I mean it, Laylay. It's not worth it. Nothing is worth being away from my sunshine." He took a deep breath. "Selma said she wants to take the tour to Europe next year. Come with me, my love."

"I don't think that would…"

"That is your problem," he said, tapping a long finger against my forehead. "Too much thinking. Whatever happens, we will face it together. Be with me, Laney. It'll be the next adventure."

I sighed. "It does sound amazing, but … let me think about it."

"Sure," he said, rolling from the bed and peeling off his ruined shirt. "But you'll say yes in the end."

"I don't know if…"

"You'll say yes," he said confidently, leaning down to kiss me into silence.

When he stood up again, he was grinning at me and tucking a semi back in his pants. It was a good thing I was well this week, because his smile told me to expect little sleep tonight.

My eyes slid across his beautiful body, a little thinner than last time we'd been together. And then I saw it.

"You got a new tattoo?"

He nodded, his eyes slanting across mine.

I looked closer, studying the intricate work in ink.

It was a depiction of the sun peeking from behind a cloud, and arcing above it in flowing script was my name.

"My sunshine," he whispered, his eyes soft.

I reached up, my arms wrapping around his neck as I stroked the soft skin, and I kissed him to say thank you.

Thank you for being my husband.
Thank you for being with me.
Thank you for being the love of my life.
Thank you for being you.

I wondered later if our love was built in tiny, paper-thin slices, moment by moment, day by day. I asked Ash about it once, when he fell in love with me. His answer was enigmatic—typical Ash.

"When I felt my heart beat again."

THE END

MORE ABOUT JHB

I was born on the 13th which explains a few things. I love the ocean, dogs of all shapes and sizes and chocolate of all shapes and sizes.

When I'm not in my writing cave, I can be found at the beach, watching surfers.

I love hearing from readers, so please do get in touch.

www.janeharveyberrick.com
www.twitter.com/jharveyberrick
www.facebook.com/jane.harveyberrick
www.instagram.com/jharveyberrick

Made in the USA
Charleston, SC
09 May 2016